SANTA'S CLAWS

David Taylor

I0672393

Delta Tango Publishing

Author details

Born in Yorkshire, where he still lives, David Taylor left school at the age of fifteen. After a brief period as a motor mechanic, he joined the Royal Air Force, where he continued his education, and saw the world, literally. During his twelve years of service - three of which were spent in Far East - he visited 38 countries.

Emigrating to America after leaving the RAF in 1964, he secured a job in the oil industry. It was to be a fleeting emigration, but a long period away from home, 30 years, during which he again travelled extensively. Ninety-six countries at the last count, some of which he knows very well, and which provide background locations for his novels.

During his free time he enjoys reading, travel, and walking - though this is very restricted these days due to health problems. His many interests include aviation, motor racing, and photography, although he admits he now rarely finds time to devote himself fully to any of them.

Santa's Claws is his second novel.

Other books by this author:

Crowning Glory - a history of the Royal Air Force in Singapore. **ISBN 1-903953-16-2**

A Suitcase Full of Dreams - Expanded & Re-Packed. **ISBN 978-0-9534082-3-8** Autobiography.

Deadly Rainbow. **ISBN 978-0-9534082-4-5** First of his Roger McLaren novels.

For the Williams in my life: father & son; & Helen, a daughter lost.

First published 2016
Delta Tango Publications
York, England, YO19 5RB

British Library Cataloguing in Publication Data.
A catalogue record of this book is available from the British Library, Wetherby, Yorkshire.

ISBN 978-0-9534082-2-1

Author Notes

Although a work of fiction, the majority of locations used in this story, relating to Singapore and Australia, are in fact reality.

A little artistic licence has occasionally been evoked so as to fit the storyline, such as that relating to the Pine Gap Satellite Communications facility, which is actually located in the Northern Territories, not WA, as hinted at, and the 1991 Australian GP was actually held in November, a month later than in my story. The area around the Whim Creek hotel is, I believe, once again subject to mining operations. Though this wasn't the case during any of my visits in the 1970s. Same goes for the Walkabout Hotel, out by the airport in Port Hedland; I believe this is now the Mia Mia.

The road from Port Hedland to Marble Bar, where it then turns South to run back down to towards Perth, is fact, but my continuation to the east is pure fiction, as of course is Silver Springs, along with Wicker's Keep, and its knoll known as Dead Man's Hill. Of course the roads I say are, or were, unsealed, are probably tarmac for their entire length these days.

A few other things may have changed also, but as for everything else, well.... the wisdom is, write about what you know, what you have seen, or what you have experienced!

SANTA'S CLAWS
INDEX OF CHAPTERS

SANTA'S CLAWS

Prologue

September 1991

ednesday had just become Thursday when a signal emanated from an office located deep in the heart of the modernistic building on the south bank of the Thames, at Vauxhall Bridge Cross. It began its electronic journey in a room that was over fourteen thousand kilometres from the theatre of intended operations. But this wasn't a conceptional signal, it was in reply to the one that had initially set things in motion some time in the past - a request for cooperation in the international fight against crime. And that request had come from an altogether more distant place.

Travelling via secure landline to Goonhilly Downs, on the Lizard, Cornwall, from where it was beamed up to bounce its way across the heavens, transferring from one satellite to another in a matter of seconds, that Tuesday response returned to earth in the dusty, dry outback of Australia. The decoded message, eventually to end up as a typewritten sheet on an obscure desk somewhere in the Australian

Capital, Canberra, was short and to the point. Basically: Operation "Whipping Boy" had received official clearance to go ahead.

This was cause enough to set secure phones in various Embassies and consulates ringing.

*   *

Chapter One

ROGER, ROGER

Tuesday October 8th 1991.

Singapore. Another day in the tropics; hot and humid. Although that was how my forth day here in this Far Eastern city began, it certainly wouldn't end as "just another day".

Alright, so that start of this particular day had been a little later than usual, a tad more unwelcome to my slightly fuzzy brain, therefore somewhat protracted.

Late, OK! Although in one way it was a day worthy of a small celebration, for it was one of those rare days when I knew things could only improve, health-wise. But the reasons for that had been pretty basic: yesterday had *ended* a lot later than usual.

*

The flight from London to Australia can be a long, boring affair; over twelve hours in the air. So, since I was not running to much of a schedule, I'd elected to make a five day stopover in the City State of Singapore. It was an option that

8

had been recommended to me by an enthusiastic travel agent, who had also been recommended to me. Both via the same source.

It has sounded like good advice, for although I did enjoy the adventure of flight, and international travel, twelve hours seated was usually more than enough without a break, despite the movies, and the meals. Large commercial aircraft were not my idea of flying, even when travelling up front, in the added comfort of Business Class.

Once back on *terra firma*, cleared through Immigration and Customs, I had taken a taxi to my hotel.

As opposed to most countries, relaxation in Singapore begins with the taxi ride along fauna-lined, multi-laned carriageways between airport and city, from where, in air-conditioned comfort, everything appears so colourful and peaceful.

It hadn't taken me long to relax completely once in my room. And although a girl named Caroline did still make an occasional, and welcome, guest appearance in my dreams, the nightmare of her loss no longer intruded in my everyday affairs, although some of the lessons learned from that liaison certainly did.

Once in the city, first Impressions of the Orient had been those of noise, hustle and bustle, and the smells; different country, different smells. Certainly not English smells, especially along the Boat Quays. The people were mainly Chinese, naturally, although I hadn't really expected that. Don't quite know what I had expected. Hadn't really thought about it until I arrived here. (I was once informed by a learned friend from Bradford, who had served three years with the RAF in this theatre, that they were really Singaporeans. "They only calls 'em Chinese 'cause they're slanty-eyed like," he'd confided in me. Harry Hargraves had told me a lot about Singapore, and his time there.)

Here, along the banks of the Singapore river, had been my introduction to trading, Chinese-style. Waterfront godowns displayed their wares: foods; spices of every type and colour; weird and wonderful mushrooms; root ginger and ginseng; garlic by the ton. There were even beetles, and centipedes fully six inches long, dried, bundled, and boxed, ready for .... Huh! Whatever. Count me out.

During my initial excursion along that riverside, a man had given me a cheery wave, which I thought unusual. One man out of many. Why him? Why me? It was the way my mind worked these days. After being involved with the Secret Service for a brief period recently, albeit on the very fringes of the SIS - Caroline's father being a one time head of that service - watching ones back had been instilled into me, to come a natural habit. But out here, I decided I could afford to carry on relaxing. After all, wasn't that the purpose of this trip? Dismiss the past. England. South Africa, a bit of amateur sleuthing, with all that that entailed. This was still a foreign place, albeit with different foreign customs. Live with it.

I had. For three days, and nothing untoward had happened.

Then came yesterday evening, when I'd stumbled across another "Yorkie" - almost a neighbour, in fact - eight thousand miles from home.

Paying regard to the local brewery advertizing, "Time for a Tiger", I'd decided it certainly was. Back home I was a "Real Ale" drinker, but in places like this, given the climate, cold, lager type beers went down much better. A host of others also agreed it was "Time for a Tiger", too, it seemed.

"Yorkie" and I had bumped into each other in the Jockey Club. At least, he had joined me at the bar, so we'd introduced ourselves. He was Henry Smith, I was Roger McLaren. I hadn't lied, felt he may have. Just a notion. There again, over the years I had become a rather suspicious person. This was especially true of the past few months. Something else instilled in me by what I had experienced during that period. Anyway, lie or not, in this instance it didn't matter, especially as he bought a round. Naturally, I bought one in return. And not to be outdone, he bought another. So on and so forth, into the wee small hours, moving from one bar to the next. Part of the relaxation, and getting to know you process; with me, this was usually associated with someone of the opposite sex.

Seemingly reluctant to divulge the reason *he* was in Singapore, I burdened him with mine: Caroline, a lost love. I must have sounded a bit down, for he unsympathetically told me I needed to get straightened out. Not the first person to push that opinion. I told him I already was. We left it at that, got on with the drinking.

'Well, what you been doing with yourself, Roger?' he'd asked.

I'd told him that too. Singapore in a nutshell.

'Don't want to miss out on the Omni Theatre,' he'd advised, setting them up yet again. 'In the Singapore Science Centre, out by Jurong. Fifteen minutes on the MRT.'

Said I'd bear it in mind.

It had been very much later when we'd finally said our goodbyes, quitting Bill Bailey's at some ungodly hour. Myself for bed, alone once again, my apparently seriously wrecked companion, to seek sustenance, he'd said.

So it was that my alarm call on this fateful day had been the general hubbub of a city fully awake, rather than the usual early morning birdsong.

On the whole I hadn't felt too bad, considering. OK, the head *was* a tad fuzzy, and my eyes took time sending their messages to the brain, but there was definitely no headache.

I contemplated the image in my bathroom mirror, interested to see how I looked. Like I said, didn't feel too bad, was relieved to see the face that stared back also looked reasonable. A strong, noble face, a girl had once told me. She'd been an 'ologist of one kind or another, or had high hopes of becoming so. An average face then - possibly strong and noble - not unlike Robert Redford, another girl had once suggested.

Bollocks! Not like Robert Redford at all, a familiar voice chirped in; my male alter-ego. Not schizophrenia, a companion, ready to offer friendly advice and opinions - well, most of the time. Minerva, I called it - after the Roman Goddess of prudence and wise council, even if I did think of it as being male. I could be a bit of a chauvinist, at times.

Who asked your opinion? I silently addressed the mirror, pulling a face at the image, thus creating lines that made me look much older than my thirty-two.

My morning ritual consisted of twenty lengths in the

hotel pool - seventh floor - which I'd already done; much too late to enjoy having the pool to myself on this day. It had been a tremendous help in the eye and brain departments though.

After the swim, I'd shower, dress, and stroll out for breakfast. I'd discovered a marvellous little diner type place just around the corner. It was much cheaper than the hotel, which appealed to my Yorkshire upbringing, it also provided both quick and friendly service, along with good food.

Lingering over coffee - today's breakfast having become brunch - I flicked through my guidebook. Now then, what's it to be? Chinese Garden; Zoological and Orchid Gardens; Sentosa Island? Done them all. I'd seen Indian temples, been "transported to a bygone era" at Tanjong Pagar Conservation area, cruised the fetid waters of that Singapore River. I'd even stopped by for a Singapore Sling, at the Long Bar in Raffles Hotel one evening. Even though Singapore had plenty of attractions as far as tourism went, some of them world class, it also had architecture worth more than a cursory glance, both ancient and modern. Especially the glass and concrete modern. But in my present mood, it seemed to me I had already done most of what was on offer; the usual touristy things. I was becoming slightly bored - tourist wasn't really me. Then I came across a reference to the Omni Theatre, at the Singapore Science Centre, recalled my drinking partner of last night recommending a visit. Well, why not? It sounded interesting enough, would fill a good part of the afternoon, and the air-conditioned environment would certainly make a welcome change to the humid atmosphere outside.

Nodding to the Chinese guy who had nodded at me when I looked his way, I paid and left. It was the same guy who had given me a wave the day I'd strolled alongside the river. Seemed this was *his* favourite breakfast bar, too. He was here most days. Had something similar occurred during the past months, I would by now have become suspicious. Very much so indeed. Prowling around dark alleys and buildings, where truth can often become fiction, reality an illusion, one can easily develop such traits. Here, being on vacation, as I was, he had meant nothing.

As Henry Smith had advised, to get to the Science Centre I used the Mass Rapid Transit system, which it was. It was also clean, efficient, and convenient. OK, the strap hangers were perhaps a little on the low side for the average occidental, but was it ever cheap! My journey was priced at sixty cents, I duly deposited a dollar in the machine. It gave me a ticket and eighty cents change. Technology gone wrong. There was a time I'd have welcomed those extra cents, but those days were now long in the past, too.

Once in the suburbs, the crowds and the passengers began to disperse station by station until, by the time I reached my destination, only a few bored-looking faces remained. Exotic. Smooth faces, with Sphinx-like eyes. Menacing? Perhaps so. Inscrutable? That may have been true, too. Certainly no one was taking an interest in anyone else. Monday morning on the Metropolitan line, I thought, feeling an affinity with home. Which is when the train slid smoothly to a halt, curtailing further recollections. The Science Centre was upon me, or I upon it.

The Centre itself was interesting enough, if you were at all technologically inclined that is, and the Omni Theatre was actually an Imax cinema. Between them they managed to hold my attention for a few hours.

*

Returning from Jurong East to Singapore's central tourist district it is necessary to change trains at either the City Hall or Raffles Place interchange, choice dependent on whether you are north, or southbound. Getting it wrong is no major disaster, as I'd already discovered. It just presented you with a long escalator up and a short one down, as opposed to merely crossing the platform. This time I happened to get it right, although later events gave me cause to reassess that opinion. They also assured me of the time necessary to carry out that reassessment.

The station was crowded. Circle line at rush hour. Not a lot of difference, except this was cleaner, more modern. It was user friendly, too, platform sealed off from track by automatic glass doors. No sudden rush of air here to indicate the train was approaching, no chance, either, of falling, or being pushed, onto the track. No bad thing, that!

13

On the flight out I'd nicked an *Economist* off the aircraft, so as to keep abreast of affairs back home. I finished it as I waited. Out here the magazine cost more than twice the UK cover price, which, my being a frugal Yorkshireman (tight bastard, some might say), went against the grain somewhat. Maybe someone else could use this copy, thought I, preparing to discard it in plain sight atop a pristine refuse bin, just as my train arrived.

Possibly they could, for it seemed everyone and his dog rushed to grab it. They weren't really, it was the train they were interested in. Hustle and bustle, polite push and shove. But then, in a move which told me he'd been awaiting his opportunity, the magazine *was* snatched from my hand, to be replaced by a briefcase, the handle of which I instinctively grasped before alarm briefly paralysed me. I glanced down, had a fleeting glimpse of a bony oriental hand. It deftly snapped a security clasp about my wrist, and there was a singsong whispering in my ear.

'What the...?' Too late, he was gone; swallowed up in the milling crowds.

A hiss signalled pneumatic doors on platform and train opening in a synchronized ballet. I snatched a quick look around: people moving purposefully about; brief glimpse of a local - Chinese - moving against the flow, towards the escalator. I, part-directed by crowd flow, part intuition, found myself on a train whose doors were now hissing closed behind me. Definitely nothing synchronised in the boarding process, and I now found myself to be underway to my hotel, chained to someone else's briefcase - a smart, slim, crocodile-skin affair, with shiny gold clasps.

Those were the stark facts, the reality - even though, as yet, that reality was something of a mystery. All I knew for certain was that something had changed in the world around me. It wasn't simply a briefcase that concerned me, or a mysterious Chinaman. Thoughts of my breakfast companion now played on my mind, as did thoughts of a second seemingly "casual" acquaintance. On that platform I was sure I had glimpsed another face; someone who'd appeared to be observing from a distance. A man who, last night, had introduced himself to me as Henry Smith.

I quickly analysed the situation. The Chinese geezer had slipped a key in my pocket, and as the case was fitted with a central combination lock - for which, I assumed, that singsong whispering to have been the number - it stood to reason the key must be for the security clasp. With which thought my mind logically ruled out ideas of bombs and booby traps. Such knowledge lowered the tension somewhat, but still left me with a sackful of questions to which I didn't have answers. Mistaken identity? That was first card to be pulled out. Then what of Mr Smith? If it had been him. Coincidence I discarded rather quicker than immediately, automatically according him the role of spotter; ie, there had been a need for identification. Scratch the mistaken identity theory. But such supposition was getting me nowhere near as close to a solution as the train was by now doing as regards my stop. The answer, I realized, probably lay inside the case. I therefore felt an urgent need to examine the contents. Sooner, rather than later. And in private.

I glanced around, as casually as was possible in my enhanced state of stimulation. Checking movements and faces. Nothing out of the ordinary that I could see. Neither was anything being logged by my sensitive, sixth sense antenna. This had been developed over the past months, was still being developed. No idea how it worked, but work it did, giving warning of my being watched, or about to step into danger. There was non of that. And apart from that case on my wrist, everything else appeared to be normal. It was the case that was not normal, but apparently only to me.

Fighting a growing impatience I detrained at Orchard, heading for my hotel, movements automatic, thoughts - directed by location - temporarily diverting me from my predicament. This was the very heart of tourist Singapore: Orchard Road, that tree-lined boulevard which stretched out to connect the junction of Dhoby Ghaut and Stamford Road, with Tanglin. Orchard Road, with its wall-to-wall, futuristic, multi-storey, super-cool shopping centres. To my mind they displayed more luxury goods than the whole world could ever use. Who bought all that Gucci, St Laurent, and Dior, I'd idly wondered during my first days here. If of course they even were the real thing. But I knew most were, at least those in shops like this. Shops dedicated to the sale of luxury items, at a luxury item price, of course.

Naturally, being in somewhat of a hurry, therefore subject to the first law of cussedness, I had to wait for the lights at the wide and somewhat dangerous Scott's Road junction. In this city, jay-walking is a serious offence; if the cops don't get you, the heavy traffic almost certainly will. A timer on the pedestrian lights advises you of the time left to complete your crossing. Or perhaps, time left to live!

As I waited I continued looking around, not as if that may help speed the passage of time - which of course it couldn't - but because I was now back in operational mode. Sight and senses were at full stretch, observing, discerning. Nothing out of the ordinary to be seen or sensed. But the time did allow my mind to be filled with worrying thoughts. I may not have observed anything, but conditions *were* ideal for a tail. Usual milling crowds, chaotic traffic, a good percentage of which appeared to be taxis. They shone like new, hardly a scratch or a dent to be seen. There again, Singapore law did not allow old bangers on the road. Once your car reached a certain age, apart from not qualifying to be re-licenced, the Government had a compensation scheme to help you replace it.

Traffic apart, construction work also needed to be taken into account. This seemed to go on all around. It was something else I'd noticed about Singapore, in certain areas the place appears to be unfinished, seemed determined to remain so. Buildings were being erected and demolished everywhere. It was like being in a combat zone, an impression the feeling in my gut served to reinforce.

'Excuse please. Copy Rolex?'

Given my heightened sense of awareness the bugger made me jump, but he shouldn't have. The question had been put to me almost continually since my arrival here, this time as I passed the entrance to the Far East Shopping Centre, my hotel but a short distance up the road.

'No, thanks. Not today,' I replied, somewhat firmly, as I negotiated yet another assault course of construction. Copy watches, Rolex or otherwise, were the last thing on my mind. For a start, I already owned a gold Omega dress watch, only

16

it was safely back home in the UK. In this day and age it did not pay to wear ostentatious jewellery in many parts of the world. Singapore I had been uncertain of, prior to my arrival here. Anyway, I may just have a briefcase full of copy watches!

Whatever, I was anxious to find out just what it was I did have.

*   *

Chapter Two

THANK GOD IT'S FRIDAY

Acute anxiety over an extended period is extremely stressful. The very reason I was to be found idly drifting later that evening. I was attempting to relax by losing myself in the fantasy-land of shopping centres and street vendors. I wasn't buying, not even looking, I was just reviewing events in my mind: the sequence, the timing, the possible people involved, and not just here in Singapore! I had others in mind too. Far, far away.

Forget it. What is done, is done.

Minerva's unwelcome reminder. Anyway, I was already well aware of that. What I was actually hoping to do was dream up a solution to the almost unimaginably dire position in which I now found myself. It was as if by so doing I could somehow reverse things; an impossibility, I realized. The whys and wherefores were irrelevant, for now. Survival was presently the dominant priority. I was also keeping my eyes open, alert for trouble. Almost expecting it. More than almost, truth be told. It was certainly coming. I could sense it. Time uncertain. Place unknown. But definitely coming. My sixth sense antenna was alive and well, alerting me to the fact. Time now to increase my sense of awareness, up the concentration levels.

Letting my feet take me where they would, I wandered along Orchard Road, using shop windows etc to watch for signs of a tail.

Trees, which offered mottled shade during the heat of the day, now created disconcerting shadows in the warmth of the evening. I wandered past restaurants and bars, shopping plazas, and hotels. The multi-storied, oriental-style Dynasty, with its green, ceramic-tiled roof, was across the way, Toys R' Us to my right, next to the Win Chou Ho Camera Emporium. The streets were teaming with life, and there seemed to be buyers for everything. Buyers for the cameras, and the electronics, for the designer clothes and shoes, the expensive jewellery, the souvenirs, even for the trivia and knick-knacks. There were buyers for the food and whisky too, and, in the nightclubs, for the cold tea that masqueraded as whisky for the hostesses. I imagine there were even buyers for the copy watches.

The Saxophone Bar, on Cuppage Road, was my intended destination, but passing Lucky Plaza I was once again reminded that, beneath all the gloss and glitter of fantasy-land lay that other, much more sinister world. The real world in fact, to which I was no stranger.

It may have been instinct, or just a hunch, but at this point I experienced a strong feeling being followed. I was no stranger to this, either. The last time it happened it had posed few problems. I had managed to pick them out and shake them off, using methods in which I'd received some brief training. But that had been on a fairly quiet street in London, amongst my own people. This was an entirely different situation. Singapore. Crowded. Noisy. Foreign. And no matter what tricks I pulled, I failed to spot anyone. OK, so I wasn't a graduate of the James Bond school of surveillance procedures, then again, neither was I a novice. I'd often been branded "amateur," and so I had been, at one time. But most of those who'd expressed such an opinion of late, now seemed to be dead. Some of them by my own hand. Funny thing, that; learning how wrong you could be being the last thing you ever learned. Probably even before you'd become aware of it!

I scanned the sea of tourist faces, recording details for later comparison. That was the easy part. As for the locals, to me they really *did* all look alike. So I studied instead the style and colour of their dress. I utilized the plate-glass windows, comparing reflected images against those stored earlier. Not one matched. Nor were there any friendly - though by now extremely suspicious - waves or nods. In fact there were no false moves at all. No sudden changes of direction, people suddenly averting my gaze as I looked round, no unlikely events. Nothing unusual at all. Either that, or the exponents had one huge advantage: they were bloody experts at it.

Still that sixth sense issued its warnings. Still nothing.

I shrugged off the feeling and continued on my way, initial conviction gradually dissipating. Which was when two things suddenly became apparent: I was hungry and, in a way, I'd been enjoying myself again. I had felt it once more: the thrill of the chase. Hard to shake once you've experienced it. A kind of sharp, intense focus, rarely encountered in normal life. Energy, thoughts, instincts, all channelled into a single purpose. The adrenalin had certainly been flowing, that was for sure, even if the cause did appear to have been based on imagination rather than something more tangible. But at least it proved I hadn't lost my touch during the months of inactivity. The only fly in the ointment being my lack of concern over a man who breakfasted where I did. His continued presence had not triggered the slightest worry. Until today, that is. A day during which a lot had happened, the majority of it, at least as far as I was concerned, not too good.

Sod it. Time to eat.

*

Engulfed in postprandial euphoria, I wandered once more, eventually deciding that perhaps another drink may help me unwind a little, and use up a little more time. I passed close by Bill Bailey's, gave it a miss; decided instead on the Far East Plaza. Although I did fancy chatting to someone, I wasn't in the mood for a repeat of last night's session - even if it now seemed highly unlikely that "Mr Smith" would turn up again. Seems he had achieved his goal. Next time, if there was need of a next time, it would be someone else entirely.

Taking the escalator to the third floor of the Plaza, almost as if programmed, I ended up in a pub I'd previously found there.

Thank God It's Friday, or TGIF, as it was known locally, and probably around the world, is a popular watering hole. During the day I'd found it to be a cool, quiet oasis. A good place for a refreshing drink and a chat. Obviously this didn't hold true at night, for it was now crowded, noisy, and hot. A good place for meeting girls, it seemed, though not exactly my type of girl. Still, it did enable me to cast aside my problems, even if only temporarily. Normality returned like a forgotten luxury after just a single glass of *Tiger*.

Ranged around the bar were well formed groups of people, from which I was excluded, so, not in the mood for drinking alone, I thought about pastures anew. Maybe I should chance Bill Bailey's after all? Drinking alone meant I was left alone with my thoughts, which is exactly what I didn't need right now. I would let my subconscious mull things over, come back to them later.

People came and left continually, even amongst the groups around the bar. Maybe I should, too. Leave, that is.

"The Holocaust is now, Hitler showed us how". The words blasted from the sound system to echo around the room, convincing me I really should leave. I could get along quite nicely without this place, I thought, and I was just about to depart when another beer was placed before me. The barman answered my silent query by directing my attention to a customer sitting opposite, facing me. Well dressed. Chinese.

I looked across to be faced by a raised glass and a toothy smile. Not my breakfast companion - the man from the riverside; different altogether, this. Well it would be, wouldn't it.

Not a member of a group, he was alone, too.

A pleasant enough smile. Expensively gold-capped, though, and - past events, along with what had already gone on today, leaving me with a nasty suspicious mind - not one

21

to be readily trusted, I felt.

Ah well, what the hell. Maybe I could learn something. I shot him a questioning glance, and he was immediately on his feet, walking round to join me. He reminded me of a mechanical toy which someone had wound up, pointed in the right direction and turned loose. He was lean and athletic-looking. He was also the kind of person I'd been wondering about whilst looking in the shops down Orchard Road. Here was one person that went for those luxury goods that were on offer hereabouts. The shirt was silk, belt Givenchey, shoes by Gucci. Hardly a hawker, I surmised.

He offered a hand, gold Rolex dangling loosely from the slim wrist. With some trepidation, I reached out and shook it. A damp hand with a limp grip. 'Fwed Lee,' he announced, having trouble with his diction.

I hesitated briefly, thoughts suddenly in turmoil. Something else had registered. In here, when I'd looked across the bar. A face. Seen but fleetingly, if at all. Peripheral to Fred Lee. Glimpsed over his shoulder. Someone in the crowd. A face I felt I should know, but couldn't for the life of me catergorize. A Caucasian face. That worried me, for I was usually pretty good at faces. I quickly glanced round the room, searching. There was nobody I recognised. Still.... Perhaps the time really had come to start treating events with a little more circumspection. The warning signs were there all right.

I shrugged inwardly, turning my attention to Mr Lee. I'd give him a hearing, but I would be vary wary.

'Fwed with an R?' I asked, smiling to show I was taking the piss, or whatever was the local equivalent.

He returned the smile to show he understood. 'Wight,' he confirmed.

'Roger. Roger McLaren. From London,' I added, thus forestalling the question. They always want to know.

'I have a fwiend in London,' he said. 'Weginald Tucka. You eva' come acwoss him?'

I laughed. This line of thought was common among foreigners, I'd noticed. It seemed to work on the principle that any two people of the same nationality would automatically be known to one another. Be they two British out of fifty-five

22

million, or two Americans out of better than two hundred million.

'Can't say I have,' I replied. Mainly because it was true, but at least it gave us a point at which to begin congenial small-talk, the trivialities that ease human intercourse.

It seemed Fred was just as much in need of a drinking companion as was I. So, for the moment, I pushed all previous thoughts to the back of my mind, and we sank a few. But I did carefully study every word he said, looking for anything that might give any clues.

There didn't seem to be any, so we became friends of convenience, and we talked. Even went to the Hard Rock Café together, for a late-night burger.

I drank a lot of water between beers. Fred's diction didn't improve at all. He still had trouble with McLawen!

*

To return to my room was to return to my problem. It was a problem that had presented itself this afternoon. Shortly after opening that briefcase, I immediately found myself with far too much on my mind. Well, who wouldn't have in my position? I'd seen the notices at the airport upon entry. In the four principal languages of the area - English, Chinese, Malay, Hindi - they left no margin for error. And here I was, in Singapore - a country in which the crime of being caught with even a small amount of a banned substance carried the death penalty - suddenly finding myself to be in possession of a briefcase full of what I could only assume to be heroin! That wasn't all. It also contained one thousand American dollars in 100 dollar used notes, a sealed envelope, and an airline ticket - Singapore Airlines, first class, Singapore to Perth. The reservation was for a flight in two days time, with an open return. The ticket also had a blank space where there should have been a name, which told me it hadn't been issued by your everyday travel agent.

Cash and ticket posed no problems whatsoever. I hadn't been brought up to worship money, there again, neither had I been brought up to reject it. Especially when it was being offered on such generous terms as, take it, it's yours. The supercilious, disapproving attitude of my younger days having melted into comprehension, the art of money management was now in my blood. Taught me by my now deceased girlfriend, Caroline, and funded by a recent windfall, in which she had also played a large part. All of it legal.

As for the ticket, well, I was going to Australia anyway, Perth, too. And travelling First Class had to be a better option than even my Business Class ticket provided. As long as I was able to change the flight, therefore the ticket, for they are identifiable.

No! The problems were in that briefcase: the note contained therein, along with drugs that must be worth a fortune. Not to me, particularly, for I was as anti-drug as were the Singapore authorities. Surely then, the solution was to turn them in. But if I went to the police, what could I say? This "Chink" - never seen him before in my life, honest - traded me a briefcase full of drugs for a week-old copy of the *Economist*. They'd be as likely to buy that as I was to buy a copy watch. Anyway, the police weren't always to be relied upon, especially in a foreign country, so what guarantee was there I wouldn't end up in the slammer? Clang! Mind your fingers. To await my fate.

From there it could be but a short trip to a hanging. And hanging was a very short trip indeed. Anyway, the note had advised against just such a move, issuing certain warnings to deter me - or whoever - from involving the authorities. It also offered a sweetener to the effect of the one thousand dollars being a down payment - balance upon delivery.

Presumed threats against my life didn't overly worry me, the money I didn't really need - especially earned this way - but.....

Not too many options, really. I could abandon the case in a luggage locker out at Changi, only that way the contents were almost sure to eventually end up back on the street. That was something I couldn't, and wouldn't, allow. Flush it down the loo then? A possibility. Wasn't that what they did in the movies, once they realized the cops were on to them? God, I thought, recalling the carefree period during which I'd sold computers by day, and toured the clubs - impersonating the rich and famous - by night. Why did I ever leave a business at which I used to earn an at least reasonable living? In fact, why did I ever leave school?

It was those thoughts which immediately prompted another: call Mike; he'd advise me. Mike Douglas, ex-SAS, now a security advisor. He'd been a childhood friend. We'd shared the same class at school, shared our knowledge during exams and, dare I mention it, even shared our first girl. Not on the same night, I might add. Anyway, I'd been there first, before he'd stepped in to take advantage of our friendship!

As it was still early morning back in London, I'd delayed calling him until this afternoon.

*

Now was the time; early evening back home. I just hoped that Mike was not away somewhere, which was frequently the case. As it happened, I was in luck.

Mike answered on the third ring, and after the usual preliminaries I explained my predicament. He at least confirmed my thinking as to method of disposal.

'Get rid, Roge,' he advised. 'Flush it down the crapper. Dump the case, keep the money. *Don't* use the ticket, unless you are able to switch flights. They're traceable, and someone's certain to meet that particular flight.'

'Um, not exactly what I wanted to hear, Mike. I've already thought all that out for myself, arrived at the same conclusions.'

'Oh, oh! Sounds like you're debating the alternative. Well, my advice, for what it's worth, don't do it, Roge. Last time you had some back up. This won't be anywhere near so simple. Don't forget, you're a long way from home.'

'I'll sleep on it.'

'OK, sleep soundly. And should you decide on.... Well... if you need help, don't hesitate to call.'

Promised I would. Then, still debating those options, but now vastly relieved, I lay my head gratefully on the pillow. Long before a solid decision had been reached, I succumbed to the arms of sleep.

It was entirely the wrong thing to do.

*   *

Chapter Three

IN FLAGRANTE DELICTO

He was Chinese; with a red face, a green face, a yellow face. Then it was red again beneath the flickering neon sign that advertised Tiger Balm. The man's head swivelled, eyes observing, watching. Never still. There would be others out there, I imagined, lots of them, ready to stop me if I ran. But why should I run? To where? Run from what? *I* knew, but how could they? It was impossible. The old onus-of-guilt syndrome, I thought.

Right on, Minerva agreed. *You're becoming paranoid. There again... Why didn't you do it last night, like Mike advised?*

Because I hadn't reached a decision then is why. The decision came later, much later, in the early hours, and even then.... OK, point taken. I'll dispose of it as soon as I get back to the hotel. Be there in less than ten minutes.

I can honestly say that I *had* intended doing it first thing this morning, but it seemed that fate had been against my decision from the start. Strange though it was, this morning there had been so much coming and going in my room I felt it should have been fitted with a revolving door. The maids were there first. Then it was the electrician, checking on a reported problem: a bedside light I didn't use, therefore hadn't reported a problem with it. Maybe the maid had, or the last guest. Whatever. The desk called next, advising that workers would require access to the bathroom. It was booked for refurbishment, the room should not have been let. Now that it had, they hoped it wouldn't be too much of an inconvenience. No, not at all, be my guest. I only have a few kilos of heroin to dump!

The thing was, I hadn't put up any serious objections. Hadn't even bothered to use the "Do not disturb" sign, which seemed to indicate that my subconscious was still debating the options. And I had to admit, I *had* consciously thought about the, What if...? Nothing to do with financial gain, everything to do with raw excitement and the thrill of the chase. Where it might lead me. Such thoughts buzzing around in my head, along with the domestic upheavals depriving me of my privacy, prompted me to stay my hand and go out. So I did. With some trepidation, I'll admit. I'd have been a fool not to have.

I'd elected to take a trip across the causeway, to Johore Bahru. But not before making sure everything was secure. Secrets well protected from accidental discovery.

*

It hadn't been a good day at all. I hadn't enjoyed anything about it. Johore was all right, I suppose. But I hadn't been able to concentrate, therefore enthusiasm had been at a low ebb. Lunch had been rubbish. Probably not. Maybe lack of taste related to lack of appetite rather than vice versa. The traffic had been horrendous; numerous delays; a sweltering coach offering me too much time with my thoughts. Time I didn't want with thoughts I didn't need. Negative rather than positive. But I had at last reached a decision. Reluctantly, I'll admit. But, as Mike had suggested, the options seemed far too fraught with danger. Then there had been all those neon-lit, imagined "watchers" on the walk back to the hotel.

So it was with great relief that I closed my door on the outside world that evening. Stopping briefly to retrieve the case - after first checking the exact position: of it, the book I'd

27

placed on top, and the old hair-across-the-lock trick - I made for the bathroom. Even greater relief to find that it actually had been refurbished: smoothly sliding, glass shower doors replacing the tatty curtain over the bath. That had given me cause for extreme concern. Not the shower curtain, the previously unannounced need for someone to work in my bathroom. That they actually had, offered more relief.

To cap it all off, it seemed my watchers *had* been imagined after all, for no one had followed me in. I'd been careful to check that. Neither, as far as I could tell, had the case been disturbed. So maybe the day wasn't turning out too bad after all. No matter, I wasn't about to tempt fate and hang on any longer. Besides, I had a flight to catch in five hours - Business Class.

Kneeling intently, I set the combination to the required number - that singsong whispering, "nine'een firy four," having deciphered, as expected, into nineteen thirty-four - clicking open the catches. Nerves a-jangle I removed the first packet and tore it open, managing to spill some of the contents. The remainder I quickly flushed down the toilet, experiencing relief as it disappeared. Only five to go.

It was a relief that was short-lived.

About to repeat the process, I found my arms suddenly pinned from behind, just as I picked the packet up. Not one of life's more exhilarating experiences, I'll tell you that for nowt. A brief and stupid thought.

Squeezing my eyes shut, I had the fleeting impression of being a character in a dream. Soon I would wake up and find myself in bed, no one else around. I'd be a tourist again. No briefcase. No drugs. Maybe not even any Singapore. Just like a movie I'd once seen, or a book I'd read. But of course, it wasn't to be. When I again opened my eyes they were still there, large as life. And they still held me. Crazy thoughts flashed through my mind at the speed of light as I tried to figure out what was happening; although it was fairly clear what had. It was also fairly clear what was about to happen, unless I could convince someone to believe my story. Thoughts like that I needed as much as the Vatican needed condom dispensers.

They'd certainly made a surreptitious entry, which

pointed to a passkey, for I *had* locked the door.

As I was hustled to my feet I did some simple arithmetic. Very simple! Four to one, at least. No problem for the likes Swarzeneger or Stallone, but this wasn't Hollywood. All I could manage was a small nod of acceptance, letting my body relax. No bloody Oscar nominations for that. The obvious question I left unasked. I was more than capable of predicting, what next?

But what did happen next caused me to readjust my thinking completely. There were no handcuffs, no uniformed officers, just a polite, "Come with us, please, Mr McLaren." Mr McLaren, eh! Like they were friends, taking me out for the evening. They were; taking me for a guided tour of the local nick. Well, I didn't actually have a lot of choice, being *in flagrante delicto,* as the lawyers would have it. Better to go quietly. Anyway, I *was* innocent. No matter how bad things looked at present.

Soon sort it out, Minerva suggested. *After all, you were disposing, not selling or distributing.*

But I *had* been in possession. That was all the law required. Despite such thoughts I made my face impassive, something I'd found myself able to achieve without too much effort. Of course, it was only skin deep. External. Inside I was in absolute turmoil.

Firmly, though without force, they took me away, quickly and quietly. They even allowed me the freedom to walk unrestrained, once it was clear I wasn't about to attempt the hundred metre sprint record. But on the way out of the room I quickly glanced round, saw what I was looking for. Another addition to the room refurbishment. What could well have been a discretely hidden camera. How had I missed that?

That camera gave me more food for thought.

Nobody spoke from that point on, but it didn't bother me. I just closed my mental doors on the outside world, deciding, for now, to accept things as they were. More often than not I'd found this to be the least stressful approach. After all, I couldn't exactly force them to tell me things they weren't prepared to tell. Not in this situation. Instead, I worked on what I was going to tell them. Quickly realized there was no way I was going to be believed.

I'd had ample time to get rid, squandered most of a day, deliberating! Or had I? Something told me they had been on to me all along, just waiting to catch me with the drugs in my hands. A very compromising position.

We left via a rear exit and were immediately picked up by an unmarked car. *Very* civilized. Strange, though. I'd not been cautioned. Nor had there been mention made of any charges. Very strange.

It was all very suspicious, and worrying. Especially as we drove straight past the local cop-shop.

*　　*

nese; with a red face, a green face, a yellow face. Then it was red again beneath the flickering neon sign that advertised Tiger Balm. The man's head swivelled, eyes observing, watching. Never still. There would be others out there, I imagined, lots of them, ready to stop me if I ran. But why should I run? To where? Run from what? *I* knew, but how could they? It was impossible. The old onus-of-guilt syndrome, I thought.

Right on, Minerva agreed. *You're becoming paranoid. There again... Why didn't you do it last night, like Mike advised?*

Because I hadn't reached a decision then is why. The decision came later, much later, in the early hours, and even then.... OK, point taken. I'll dispose of it as soon as I get back to the hotel. Be there in less than ten minutes.

I can honestly say that I *had* intended doing it first thing this morning, but it seemed that fate had been against my decision from the start. Strange though it was, this morning there had been so much coming and going in my room I felt it should have been fitted with a revolving door. The maids were there first. Then it was the electrician, checking on a reported problem: a bedside light I didn't use, therefore hadn't reported a problem with it. Maybe the maid had, or the last guest. Whatever. The desk called next, advising that workers would require access to the bathroom. It was booked for refurbishment, the room should not have been let. Now that it had, they hoped it wouldn't be too much of an inconvenience. No, not at all, be my guest. I only have a few kilos of heroin to dump!

The thing was, I hadn't put up any serious objections. Hadn't even bothered to use the "Do not disturb" sign, which seemed to indicate that my subconscious was still debating the options. And I had to admit, I *had* consciously thought about the, What if...? Nothing to do with financial gain, everything to do with raw excitement and the thrill of the chase. Where it might lead me. Such thoughts buzzing around in my head, along with the domestic upheavals depriving me of my privacy, prompted me to stay my hand and go out. So I did. With some trepidation, I'll admit. I'd have been a fool not to have.

31

I'd elected to take a trip across the causeway, to Johore Bahru. But not before making sure everything was secure. Secrets well protected from accidental discovery.

*

It hadn't been a good day at all. I hadn't enjoyed anything about it. Johore was all right, I suppose. But I hadn't been able to concentrate, therefore enthusiasm had been at a low ebb. Lunch had been rubbish. Probably not. Maybe lack of taste related to lack of appetite rather than vice versa. The traffic had been horrendous; numerous delays; a sweltering coach offering me too much time with my thoughts. Time I didn't want with thoughts I didn't need. Negative rather than positive. But I had at last reached a decision. Reluctantly, I'll admit. But, as Mike had suggested, the options seemed far too fraught with danger. Then there had been all those neon-lit, imagined "watchers" on the walk back to the hotel.

So it was with great relief that I closed my door on the outside world that evening. Stopping briefly to retrieve the case - after first checking the exact position: of it, the book I'd placed on top, and the old hair-across-the-lock trick - I made for the bathroom. Even greater relief to find that it actually had been refurbished: smoothly sliding, glass shower doors replacing the tatty curtain over the bath. That had given me cause for extreme concern. Not the shower curtain, the previously unannounced need for someone to work in my bathroom. That they actually had offered more relief.

To cap it all off, it seemed my watchers *had* been imagined after all, for no one had followed me in. I'd been careful to check that. Neither, as far as I could tell, had the case been disturbed. So maybe the day wasn't turning out too bad after all. No matter, I wasn't about to tempt fate and hang on any longer. Besides, I had a flight to catch in five hours - Business Class.

Kneeling intently, I set the combination to the required number - that singsong whispering, "nine'een firy four," having deciphered, as expected, into nineteen thirty-four - clicking open the catches. Nerves a-jangle I removed the first packet and tore it open, managing to spill some of the contents. The remainder I quickly flushed down the toilet, experiencing relief as it disappeared. Only five to go.

It was a relief that was short-lived.

About to repeat the process, I found my arms suddenly pinned from behind, just as I picked the packet up. Not one of life's more exhilarating experiences, I'll tell you that for nowt. A brief and stupid thought.

Squeezing my eyes shut, had the fleeting impression of being a character in a dream. Soon I would wake up and find myself in bed, no one else around. I'd be a tourist again. No briefcase. No drugs. Maybe not even any Singapore. Just like a movie I'd once seen, or a book I'd read. But of course, it wasn't to be. When I again opened my eyes they were still there, large as life. And they still held me. Crazy thoughts flashed through my mind at the speed of light as I tried to figure out what was happening; although it was fairly clear what had. It was also fairly clear what was about to happen, unless I could convince someone to believe my story. Thoughts like that I needed as much as the Vatican needed condom dispensers.

They'd certainly made a surreptitious entry, which pointed to a passkey, for I had locked the door.

As I was hustled to my feet I did some simple arithmetic. Very simple! Four to one, at least. No problem for the likes Swarzeneger or Stallone, but this wasn't Hollywood. All I could manage was a small nod of acceptance, letting my body relax. No bloody Oscar nominations for that. The obvious question I left unasked. I was more than capable of predicting, what next?

But what did happen next caused me to change my thinking completely. There were no handcuffs, no uniformed officers, just a polite, "Come with us, please, Mr McLaren." Mr McLaren, eh! Like they were friends, taking me out for the evening. They were; taking me for a guided tour of the local nick. Well, I didn't actually have a lot of choice, being *in flagrante delicto,* as the lawyers would have it. Better to go quietly. Anyway, I *was* innocent. No matter how bad things looked at present.

Soon sort it out, Minerva suggested. *After all, you were disposing, not selling or distributing.*

But I *had* been in possession. That was all the law required. Despite such thoughts I made my face impassive,

33

something I'd found myself able to achieve without too much effort. Of course, it was only skin deep. External. Inside I was in absolute turmoil.

Firmly, though without force, they took me away, quickly and quietly. They even allowed me the freedom to walk unrestrained, once it was clear I wasn't about to attempt the hundred metre sprint record. But on the way out of the room I quickly glanced round, saw what I was looking for. Another addition to the room refurbishment. What could well have been a discretely hidden camera. How had I missed that?

That camera gave me more food for thought.

Nobody spoke from that point on, but it didn't bother me. I just closed my mental doors on the outside world, deciding, for now, to accept things as they were. More often than not I'd found this to be the least stressful approach. After all, I couldn't exactly force them to tell me things they weren't prepared to tell. Not in this situation. Instead, I worked on what I was going to tell them. Quickly realized there was no way I was going to be believed.

I'd had ample time to get rid, squandered most of a day, deliberating! Or had I? Something told me they had been on to me all along, just waiting to catch me with the drugs in my hands. A very compromising position.

We left via a rear exit and were immediately picked up by an unmarked car. *Very* civilized. Strange, though. I'd not been cautioned. Nor had there been mention made of any charges. Very strange.

It was all very suspicious, and worrying. Especially as we drove straight past the local cop-shop.

*   *

Chapter Four

SINGAPORE SLING

In the eyes of most people, I suspect, police stations the world over are more or less the same; austere, inhospitable, unwelcoming kind of buildings. The sort of place one would not voluntarily chose to visit, especially so if you did have a choice in the matter.

Fact or fiction. The Police Station which I now found myself visiting, lack of choice in my case, certainly ticked all the boxes: bare floors; walls decorated with notice boards filled with posters and photographs, the latter of unsmiling faces. Swing doors frequently creaked and clacked with the various comings and goings, and there were starkly furnished rooms in which reports were probably being compiled on ancient typewriters.

Policemen are also comparable the world over, the difference being in the type of treatment you are likely to receive in the various countries. Civilized and reasonable; entirely the opposite; or something in between. Rubber hoses and the rough stuff, or the reading of your rights, with access to a lawyer.

In my case I'd have to go for the "in between" category, for although nobody spoke to me, I was treated, it seemed, with some deference. Although the treatment was firm and decisive, leaving me in no doubt that I was a prisoner. Although there was no rough stuff, no handcuffs, nor did they remove my belt and shoelaces before the door clanged shut on me. But neither was the offer of legal representation made, and the offer of a cup of coffee seemed equally unlikely. Oh, there were whitewashed walls in my windowless private suite all right, and the door did clang shut with the air of finality one would expect in such a place. It was prison lit, too: a dim, shielded light, up out of reach. A small, barred window, through which only blackness was visible, was also set up high, well out of reach. The place smelled of cheap disinfectant - no doubt meant to subdue the stink of urine, but failing miserably. I'd heard tell you get used to it in time. But how much time? Hoped I wasn't in here long enough to find out.

On a wall by the bunk, someone had kept tally of the amount of time they had spent here. No problems with language, just scratched lines in groups of five, last group incomplete. There had been an attempt at erasure, only partially successful, and I was able to discern that the total amounted to seventeen days, which didn't exactly ease my anxiety any. I tried to imagine what could happen to make my situation worse, couldn't think of a single thing at present. My earlier confidence was fast fading, to be replaced by anxiety, but also deep thought.

Something did not add up, and as yet I couldn't figure out what. Although the inkling of an idea appeared to be germinating at the back of my mind. Almost unthinkable. At least it would be to most, but, taking into account my recent background, I now saw it as a remote possibility.

I had expected to be driven directly to the station in Tanglin - close to the hotel, but they'd taken me instead to Central, close by, if not in, Chinatown. An area known as Novena, according to a sign I'd seen. It made sense when thought about. This would be the home of the drug squad, and that did have me worried.

Drugs! Singapore. The death penalty. I shuddered at

the thought, the reality of my predicament finally striking home. This wasn't England, and I had absolutely no viable proof whatsoever as to how I came to be in possession of that briefcase. I did wonder - under Singapore law - was I even entitled to consult a lawyer? Not that I knew any out here, but if I was allowed a phone call, I did know a couple of people in England with a modicum of authority. Though whether or not they could, or even would help in this situation, was another matter altogether. Still, all that would have wait until later. Didn't seem to be a lot going on round here just now, in the middle of the night.

Although, at times, I was a bit of a loner, there's a world of difference in being alone through choice, and having loneliness thrust upon one. This was loneliness of a different kind. I was alone with my thoughts and, given present circumstances, they were not exactly the kind of thoughts one would have wished for. My life stretched emptily ahead, so I left it there, thinking instead about what had led me here in the first place.

It all flashed back in a series of brief images, and snatches of dialogue. Just like the resume of a TV mini-series at the end of an episode, or prior to the start of the next: Assassination in London, witnessed by myself, an innocent passerby. Witness, shot and wounded by assassin, meets nubile young nurse who, in turn, is killed in mistake for him. Enter a heroine; the SIS; and South Africa. Throw in handfuls of diamonds; a cast of thousands; stir well. Stock storyline; adventure, exotic locations, sex and sadism. Good eventually defeats evil, but at some considerable cost. Myself attempting to cast those thoughts from mind. Impossible, for I was at the time busy detailing the facts in the form of a novel, an activity that kept me sane, at the same time helping me along the road to recovery. Successful publication. Agent and friend, Freddie Pratt, attempting to encourage me to go for a second. Greeting me one day in his office. Almost unbelievably, less than a week ago, now I thought about it.

`Roger, hi! Got something for me?'

`Afraid not. Seem to have run out of ideas. Just calling in as arranged. Off to Australia. Tonight, in fact.'

`Not emigrating? Holiday, you mean?'

`Of course, holiday. I couldn't very well call him a prat, for that was his name. Pratt, actually.

'Visiting a friend in Perth. If you cast your mind back you will recall I did tell you. Fact is, that's why I'm here. You promised to take care of Copper and Polly whilst I was away.'

`Perth, WA eh?' he said, his mind seemingly on other things, or deliberately ignoring the reference to my inherited pets. 'Now that *is* a coincidence. Another friend of mine is on his way there even as we speak. Travelling via the States. Freedburg Hoving. Professor,' he explained, as if explanation were a prime requisite for a name like that.

`Bit worried about him, to tell the truth. You know the type: probably fully conversant with the subatomic structure of a Mars bar, but ask him to pop down the road for some fags and he'd likely get lost. Not used to travelling, you see, or of life in general come to that, outside of a lab. And as forgetful as a dead elephant. In fact, I was just about to post this.' He reached into a drawer, extracting a large manila envelope. `Lecture notes. He's supposed to speak at the University of Western Australia. Probably won't notice their absence until he needs them. Perhaps you could pass them on for me?'

'Need to know exactly what is in there Freddie. You know all about airline security, so I will ask the same questions. Not that I don't trust you. But did you pack it yourself, or the did the absent-minded Professor pack it?'

'I can see exactly where your coming from, Roge, but it's not actually sealed, so take a peek', he said, handing it over.

I did take more than a peak. 'Ah, that's OK then, I'll leave it like that, open.' I handed it back.

Freddie then gave me a description of this Professor Hoving. `Impossible to miss,' he assured me.

`Well... er.. Are you certain he's actually left?' I had difficulty believing people could be like that. I could pick up my passport and fly anywhere at a moment's notice, no problem.

`Definitely. I checked. Not due "Down Under" until next week though. He'll be staying at the... Dampier Lodge, South Perth,' he read off the packet before handing back it to me.

38

'OK. But you won't forget the....'

'Yeah, I know, dog and cat.'

'Parrot, Freddie! It's a dog and a bloody parrot.' I handed him my spare key.

'Parrot? OK, I'll collect 'em tonight.'

That had sounded simple enough, last week, in England. Now here I was, five days on, and it looked as if the Professor wouldn't get his papers after all. It seemed I was about to disappear from circulation before I'd even reached Australia. In fact, it was at this very moment I realized my flight would already be airborne.

Despite the thoughts, and my surroundings, I slept, albeit fitfully, and briefly.

It was a dream that jerked me awake. A face within that dream. "Spectacles of such magnification they make his eyes look oversize. With his white hair and tufted eyebrows, he rather resembles a large, myopic owl," I recall Freddie telling me, when describing Freedburg Hoving.

The very same face I thought I'd glimpsed in TGIF! Not imagined, then.

But that had to be some kind of mistake, surely. My mind confusing a face with an image in my head. The Professor couldn't possibly be in Singapore. It was way too far off track. Even for someone like ... how had Freddie described him. "Not used to travelling, or of life in general come to that."

*

Bacon and eggs next morning were but a memory which lingered in my head. All I'd been offered was a cup of something warm. Hard to tell if it was supposed to be coffee, tea, or...well... neither of the above! Still, it's amazing how deprivation can make even the most unlikely item seem like a luxury. And whatever else, it did serve to kick-start my body into life, en-route a very uncertain future.

The worrying thoughts had returned with a vengeance.

They came for me later. Still silent. Still refusing to answer any of my questions. Still refusing me a phone call. Pretending they didn't understand, like I was a being from another planet, or something similar. Yet that didn't fit either, for the prime language in Singapore was English.

I was taken from my cell only to be handed over to another group of voiceless people, Caucasians this time. Leading me to suspect that questioning was to be carried out by the British High Commission.

Hope surged. Certainly a less daunting prospect. Surely my own people would believe me? Especially the people I knew back there.

Wrong on both counts, I was soon to discover.

*   *

Chapter Five

BOTTOMSWORTH OPENS THE INNINGS

I was driven away in what looked decidedly like an embassy staff car, as opposed to a taxi, or personal transport. Very strange for a start. But this was a shiny, black, chauffeur-driven Holden, rather than the expected Jaguar or Ford. Those facts immediately set me to thinking along entirely different lines to the British High Commission.

Neither was there an escort, other than the two burley, speechless Caucasians, who positioned themselves either side of me on the roomy rear seat.

By the time we set off I had the inkling of an idea as to where we may be heading, although I knew not where it was located. So this was a bit of a sightseeing tour for me. We passed through many green areas, past shopping centres and hotels, of which Singapore seemed to have an over-abundance, although I knew this not to be the case. This was a popular tourist destination, becoming more so with time it seemed from all reports. I could well imagine why. Despite my current predicament, I had grown to like it too, even in the short time I had been a free man here.

Then we were in Tanglin, close by my hotel, and the police station to which I had expected to be taken originally. But even now we passed it by as we entered and drove along tree-lined Napier Road. This was a pleasant garden-like district, buildings almost hidden amongst nature's bounty.

We turned off, onto an uphill drive, and then I saw the sign I had by now come to expect: Australian High Commission.

We pulled up by what appeared to be the main entrance, but were treated to the kind of reception no tourist could expect. The car door was opened for us, not by the chauffer, who remained seated, ready to drive off. One of my escort climbed out and started up the steps, the one remaining, blond haired, indicated I should follow. I did so, and he followed, though not closely. All very civilised, as if I were an important guest rather than detainee. This attitude changed only slightly as I followed, as directed, to enter a room, told to take a seat.

Then began the routine, one guy standing, the other also seated. Was this to be the good guy, bad guy routine, I briefly wondered. The guy standing flicked through my passport, as though he had never previously seen it. It was his opening performance. For as I was soon to discover, he really did get into playing the part.

'A yarnspinner, eh?'

'Passport says, author,' the standing man explained to his partner. He then tossed the document onto a table, hand reaching for his pocket.

The "yarnspinner" was a flat statement. He sounded as if he didn't believe it, or that "author" was synonymous with a low IQ. Though to my mind, it was all part of his act.

The blue and gold document spun twice, sliding neatly to stop, albeit upside down, in front of a shorter, darker man, who was seated to one side.

The small rectangular room to which they'd brought me was well lit, though sparsely furnished. Apart from three chairs, the table, and what looked like piles of tourist brochures, it contained nothing but the three of us. Not a lot of room for anything else, either.

'Fancy a cup of tea, do yer,' the standing guy - who was obviously in charge - asked.

'Said I did,' and he looked as if he were about to produce one out of his pocket! But no. The hand emerged clutching a cricket ball.

I threw him a questioning look as he indicated for his mate to drum up the tea. The ball spun neatly from one hand to the other.

'Play, do you? Coming from Yorkshire, I imagine you'd at least have an interest.' The voice was crisp, the language Australian, naturally. Other features more or less confirmed the fact. He was tall and fair. Blond hair, golden skin, and freckles. Around thirty-five, I judged. Probably a surfer a few years ago, definitely still a sportsman, for between fingers and thumb he now held up the familiar, red, leather covered ball.

I nodded my head, at the same time wondering what the hell cricket had to do with anything. But if he was trying to establish a rapport between us, I'd go along. One thing I needed right now was a friend, or at least someone who would listen. More than listen, believe.

'Don't play, though I do watch a lot. One of the few things in life worth bothering about, sex apart.' It was an answer that seemed to please him, I noted, for he nodded his head. But which? Cricket, or sex? Or maybe both.

I assumed he'd learned my place of birth from the passport. Then an altogether different thought presented itself. Something that would have accounted for the ceaseless activity in my room today ....yesterday, I corrected. Easy to loose track in this situation. I was supposed to be landing in Perth about now.

Blondie transferred the ball to his left hand, wrapping the fingers of his right, round the circumference, across the seam, thumb below, the accepted manner for a leg spinner. Gripping it firmly against the third finger, his arm described an arc, as though making a delivery.

'Right arm. Slow to medium,' he declared. 'Been known to go through a wicket or two in m' time.'

'I'll just bet you have,' I said. 'I take it you, or your friends, also went through my room yesterday. Maybe the evening before, while your Fwed Lee kept me occupied?'

'Ve..ry go..od,' Blondie replied, tossing the ball in the air and catching it. 'No flies on you, sport,' he declared, confirming my thoughts.

'Well, passports don't tell you a lot. But I suppose the number could come in handy, if you have the right contacts. Which I assume you do.'

'Oh, yes indeed. No worries there, sport.' He sent down another imagined delivery, arm straight, wrist flicking through on completion of the swing. 'Ran a check on you, through a certain section of your High Commission. Seems *your* passport number triggered all kind of alarms, bells, and whistles. The whole bloody shooting match. They even supplied us with a copy of your dossier, from which, I gather, you haven't shown up too badly when faced with.... well, let's say "the forces of evil!"'

So, things had been happening during the hours of darkness, as I festered in my cell. I felt better about that, especially the people he'd apparently been in touch with. My thoughts had briefly touched upon such people. The worrying part was the way things were shaping up now.

I made a disclaiming motion with my hand. 'Then you don't need me to fill in the details.'

The door opened and in came the tea, his silent partner, returning from his allotted task.

This was not afternoon type tea, but real tea, served in mugs. It looked strong, was certainly welcome. A bowl of sugar was provided, though I didn't use it, and they had already assumed I did use milk. There were biscuits, too. I took one, then a sip, and it was glorious. I nodded approval.

The conversation then carried on as if there had been no interlude, slight though it had been. But with the arrival of that tea I now felt much more human.

'Trouble with dossiers,' Blondie stated, brushing my previous reply aside as though I hadn't spoken, 'yuh can't ask 'em questions.' He checked his grip on the ball. 'You appear to be well versed in ...er, security procedures, Mr McLaren.'

'I read a lot.'

At this, he expressed profound disbelief. At least I assumed that's what was implied. 'Bollocks,' he said. Quite loud. 'Some of the things you know can't be picked up from

44

even the best of fiction.'

'Some,' I admitted, the situation now becoming much clearer in my mind.

'And you appear to have remarkable powers of survival,' he stated, giving me a verbal bow. The ball again spun neatly from one hand to the other.

'Well, let's not discount a certain amount of good fortune, and backing. Look, I'm getting fed up with all this. As I haven't actually been charged with anything, isn't it about time someone answered some of *my* questions?'

'Because you're innocent, eh?'

'Yes. Because I'm innocent. As you well know,' I said, emphatically, deciding to play along for a while. 'Pretty obvious, isn't it? It was all a mistake....'

'Strewth, Dunc! It was all a mistake!' He hammed it up, like a bad actor affecting incredible astonishment. And at least I now had one name.

'Hah! That's what they all say, sport,' Dunc advised, shaking his head sadly at what he apparently saw as a lowering of moral standards. A drug smuggler caught red handed, then refusing to admit to the fact.

'Well, this time, it happens to be true, if you'd care to listen.'

'Try us,' Blondie offered. So I did, his partner taking notes the whole time.

'And you expect that to be believed?' he asked, once I'd finished. And, to be honest, this was one of those occasions when the truth *did* sound rather hollow. Even to me. There again, hadn't I suspected as much when I'd originally decided not to go to the police? Now it seemed the police had come to me, and I smelt a set up. OK, let's see.

'Look, you've got my dossier, therefore you obviously know all about me.'

'Pretend we don't.'

'Well, I'm not into drugs, for a start.'

'Nothing to say y'are, nothing to say y'ain't. Brilliant switch, by the way. Nice touch that, pretending to dispose of your magazine just as the contact approached.'

'Come on. I'm no more a drug runner than... well, than you are.'

'Yeah, I imagine so.' he said, not looking at me, fingers polishing an imagined defect on the ball. 'But *they* aren't to know that.'

Ah! Here it comes. Just as I'd so recently figured. Though it still seemed I had little choice but to play along, at present.

'*They?*' I questioned.

'Yeah, they. Whoever that stuff was meant for. They don't know who yu' are. Therefore, it leaves 'em wide open. We've been waiting for a chance to infiltrate this mob. Bloody difficult. They can usually spot it a mile off. Yet here we are, presented with the ideal opportunity.

'This particular shipment. A mistake. Not big. Hardly in their league at all. Fact is they rarely import anything but opium base, and never by hand, so why bother with this? Definitely a mistake by someone. But it does give us an unexpected opening....'

His voice trailed off, but it did contain the hint of a challenge. So, sticking to my script, I contested the situation. Only way to find out exactly what was going on.

'Oh no. Not again. One of the reasons I'm travelling to Australia is to escape from the consequences of something like that.'

'Ah, yes. Miss Caroline. The Colonel's daughter. Read about that, too. Unfortunate affair, her getting shot.'

So, he did have a file on me, or had been in touch with certain people back home, likely via his opposite number in the British High Commission.

Excitement had recently been part of my life, it was something I had enjoyed. But that excitement had died, along with Caroline, or so it had seemed. Until now. With the memories of that incident fast-fading, I was rediscovering that excitement. Maybe I *was* in trouble, maybe not. The odds now heavily in favour of not. I decided to find out.

'A good enough reason for my not getting involved in that kind of thing ever again, don't you think?'

'Not a lot of choice this time, sport.' You've *got* to help.' He was emphatic. Not the best way to win my cooperation.

'I don't *have* to do anything I don't want,' I stated, just as emphatically. Asserting what I saw as my rights, especially now, knowing I'd been set up. Next thing I needed to know was how far they were prepared to push.

'N..oo,' he said, as if in resignation, 'course yu' don't. Well, we tried to help, can't say not. But, as this is really a problem for the Singapore police, I'm afraid that leaves us no alternative but to throw you back in....'

Which told me just how far they *were* prepared to go. All the bloody way. Even though I couldn't see them getting away with it. There again, one never knew with people such as these. Especially in a foreign country.

'On the other hand,' I cut in, 'What exactly is it you want me to do?' There was no way I was going to end up back in that police cell. Even for one more night, which I was pretty sure wouldn't happen anyway. But there was no point in my rolling over, making things easy for them. Two could play this game.

He gave me a regretful smile. 'Good on yer, mate. That's more like what I wanted to hear.' This was now straight business. Even the cricket ball had returned to a now bulging trouser pocket.

'Isn't that what's known as blackmail? You know I'm not involved, yet....'

'Save it, Roger, I've heard it all before. I may call you Roger?' he asked, electing not to await a reply. 'Duress more like. No such thing as blackmail in our business. You know that.'

I was now sure he also knew that I knew what was afoot. But I'd play along with them a while longer.

'And just what is your business?' I had absolutely no option but to ask. Didn't expect a straight answer, didn't get one. Didn't really need one.

'Sort of cops, Roger. In a manner o' speaking. So no blackmail. The fact we're willing to pay, rather than demand money, testifies to that.'

'What! You mean....?'

'Twenty grand,' he interjected.

I glanced at my watch, not that it told me anything. It was a tactic I often used; buying a couple of seconds more time. Stupid. There was nothing to think about. I didn't need the money. Anyway, I was on holiday.

'Australian or Sterling?' I heard myself ask. Well, the way I saw it, I still wasn't exactly bargaining from strength.

'Sterling. Natch. Plus expenses,' he added, still not quite sure he had me hooked. The very impression I'd aimed for.

'Plus expenses. Of course!' I threw in sarcastically. 'I'd still like to know who you are. You don't look like cops to me, so who exactly do you work for?'

The forefingers of the proffered right hand were heavily callused I noticed as he reached out. 'Robert Bottomsworth,' he announced as I shook. 'Unfortunate surname, but there we are. Call me Bob.'

'Dunc,' his mate advised. 'Duncan Bradley. We're with... er..' He looked across at Bob, as if for clearance. 'A government agency.'

'Ah! Like the Post Office, you mean?' That drew the kind of look I'd expect had I offered him a dose of Aids.

'Not posties, no. Federal Police. Narcotics Division.'

No! Never! You're kidding! Didn't really say those things, but I felt like I should have.

Then Bob took control again, going on to give me a brief run-down on what they knew about "this mob". Either, not a lot, or they weren't giving it all. I suspected the latter. Same every time with these people. Need to know, was the term they used to hide behind.

Next came, 'A bit of background, Roger.' A sort of layman's guide to *Papaver somniferum* - the flower of sleep. Opium poppy, as opposed to the common or garden variety.

'Opium, with its sweet, pungent odour is a morphine base. And morphine, when treated with acetic acid, produces heroin, in the form of liquid or powder. That's the easy part. The difficulty is in transporting the product from producer, to laboratory, to market. Route, method and means, that's the info' we need. Stuff like that.'

Of course, they knew I had little choice but to agree, eventually, saving myself any hassle they could cause if they wished to. Maybe even suspected I'd be willing to go along with it. But I wasn't about make it easy. Only slowly did I allow myself to be persuaded. Besides, I could agree to anything right now. Find a way out later, if that was the way I chose to play it.

'Tell me exactly what it is you expect. And if it's not a better alternative to a Singapore jail, forget it.' I realized that probably gave them infinite leeway.

'Your remit, in short, is just to deliver that briefcase. Then, worm your way in, if at all possible.'

'Just like that, eh?'

'Not just like that, no, Roger. Not at all. Things rarely work that way, as you well know. It may not be possible. But let's make the effort eh! Deliver the case and .... well, whatever. Just do as they ask, take the money, then sit back and see what develops.'

'Do as they ask?'

'Insofar as conscience allows.'

'Huh. I may have a problem with that.'

'Yeah, well, never forget, Roger, it's gonna be done whether you're there or not. We can't rule out the fact that people may die. Many more *certainly* will if we don't stop them. Maybe they'll invite you in, maybe not. It'll be difficult. But give it a try. That's all we ask. This is a one off opportunity. Could be years before we get another chance. In the meantime.... well, you know.'

'That's an awful lot of unknowns. Especially when my life could be at stake. I wouldn't imagine they're about to write out an invitation. Especially to a stranger. Won't they be expecting someone who's.. well... known to them, for instance?'

'Good thinking, Roger. But we do have some answers. You weren't the only person on that station with a magazine tucked neatly under his arm. Or hadn't yuh thought of that?'

'I had wondered. What had happened to him?'

'Aw, no problem. The authorities have *him* nicely tucked away. Along with the guy who gave you the briefcase.'

'But they can't hold them forever. What then?'

'Look, sport, this isn't like back home. Here, they can do mostly as they please. Especially if it concerns security of the nation, or drugs. Those two could just disappear.'

So it would seem. I thought it, didn't put it into words.

'OK. What about background? That they are sure to check. And it won't just be cursory.'

49

'Use your own, she'll be right. Nothing'll show that shouldn't, we'll make sure o' that. A successful writer, visiting an old school friend, making a little extra on the side. Not exactly unheard of, y'know.'

'You make it sound so easy.'

'Jeez! Give it away, sport. Nothing that's worth doing is easy. Have to watch every step closely, otherwise you'll be in for a bit of aggro.'

'Why don't you spell it out? "Aggro", that's a bit like gift-wrapping a cut-throat razor. If you mean I could get killed, say so.'

'If that's what you want.'

'It's what I want. All the cards face up. And talking of watching every step, let's start with the ... er.. consignment. We're a packet short, you realize. That's not likely to go unnoticed.'

'Baking soda, sport.'

'Baking soda! That *certainly* won't go unnoticed.'

'Nah. Baking soda's what you flushed down the dunny. We had the real thing safely stashed by then. No.4 heroin, also known as China White. Strewth, couldn't take a chance on *that* ending up in the wrong hands. It'll be back before you leave.'

I mulled that over, decided to test them once more. 'So, if the cops have only got a case full of baking soda...,' I began. But he was way ahead of the game. Even smiled to let me know it.

'No, Roger lad, yuh got it wrong. Cops have got the real thing all right. Every packet, some with your prints all over 'em. Good background for prints, this polythene.'

'Huh!' Another switch somewhere down the line, I assumed. So I tried another tack. 'What about airport security?'

'No worries. We'll fix it so the case looks normal on the x-ray. Nothing much'll show. Just the usual: documents, books, pens, etc.'

'And once I'm in - *if* I manage it - who will be my contact over there?'

'Guy at the Transit Inn. It's a popular pub in central Perth. He's a barman there. You can trust him implicitly.'

'Umm. What about a silly password, then?'

'Silly, Roger? Possibly. But important, as you well know.'

'And?'

He suddenly pulled out the cricket ball, tossing it in my general direction, fast, lot's of spin. He nodded approval as I caught it at arm's length. It told him there was nothing wrong with my reactions or eyesight.

'Should have played,' he suggested. 'Barman'll ask if you do. Your answer? I watch.' Not even the hint of a smile.

Next came a brief rundown on establishing drops and using cut-outs - terms with which I was familiar through the novels I read, and the little insight I had been given by the SIS. It was at this point they allowed me to leave. Just like that. I was free, about to become a tourist again. Back to my hotel. That was definitely a great relief. Even though I'd long ago figured it would happen, eventually. They'd concocted things in such a way they had a kind of hold on me, but nothing that would have stood up to a good lawyer, I thought.

'Check back tomorrow, Roger. I'll update yuh before yuh' leave. Yu'll be expected.'

'Haven't you forgotten something?'

'No. Just checking to see if you had,' he said, handing me a stack of tourist brochures. 'In case anyone raises the matter of a visit to the Australian High Commission? Good thinking, Roger. Keep it up.'

From someone like him, praise indeed. Maybe I wasn't as rusty as I'd imagined. I had a strong feeling that I couldn't afford to be. Especially as I was about to become fully operational again.

*   *

Chapter Six

SANTA'S CLAWS

Named, Wicker's Keep, after the 18th century prospector who had built it, the ancient stone tower sat atop a knoll known as Dead Man's Hill, a low outcrop of reddish, rocky bush which, although it did dominate the surrounding flat countryside, hardly warranted the label "hill," Dead Man's or otherwise. Located off the Kalgoorlie road, east of Perth, in the state of Western Australia, the very origin of the hill's name had long been lost in the sands of antiquity.

*

Friday October 11th 1991.
The morning forecast had promised yet another fine, dry day, though that was almost guaranteed. Easy enough to predict in this part of the world, at this time of year: late spring in the southern hemisphere.

Without fuss, they'd quickly seized him as he took his early morning exercise, there being few people around South Perth at six am. None at all in this particular area, the very reason it had been selected. They had done their homework.

Approaching from behind, from out of the bushes, one hand grabbed a wrist, locking it, effectively bringing him to a halt. Another hand was clamped over his mouth. A right hand, thumb uppermost, fingers smelling strongly and revoltingly of tobacco. Over his shoulder drifted the acrid fumes of garlic and stale alcohol, and the heavy, musky smell of equally stale sweat. There had been no chance for him to call out before the gag was in place, no one to hear anyway. The gag had been quickly followed by a blindfold, to eliminate the possibility of recognition, he'd assumed, but, with his high-correction glasses being crunched underfoot during the melee, he'd have had problems in that department anyway.

These people certainly seemed to know what they were about, he thought. He only wished *he* knew.

Once secure - wrists bound behind his back, uncomfortably tight - pressure on his arms, along with a fist to the kidneys, forced him to move. From then on he decided not to struggle but to obey the pressures as they directed him. Obviously the least painful option, and, being cursed with a low pain threshold, pain was something he just couldn't stand.

As an intellectual, he attempted a deduction as to what it was all about, found it almost impossible to over-ride the fear and pain. His first thought had been a mugging, but not now. They'd know he carried little when dressed for exercise. So this was something much more serious than a mugging. He was in his own black world. A totally unfamiliar, alien world. If only he could see, or speak. If only they would.

The almost total lack of speech after the initial assault hinted at professionals, for among a group of amateurs - he'd heard tell, and could well accept - silence was almost impossible to achieve.

Deprivation of sight and speech only served to intensify the fear he felt; a cold, gnawing fear. The blindfold made him feel insecure, vulnerable, which of course he was. The only remaining sense capable of tendering anything new, offered solely that which he didn't wish: the sour taste of defeat, of helplessness.

A strong pair of hands roughly gripped his biceps from behind, turning him left. Forward a dozen paces. There was the sound of a car approaching, and stopping, doors opening.

A hand on his head forced him down as they thrust him into the rear. One person settled either side of him. The doors closed. Then they were moving off. Now, no one bothered him.

Not one word had been uttered since those initial guttural commands, though the driver did whistle nervously.

The man was a prisoner in body, but not in mind. The mind was free to wander. Either aimlessly, or to apply logic; the decision was his. But as far as he could tell, there was no logic to it. He was a stranger here. Not just to the situation, to Australia itself. He'd been in the country less than two days. And during those two days he had done nothing that would warrant such treatment, as far as he could tell. All he had done was check into his hotel, advise someone at the University of Western Australia of his arrival, and made some arrangements, via the Bursar.

The atmosphere in the cramped interior was as tense as he himself. He could sense it, despite his confused thoughts.

How far, or how long they drove, he had no idea. Five minutes? Fifteen? Having not thought at the outset to try and keep track, there was no way of knowing. Apart from which, his brain had been otherwise occupied, and knowing wasn't important. One thing was certain, they had now departed the metalled surface and were heading across rough ground. They had to be clear of the city, for as he understood it, you didn't travel far from Perth before you *were* in the countryside. Perth itself almost was the countryside: green and pleasant, parks, river and bush. But he suspected this to be that other countryside - the start of the Outback, of which he'd heard so much. The thought caused a shudder to run down his body. He was a city person.

Eventually they bumped to a halt. There were sounds of doors opening, of bodies piling out, the car rocking on its springs as they did so. One reached in and roughly dragged him after them. Now he could smell the country; the quality of the air. Fresh, yet bone dry, despite the fact that the sun had yet to cast its full authority. It was still, too, and eerily quiet. Despite the still mild temperature, he broke out in a sweat.

*

The dead stone of the old tower of Wicker's Keep marked the location of disused mine workings which, up to moments before, had long been deserted. Indeed, the area had not seen activity on such a scale for years. Few came out here, apart from the odd, ambitious fossicker, seeking an overlooked nugget of gold, or young lovers, seeking seclusion.

Tower notwithstanding, there was not much else around but bush and scrub; a few clumps of eucalyptus; the thread of an empty river; a hole in the ground; and some long-abandoned machinery, silently rusting and corroding away to nothing.

*

Once on his feet, and turned to face a certain direction, the hands left the man to his own devices, no one to hold or guide him. In an unknown, unloved, unseen environment, he found that unsettling. His facial muscles twitched with apprehension.

Out here the sky was vast, and blue. A darker, denser blue, perhaps, than one somehow expected. Or maybe it just appeared so when viewed against the silver and green of the eucalypts. But, of course, the man couldn't know anything of this.

He was told to walk. The first words he had heard since this affair began. He stood his ground. A defiant protest at the treatment he was receiving. It was all he was able to offer. Big mistake.

A fist to the kidneys again. Protest noted; not accepted, it crudely, but silently, advised.

'Walk.' The order was again barked out, and this time he did, though tentatively. What was out there? Where were they going? Why? He'd heard mention of the snakes that lived on this continent, most of them deadly. What if he were about to step on one, would they warn him?

After a few paces, the order was 'Stop!' He did so, thankfully, for it was an unnerving experience for a sighted man to walk unsighted. The ground felt fairly level beneath his trainer shod feet. Sort of sandy and rough, he thought. Committing even the tiniest of details to memory was automatic for a man of his ilk. File storing. This data joined the few other positive scraps of information he'd been able to glean. They were Australian; deduced from their accent. But, this being Australia, that would be natural, wouldn't it. One of them was bearded and wore a moustache, both of which matched the explosion of red hair on top of his head; briefly noted before his glasses had been dislodged in the initial scuffle, and the blindfold put in place. A quick, though possibly vital, glimpse.

'What made them decide on this method, Jonesy?' one of the abductors suddenly asked, breaking the near perfect silence. It almost sounded like a protest rather than a question, but the voice had a nervous edge to it.

Unbeknown to the man, the person to whom the question was directed - well-built, arrogant and officious-looking - slowly turned to face his questioner. Like some third-world general, he didn't care to answer the questions of underlings. He *asked* the questions, didn't answer them. But this time, because it served a purpose, he'd let it go.

'A warning to any other bastard,' he answered. The voice of the red haired man was matter-of-fact.

One of them is a Jones, then; another brief thought. About as common over here as it was in Wales, or Smith, back in England, he'd heard, but it could help. He committed that to memory also, to be added to the file, just as the silence was broken by a harsh, metallic, double click.

Although he had never before heard the sound of a weapon being cocked, he somehow sensed that was what he was now hearing. The thought therefore brought with it a whole avalanche of fears.

Fear also escalated in the mind of one of the man's abductors. This wasn't a place he wanted to be at, either. Aware of what was about to happen, he wondered why his presence had been required. Did they suspect something?

His fear was overwhelming enough to contemplate making a break for it; of running. But run to where? The question stilled his hand. There was nowhere *to* run. Running would be his death warrant. He wouldn't get far before he was caught, tripped, or brought crashing to the ground by a bullet.

The gagged and blindfolded man experienced thoughts of a similar nature, only his were extremely short-lived, for the metallic sound was quickly followed by the crack of a shot; an epilogue whose message reverberated through the still air. The shot had been surprisingly loud. The sound would carry far out here, but there was no one else around to hear it.

Even the man didn't hear, or if he had it was the *last* thing he heard, for it was the shot that ended his life. His body now lay in the angular repose of death at the base of the tower. Limbs twisted in dramatic, ungainly angles. The memory wiped clean.

Beneath the body, the bright red stain of what had so recently been a life, now darkened to a morphogenetic memorial in the dry earth.

From that moment on, Dead Man's Hill had every reason to be known as such.

Files had been erased. Not just erased, obliterated.

* *

Chapter Seven

THE ROMANCE OF FLIGHT

After leaving the High Commission yesterday, I'd eaten and drank at the usual places, done the usual touristy things: looking round the shops, taking photographs, even buying the odd trinket. But I'd been alert all the while. I was looking for someone in particular, or for anyone following. I was sure no one did. Now I was "operational" again, I saw things in a different light; imagined myself being confronted, noted possible escape routes. I paid attention to the layout of streets and buildings, filing data away for possible future use. Scraps of information, some useful, some maybe not, some meaningful, others would possibly become so in time, but above all, being first hand, all reliable.

I'd called at the Mandarin Hotel, Singapore Airlines office, to confirm my reservation and have the ticket validated in my name. It didn't seem to pose any problems at all, so I assumed certain people had been wielding a little of their power. But from which side of the fence I wondered?

I then returned to TGIF, in the forlorn hope of running

into Professor Hoving. I saw no one even remotely like him so, after one long drawn out beer, I called it a day, took a slow walk back to my hotel.

*

Feeling much more relaxed after a worry-free night's sleep in a comfortable bed, and by now familiar surroundings, I was back into my pre arrest routine next morning. Pool, shower, shave, etc. Then a fresh start. For breakfast I sought out a new venue, not that I expected my past breakfast companion to still be in residence, as it were - his usefulness had surely come to an end - but as a matter of course. I was again in operational mode, so was no longer prepared to allow myself to become predictable. If *I* wasn't aware of where I was going, nor could anyone else be. Unless I was being tailed. But by now I was being really careful, thus reasonably satisfied such was not the case.

The offerings at my new choice of eatery - selected arbitrarily, as I chanced upon it in passing - were more or less on a par with the previous venue anyway, so no complaints there. I left feeling much better.

Next I returned to the High Commission, as previously arranged.

This I found to be far different from yesterday's visit, for I was escorted upstairs and through a labyrinth of corridors, before being directed to the open door of an office just ahead, then left to my own devices.

I found this to be Bob's lair. He stood side-on to me, using the sunlight which poured in through a window he concentrated on the open file in his left hand. The cover was stamped in red, "CONFIDENTIAL", large block letters. He frowned, shaking his head as if having trouble believing what was written there. His right hand subconsciously polished the cricket ball on the crotch of his trousers.

'Want to be careful down there. You know what they say, "Two's company, three's a crowd."'

He raised his eyes and looked in my direction, suddenly all smiles. 'Hey, Roger, g'day. Ready for a briefing? Though I imagine you're pretty familiar with most of it.' He nodded at the file. 'How'd you become involved with you-know-who, anyhow?' He asked. There was no mention made

59

about my mode of dress.

I avoided answering directly, by the simple expedient of asking a question of my own. 'That my file?'

'Ain't Ned Kelly's.'

'And the details aren't there?'

'Some. Not all. Sir James made sure only the relevant information was available.'

'The Colonel, eh! Well, well, well, as I thought. And just why would he do a thing like that?' I posed, rather sarcastically. I'd long since come to suspect SIS involvement. Few people even knew I was in Singapore, but in this day and age the SIS could easily have found out, should they have a need to know.

Bob tossed the ball in the air, catching it in the same hand. 'I suppose, if it were in his interest to do so.'

'So this involves the UK, as well?'

'And the rest of Europe. That's where most of it seems to end up.'

Bastards! I thought. Now the picture became crystal clear. Confirmation that I *had* been set up, to be used once more. Well before I'd even arrived in Singapore, no doubt. Once here, spotters apart, my "Yorkie" friend had been waiting; mainly to ensure I rode the MRT. But they'd have had a back-up plan, just in case I hadn't been so gullible. A restaurant I visited, my hotel, a bar - TGIF maybe. No! more than maybe. After all, that was where they'd set me up with Fwed. This made it possible... likely even, that the man on the MRT had been one of theirs, too. I'd bet they'd already had the real carrier, and receiver, in custody. Nor, I suspected, had they been in my hotel room to switch anything. At that stage, despite what they knew, they wouldn't have trusted me with "real live" heroin. And the Singapore Police had to be in on it, too. No way they'd release me to a foreign power if they even suspected I might be involved in drugs. So, *if* I was right, the situation had changed somewhat. "No choice" suddenly became "my choice." I hadn't needed to come here today at all. Could have called their bluff, fairly confident they were bluffing.

Could, but you didn't, Minerva offered. *After the previous experience, imagined you'd have screamed and shied away from anything similar. That episode cost the lives of two people you'd been very close to.*

Not wrong. But, let's face it, life became boring if you allowed it to, and that's just what I'd done of late. I'd had four days playing tourist, and it really wasn't me. Now I felt something I'd almost forgotten existed; sheer exhilaration. But there was something else as well. Something Bob had said. 'Overall, they're changing thousands of young lives. A lot of those will die young.' SIS involvement signified that some of those would be young Brits. That's what struck home. It was as if he'd pushed a button on me marked "Patriot", for I happen to be one of those old fashioned people that believe I owe my country, not vice versa. I did, too. I'd become rich working ad hoc for the intelligence services. Didn't feel bad about taking the money, either. It had been earned. In their minds the job came first, people second. One of the reasons I never fully trusted them. Never would. Which got me to wondering about the person who had recommended I indulge in a Singapore Stopover in the first instance! In fact, thinking about it now, the recommendation to use that particular travel agent had probably come via the SIS. Surreptitiously, of course.

I filed the thought, quickly reverted to the here and now.

'Not very subtle, Bob, the MRT setup. In hindsight, of course.'

'Yeah, well, we had to dream up something in a bit of a hurry. Situation was there, you were there. Only the Colonel suspected you might prove difficult if we'd approached you cold.'

'Seems the Colonel knows me better than I know myself,' I admitted, knowing I would have been reluctant had they made a direct approach. Natural reaction; kicking at traces. Now things were a little different. Everyone happy. After all, wasn't this just what I wanted. What I thought I'd been missing?

Apart from all that, the flight I had originally been booked on had left days ago. Cash for my ticket already refunded.

We tided up a few points, then made arrangements for

me to pick up the briefcase later on in the day. No way I wanted to wander around town with that lot in my hands. Nor was I willing to leave it unguarded, in my hotel room. Too much riding on it this time.

As for my packing, most was already taken care of, the final touches would come later, after my visit to pick up the briefcase, and receive a final briefing, scheduled for late in the afternoon. I would then change into something better suited to first class travel than the shirt, shorts, and sandals I now wore.

The rest of the time I gave to walking around town, taking in various sights. This included a park or two, of which there were many in Singapore. Fauna filled oases of relaxation, like their Orchid garden. Lots of open space, where to tail anyone would be nigh on impossible.

*

After my post breakfast visit , I had no need to call in at the High Commission again. For security reasons, being as our final meeting was scheduled for long after the building had closed its doors on normal business, therefore the public - the issuing of visas, etc - Bob had arranged for us to meet at an end of day place of relaxation far removed from Embassy Row, which is what the Napier Road area essentially was.

I took a taxi, arrived slightly early after allowing for the evening traffic and getting it wrong. Even so, Bob and Dunc were already in place, probably so as to observe my arrival, checking I was clean, ie, not being tailed.

It was a routine meeting, for there had been no last minute changes, no alerts, no additional information or instructions to pass on. So we had a drink, passed a little time together, during which I assumed charge of the briefcase. The ticket, I already had, now correctly administered. So we said our goodbyes and parted. Although I assumed, and hoped, that Bob's goodbye had been au revoir.

I had arranged with the hotel to keep my room until well past check-out time, so was able to shower, change, complete my packing, and even have a leisurely meal before departing for the airport at Changi.

I checked in early. Not early in the day, for it was a night flight, so time-wise it was almost midnight.

Using the ticket supplied to me, I exchanged my suitcase for a first class boarding card. That briefcase I hung on to as if my life depended on it, for I was sure that could well be the situation. The threat would come, I realized, not necessarily from anyone known to me, but from those who weren't. Unknown people in an, as yet, unknown country. The worst possible scenario.

I was excited as I approached security, and, yes, a little nervous, too. But all went well. Bob and Dunc obviously exercised some influence around here. But I had already been made aware of that fact.

*

As I boarded this particular Boeing 747, turning left, and upstairs, for the very first time, rather than the usual right, I was surprised at the change up here, even when compared to Business class.

Placing my briefcase in the overhead locker I chanced a glance at who was to be my companion on this flight, knew immediately I was in trouble.

I had been hoping for a trouble-free flight, during which I could probably relax, to finally shed any remaining tensions and worries of the past couple of days. Even though they were mostly no longer tensions and worries, never really would have been had I known then what I did now. Almost laughable.

What actually lay ahead was not worth worrying about just yet. I'd play that as it came.

*

I never accept anything at face value without question, never trust immediately without suspicion. It was a defence system I'd devised at school, and it served me well, then and now. Most of the time, anyway, although there had been occasions earlier on in life where the system had back-fired on me. Therefore, what I saw here gave me cause to wonder if anyone had pre-arranged the seating plan. Or was it just the plain old McLaren' good fortune at work. That said, I suspected things could go either way from this point on. Very good, or infinitely bad. I hoped for the former.

I'm usually pretty well laid-back, even when the

pressure's on, but there is one thing that's almost guaranteed success in penetrating my defences. Women.

There had been rather a lot of them over the years. Some, pleasant dalliances of little consequence; others rather more serious affairs.

Anne had been one of the former, I recalled. One of the early girl friends. One out of many. She'd been a "tack" girl with one of the local trainers, back home in the "Newmarket of the north". Definitely a stable relationship, that, for we'd often end up there at night. And it hadn't been to bed down the horses! Then there had been Jennifer, lovely girl, but rather too keen on marriage once we had got to know each other probably far too well! Just two of the many, I mused. There had been plenty more affairs, none seeming to work out quite the way I would have wished. Two eventually had. Then they'd been taken from me. Cataclysmically and forever. What I needed now was direction, and that certain someone. Yet I wasn't sure there was enough love still remaining for that. Maybe it had all been used up along the way.

Others, more recent, came briefly to mind, but were now swept aside, for the example of the fair sex seated here seemed almost too good to be true. Kind of girl that's always previously spoken for. But although these dainty hands were heavy with rings, there appeared to be none on fingers that mattered. To my mind, especially with a looker like this, that immediately gave cause for hope.

Around her throat she wore a silk scarf, probably St-Laurent, or of similar quality.

As I took my seat, strapped in and made myself comfortable, I also made a quick visual survey, as surreptitiously as possible. A youngish - say mid-twenties - healthy-looking person, who certainly wasn't strapped for cash was my instant opinion. In the same quick glance I could hardly avoid taking in the outline of shapely, well-defined breasts. In fact, because I'm made that way, I felt it my aesthetic duty to savour the sight. Besides, they were just demanding to be admired.

And she did look stunning. Ok, to me most girls look stunning at first glance, that's the way I am, but this one looked exceptional, despite being seated, therefore her full length not totally in view.

'Champagne, Miss Hamilton?' the stewardess asked, innocently surrendering my companion's identity as she proffered a tray of fluted glasses, along with a wide, reassuring smile.

Orange juice was also on offer.

So! Miss Hamilton. Either a frequent traveller on the route, or the stewardess was on the ball. Or was this standard First Class procedure?

'It might help pass the time,' Miss Hamilton replied, accepting the glass with an admirable lack of pretension. The plaintive voice of an insecure, lonely person, was the impression given. All her vanity, apparently, was in her clothes, and the jewellery she wore.

'And for you, Mr McLaren?'

My! Standard procedure or not, this stewardess had certainly done her homework. Not something that happened down the back end, where I normally travelled. Or had done, previous to my bank account recently receiving an injection of a not too unsubstantial amount of cash. Then I'd promoted myself to the Business section. But this was another level entirely.

'Champagne 'll be fine. Thank you.'

The aircraft lurched slightly as it was pushed back from the stand.

'Not bad,' I commented conversationally, after taking a sip; champagne and flight at present offering the only common links. But the remark elicited no instant response, although she did turn to look at me. A double take, in fact.

Her hair was a silky, ash-blonde, eyes blue. So blue, in fact, I suspected contact lenses. Was to be proved wrong when I put the question to her; another attempt at drawing her into conversation.

'Certainly not.' There was no trace of malice in her voice. A lack of interest, perhaps. Her thoughts elsewhere. Her enthusiasm just bowled me over, despite that quick double take indicating a possible show of interest.

I tried again, a different tack this time.

'And is Miss Hamilton going all the way, to Sydney?' I

gave the question added fervency by use of the slight break, and raised eyebrows.

The engines spooled up - a subdued whine up here behind the cockpit - brakes released, and then we were taxying.

Aware she was stuck with my company for some time to come, she now turned her head, examined me in depth. Not unfavourably, I decided. At least, she seemed on the edge of being interested, so I also indulged myself. I suspected there was a good body hidden beneath those fashionable clothes. The pointers were certainly there; if one can be excused a pun.

'Miss Hamilton is... going all the way,' she said, the slight hesitation seemingly deliberate. And then she smiled, all the warmer for being so genuine. It was like the sun coming out on a dark, cloudy day.

'How about Mr McLaren?' she asked.

A severe twist of gold glinted in each earlobe.

'Roger,' I insisted. 'Only as far as Perth, I'm afraid.'

Was that a brief flicker of disappointment I saw in her eyes, on her face? I was almost sure it was. It was the old McLaren thing with women. It happened often. They seemed to be strangely attracted, without me having to try to much.

The aircraft lined up on the runway and there was a long silence, but one full of thought, on both sides, I imagined.

'It's where I'm going,' she suddenly said, ice now broken. She gave an overall impression of well-to-do youth, with flashing white teeth and a Liverpudlian accent.

'But I thought you said....?

'Eventually,' she interrupted. 'Sydney first, just a day, then back t' Perth. West Oz is where I live.'

'Ah.' She still seemed slightly hesitant, and perhaps a little uncomfortable in my presence, but she was definitely coming round.

'You don't by any chance suffer from androphobia?' I asked, using a word I'd only recently come across. I'd read it somewhere or other, looked it up, out of curiosity. Not a word you'd become aware of at the type of school I'd attended. Or that of my near companion, I was soon to discover.

66

'S'pose it's possible.' She examined her hands. 'Depends what it means like.' Not perfect English, and it was said with effort. It then seemed she could find nothing more to add.

'It means a fear of men. Do you suffer from a fear men, Miss, er Hamilton.' A bit pretentious, I suppose, but it seemed to be working.

'Yuh don't miss much do yuh? Don't waste a lot of time either?'

'I don't suppose we have a lot of time.'

'We don't?' The challenge roused her, but I noticed her hands grip the armrests as the aircraft surged forward.

'Yeah, well, it's not as long a flight as my last one,' I said, leading her on, but she delayed replying until we were actually airborne, earth and its lights falling away below as we cleared land and headed out across the sea. We were about to exchange one island for another. The next an island continent.

'Oh, and 'ow long was that then?' she asked, relaxing slightly as the aircraft cleaned up - slats, flaps, and landing gear all tucked away - flight becoming quieter and much smoother. Her wrists also jangled with gold.

So I told her about my trip out, relating my Singapore stopover, with certain omissions, of course. And within a short space of time I learned she'd been born in Kirby, Lancashire, "over twenty-five years ago" being as far as she was willing to admit to. But there was one thing she never told me, so I asked.

'And who is, Miss Hamilton? You surely don't wish me to use anything so anomalous for the next five hours.'

'Kimberley. Judy, actually, but I don't use that 'cause it's common where I'm from. No idea 'ow I come to 'ave such a posh name as Kimberley. But I do quite like it.'

'I do, too,' I told her. 'It seems to have an air of mystery about it.'

'Judith Kimberley Hamilton,' she proudly announced, emphasising each, as though I should be familiar with the name as a whole. 'Nothing mysterious about that.'

'Well, Kimberley, is one supposed to be impressed or something?' I asked, testing the use of her name for the first

67

time. It felt right.

Rather than answer, she put a question of her own. 'Where yuh from?'

'England.'

'I *know* that. T'other side of t' Pennines,' she guessed. 'But where exactly?'

'Live in Chelsea, London, born in Scarborough, Yorkshire.' That I at present lived in the East End rather than Chelsea was a moot point. I was seriously thinking of moving into the large house Caroline had willed to me.

'Figures.'

'What makes you say that'?

'Yuh talk posh, but with a Yorkshire accent.'

'Me, lass? Nay, nivver.'

Her reply only served to demonstrate that to have labels which bore words like London, Paris, and Milan stitched into one's clothing, didn't automatically elevate one to the upper classes.

'Crap!' she said. 'For starters it's *one* this, and, *shouldn't one* that. Just like Prince-bloody-Charles. And what the fuck is anom.., whatever yuh said, supposed to mean?' She rummaged about in her handbag, as if searching for something, failing to find it. Certainly nothing was removed. No comb, no lipstick, no mirror. Diversionary tactics, I assumed. Seems she'd actually embarrassed herself.

'Irregular,' I replied simply, somewhat taken aback. Though, in a way, I had asked for it.

'Do you often talk like that, by the way?' I said.

'No, not really,' she admitted, screwing up her nose. 'S'pose I threw it out just so's you know it's there if needed. Never did talk flash in Liverpool; never found t' need out in Oz.'

I was beginning to enjoy this, and not solely because it took my mind off what the future might hold.

Next followed ten minutes of family history.

After a rather austere upbringing in Liverpool, her father had left home ten years ago, a postcard from Suez bringing the news he wouldn't be returning. Her mother had apparently been glad to see the back of him. "Nivver was any good," she'd told her daughter, "Nivver will be. He's a wrong 'un, despite t' pieces of paper from his fancy college."

Five years later a cheque arrived, from Australia. "Ten thousand pounds conscience money," her mother had said. There was also a ticket for Kimberley to go and visit, which she had done, flying out almost immediately.

'I'd missed him,' she admitted. 'We allus did gerron well together. Much better than I did with me mum. Only been back 'ome once since then,' she said, stuffing an inelegant handful of peanuts into her mouth. She then proudly handed me a business magazine, opened to a particular page. Robert K Hamilton's "pieces of paper" had finally come good, it seemed. He was chairman and managing director of Hamilton Resources Pty. A conglomerate which was into property, freight, pharmaceuticals, mining, and the media, among other things. Not bad for someone who "Nivver would be any good!" I had to admit. So, I imagined, would Kimberley's mum have been.

He was now part of the establishment, it seemed. Could be seen at the races at Belmont Park, cricket at the West Australian Cricket Association ground, in true Australian fashion, known as WACA. He was also a motor racing fanatic. That got my attention, for so was I. In fact I was a bit of a frustrated racing driver, truth be told. Which probably went some way towards explaining why I was occasionally willing to risk my neck in search of thrills and excitement.

I was by now somewhat impressed by the Hamilton name. More than impressed. Interested too. And from this point on things advanced rapidly.

During our conversation I noted her Liverpudlian accent was not always so prevalent. At times she seemed to speak quite well. It was as if she had forgotten about, or was trying to overcome, her scouse dialect.

*

A beam of light caught the diamonds of Kimberley's ring, causing them to flash and sparkle a brilliant fire. But the fire was extinguished as she switched off the reading light and lifted the blind. Dawn was fast approaching out there, and it could be seen that we were descending into the thick, grey clouds that massed below.

The aircraft bucked and shuddered with sickening

unpredictability, massive engines swaying alarmingly on their underslung mounts. The extremities of the wings - flexing to take the load like the gigantic shock absorbers they actually were - lost in dense cloud as violent currents punched us aloft one minute, then, with contemptuous ease and a sickening lurch, threatened to drag us out of the sky the next.

As someone with a developed interest in all things aviation, I was well aware that aircraft are designed to withstand all but the very extremes of the weather. Extremes admitted, that could pluck it out of the sky and tear it apart as if it were a plastic model. But you had to trust the pilots not to endanger their craft to such forces. After all, loss of control would be just as fatal to crew as to passengers. By use of weather radar, they would guide the giant aircraft around the most vicious of the storm cells, their course a slalom through the dark and troubled sky.

I looked at Kimberley. She smiled nervously, white-knuckled hands again gripping the armrests. So, taking one in mine, I squeezed gently, an assurance there was no need to worry. It appeared she approved of the gesture. Nature, it seemed, intent on us becoming bosom friends.

'What happened to your hand?' she asked, staring at the one that held hers.

'The missing finger, you mean?' Slight accident.' I left it at that, so did she.

Gradually, the turbulence became less violent. Passengers began to relax again, suddenly aware they *had* been tense. Small, nervous smiles spread throughout the cabin like a virus as the aircraft banked steeply, lining up with a runway which lay unseen somewhere ahead.

The greyness became translucent, but still nothing was visible, a muffled thump, felt through the airframe, signalling the lowering of the landing gear, the only indication we were getting close.

Runway lighting flashed past. The aircraft floated over glistening black tarmac, before settling smoothly, wings sagging, as if they too were relieved it was all over. Then, with the sudden, seemingly panicked scream of reverse thrust, it almost was.

*

'You will call?' Kimberley asked as I retrieved the briefcase from the overhead locker, offering her the only other bag it contained. It was hers, but she didn't thank me.

'I aint gettin' off,' she reminded me.

'No, of course. Silly me,' I said by way of apology. I replaced it, wondering if that had been wishful thinking on my part!

As I picked up the briefcase and prepared to depart, the adrenalin was once again being released into my system.

'I'll think it over,' I told her. Hardly helpful. She *was* coming on a bit strong, but the real reason for my apparent hesitation was that I did not wish to appear too eager. There again, I wasn't yet sure of my scheduling, or that of others I had yet to meet. But if the chance was there, no doubt so would I be. That was guaranteed, if it were at all possible. Especially so in this particular case. For someone of her stature in society could possibly be of some help to me in my quest for information, I ungraciously thought.

Her big eyes, bright and impudent, turned searchingly upon me. 'Aw, go on,' she persisted, 'take a chance. You never know, maybe next time we *will* go all the way together.'

Now, to me, that sounded like plain old-fashioned lust. She took some figuring out, this girl. Apprehensive when I boarded. Not even a cautious glance as I took my seat. And here she was, five hours later, almost inviting me into bed, if I was reading her correctly. And I knew for certain I was.

'Well, put like that.... But I have business to attend first. Then ..., who knows?' I smiled and gave a *que será* shrug. 'I have your number. And as I said, I'll think it over, so don't give up hope.' I gave her another smile, along with a reassuring wink, for I knew I would call, and soon, for despite her rather melancholic attitude, she looked like she'd be fun to be with. And once she stood to stretch her legs, displaying her complete form for the first time, I was doubly certain. The lower half appeared to complement the upper to perfection. Quite exceptional. Anyway, that was for the future. Kimberley was not due back in Perth for a couple of days. A lot could happen in two days.

There you are, Minerva told me. *Good fortune does occasionally shine upon one. Besides, when faced with danger, a man needs to relax now and again.*

Which was enough to remind me of the amended reasons for my visit. The game was afoot.

Up to now it had all been fairly informal and low key. The briefing; peaking myself up so as to be in operational mode; even passing through airport security. But from here on I was on my own, in charge, master of my own fate.

I was almost in enemy territory. Things were about to become a little more serious.

But first, customs and immigration.

I just hoped Bob had completed all the "formalities."

*　　*

Chapter Eight

CAUTIOUS RECEPTION

Although the sun had begun its lazy, inexorable climb, the air was still cool, though the temperature was quickly rising from its nighttime low.

It was the morning of the twelfth day of the month when we landed. Saturday. The beginning of a long weekend, as it happened. Not surprising, I was later to discover. Difficult for it to be otherwise in a country where every other weekend seemed to feature an extra day or two, so as to celebrate one event or another. This time it was the Queen's Birthday, I thought I overheard someone say. Or perhaps that of her son's brother's mother-in-law! No one really seemed to know for sure, or to care. That was easy to believe, too, for the Queen's Birthday I knew to be in June. At least in England it was. Perth may be nine hours ahead of GMT, certainly not four months behind.

'Yuh have a prison record?'

It was the Immigration Officer at Perth airport that posed the question. Some kind of greeting that was, even if he was asking, not stating a fact.

73

Didn't realize it was still a requirement. Although I briefly toyed with giving that as my answer, I didn't, even though I felt like doing so. As it would certainly not have scored any plus points towards my being allowed entry, I kept my silence, and was soon on my way. No point wisecracking with someone who may have no sense of humour, especially with that briefcase in my hand!

As a precaution, before leaving Singapore I'd called Tony Higgins, the friend I was here to visit, advising him I expected another slight delay. I had the address, would make my way there as soon I was free, I informed him, giving the impression I first had business with the local office of my publisher. Not being aware of Australian weekend working practices, I had deliberately been rather vague on this point, hinting that the publisher would be meeting me. Fortunate, that, in more ways than one.

Tony was a man of the world. I had already missed my first schedule, was supposed to have met up with him two days ago. He'd accepted this latest delay without question. Was looking forward very much to meeting up, whenever that may be. To show he wasn't unduly worried, he signed off with a colloquial dingle; 'If you were here we'd have prawns and beer, as you're not I'll have the lot.'

So now I knew exactly what to expect when we eventually did meet up.

*

He was aged about forty. Of average build for his height, which is to say, at an estimated six foot six, there was rather a lot of him. He was holding up a card with my name on it, so I assumed someone had been checking with the airline. He also carried something in his hand. It looked like one of these recently introduced cell phones I'd read about. He was also checking anyone carrying a briefcase, I noticed. Looking for a particular style of case, no doubt. A crocodile-skin affair, with gold clasps, maybe? Just like the one I carried.

I saw from his eyes he'd spotted it, so walked over and introduced myself, saving him the hassle. He didn't reciprocate. Not with a name, and I couldn't very well ask. There remained the possibility I was supposed to know him. In fact, in a way, I did, though not by name. I *had* seen him before - in almost every movie ever made which featured Australia. Craggy, bronzed features, khaki shirt and shorts, knee length socks, sandals and the inevitable Aussie hat. No corks though. Apparently the fly problem mainly arose out in the bush. Besides, the corks were a fictional thing, I was later to deduce. The Aussies were more sophisticated than that.

`Good flight?' he asked, slipping the slender black item he carried into a pocket and out of sight. Not a cell phone then!

He threw me a brief smile. It was the smile of a man who didn't know who he was smiling at, I could see that, in his face, and in his eyes. Was I important, or was I not, he seemed to ask himself. Then he remembered; I was not. But apparently that would only apply after I'd handed over that case.

`Until we arrived in the area. Bit lumpy on the approach, I told him.'

`Not surprised. Seen the airport closed for less. Boomer of a bloody storm, but she's clear now. Gonna be a beaut day from hereon in.'

Amiable small talk, which I found myself having to decipher as we walked. "Boomer" I took to mean huge. But he wasn't interested in my answers, didn't even seem interested in what I'd brought with me, either. But I could see that he was. His eyes were everywhere. Obvious to me, but wouldn't be to anyone watching from a distance.

He didn't offer to carry anything, even *that* case! I could well understand that. Until we were clear, it was *my* case rather than his. This would be especially true if anything untoward happened. Of that I was sure!

He didn't offer to shake hands either. Offered to buy me a drink instead. Very civil. Only I wasn't in a civil mood, myself. I was annoyed. Not with him, with Bob and Dunc. They'd slipped up already, almost putting me at risk. A drink was just what I did need right now. Ideal situation really. Get him to relax, maybe drop his guard. Perhaps I could find out a thing or two.

Only I wasn't given the chance.

`Car's over there,' he said, pointing to the parking lot as we exited the bar a quick two beers later.

Yes, well it would be wouldn't it, hardly likely to be in the bloody terminal, I thought, somewhat foolishly, struggling along in his wake. I felt like a sleepwalker. Shouldn't have had that second beer, even though the glasses were ridiculously small. Gone straight to my head.

`And now, I'll take that if you don't mind,' he insisted, reaching out a hand for the briefcase. That told me the coast was clear. He hadn't been about to take delivery until he was sure of that. If we'd been caught, it would have been my hand holding the case. He would have pleaded innocent. Just someone sent to pick me up.

`1934,' I said, surrendering the briefcase.

`Eh!'

`Combnation,' I advised, slightly mispronouncing the word. My mouth felt strange. As though I'd been given an injection at the dental surgery.

He nodded curtly. It was enough to tell me he was already aware of that.

After dumping the rest of my bags in the back, I wasn't exactly forced into the car, though "hustled" would not be a misplaced word, I recall myself fuzzily thinking. I was seated rear centre, one person either side of me.

Then, just as the extra from Crocodile Dundee slipped behind the wheel, I slipped into oblivion.

*

`You'll have to excuse the preliminaries,' he explained as I climbed back into my clothes, sneaking a glance at my watch as I did so. I'd been out of it for quite some time. Four hours had elapsed since we'd left the airport. Even so, I was surprised my recovery had been so complete, so immediate. God knows what it was they'd given me. There were none of the usual side-effects: disorientation, dry throat, dizziness, or blurred vision.

`Life has taught us to be cautious about strangers. Could be you were with the cops.'

`You really thought so?'

`Who's to say. We've got people everywhere, but so do they. Sneaky bastards.'

`And if ...?' I stopped there. Pointless to complete the question.

`That about gets it,' he confirmed.

`What he's saying is, yu'd now be cocking yur toes.' The comment carried with it a distinct lack of goodwill.

`I'm sure Mr McLaren is well aware of what was implied, Bruce.'

Mr McLaren certainly was, but didn't turn the thought into words, turned instead to see who this belligerent voice belonged to. Who in fact was this Bruce. He hadn't been at the airport, that much was clear. I would certainly have remembered the red hair, with matching beard and moustache. And his head looked shrunken, almost too small for his body. The glassed-in eyes were deep set, so much so it was difficult to make out their colour, let alone read anything in them. He looked psychopathic, and I knew the trick with the likes of him was not to stare.

It was a collection of features which made me realize God actually did have a sense of humour. He looked like a genetic experiment gone awry.

Some thoughts are often best left unsaid, it was something of which I had always been aware, often shortly after I'd said them! Though not being of frivolous mood at present, this time I declined. The mood arose from the fact they'd taken me so easily. The arrangements to make sure I didn't slip past at the airport; the almost too friendly reception; the drugged beer. I wasn't anywhere near as sharp as I'd thought. I really should have expected something of the kind, but hadn't.

`You guys don't piss about, do you.'

`Too bloody right", Pommy bastard. One night you never returned to your hotel in Singapore. How come? Answer that.'

Charming! The request... no, order, came from the shark like mouth located beneath the red moustache, his matter-of-fact manner sending a chill through to my bones. A misshapen nose and a wicked scar across one eye suggested his formative years had not been spent at a desk in the city. Just as well I'd kept my previous frivolous thoughts to myself. I imagined there was a faint chance Brucie boy wouldn't have seen the humour in it!

`Well, if you can't *guess,* I can explain. After all, a man has to relax now and then.' I threw them an understanding smile to give credence to the lie. I then started to collect my belongings and re-pack my bags. Someone really had been keeping an eye on me, or at least on my hotel. Luckily, not the rear entrance, it seemed.

*

The extra from Crocodile Dundee later drove me into the city, introducing himself on the way. But not immediately. It was by now obvious I wasn't expected to know anyone, so I dropped a delicate hint or two, which he apparently chose to ignore. That left me little option but to ask outright, and, surprisingly, he told me. He also offered me another drink.

`Just a drop of the amber nectar this time, Roger, trust me.'

For some reason, it appeared he had taken a shine to me. And as he, from all evidential indications, was running this particular part of the operation, I felt it a friendship worthy of an attempt at cultivation. Just as long as I remembered to take any information offered, without giving anything useful in return.

It was a typical Aussie pub, stripped to the bare essentials: a bar of vast length; a telly - for watching the footie, cricket, and the gee-gees - and the odd seat. Though most of the clientele chose to stand. The men wore a tee-shirt or singlet, shorts, footwear, and the Aussie hat - in most cases, sweat-stained, battered and shapeless. And the women? Well, there weren't any, at least not in this bar. The glasses were chilled, beer almost cold enough to crack the teeth. But boy, did it taste good.

We positioned ourselves at the far end, clear of the TV, and out of earshot of the other customers.

`Back there,' I said, middie to hand, `what was that really all about?'

`Like the man said, we had to be sure, you understand.' There he was, almost apologizing again.

`So what's with this Bruce guy? He didn't strike me as being the friendly type.'

`Always a problem with Bruce.' He was normally right handed, but when it came to hefting a beer glass, quite ambidextrous, I noted. He eyed me over his drink. Weighing

78

me up, just as I was him. 'If you know what's good, you'll keep well clear of Bruce,' he advised.

That sounded promising for a start. To keep clear, I'd surely have to be among them.

'Yeah. Well, seems to me if I *had* been with the cops, they'd have been swarming all over that place long before you got round to searching me.'

'Not if you'd been sent to penetrate, they wouldn't.'

'Ah yes. Suppose not,' I agreed, as though the thought had just occurred. 'But you can forget about that. What I did fitted in with my plans. Now, the balance of my fee, if you don't mind,' I held out a hand. Testing time. Could they be trusted to keep their word?

Seems they could, for after quickly surveying the room, he reached in his pocket and came up with a thick, brown envelope, which he handed to me.

I slipped it into an inside pocket, not even checking the contents. A show of trust, I hoped.

'Cheers,' I said, saluting him with my glass. 'Now I'm on vacation. That's it. End of story.'

'You don't have any scruples about that?'

'None whatsoever. I have few scruples about anything. Especially if it provides me with first class travel, and expenses. Money's the key that unlocks all. Everything and everyone has a price,' I lied - something that, until a few months ago, I'd have found difficulty with, for I'd always tried to remain honest and truthful. At first I'd marvelled how easy it was to tell lies, to make them up so readily, and in such a way they sounded plausible. But I soon realized that was what worried me about it also. So I only lied when not doing so would endanger me, or someone close to me. Or if there was a possible advantage to be gained, like now.

'You're obviously not aware of the risk you took.'

'Oh, I was aware all right, very much so. Every second of every minute. Just thankful it all went off OK.'

' Yeah, Me too. We rarely have goods hand-carried for that very reason.'

'Oh! So why this time?' I asked, as casually as possible.

It was obviously one question too many.

79

`You don't need to know,' he replied, rather abruptly. With which we drank up and left.

There were no handshakes or goodbyes. No mention of the possibility they may be in touch. Things seemed to have taken on a slightly different perspective with my last question. Had that been my mistake, pushing too hard, too soon?

I was dropped at a taxi rank just after midday. Felt more like midnight to my sleep-starved body.

First thing was to call Tony, advise him of my arrival, and inform him I was on the way. He sounded very pleased.

On the drive out to Maida Vale I sifted through my thoughts, replaying my performance, assessing my chances. None, I concluded. Overdone the indifference bit, or just the opposite? Either way I'd blown it. Contact gained, and lost. Hadn't even established who they were. Obviously the building I had been taken to had been unimportant, otherwise they would have used a blindfold. I did have a name, but doubted *Norman Holman* was real. Even so, I certainly couldn't call, offering my services. I also dismissed thoughts of them contacting me. One reason I hadn't taken the precaution of switching taxis. Pointless, for I'd deliberately made them aware of my plans, even though they had probably learned of them from the search, just as they had probably learned a few other things. Conclusion: I clearly hadn't done enough to increase my chance of employment.

Well, there was one possible good prospect in the offing, in two days time, when Kimberley Hamilton was due to arrive back from Sydney. The thought of that excited me a bit. Lifted the spirits.

As far as today's crowd went... Well, I *could* recognise them, but had no way of putting names to faces. Faces which could well have been disguised, especially that of Bruce. But something told me it wasn't so, and I was something of whiz when it came to make-up. Had at one time earned good money at it.

There was one more thing I had; the registration of a white Ford Falcon. I'd memorized it, and now I wrote it down.

Next I reassessed Bob and Dunc. They *had* been in my Singapore hotel room. I was absolutely sure of that now.

Either them or some of their compatriots. They'd at least have checked my bags, ensuring I carried nothing I shouldn't, positive in the knowledge the bags would be checked upon arrival. As they had been. Rather thoroughly. Even Professor Hoving's notes had not been spared. That had been plain to see.

With which thoughts I arrived at my destination.

* *

Chapter Nine

SETTLING IN

'**H**ow's it going, Tony?' I asked, greeting him like I'd seen him only yesterday, not fifteen years ago.

'Going good, doncha know. Hows about yourself?'

'Very well, thanks.' We shook hands.

He looked older than I had imagined he would, and he'd fleshed out, looked fit and well. The once thin and scrawny figure - which at school earned the sobriquet, dipstick - was now average. In fact he was average everything. Average height, average build, average looking, average personality - in itself, a welcome change of late. But, though reasonably dressed - the inevitable shorts, shirt, and sandals - he still wore yesterday's beard, flecks of grey evident.

'Well, don't just stand there gawping, come on in. It happens to be my birthday. Thirty one, would you believe.'

'Oh!' I said, unable to conceal my surprise. I knew him to be within a year or two of my age, but, obviously, had wrongly remembered him being ahead of me at school. 'Must confess, I assumed you to be older than that.' I realized it was rather tactless of me to say so, but the difference between estimate and truth being so unbelievable, I couldn't help myself. Luckily, he wasn't a vain man.

'Aw, don't worry. Tomorrow I will be. Meet the wife.'

Marge. The name didn't fit. She had a snub nose with a scattering of freckles. A bubbly, relaxed creature, glowing with vitality, and she moved with a quiet, efficient grace.

'Pleased to meet you, Roger,' she said, offering me a polite, well-manicured hand, and sounding like she really meant it. 'Bring your bag and we'll get you settled.'

I rinsed my face and changed into something more appropriate; casual, sports shirt and shorts, sandals, just like Tony. Felt much better for it. And, being Australia, next thing to be organized were the drinks.

'Beer, Roger? Or would you prefer wine? We produce some cracking stuff over here.'

I opted for wine, then we sat around and talked of this and that. Of former days, and characters we'd known. Where they were now, and what they were all doing. I was actually still in touch with only a few, but I brought him up to date on those. Mentioned some of the things we remembered them for. Tony was in touch with other mutual friends from the old days, so he reciprocated, brought me up to date on those. They in turn evoked yet more stories from the past.

A brief smile touched Tony's face, as if he were recalling fond memories. 'Those were good times,' he said.

'And now is not so good?' I questioned, opening my arms so as to encompass the fairly luxurious surroundings. The pool, barbecue area, extensive grounds and garden.

'Good, yeah, sure. Wouldn't trade it for anything. But the past is always something special, don't you think?'

'Not always all of it,' I opined.

'I suppose. Anyway, what about you? Quite wealthy, so I hear.'

'Oh! Where did you hear that?'

'Ah! I keep an ear to the grapevine, still get the occasional visitor from back home.'

'Tell you one thing, Tony. My apartment is built to slightly less demanding specifications than this place, that's for sure. But I admit, I do use an accountant these days. So I must be reasonably well off, I suppose. Not rich, you understand. I *go* to an accountant. The rich have accountants who come to *them.'*

'Yeah, and the super rich have their own. Like my employer.'

'Who is it you work for?'

'Offshore Marine Services. Melbourne based, but we're mainly located up in the northwest.'

'Why so isolated?'

'The gasfields are up that way, Northwest Shelf. After the Bass Strait, on the south coast, between Melbourne and Tasmania, Northwest is where a lot of the action is now. We keep the industry up there supplied, so it's convenient. Land's cheap, and there are generous tax concessions to be had north of the 26th parallel. But we're not as isolated as some. The Yanks run a secret communications base up that way. A place you may have heard of, Pine Gap. Makes the headlines now and again. And there's a pharmaceutical research facility way out in the bush at Silver Springs. Makes sense really . Distances them from protesters. You know, peaceniks, animal rights, environmentalists, that kind of thing. We have 'em all here as well. You didn't think the British had a monopoly on that kind of crowd, did you? There's lots of acreage on this island, so we can spread ourselves out. For instance, did you know that Perth is the most isolated city of any country in the world? Adelaide, our closest Aussie neighbour, is over two thousand kilometres away. Sydney is four hours by air.'

Which reminded me of something that had slipped my memory until now: Tony's predilection for both gathering and quoting, trivial data. These facts he was able to recall at will, and, given the slightest opportunity, would readily do so, exposing his knowledge to all. It was something else for which he'd been noted at school.

While Tony and Marge sorted a few things out in the house, I sat out in the sun and relaxed, ready to read the paper. Tony noticed I was out of wine, came out and recharged my glass.

'Always a good introduction to a place, the local

newspaper,' I said.

'Right,' he replied. 'Cept *The West Australian* isn't exactly your local rag. It covers a lot more than the Perth area. West Australia is the country's largest state.' he added. He then returned to his duties, left me to get on.

The lead was a political story; one politician accusing another of dirty tricks - so what's new in the world. Hamilton got a mention. Two, in fact, one business, one social. There was a piece about the Silver Springs place Tony had mentioned, and also somewhere with the unlikely name of Tom Price - a huge mining project. But the real facts about a place are to be found in the adverts - food and consumer goods prices are suitable pointers to cost of living - and from news of local events and happenings. Those kind of things give you a feel for a place, so those were what I read. I'd get to the business section later. I needed to know about that as well, for big business had to be involved in this drugs thing. Stands to reason. Too obvious if a small company were to experience a sudden, unaccountable influx of funds. Big business would find it much easier to conceal and launder large sums.

*

Later in the afternoon, under a sky swept clear of clouds, we lit the barbie - not a doll, Aussie for barbecue - and with that our numbers increased. They'd invited a couple of friends; Fred Manning, whom I understood to be a policeman - could be useful, thought I - and Alf Todd, bosun on the supply boat of which Tony was First Mate. First Mate was more or less the equivalent of being Co-Pilot of an aircraft. Tony actually held a Captain's ticket, but at present there were no vacancies, so he had to settle for the lower post. 'Common practice at sea,' he said.

They worked the Rankin Field, 'month on, month off,' he told me. 'West Coast, all the way up to Port Hedland, and above.'

'Interesting job?'

'Routine most of the time really, unless a cyclone pops up, which they now and then do, in the season. Otherwise, it can get boring, running back and forth. But occasionally something different pops up. The odd seabed survey, help with a seismic survey, things like that. Any change helps break the monotony, which now and again occurs. Like I suppose it does in any job. Last trip we had to recover a current-meter. That was something we'd never done before.'

'Just worked out that way, Tony. So the other crew tell me,' Alf said. 'Don says they pick 'em up on a regular basis. Well, 'bout once a month. So it usually occurs when we're on break. He says they've never deployed one though. Often wondered who did that. Thought we were the only other vessel fitted with DGPS.'

'DGPS?' I questioned.

'Satellite based navigation system. The future,' Tony explained. 'Can be accurate to within five metres or less. Land based systems have problems over around thirty miles offshore, so satellite is the way to go. Out of sight of land five metres is extremely accurate. Needed to be, for it was a Doppler acoustic meter, located on the seabed.'

'So how do you recover them?'

'Ah! That's the clever bit. They recover themselves, see. Radio recall. Tune in, press a button, and provided you are within range, bingo, it releases and floats to the surface. Technology, eh!'

'So what do these current meter things do?'

'Collect data on currents of course, and sea conditions. Temperature and the like, also. They can't transmit, so have to be recovered to download the data. I guess transmitting it to a satellite will come in time. One less job for us.'

*

'No Hoving here,' the receptionist at the Dampier Inn advised when I phoned, later that day.

'Not there? How do you mean, not there?'

'Not here, sport. As in gone. Pissed off! Checked out this morning. At least, he had someone do it for him.'

'Oh! He leave a forwarding address?'

'Afraid not.'

'OK, thanks.' I hung up, the call having eased my mind a little. If Hoving was in Perth, he couldn't be in Singapore. And being in Perth myself, I'd find him eventually. It wasn't a large city.

'Well, at least he's arrived,' I told Tony. 'Probably

moved in with someone at the university. I'll check with them tomorrow.'

'Yeah, do that. Run you in if you like, show you round town a bit. Sunday. It'll be fairly quiet.'

And so we settled down to barbecued steaks and prawns, with plenty to drink.

The prawns were out of this world, far better than any I'd had back home, and I commented on the quality.

'We buy 'em fresh from Sealanes, South Fremantle, Marge said. 'Get most of our seafood there. Well worth the extra distance.'

Along with the drink, Tony dispensed more tips and trivia, stirred on by me, especially when I addressed him as "cobber".

'Never "Cobber," Roger, that's pure bloody fiction. Aussies never use the word. Another thing: it is acceptable to call your best mate a "right bastard," whereas you need to watch out for anyone who is said to be "a bit of a bastard."' And by night's end I was prepared to believe almost anything of a country which hosted such oddities as a beer-can regatta, and the Todd River Regatta.

'The former,' he proudly informed me, 'is held offshore Darwin, and features boats constructed entirely of empty beer cans, while Alice Springs is the location of the Todd River. The oddity being that their regatta is held during the summer months, when the river-bed is so bloody dry it looks as if it hasn't even a recollection of the feel of water.'

He could go on and on, Tony. A fantastic memory for lots of interesting trivia. Crap, most people might say.

We saw most of the evening out, but here the sun sets early, and along with dusk and darkness came weariness I was finding it hard to retain control. A long night-flight; the rather unconventional arrival procedure; the excitement of meeting up with an old fiend; the heat; beer, and the wine; a long, eventful day, along with the length of time since I last saw a proper bed, all combined to tire me out. I made my apologies and retired fairly early.

*

Next morning I awoke just after six. Or should that be, was awoken; a rather unusual noise the cause.

It wasn't a shock awakening, therefore not quick. My eyes opened, but it was some time before the brain was fully functional, so I lay there awhile, letting things slip into place. It happened quite slowly, the way things sometimes do the first time you open your eyes to unfamiliar surroundings. By slowly, I mean relatively so, quite a few minutes rather than the usual one or two, that kind of time scale. Nothing drastic then, though it had been quite an early night, relatively speaking. Even so, given all the excitement and recollections, the catching up, consumption had been rather on the high side, too; ample corks to hang around someone's hat. But at least for me it hadn't gone on past ten pm, and my nine hours in bed had been the sleep of the dead. So there were few after effects.

There it was again. Tap, tap, tap, a pause, tap, tap, tap.

No response from elsewhere in the household, so I assumed it to be the wind blowing a branch against a window.

Tap, tap, tap. Seemingly more urgent this time. But apart from that, there was just stillness and silence.

Stillness and silence!

In my mind that equated to no wind to blow branches against anything!

*   *

88

Chapter Ten

ANTIPODEAN ATTITUDE

*T*he drive in to Perth was a trip that urged me to think seriously about staying here forever. But it was an instantaneous thought, therefore possibly not serious at all. The atmosphere was just so peaceful and serene, it aroused similar feelings within me.

Tony took a roundabout route so as to show me a little more of the area: Kalamunda and Mundaring Weir, situated in the hills east of the city, as was Maida Vale. He also brought to my attention a varied selection of desirable properties, at unbelievably cheap prices when compared to the UK, so once again I found myself briefly toying with the idea of one day possibly moving out here.

A lifelong dream I had - given I was still only in my early thirties - was to retire somewhere on the Cote D'azur. A small cottage up in the hills of Provence, situated amidst the olive trees and cork oaks. A million miles away from my present location. Only this seemed more practical, given the language, even if just as unlikely. Especially so being that, at my age, retirement too seemed a million miles away. I was nowhere near ready for that kind of thing. Too much yet to be done. Still, it cost nothing to dream. Or to make enquiries.

On the other hand, enquiries as to the whereabouts of Professor Hoving proved only to indicate that he was hard to find. Impossible, in fact. No one at the university had heard from him since the day he arrived; Friday, when he had checked in by phone. Yes, they were expecting him. Soon, they hoped. Otherwise there was a lot of rescheduling to do. He'd made arrangements to call at the bursar's office yesterday, but had failed to show up. It really wasn't good enough.

I said I would check with them again, tomorrow. They said they hoped to hear from someone before then. We departed, neither of us exactly happy bunnies, I thought.

Next stop was the Dampier Inn. Different person from the voice on the phone - this one female, and so much more polite. English origin by the sound of things, though probably naturalized Aussie by now - but, once she had checked the records, same message: "I'm afraid Mr Hoving has checked out."

She turned the register to face me, pointing at the entry. The signature was undecipherable.

My anxiety returned. It wasn't really my problem anymore. There again, it wasn't my way just to let things slide. I'd made a promise to a friend, had some notes to deliver, personally.

`Maybe I should check with the police,' I suggested to Tony. `How about Fred? Will he be on duty?'

`Fred? Fred's not a copper. You must have misunderstood. He's *with* the police, not *in*. He's a civilian clerk. Anyway, you'll not get much joy on a weekend. This is Australia, remember. Best leave it till tomorrow. I have business to attend to in town anyway.'

He consulted his watch. 'Tell yuh what. I know a pub serves the best fish and chips you'll ever taste. Let's go there for lunch,' he suggested. So that's what we did.

Left Bank was. On the left bank of the riverside, closer to Fremantle than Perth, and even though the place was heaving, we managed to secure a table after a short wait, during which we had a drink.

'This fish is so fresh I'll bet the next of kin have not yet been informed!' I suggested, once we'd been served and I got stuck in.

Yeah!' Tony agreed. 'And although serving them in newspaper is probably seen as a gimmick, to my mind, it's how fish and chips should be served.'

'That was excellent, Tony,' I said as we left. 'Beer wasn't bad, either.'

'Fish and chips better than back home?'

'Wouldn't say that, especially up on the Yorkshire coast. But they came close.'

We then drove back to Perth, proceeded to make a foot-tour of the city. Which suited me fine. You can always see much more during a slow stroll. Or be seen, come to that.

Another of the reasons for wanting to come into town was to show myself around, in the vain hope someone may wish to talk to me, or contact me. It was the only hope I had of regaining touch, for I suspected that if they did wish to communicate, they'd be reluctant to call at Tony's. Now, in the bright light of day, I cursed myself for not pushing things when I'd had the chance. Or possibly I'd pushed too hard! Penetration is looking less and less likely, Bob boy, I thought.

'Everything's so new and fresh-looking, Tony,' I remarked of the city. 'Sparkling, modern, not quite what I'd expected of this country.'

'What had you expected?'

'Don't really know. Possibly a bit of the Wild West. Suppose like everyone else I'd assumed Australia just to be birthplace of such as Don Bradman, and Clive James. Home to Sydney Opera House, and the Barrier Reef, along with the Outback.'

'So it is,' Tony advised. 'But they're thousands of miles away. Here in Perth you got the west bit right, maybe not so wild though. It is the birthplace of Rolf Harris, and we do have a mock Tudor shopping arcade to remind you of home. Look. Circa 1937,' he said, pointing as we passed beneath the castellated arch upon which the date was boldly emblazoned.

'Fifty-four years. Not even a lifetime,' I reminded him.

'Right, mate, but that's Perth for yuh. Founded 1829. Not a city of old, timeworn structures, and a history stretching

91

back over centuries, for sure, but there are some *interesting* buildings. The Mint, for instance, even if it does only date back to 1899.

As usual with Tony, dates and data rolled effortlessly off his tongue.

'It is a new country,' he stated. 'From the white man's point of view, that is. The Abbos have apparently been around for millions of years.'

Naturally, the sun was shining. A sun that was hot enough to make it almost mandatory to have a glass of something cool close to hand. In this heat, another beer would be right. Perfect, in fact. So I agreed with Tony when he later suggested we "go rip the tops off a couple of tinnies."

Hard to believe this was the same sun that occasionally shone over England. Something else was different, too. Patently obvious. Out here, everyone had a shadow! Not that they didn't back home, but here, shadows were dark and solid looking, not wishy-washy grey, if there at all. Out here, shadows accompanied everyone, everywhere. Sometimes leading, sometimes tagging along behind. But, during hours of daylight, almost always in sight.

*

Visions of a different type of shadow had been generated as I lay in bed that morning, my mind attempting to focus on reality, after hearing the tapping noise that awoke me. No gradual, sleepy-eyed, sitting up, hands running through tousled hair surfacing, this. Even though I didn't immediately leap out of bed for a while, I was awake instantly. Senses alert, ears straining.

Curious, yet not without some trepidation, I eventually slipped out and padded across to the window, to peer out on a beautifully clear morning. The air was absolutely still.

Tap, tap, tap. There it was again. It appeared to be coming from the kitchen, so I threw on a pair of shorts and made my way out there, muscles tense as coiled springs, yet there was none of that familiar prickling of the skin, warning me of possible danger. Still, I remained cautious.

I carefully stuck my head round the door, only to find three seemingly smiling faces greeting me from the window-sill. Huge, black and white kingfisher-type birds, which I recognised as being kookaburras.

With some relief, I breathed deeply, unaware until then I had been holding my breath. A good sign. It had been automatic. As had been my silent and cautious approach. Unthinking instinct. It showed I was in operational mode.

Tap, tap, tap. They pecked at the glass, three beaks in sequence.

'Oh, did they wake you, Roger? Sorry.'

I feigned shock upon hearing the voice, but I'd been primed, the approach not at all stealthy. I turned to find Marge standing there in her dressing gown, tousle haired and bleary eyed.

'My mistake, I should have warned you. Most mornings I feed 'em scraps of meat. Encouraging 'em, I suppose. But weekends we let 'em tap away and eventually they get fed up and leave. May as well feed them now, and have a cup of tea ourselves.'

'A cuppa I could use.' I'd said. Naturally, I hadn't elaborated on the reason.

*

As we continued our tour, my thoughts were returned to the present by a Qantas poster in a travel shop window. It depicted Windsor Castle, and Beefeaters. In London it would be Ayers Rock, or the Harbour Bridge in Sydney, I thought. Then another poster caught my eye. Jumped out at me really, being a bit of a fanatic: Foster's Australian Grand Prix. It was being staged in Adelaide, three weeks today. With all that had gone on, that had slipped my mind completely. Now, not only did that poster remind me, it planted the seed of an idea. It was something I'd need to work on. But that would have to wait until tomorrow, at least, before I could test the feasability of putting such a plan into action. Just the glimmer of an idea at present. Providing certain things turned out as planned.

*

Compared to the Sheraton, and the Parmelia Hilton, the Transit Inn on Pier Street was old and faded. But what it lacked in glass and chrome it made up for with good old-fashioned comfort, it's semi-circular bar a particularly welcoming oasis.

It was here that Tony and I chose to ease our thirst.

But that hadn't come about by chance. It had taken a street map, and some fairly surreptitious navigating on my part, along with a little gentle persuasion, for us to end up in this particular area. Not too difficult a thing to foist upon an unsuspecting, but thirsty friend.

The place was lively - people continually coming and going - though not unduly crowded. We managed to secure a couple of seats, and over a beer we sat and talked, and I observed.

I hadn't abandoned all hope of being contacted, but had more or less pushed such thoughts aside, for the time being. I was now in the process of thinking about that Grand Prix, and of how I may just be able get there.

Then I noted the barman seemed particularly interested in either myself, or someone close by. I casually looked around, saw no one in the vicinity sitting on their own, nor was there anyone to raise suspicions. So I decided maybe it was time for me to establish contact of my own.

I waited for Tony to answer the call of nature before approaching the bar to order more drinks, at the same time toying with the cricket ball I now carried. It got the barman's attention, right away.

'Yuh can stick that thing away, mate. Where d'yuh think y'are, bloody WACA ground?'

Obviously not who I was expecting, so I meekly complied. Pocketing the ball, ordering and collecting our drinks, I returned to our seats.

Tony returned too, after first stopping off to acknowledge a group on the way past. 'Some of the guys from Port Hedland,' he explained. 'Popular place this with the oilfield crowd when in town.'

We walked some more upon departing the Transit Inn, which was by now becoming slightly more boisterous.

Perth town centre is not that large, but there is a lot to be seen that is of interest. Down by the Swan River, actually in Barrack Square, on the riverside, Tony pointed out the Swan Bell Tower, a modernistic structure that houses 18 bells, 12 of them originally from St Martin-in-the-Fields, back in home in Trafalgar Square. Apparently they had been presented to the State of Western Australia as part of the

Bicentenary Celebrations of 1988. The main attraction of this tower is the level 6 observation deck, which allows 360 degree views of the city, and beyond. Unfortunately we were not around when the bells were rung, which they frequently are.

After this, we left Perth behind and drove south back down to the coast to the docks area, and the old town that is Fremantle. In my view we didn't stay here long enough, for it appeared to be an interesting place at first glance. Although we did visit the market there. It was tastefully set out in one of the old warehouses, a wide range of products being on offer, so I took the opportunity to buy myself a genuine, wide-brimmed Aussie hat. Not out of a desire to look the part, or any vanity thing, simply for protection. Out here, a seriously hot sun beams down for a majority of the daylight hours, along with its associated cancer-causing UV radiation. A hat is almost a necessity.

Later, back in Maida Vale, it was barbecue and wine time once again. I was definitely starting to embrace the Antipodean attitude it seemed.

*   *

Chapter Eleven

BIT OF A DING

The following afternoon - still with no sign of contact, nor any word on the whereabouts of Professor Hoving - Tony and I were back at the Transit Inn. We were in town for some business Tony needed to take care of, so had decided to make a day of it.

Business now complete, along with some suitable exposure on my part, we had taken lunch at a pleasant little place that went under the name of Fast Eddies. From that point on we walked around for a while, then it was the usual excuse on a hot afternoon, we fancied a drink. We were in town, the Transit Inn was close by. So we called in. But I really needed to take care of other business, too. And being as things weren't exactly going to plan on the "Bottomsworth initiative", I figured now was as good a time as any to invoke the back-up plan. Hopefully the much better option anyway.

There was a good possibility I'd blown any chance of penetration on the drugs ring front, plus I'd failed to deliver Professor Hoving's notes. I had debated passing them on to the university, leave them with the problem, but that wasn't really my way. I had promised Freddie I would deliver them, personally, and if at all possible, I would.

Some trip this was turning out to be. Well, I'd give it a few more days before contacting Bob. There was always the likelihood they were checking on my background before deciding anything. In fact, thinking about it, that would be a certainty, and they had probably copied all the details they required from my passport. Such thoughts raised my hopes again, if only fractionally.

Yeah, give 'em time, Minerva agreed. *Foolish to expect them to act impulsively. These are very serious people.*

And I'm not?

So, in the meantime, nothing for me to do except play tourist, and hopefully still deliver the Professor's notes.

Huh! That's looking less and less likely, too.

Right again. But there was one more thing, and I just hoped the telephone was able to deliver more positive results on this front.

I excused myself for a or two minute, made the call, and for a change, was rewarded. That minute or two was all it took.

*

'Strewth! Perv that will yuh! I'd crawl half a mile over broken glass just to sniff the exhaust fumes of the van that carried her laundry,' Tony crudely remarked not too many minutes later. He motioned with his head towards the door. He hadn't needed to, I'd been watching.

What appeared there was a sight which painted a smile on my face. 'You and everyone else,' I said, getting out of my seat. 'Hang on here and I'll introduce you.'

'What! You know her?'

'Yeah, but don't get any ideas about slipping your shoes beneath *her* bed. She's here looking for me,' I told him. And the speed with which she had arrived suggested she'd been eagerly awaiting my call. Good news indeed. I'd figured she might have been off with someone else by now; imagined she could take her pick. She certainly could have in here, going by the looks on most men's faces.

When not travelling, Kimberley obviously dressed to be admired. Today she wore a white cotton blouse - obviously

97

nothing beneath - and a skirt so short it left little to the imagination. Clothes which allowed her body to be displayed in public. It was better than I'd imagined; those legs went on seemingly forever. I hoped I may get to check them out sometime.

She was absolutely stunning. She also wore a Cheshire cat expression, so maybe things were about to change for the better. My thoughts back there regarding lack of penetration may possibly have been a little hasty. Albeit they'd been meant in a different context entirely.

'Hi, Kimberley. Glad you could make it.' I greeted, pecking her cheek.

'Well hello Roger. Love the hat. Suits yuh.'

'Bought it when we were in Freo the other day. Yesterday, in fact. Keep getting screwed up with the days.'

'Well, good choice. It suits yuh.'

'Necessary I've found, given the weather here. Anyway, come and meet my ex school pal, Tony Higgins. I'm staying at his place.'

We wandered back over to where Tony sat, many envious pairs of hungry eyes following us as we crossed the room. I say us, but me only because I had the delightful Kimberly on my arm. Most were probably wondering who the hell I was, but they certainly wouldn't be thinking the same about Kimberley. They wouldn't care who she was, just that she was who she was!

'Tony, meet Kimberley Hamilton, I said.'

He rose, held out his hand. 'Hamilton?' he questioned. 'Not related to *the* Hamilton? The one who appears to own whatever Alan Bond doesn't?'

'The very same,' she proudly replied. 'My father.'

Tony gave me a look of admiration when I told Kimberly she looked decidedly sexy, which was true. Only to be expected with a body like that. And I'm sure she was aware of it. Certainly a different take on the girl I'd first sighted when boarding that aircraft in Singapore.

'What would you like to drink, Kimberly?' I asked.

'Could I have a Glenmorangie, please Roger. Ice and water?' Was that her public voice, I wondered.

'You can have whatever you like love, though I suspect

a purist would shudder at the Ice and water bit.'

'It's how I like it.'

'I don't have a problem with that.'

I went and got the drink, then, there being only two seats where we were, we swiftly moved over to a corner table that I noticed was just being vacated.

Although Kimberley and I didn't intentionally exclude Tony, we did seem to spend a lot of time communicating solely with each other, holding two conversations at once, one with voice, one with eyes, both full of promise. And in time, Tony diplomatically made an excuse and left us to it.

'What would you say to dinner?' I asked, sometime later.

'Bloody oath. I could eat a scabby dog.'

'Great language, Kim. You should have been a diplomat. You don't mind if I call you Kim, do you?'

'Not at all, Roger,'she replied. 'I prefer it.'

We decided on the hotel, the restaurant having a good reputation, Kimberley informed me. Knew it well, she said. 'Besides, it's licensed. Gets away from that Australian phenomenon of BYO - bring yer own,' she explained.

She ate with little finesse. That is, she enjoyed her food - tonight, lobster thermidor - but it could just as well have been a meal from a chippie in Kirby. And she acted as if we'd known each other for years. No first-date nerves, no shyness. In fact, she tended to speak her mind, as I had already gathered.

During the coffee and cognac stage we discussed this and that, and I awaited my moment. Kim, as I hoped she eventually would, provided it.

'So, what are your interests?'

'Apart from life in general? Oh, this and that. Motor racing in particular.'

'Ah! So you'll be off to Adelaide for the Grand Prix?' she said, playing straight into my hands. And although I felt bad about it, I decided to go ahead anyway, after first squaring it with my conscience.

'Hoping. But it's probably too late to get reservations this late in the day.'

'Oh, no problem, Roger. I may be able to help there. At

least Dad can. He owns a hotel in the city.' She giggled at that. 'Probably arrange tickets and passes as well, if I asked him to.

Hope soared. Go for it, I thought. 'Oh, would you do that for me?'

'Course I will. For two?' she questioned.

'If you'd like to go, certainly. That would be perfect.' I felt a twinge of shame at using her in this way. There again, as far as she was concerned, she'd offered to help. And now she was offering to accompany me. Couldn't be better.

That little discussion appeared to have automatically established us as an "item". At least to Kimberley's way of thinking. For then she was offering again. At least I presumed so.

Speaking with remarkable laxness and imprecision, yet managing to express herself with wondrous subtlety, she caught me completely by surprise.

'Well, Roger,' she said. 'Get drunk up and we'll go back to my place.' The words had a kind of finality about them: decision taken, no arguments accepted. Not that she was going to get one from me!

I held a brandy balloon in one hand, swirling it around, but the proposal so surprised me that, as a consequence, some of the precious liquid swirled itself right out of the glass. Never having been one for waste, especially as it was quite a good cognac, not to say splendid, I allowed myself time for thought, sucking it off the back of my hand before it evaporated completely. I then drained the glass, pretending to deliberate. But not for long.

'Ah, well,' I said, 'why not. Days like this don't happen too often.' I rose, fumbling for my wallet.

'Put that away, Roger. This is my treat.'

'Wouldn't hear of it,' I said, 'I invited you.' To which she replied she wouldn't hear of me not hearing of it. She simply lead us away from the table and out of the restaurant, making no effort whatsoever to settle the bill. The maitre d'hôtel smiled, bowing deferentially as we passed by, plainly not expecting to be paid.

I just looked at Kim, smiled, didn't need to put the question.

'When you can easily afford to pay, Roger, quite often you find you don't have to. But don't worry, it'll end up on Dad's account.'

Kim took the initiative, arm tucked into mine, pulling me close. I was feeling euphoric. I hoped. Wouldn't do to...

I felt it immediately we stepped outside, the old sixth sense thing, that prickling sensation in the hair at the back of my neck; a warning. I attempted to ease Kim away but she was having none of it, just clung on tighter. I looked around. Nothing out of place, nothing unusual, nothing to cause undue worry....

Then, suddenly there was, interrupting my thoughts as a man appeared as if from nowhere. He stepped right out in front of me. A big man. Bush hat, tee-shirt, jeans tucked into suede boots. We collided lightly, and I was about to utter something flippant when the warning bell sounded again. The timing was too perfect for it to be coincidental.

'Sorry mate,' I offered, knowing an apology where there was no fault usually defused things somewhat.

Not in this case it didn't. And I knew immediately I'd drunk one Cognac too many. Not that I was drunk, but neither was I fully alert. At least not as alert as I suddenly knew I needed to be. A major blunder in this situation.

There was a fractional moment of indecision during which I was briefly tempted to turn away, but having Kim on my arm precluded such actions. Anyway, from a macho point of view I decided it would be better to stand my ground. I forced myself to concentrate, but was somewhat hampered by my condition, and the fact that Kim was still restricting my movements.

'Excuse us, please,' I said. It was another attempt at pacifying someone who had no intention of being pacified. Just the opposite.

He managed an unconvincing smile before opening his mouth to speak, and he wasn't what one could call prolix.

'Fuck off,' he said.

As good a time as any to take his advice, I thought, as I attempted to do just that. But he moved also, again blocking our path. So, after finally prising myself free of Kimberley, I eased her to one side. It was obvious the gloves were off, so

101

I decided to get straight in whilst he was thinking.

There's a lot been written about instinctive reactions, some of it true, most not. Whatever, I was far too slow in the circumstances. Further hampered as Kim again grabbed my arm, and shouted.

'Come on, Roger, forget it.'

Rather than a well aimed kick at his most vulnerable area, she caused me to stumble slightly, throwing me off balance. Now I knew I was in trouble.

'Careless,' my aggressor tut-tutted, taking advantage by following up immediately.

When he moved he did so very quickly for so vast a man, and the blow that caught me was low, hard, vicious, and surprisingly effective. I could possibly have parried it had I been fully sober. I wasn't, so it forced the air from my lungs, and I almost blacked out as I slid earthwards, probably the best place for me to be, I recall thinking. Then I was, eyeball to eyeball with the pavement, knowing I should be doing something to retaliate, finding myself unable to. My skills appeared to have deserted me. That blow had been a crippler.

'That's just for starters, shit head.' He spat it out, full of contempt. The words echoed in my ears. Woolly and indistinct, yet replete with intent. And there was little I could do about it.

I looked up, noted that Kim was nowhere to be seen.

Then, without hesitation or warning, he followed up with a boot to the ribs. Despite being soft suede, it bloody hurt. Felt like those boots could be steel capped.

The foot swung in again and again; ribs, legs, arms, but only one blow directed at my head. I protected myself as best I could; arms over the face, legs together, knees drawn up. Of course, that left the kidneys wide open.

I felt myself going; drifting into unconsciousness.

The last thing I recall was hearing was Kim's voice. Away in the distance. The only thing I was able to put together was that it sounded like a strangled cry. But, to my tortured mind, it could just as well have been one of successful accomplishment!

*   *

102

Chapter Twelve

FATE INTERVENES

I didn't need to visit the police after all. They visited me. The very next morning, whilst I was still in hospital. Nothing serious. Nothing broken. No damage to the head. In fact surprisingly little damage at all. There were bruises to the body though, and they were rather painful. Though nowhere near as much as I expected, strangely enough. What little pain there was could be easily pushed aside. Mind over matter. The reason I was even in hospital, it seemed, was the fact that the police had requested it. Though how they got away with that I had no idea. Still, this was Australia, not England.

It was an inspector who eventually asked the questions, and he didn't exactly endear himself to me. A rather pompous man who, despite the name labelling him as originally of Scottish descent, was obviously nowhere near first generation Australian. His voice was flat, a distant monotone. It was a voice to which I took an immediate and instinctive dislike, as I did to its owner. I imagined he could be a real nasty piece of work, and his bedside manner only served to ally that opinion.

`Name's McRobertson. Inspector. Like you to remember that Mr... er...?' His pencil hovered over his notebook, awaiting my reply.

`McLaren. Roger.'

`Ah! A pom!' he said, running a hand over where his hair would have been had he possessed any. His tone seemed to suggest that my being English automatically explained everything: a foreigner in *his* country, causing *him* problems. Not just any old foreigner, a pom. Probably had me tagged as a football hooligan or similar. Seemed to be an automatic thought these days. Or maybe he was just jealous of my hair.

They were looking to verify Kimberley's statement on last night's events.

`Can't help, I'm afraid. Last thing I remember was this guy laying into me with his boot. Steel-toed by the feel of it.' I was laying it on a bit, for it hadn't been that bad. Had they been steel-capped, I knew I'd have suffered far worse. As I would if they had been leather.

McRobertson's flat, broad, ugly face peered at me through pig-like eyes that were not exactly filled with compassion.

`Why'd he wanna do that? Musta' give him good reason.'

`No way. We were just walking along when he contrived to bump into me.'

`Contrived?' It sounded at first as though he was questioning the meaning of the word, but he then continued. `Anyone around to verify that?'

`Miss Hamilton.'

`She's no bloody good. Prejudiced witness.'

`No one then, as far as I was aware.'

`Pissed, were yuh?'

It was rapidly becoming clear that the inspector had an aversion to the British. Myself in particular, it seemed.

`Look! *He* attacked *me*.'

`So yuh say. Take it yuh can you substantiate that?'

`I'm the one in hospital, aren't I!'

`Yeah! Other bloke's in the morgue.'

`What?'

`S'right. Hit and run.'

The same man who'd attempted to present me with a Glaswegian uppercut, I gathered. The description fit to a tee.

`Bloody hell. Seems like you should be looking for whoever it was put him there, then. Certainly wasn't me.'

`Time 'll tell. Who's to say you weren't the cause? Anyway, that about gets it, *for now.*' Come down to the station and sign a statement, later. Today, if you're not feeling too crook.'

It sounded like an invitation, though it was made fairly obvious that had I been citizen rather than tourist, the invitation would have been an order. But it did fit in with my plans. I'd intended visiting them anyway.

After he'd gone I lay back and thought about things, whilst I awaited the arrival of Kim. Despite brief negative thoughts last night, I felt sure she would soon be here. If not, it was a taxi back to Tony's.

I'd been lucky, it seemed. I figured that first blow had more or less saved me. Apart from rendering me almost unconscious, it had prevented me from retaliating. No bad thing given my state of unpreparedness, for it had limited his options. There again, had he not got careless, I could have been.... Could have been what? And why? Had it been an attempt to frighten... or injure? To abduct... or to remove me from the scene permanently? Whatever, I couldn't rely on luck again. From now on I'd better be careful. Very careful indeed. It seemed my survival could well depend on it. But it did mean someone had an interest in me, even if not in my well-being. Maybe someone *had* been checking on my background, and had stumbled across something they didn't like. Something someone had overlooked, maybe?

Kim must have been waiting close-by, for she bounced in almost immediately, and I felt a slight twinge of guilt at my thought, however brief, that she may have set me up. Not very charitable, I'll admit. But for me, a natural thought. The moment danger lurked I was ready to believe the worst of anyone, until they proved otherwise. It was the way I'd been trained to think. Trust no one.

`Good God, Roger. You look like you were in a war.'

`Feel like it, too.'

'Oh dear. That bad is it?'

'No, not really. Just kidding,' I assured her.

She looked vibrant and infinitely desirable. Sunglasses pushed up in her hair, and my last remark had brought about a wide smile. My mood brightened; the sight of her recalling not what *had* happened, but what *hadn't!*

`Sorry, about last night, love. Seems someone doesn't love me. I threw her a smile.

`Probably too pissed to do me any good, anyway. How d'yuh feel now?'

`Relative to a dead man, pretty good. Actually feels like a bus ran over me. But I'll live.'

'Yuh sure about that?'

'Reasonably so. Must have been a very small bus.'

`Good. Climb into yur strides and let's go,' she said, handing me my clothes. `They've released you into my care, and I have transport. Called Tony, by the way. Told him you were dossing down with me. Hope I was right.' She didn't pause, presumably in case she wasn't right. `Didn't sound like he expected you back anyway. We'll call in and pick up your gear on the way.'

`On the way? To where?'

`Got a day out planned. You don't mind, Roger, do you?'

`As long as it's not too strenuous. And I *am* supposed to visit the police later.'

`Fuck em. We will go. Only much later. It's a beaut day, so we're off to relax in Freo. It's only a couple o' miles down the coast,' she added.

Out here, every day seemed to be a beautiful day to me. Weather-wise, that is.

Her choice of transport was the next surprise. I imagined she could have any car she wanted. What she did have was a Ford pick-up. Metallic blue, with a four-seat cab, and extra steelwork.

I ran my hand over the front end.

'Roo bar,' she explained. 'A bloody kangaroo can do huge damage. Stupid animals. They tend to leap out in the road if the see headlights.'

106

A Ute, she called it. For utility, I surmised. That was the way with Australians.

"Speech is simple," I recall Tony expounding. "We avoid all extravagant adjectives and superlatives. Country, and language, for example, are reduced to `Oz'. Though the latter can also be `strine'."

As promised, we first stopped off at Tony's, where I picked up my things. They understood, they said. Well I knew Tony would, and from the look Marge gave me, I could see she did too!

'Anyway, you're both welcome round here anytime,' she said.

'Just remember though, I'm back at work next week,' Tony said. He gave me a couple of phone contacts. `If you fancy a trip up there, call either of those. They'll tell me, and we can get something organized. Well worth it, Roger. Lovely country.'

`I'll bear it in mind,' I told him. 'But don't bank on it. Depends on how things play out.'

`Ah! I'm sure it does.' He grinned, and gave me a wink. `You still be here in a month?'

`I'd say that is quite possible. Again, depending on how things pan out. I'll keep in touch. You never know, may just stay for ever.'

With which, Kim gave him her phone number, we said our goodbyes, and parted.

During the drive Kim supplied details of how I'd ended up in a hospital bed, rather than hers. She'd rushed back inside the restaurant and immediately called the police, but by the time they arrived my attacker was seriously dead. He'd apparently got carried away, misjudged his footing and fallen into the path of a speeding car. All she'd seen as she came back out were tail-lights disappearing down the road.

I, apparently, hadn't stirred until they got me to hospital, which the police had arranged.

It occurred to me then that Kim was unlikely to have set me up, then called the police. But it did explain why I hadn't seen her when I'd glanced round.

That was basically the how. It didn't explain the why.

*

I was once again impressed by the new-look/old-look Fremantle, principal port and docks area of West Australia. It was a place which, after the previous brief visit, I had already found to be much more interesting as a tourist venue. Although I doubted it would be likely to aid my desire to be seen, or to be contacted by certain people in Perth. But it *was* relaxing, sitting outside on the wooden boardwalk at Kailis. Here we lunched overlooking the Indian Ocean, fish and chips again for me.

Fremantle, especially down here onthe waterfront, appeared as if a picture from a children's book, drawn with the intention of convincing the kids that there had been better times; sun, sea, golden beaches, smiles and laughter. Seagulls wheeled overhead, ever watchful. One presumed they wanted fish, but they seemed quite prepared to settle for chips. The fish and chips *were* very good, but I knew of a place where they were even better. Not too far away either.

`I was wondering, Roger. How come you aren't married?' Kim suddenly asked, breaking in on my peaceful solitude.

Oh, oh. Here we go again. Women passed through my life with a kind of regular frequency, but the last three I'd got to know very well had all been taken away from me. Violently, and forever. And recalling my wife, what not revealing the truth had almost cost me, I decided to come clean this time before getting too deeply involved.

'Was once. Lost her in an accident.'

`Ah, sorry. But it sometimes happens.' Apparently not interested in the hows, whys, and wherefores.

`No women since?'

`A couple. One another possible future wife. They're also .... well..'

`Dead! Not more accidents?'

`Sort of.'

'Jeez! Is this where the lack of a finger comes in?' she asked, pointing to my left hand and its missing little digit.

'Somewhere around that phase of my life.'

`Jeez!' she said again. 'Maybe we should forget the whole fucking thing.' She uttered the words, But I knew she wasn't serious when she failed pursue it; waiting to see if I would. Which I did.

'Suppose I could ask the same question of you. Rich, got the looks, and figure, dresses well, fun to be with. I'd think there would be no shortage of offers.'

'Well thank you,' she replied, actually blushing. 'Just never came across the right fella, I s'pose. There 'ave been one or two got close, ' she admitted.

Yeah, I'm sure there have! Something drastically wrong somewhere if there hadn't been.'

'Maybe I'm a bit too choosey.' She paused, as if waiting for me to follow up.

'Mayb...' I was suddenly prevented from continuing, being overcome by a strange feeling. Maybe it was the effects of my injuries... the first drink of the day... too much sun?

None of those, I realized. Something else entirely. Very close by. Something had registered itself in my mind. A presence announced, peripherally.

'Maybe what, Roger. What's up?'

I held up a hand, signalling a halt to the conversation. I looked around. People, buildings, seagulls, traffic. Nothing unusual there. But... Yes. People. A *particular* person, in fact. One of a group, seated a couple tables away. Dark hair, back to me, head turned to show an oblique profile. Could that be...?

'No,' I said. 'Impossible.' Or was it? I thought. Which was when I realised I'd been talking out loud.

'No what, Roger? What's impossible?'

My hand was up again. 'One moment, love.'

Not wishing to appear a fool, I excused myself and headed for the loo, glancing at him on my way past. He turned to look me right in the eye. He showed no sign of recognition, which introduced a degree of doubt in my mind. Now I wasn't so sure. Well, he certainly bore a close resemblance to old Foxy Reynolds, I thought. Very close. Similar features: the dark, naturally wavy hair, liquid brown eyes, broad face. Understandably a few years older, with a touch of grey around the temples. Only this guy wore a moustache. Even so, I'd almost swear it was Foxy. At least a very close likeness, almost a doppelganger, I thought. And I should know, Foxy and I had been very close friends at one time. Besides, a moustache meant nothing. Easiest feature of all to change, most obvious, too.

I decided to take a chance and introduce myself on the way back. But when I came out they'd left. Sod it, I was sure.....

'What's going on, Roger? `Bloke slipped me this on his way past,' Kim said as I arrived back at our table. 'Said he knows yuh.'

She handed me a scrap of paper. 'He seemed very cautious about it, fiddling with his clothes and hanging back until the others had gone by.'

I unfolded it to find a somewhat cryptic message. "OBH 14:00 tomorrow". It was signed, Foxy. Well, well, so I was right. It had been him. I showed the message to Kim, not doubting she'd already have looked. I would, had I been in her position.

`Foxy? That his name?'

`Daniel Reynolds, actually. Dan. Foxy's how he used to be known.'

`Would be wouldn't he, with a name like that.'

`Reynolds, not Reynard. But close enough for kids I suppose. You know what OBH means?'

`Yeah, sure. Ocean Beach Hotel. `Cottesloe,' she explained. `A right popular place, 'specially on weekends. But no one calls by its full name. Allus referred to as OBH. Drop by if you like. Or we could go tomorro'. Going into town anyway. I mean, you are staying with me, aren't you?'

'Dossing down, you mean?' I suggested, laughing.

'Right,' she confirmed. 'I'll soon have yuh speaking Oz.'

It was the kind of question that definitely set the heart beating faster - made me feel good as well. At least, better than I had been feeling of late. I figured she could easily make me forget my woes.

`It would appear so,' I was happy to answer. `If that's an invitation for me to do so. Just so long as you promise not to beat on me. I'm a little fragile at present.' It was an answer that appeared to make her feel better, too, for she smiled and clung to my arm.

`Oo, goody, goody,' she said, childlike, but sounding

like it was what she had always wanted. 'And I do promise. Not too hard, anyway.'

We spent the next hour wandering round, soaking up the atmosphere, looking at the fine old buildings. Myself meantime thinking about Foxy. Not particularly good thoughts. His haunted look. The failure to acknowledge me face to face. His secretive message and curious use of the twenty-four hour clock. Little bits of information that didn't seem to add up.... Unless?

We stopped by at Pappa Luigis for an afternoon cappuccino. After which, it was back to Perth, and the police.

'They released yuh this morning, where the hell yuh bin all day?' was how inspector McRobertson greeted my arrival. He then took me to a small office where I read and signed a prepared statement.

'That's all it needed. Should have come right away.'

'Felt a bit crook,' I lied, throwing the colloquialism back at him. 'But now I am here, there's something else. Meant to call in on Monday about it, but...' I shrugged and explained about Professor Hoving. McRobertson didn't appear in the least interested.

'Yeah. What yuh want me to do about it?'

'Well, he came to Perth, and he didn't leave. Just vanished.'

'Poms come out here all the time and go walkabout. Nothing unusual in that.' The reply, whilst not exactly impolite, was certainly not intended to be helpful.

'Not university Professors, with meetings to attend, lectures scheduled. Something strange there.'

'To you, maybe.' His closed expression told me such a thing was not possible. "Not in my territory," I read as the sub-text to that.

'Well,' I said, looking thoughtful, 'If you add up all the facts, even though there's no hard evidence, nothing substantial anyway, you do at least come up with a question mark or two. Maybe I should take it to the Federal Police.'

'Just think on where yur' at. If there *was* anything, it'd be local. Doesn't involve the Feds. And don't assume yuh can go around bypassing official channels. I'll ask a few questions,' he said. But he didn't look or sound like he meant it.

He dismissed me by collecting his papers together, and I wondered what would it take for him to believe a member of the public. He was treating me as if I were making everything up, as if the facts were mere speculation. The facts were, Professor Freedburg Hoving had completely and thoroughly disappeared. Well, I had my own life to attend to, so when we got to Kim's, I placed a call to Freddie, back home in England, setting him the problem of coming up with a reason for the Professor's disappearance. There had to *be* a reason, as it seemed he didn't *want* to be found. Otherwise, why had he disappeared so thoroughly?

There was of course another possibility. An as yet unspoken one. That of the Professor being dead.

*   *

Chapter Thirteen

FOXY, FOXY

Upon leaving the police station we abandoned the centre of Perth as evening stole in, and headed for the hilly suburbs and country surroundings to the east. With Kim at the wheel, the Ute followed what for her would be a familiar route.

It had been another long, tiring day as far as I was concerned. My bruised and battered body not standing up well to even the minor movements of the vehicle. But we were soon safely ensconced in Kim's rather remote property. With the sun now well below the horizon the lighting was too dim for me to get a good view of the outside, besides, I wasn't exactly in an interested mood. It was great inside, from what I saw, lavish in fact, though all I really wanted right now was rest.

But as far as Kim was concerned, it appeared that wasn't about to be allowed anytime soon.

A short time later I was to be found wagging a finger at her in disapproval. A purely token gesture. 'You said you had something that would help ease my bruising,' I said. She had undressed me, and I now lay back on her bed. Fair enough. But what came next didn't fit in with the scenario of the rubbing in of healing lotion.

'Not too sure this is a good idea for a man in my condition,' I told her. Another token protest as, with an atypical lack of female ceremony, Kim's skirt fell to crumple around her ankles. Naturally, already being naked myself, visual evidence was now well enough advanced to give lie to my words.

'How do you mean?' she asked, managing to maintain the pretence.

Well, if she could, so could I. 'I'm badly bruised. You said.....'

'That comes later. You is first. OK?'

After a little, slightly-exaggerated bottom wiggling, something flimsy followed the skirt to the floor, leaving a shirt-tailed blouse to cover the rude, and to me, very exciting bits.

'Well, I feel terrible. How do I look?' I managed to blurt out. Horny as hell was how I really felt, despite my medical condition.

She somehow managed to stifle a laugh. 'Well, tha certainly don't look as if yur about t' drop dead at me feet.' she said, climbing onto the bed to kneel astride me.

'Not bad then, huh?' God! she exuded sex. Terrible though I may have said I felt, by now I was about ready to rape the Statue of Liberty.

'Not too bad, no.'

'Right! So just lay back and leave things t' me fer t' time being.'

'Funny you should say that. Want to hear my philosophy on life?' I told her anyway, saving time. Had to, before the vocal cords seized up completely. 'When it's good, lay back and enjoy it. When it's bad, lay back regardless, that way you're less likely to get hurt. Me thinks this is a time for enjoyment,' I managed to mumble.'

I think she agreed, for she reached up and pulled the silk top over her head, and discarded it. Consigned it to a floor awash with sheepskin rugs.

As for Kim she emerged sporting a nice line in nothing at all; apart from a wide smile, that is, breasts and buttocks

114

firmer than a politician's handshake. And if awards were given for good bodies, in my book, Kim would have qualified for a gold. Possibly diamond studded. There again, it could be said I was a biassed judge, given the current view I had of this one.

'Goodness me!' she said, as if noticing my lower quarters for the first time. 'Thought you said you didn't think this was a good idea? Doesn't look to me like that's what yu're thinking.'

'Oooh. That was before. Right now I, aah, I like the ide..aaah.'

She *did* agree, for she was now away, riding off into the sunset, and all intelligible sounds from her lips ceased. They were replaced instead by a series of oohs and aahs, grunts, groans, and animal-like whimpering noises. Her eyes were tightly closed, face an expression of intent concentration. She was lost to all but pleasure.

And she was wonderful.

Made me feel so much better, too.

*

Kim apparently also enjoyed life's other little pleasures, for on the bedside table was a silver tray. It held a bottle of ten year old, single malt Glenmorangie, glasses, and an ice bucket. She poured some of the amber liquid into a crystal glass, added ice, and offered me it.

'Not me,' I said, wrinkling me nose and shaking my head. 'I'm a Calvados or Cognac drinker.' Whisky, I hated the stuff. She obviously didn't, although I doubted she was much of a connoisseur, for I was reasonably sure a true connoisseur would never have added ice to a decent single malt.

She also possessed one of those modern multi-deck, Japanese stereo systems. Type of thing that looked like it required a course of instruction at the manufacturers, rather than merely a simple on-off switch.

Speakers were located throughout the house, the style of which was open-plan - upper floor rooms apart: bedrooms, this master, plus two more, both with a small en suite. There was and a separate, rather luxurious shower down the hall.

The music centre itself sat on the upstairs landing. As

we'd passed by, myself being almost dragged along on the way to her bedroom, I'd noticed Kim stop, flick a couple of switches, punch a button or two, and adjust some sliders. But as no music issued forth, I'd assumed her to be putting it to bed, also. "Night, night, stereo", kind of thing. Wrong! For now, after fiddling with the remote control, Sinatra's voice burst into the room. That was a surprise. As the stereo was nowhere in view I figured it had to be a radio-frequency remote, rather than the usual line-of-sight, infra-red system. Trust Kim to be different. There again, it did give her the added luxury of being able to control the music from anywhere in the house.

Sinatra was a surprise, too. I'd have expected Pink Floyd or some such to be her kind of thing. But perhaps not, post-coital. Currently, Frank rearranged Lennon and McCartney's "Yesterday", without detriment to either.

We lay back and let the music wash over us. Kim didn't say a word, just stared at the ceiling, a look on her face. Pleasure? Approval? Something of the sort, I was sure, for that's how I felt. I basked briefly in imagined praise before speaking.

'Could almost have you charged with rape. You realize that?' I told her.

She looked at me in a puzzled kind of way. 'Why *almost?*'

'Well, the police would take one look at you and ask why I was complaining.'

'Think I've just been paid a compliment.' she said.

'You have. It also reminds me of a joke about the ugly, fat girl who was stopped by a police patrol down a dark lane. "Excuse me, miss," one constable said. "Don't you know this is a dangerous place to be?"

"Oh yes," she sighed. "Been down here twice before, got raped both times. So here I am again."

Kim giggled, and snuggled close. Sex, companionship, and sleep were just what I needed at the moment. To take my mind off my aching body, and thoughts of what tomorrow may bring.

But Kim wasn't quite finished with me yet, for she now produced a bottle of lotion with which she anointed me, both front and back. The feeling was both wonderfully soothing and relaxing, so I told her so. She said it would help with my healing, and take the pain away. At least I think that was what she was saying, for I suspect I was sound asleep even before she had finished.

*

The Ocean Beach Hotel is located slightly north of the suburb of North Cottesloe, on the landward side of the beach road, overlooking the sea.

I asked Kim to first drive slowly past, allowing me time to recce the place. I then had her drive round the block, checking for alternate exits. Finally, I requested she drop me a hundred yards up the street. I'd arrive on foot.

'Why the caution Roger? What yuh up to?'

Natural she would ask, so I gave her an answer she could believe, almost the truth. 'Foxy acted cautious when he passed you that note, didn't he? The reason must be with him. He didn't wish to be seen, so I need to be just as cautious until I find out what's going on.'

It seemed to appease her, for now, I suspected. She did as agreed to my request, dropped me off, and then drove away. We had already arranged to meet up later.

It must have been all of five years since I had last exchanged civil words with Daniel "Foxy" Reynolds, so we would have a fair bit to talk about. At present he was classed as, ex-friend. We had been close at one time, until, returning unexpectedly from a trip up north one evening, I'd caught him in bed with my girlfriend. Naturally, we'd parted then, the girl electing to go with him. But they hadn't stayed together long.

I'd been about to break it off anyway, so hadn't been too upset. He'd probably saved me some strife, though I hadn't told him so. It had been my bed they were in.

These thoughts passed through my mind as I sat outside, on the upstairs, open air veranda of the OBH, drinking, watching life pass by, waiting. I'd purposely arrived early to enable me to do just that.

A hot sun blazed down from an otherwise empty sky, its heat, dry, thirst creating. Far removed from the cold they would be experiencing back in this city's namesake, twelve thousand miles away. Which made it quite a coincidence. For the last address I had for Foxy *was* Perth, Scotland.

He arrived on time.

I watched as he stopped and paid off his taxi, half a block away, glancing around as he continued on foot, cautious as a deer at a waterhole. Lightweight slacks, short-sleeved shirt, sandals. Casually smart, no bright colours; as if not wishing to stand out in any way. So the jewellery didn't help!

Once inside I went down to meet him. Yes, it would be some reunion all right. First he'd refused to acknowledge me in front of his friends in Freo, apparently preferring the intrigue of something more covert. Now here he was, making a surreptitious entrance to the OBH. Why? It was the obvious question that sprang to mind as I made my way down to meet up with him.

'Buy you a drink, stranger?' I asked, approaching from behind. He almost jumped out of his skin, effected a recovery when he saw who it was.

'Hey, Roger. Long time no see. How's it with you?' Attempting to sound casual, but failing miserably, his relief obvious. He'd never make it in Hollywood.

I shook the proffered hand. It was cold and clammy, despite the weather. His wrist, I noted, carried a watch that must have cost more than my London apartment. Couldn't very well have missed it.

'Not too bad, stranger.' Didn't ask how he was, he'd have lied anyway, told me life was great, when it so obviously wasn't.

I got the drinks and we secured a window seat. I positioned myself back to the wall, window to my right. Foxy had the glass at his back. The sun streamed in, drawing my eyes to the ring on his right hand, couldn't have missed that, either; diamond that would have attracted the attention of Richard Burton! It glittered, flashed, and sparkled in the sunlight. But despite this brash display of wealth, he was obviously very unhappy, that was plainly evident from his body language. His arms slumped loosely from his shoulders, as if his brain had forgotten they were there. His eyes were evasive, looking everywhere except directly into mine.

'So, tell me a bit about yourself, Foxy. When did you

come out to Oz?' Only been here four days myself and already the colloquialisms were rolling off the tongue.

'Oh, about a month after you met up with that dishy Simone.'

'If you remember, I was with Simone because some turd went off with Janet. Still, on reflection, you did me a great favour there.'

'Yeah, I must admit, Simone did seem to be a big improvement on Jan. What became of her?' A fire-opal nestled in chest hair. It hung from a gold chain around his neck.

'We eventually got married. Then there was an accident. She was knocked down by a truck, and killed.'

'Jeez, Roger. I'm sorry.'

'It was a while ago now. I've recovered. Water under the bridge and all that.' It was a pretence I lived, so not exactly a lie. I just didn't allow myself to think of her, though the visions did occasionally creep into my dreams, as did those of Caroline, another of my girlfriends who had been laid to rest.

'I wondered for a second there,' he replied. 'When you said you were married. And here I see you in Freo with JKH.'

It took a couple of seconds to click. Judith Kimberley Hamilton. 'You know Kimberley?' I asked.

'Ha! Chance would be a fine thing. Know *of* her, never had the pleasure. Know lots of guys who've tried, without success. How did you manage to latch on to that gorgeous piece of totty? There again, you always were one for the women, Roger. You and your magnetic attraction. Still as popular as ever, I see.'

'Just lucky. Happened to sit next to her on the flight from Singapore. Had five hours to charm her over.'

I realized my mistake too late, immediately prepared an alibi. Just as well, for despite his nervousness he was on to it like a lawyer in court.

'Would have thought a Sheila like her must travel first class. Writing must pay well, eh?' He glanced at his watch. Not for the first time. He was continually doing so.

'I wish. But no. Economy was over-booked, so they upgraded me. Just one of those things. Couldn't have worked out better as it happened. It was small talk, but he was leading up to something.

119

He stole another look at the Rolex.

'Pushed for time are you Foxy.'

'No,' he said, realising I was watching. 'Just can't stay too long.'

His actions were not those of the average man. He noticed things that normally went unnoticed, except by people like me, who had been trained to notice them. I decided to push him along.

'Anyway, what're you doing these days?'

'Me. Oh I work for AA&M.'

I shook my head. 'AA&M?'

'Armadale Air and Marine. Freight handlers. I work on the aviation side, out at the airport.' He didn't offer any more. 'And you're here doing what, Roger? Research?'

'Some, hopefully. Visiting another old school friend as well. You recall Tony Higgins?'

'Can't say as I do. There again, you were a class ahead of me.'

'Or was I behind? Can't remember now. Anyway, did you say you read my book?'

'Yeah. Enjoyed it too. Where d'yuh get your ideas. It read like you were writing from experience.'

'Some, though not all. Fertile imagination,' I averred. 'But if you stay alert you pick things up here and there; books, movies, newspapers, real life.'

'Suppose so. Like sitting facing the street so nobody can sneak up without you seeing them, for instance?' He turned to look out of the window.

'Was I?' I threw him a smile. 'Well, you often find yourself relating to your characters without even realizing it.' He wasn't quite as astute as I'd thought. He hadn't realized I was also using the window's reflections to check on what was happening behind me, in the bar, so I pretty much had the place covered. All clear at present, nothing and no one that raised any suspicions.

And that was it. Almost. We talked a while longer before falling into an uncomfortable silence. He'd obviously been sounding me out for something, had yet to reach a decision. Not sure. Needed more time. But obviously not here.

We only drank one toast: to the future. Then, just as I

was about to give up and leave, it seemed he had decided. I was to be trusted.

'Roger? Could we meet again? Somewhere more private? Tomorrow, maybe?'

That saved me from asking. Thinking what I was, I really did need to talk to some more to Foxy. Better it be on his terms.

'Sure, Foxy. Always time for old friends. But why the cloak and dagger stuff?' I asked. Although by now I had a good idea why. Could this be the break I'd been hoping for? Fortuitous, that, if my thinking was correct. But fortuitousness could often be the way of life, I'd found.

'Tell you tomorrow. OK?'

'All right,' I agreed. 'Time and place?'

'King's Park. You know where it is?'

Heard of it, not hard to find, so I'm told.'

'Right. The cafeteria; fourteen hundred.'

'OK Foxy. See you there. Oh, and by the way,' I said. 'If you're worried about being seen, don't wear the jewellery. I'd never create any my characters doing that.'

He looked at the watch, then just nodded.

I let him leave first, finished my drink as he did so. The car didn't follow him. So it must be me someone was interested in.

I'd watched it park, down the street, well clear of the hotel. My eyes had been drawn to it. Not because there was anything unusual about the colour or make - grey, Ford Falcon - but the registration caught my eye; registered as it were. I'd already seen it twice before during the day. Coincidence, or what? Hardly. As far as I was concerned, coincidence dealt itself out of the equation after the second appearance.

They were easy enough to shake. No one had left the car, and there were other exits, leading onto other streets, as I had learned from my earlier recce. I chose to leave through the back, walked away up the hill and caught a taxi.

It had been a fairly relaxing day, as far as my days ever had been, since Singapore. Previous to my meeting Foxy, I'd spent the morning in town with Kim: her shopping, me familiarizing myself with the area. After three days with Tony I'd become fairly well acquainted with the layout, was now dotting the I's and crossing the T's, so for sure I knew about Kings Park, even though we never went there. Couldn't really not be aware of it. At over four square kilometres it is said to be one of the largest inner city parks in the world. It sits on a bluff, overlooking Perth, its Swan river, and the Indian Ocean.

*

Kim hadn't arrived at our rendezvous point, the Transit Inn, so I ordered a beer. Same barman, no one else around.

'No cricket ball?' he asked.

'Left it at home.'

'Play, do yuh?'

'I watch.'

'Need to watch yur back. Fella followed yuh in last time. 'S why I didn't respond.'

'Anyone you know?' I silently cursed myself. I'd slipped up there, missed him.

'Nah. Never seen him before.'

'Well, if he appears again give me the nod.'

'Natch.'

Then I thought about that. 'Have a description do you?'

'BB does, and he's due tomorrow, by the way. Wants a meet.' He looked up at the ceiling. Room 17. Around ten. He'll be waiting.'

Bob Bottomsworth, I translated. Wishes to talk with me.

By the time Kim finally put in an appearance - a clutch of department store bags suitable enough explanation for her lateness - I had become reasonably well acquainted with the barman.

I greeted her with a kiss, but she didn't wish to stay for a drink. Didn't fancy alcohol, she said. Didn't want a coffee here either. 'I know a better place, lover,' she told me. 'I can call you that now that we are, can't I.' She smiled.

En-route back to where she had parked the car, we called in at a little café in London Court, for a sandwich and a cup of tea. We took an outside table - where I sat, back to the wall, as was my wont - and relaxed in the sun, whilst she enthused to me about her purchases. There were plenty of reflecting surfaces around that allowed me to keep an eye on things without making it apparent: shop windows, nice shiny chrome tea-pot, things like that. Relaxed or not, it was time for increased awareness now someone appeared to be taking an interest in my movements.

After half an hour we picked up the Ute and left for her place.

*

I was back on Pier Street shortly before ten the following morning. Entering the Transit Inn as if I owned the place, I made my way to the first floor and followed the numbers to the designated room. Here I knocked and waited.

No reply.

Should have called from the desk, Minerva advised. *Maybe he's in the shower.*

I tried the door. Open, so I knocked again and walked in, calling as I did so.

'Bob?'

It was a suite: sofa, a couple of chairs, coffee table, desk, mini-bar, bedroom door - closed. No one in sight and still no reply. I walked across an expanse of Axminster to the bedroom and was about to knock, when there was a thump as something was tossed into the room behind me. Something that landed heavily and rolled across the floor. Something that behaved and sounded very much like a hand grenade!

*   *

Chapter Fourteen

A WALK IN THE PARK

*W*ithout hesitation, or time wasted on a backward glance, I dived for the sofa, pulling it away from the wall and sliding into the space created in one smooth, though rather painful movement. I was counting the seconds in my head as I did so, heart in overdrive. *Four.. five*, by which time I was in place; secure, but my body crying out, reminding me that I was still badly bruised. *Eight... nine...* Nothing. If it was a grenade it was on a very long fuse. *Ten...* Extremely long. A dud... or?

I eased my head forward, slowly, inch by uncertain inch, thoughts in a whirl. Nothing added up. And because nothing added up, it suddenly did. Bloody wanker.

I peered out, still cautious; training coming into play.

'Boom!' a voice cried. Then a familiar tanned face grinned at me from the doorway. The cricket ball lay in the centre of the carpet, looking like maybe it was wondering what it was supposed to be doing there. Possibly wondering what I was doing throwing myself behind the furniture.

'Pretty impressive, sport,' Bob Bottomsworth said,

entering the room. 'Saw yuh disappear through the door just as I came up the corridor. Ideal time for a little refresher, I thought. Like to keep on top of things.' He closed the door and walked over to retrieve the "grenade". With an impressive foot movement he flicked the ball into the air and caught it, automatically wrapping his fingers around it as though about to begin his run up.

'In my condition I can well do without having to fling myself around unnecessarily.'

'One would imagine you've been doing something like that anyway, given the Sheila you're shacked up with.' Then, reluctantly, it seemed, he ended his judicious contemplation of sending down the perfect delivery, pocketing the ball instead.

'Feeling a bit fragile, are we? Well, grab a pew, Roger.' And as I did. 'Fancy a frostie?' he offered, reaching into the mini-bar.

'Too early for me, but you go ahead. You can drink as you listen.'

He caught my mood, became sincere. 'I'm listening.'

'There was a tracking device in that briefcase. If you're on top of things, how come you missed that?'

He cracked the can open before replying.

'Didn't miss it. Just didn't tell yuh. We wus tracking it as well. Needed a guarantee yuh wouldn't shoot through with that lot, try to sell it?'

'You mean you didn't trust me.'

'Back then, not entirely,' he admitted. 'It's serious business, Roger. We had to be sure.' He put the can to his mouth and tilted his head back, Adam's apple shuttling to and fro like he hadn't drunk for a week.

'And now you are?'

He wiped the back of his hand across his mouth before answering. 'Fair dinkum,' he said. Which I encountered a certain difficulty in accepting; knowing it to be nowhere near the truth.

'So why the tail? Don't think I didn't notice. Couldn't very well miss. And neither will the opposition, if they have me tagged. You could be putting my life on the line, or at least the possibility of me being invited in. Probably already have. Know anything about a case of hit and run?'

125

He shrugged. 'Sort of thing that could well befall anyone who happened to be kicking a man when he's down. Yuh got lucky.'

That set me thinking. Accident or intent, it didn't make the slightest difference to the subject in question, he was no longer a factor to be taken into account. But the implications of his demise were. Seemed like Bob's people had known something about him, probably something that threatened our operation. That they were prepared to kill like that told me they also were very serious, despite his laid-back attitude.

'What caused the threat to my life? What does someone know?'

'Don't think they know anything. Suspect they weren't sure, easier to silence you than worry about it. With any luck they'll see it as an accident, by which time they *will* be sure about you. Maybe they'll decide it's better you work for them. That way they can keep you under control.'

'How do you mean, "they will be sure"? What makes you think so?'

'There's been feelers out, about your background.'

Just as I'd hoped, they *were* checking. Which seemed to point at them coming back to me. But would it be for the right reasons?

'That so? Then let's hope they don't find anything they don't like,' I told him.

'They won't.'

'All right,' I said, not feeling that "all right" about it at all. 'What's next?'

'Keep plugging away, stirring them up, asking questions. Seems to be working out.'

'OK, so we carry on. I admit I was bloody stupid. Careless. It won't happen again.'

'Easy to be careless when there's a Sheila involved, Roger. Hope you know what you're doing.'

'Oh, I do, believe me. So call off the tail.'

'Consider it done,' he said, dismissing the subject by reaching into the bag he carried and placing a small, black object on the table. It looked like a Walkman, or a micro-recorder.

'Kind of answering machine,' he explained, noting my

look. 'Only it doesn't answer.' He handed me a pen; Singapore Airlines logo. 'Just records anything this picks up. Fully functional, but go ahead, take it apart.'

Cautiously, I unscrewed the top, revealing a thin sliver of perforated metal with wires running down into the barrel alongside the refill. No doubt to a micro transmitter, located in the depths. It would be difficult to detect if you weren't specifically looking for it. I reassembled the pen.

'Range? About a hundred feet,' Bob advised. 'Clip it in your shirt pocket,' he suggested, as he switched the receiver on. So I did.

'What's with this Hoving guy, Roger?' He slipped it in so shrewdly he almost caught me off guard. No doubt meant to. But I had nothing to hide from him there.

'I have a package for him, is all. Like to get rid of it. A favour for a friend.' My words echoed from the table-top receiver, the voice kind of scratchy, but loud and clear. Bob was slightly muted, though still audible.

'Had this faxed from London,' he said, handing me the sheet. The quality was so poor - smudgy and indistinct - it looked as if it could have been beamed down from a distant planet rather than a man-made satellite. It was a photograph of a face. Presumably the professor's, but not much use as such, although it did trigger a memory. A face, glimpsed briefly in a Singapore bar. Not imagined then. And it did point to something else: the fact they had Tony's phone bugged! I could accept him learning of my interest in the professor, via the police. But the police couldn't know I'd phoned Freddie, asking for a photograph.

'According to the local constabulary,' Bob continued, after taking another long draught from his beer, 'no one even thinks they've seen him. There's been no reports of anyone wandering. And he did check out of his hotel. This McRobertson guy is a bit touchy; very anti-Brit, and unscrupulous,' he advised. 'But he does carry a lot of weight locally, so don't give him cause to divert you from *our* project, if you know what I mean. As far as the Federal Police go, they are totally isolated from this, as are the local cops. And, for obvious reasons, must remain so.'

'I'll bear that in mind.'

'Do that. And take these, you may find them useful.' He passed me a couple of the recorders, half a dozen pens, and a handful of small plastic squares, maybe half an inch across, different colours. They looked like something you got free when you sent in ten special coupons from the back of a cornflakes packet.

'Transmitter relays,' he explained. 'Each is capable of tripling the range. Match the colour to the background. We need information from somewhere.'

'Yeah, ain't that the truth,' I said. 'I don't have much at all. A couple of possibilities, maybe. Some ideas forming, but nothing positive. Not even a contact, as yet. But things are starting to move, into the danger zone, it would seem.'

'You want out, Roger?'

'Want out! What do *you* think? I figured at the start you didn't have anything to hold over me, remember. Yet I still went along with it. Why would I want out now, just when it's starting to get interesting. Besides, I intend to hold you to that twenty thousand.'

He seemed relieved at that. He finished the beer, crushed the can in one hand and shied it at the waste basket. It was an oblique shot and he barely glanced at the target, yet it hit dead centre, never even touched the sides. He looked at me as if seeking approval. He didn't get it. 'OK,' he said, 'had to ask. They've got to make a move soon. Drugs don't make money in storage remember, they only present a danger. It's a rush business. They need to get the stuff processed and out of their hands quickly. The more the pressure, the more the hurry to move them on, the greater the chance of a mistake.'

'Like hand-carrying from Singapore, for instance?'

'Got it in one.' He reached over to the fridge and helped himself another tinnie.

'So we have the luxury of being able to move cautiously, whilst trying to force them into a mistake.'

'Well, yeah. Move cautiously, but we have to take some chances. Got nothing at present, when what we need are details. Who? How? By what means? Where? And particularly, when? But remember, Roger, you're just there to collect information. Nothing complex. Maybe get them worried, push them into a mistake.'

128

'Seems I've heard that tune before.'

'Well listen good. As soon as you have anything solid, pass it back. We'll take it from there. You don't have authority for anything else. Unless your life happens to be at stake, that is.'

I figured he'd added the last to give me some leeway. But only because it would be in *their* interest to do so.

'Roger,' he said as I left, causing me to glance back. 'Be careful,' he warned. The second empty tin followed the first to oblivion, spot on once again. He had a good eye, Bob. I could imagine him being devastating on the field of play.

Whilst I was relaxed enough to be seen as treating this thing as an adventurous lark, I wasn't so stupid as to fail to see the risks involved. Yes, I would be careful. Very careful indeed.

Back on the street, my first action had been to check on Bob's tail, but it seemed he'd been as good as his word, no sign of them, or of anyone else taking an interest in my movements.

*

King's Park was one place Tony had missed out on during our touring around, though he had directed my attention to its existence. Sited on a hill, overlooking the city and the Swan River, I now discovered it to be much larger than I'd imagined. Part garden, part bush, part play and picnic areas, it could well have been a corner of paradise. Up here the sky appeared maybe that much bluer, the grass unnaturally green, the air hot and dry.

I noted the gardens hosted Kangaroo Paw - the floral emblem of this state - and there were kookaburra's, Norfolk pine, and the ubiquitous gum tree, their trunks a kind of luminous blonde, flaking like sunburnt skin. Given such conditions, life seemed even more relaxed and laid back. Difficult to imagine anything incongruous happening up here. The only reminder that things are not always so, was a small plaque set beside each gum tree. Lining the road through the park was an avenue of such trees, each dedicated to an Australian killed in the wars. The West Australian State War memorial was sited here, too, along with its eternal flame. Back to the reality of life.

I didn't notice a McLaren amongst the names

mentioned around here, hoped things would remain that way, whatever cause he fell in, or the politics of his commemoration.

I'd arrived well before the allotted time of our meeting, had the taxi drop me by a memorial to Queen Victoria, and from there I set off on my usual journey of discovery. I stopped abruptly a couple of times, turning to retrace my steps, observing other passers-by carefully, looking for the unnatural or sudden movement. I checked the toilets, scouted the parking area, the back of the building, and the surrounding bush. Anywhere a man could hide. I studied faces, and modes of dress, looked for any unusual signs of movement, detected no signs of surveillance at all.

Standing in plain view outside the cafeteria entrance, I again watched Foxy's arrival, making sure he was clean. It appeared he was. I noticed he'd even dispensed with the jewellery, now wore a simple digital watch. Black, just like mine. So not only did he listen, he took note, I thought.

He must have felt he was not being followed, too, for he wasted no time with preliminaries. But he was so tense one could almost visualize stress lines in his make up. Like a block of ice, I thought. Tap him in the right place and he'll shatter.

I still didn't know what Foxy's problem was, but boy, did he have one. That was plain to see.

'Suppose you're wondering what this is all about?' he began.

'You might suppose that, yes.' I took his arm, steering him away from the building, walking across the grass to a clear, open area. The Swan river was visible through the trees, down there beyond the city centre, its waters a mass of colourful sails. Difficult to imagine danger lurking in this sylvan setting, but I needed to believe that it was. An absolute necessity, that. Everything could depend on it.

'I'm in trouble, Roger. Don't know who to turn to.'

'What kind of trouble? And what makes you think I can help?'

'Can't talk to anyone else because I don't know who's not involved. You've just arrived, so you're obviously in the clear. And, being a writer, I... well, hoped you might have some ideas or thoughts on the matter.'

The very first thought that came to my mind was that,

providing I was correct in my thinking, he couldn't be more wrong about me being "in the clear."

'In the clear about what, Foxy? What's going on?'

'I got involved with some people, and... well, it was a mistake.' He was continually glancing around, like a nervous dog.

'So? Become uninvolved. Where's the problem in that?' By now I had a good idea, but I wanted him to spell it out. It looked as if I had an ex-friend who, albeit having made his pile out of it, was now faced with a crisis of conscience. I felt it right to exploit the situation.

'It's fucking drugs, Roger. And you don't just pack up and leave. This mob's like the Mafia, once in, always in. I've seen too much for them to let me leave now.'

'Don't imagine they'd be exactly thrilled at the idea of you talking to me then.' I stopped, sinking down to sit on the grass, well clear of anyone else; the picnickers, strollers, and the frisbee throwers. It was that kind of place, a family place. Grass neat and trim, like a well-kept garden. Albeit, a very big garden.

'Ain't that the truth.' He forced a smile as he joined me, down on the greenery. 'In fact, were it to become common knowledge, I dare say it could seriously affect my health, as they say.'

'Then leave the country. Go where they'll never find you.' My eyes kept returning to a particular area. Drawn there by the figure which occupied that spot. He'd appeared suddenly, been standing there for some moments.

'Try and smile, or laugh now and again whilst were talking, Foxy. Like old school friends catching up on lost years.'

He immediately looked worried. 'You've seen something haven't you,' he said.

'Take it easy, Foxy, and listen to what I say. Not just listen, do it. Let's see you laugh. And no, there's no one around. No point waiting until there is though.'

'Anyway, as I suggested, why don't you leave the country, go somewhere where they're unlikely to find you.'

'Ha! And where might that be? Oh, they'd find me all

right. Johan tried, they found him. Admitted, he didn't leave the country. Picked him up in Perth would you believe. Incredibly stupid. Especially for someone that stood out like he did.' Now he did actually laugh. Not perfect, but it would do.

'Stood out?' My mind was only fifty-percent with Foxy. The man was still there, lighting a cigarette now. He had the other fifty-percent.

'Yeah. Like a myopic owl.'

Well, that got my attention all right. All one hundred percent. Jesus, yes! I latched on to it immediately, alarm bells ringing. 'Like a myopic owl,' I repeated. The very words Freddie used to characterize Professor Hoving.

I pulled out the fax. 'Something like that? '

'What the..! Well... not very clear, but basically, yes. Where did you....?'

'Friend of a friend, who happens to be missing.' I relaxed slightly. A large Alsatian went bounding up to the man and they walked off together.

'Guy at the airport was a friend of Johan's, maybe he has a picture. Would that help?' Foxy asked.

'Might help me, not you. But ask anyway. You say you actually saw this Johan?'

'Only once. I was there when they.... dealt with him. In fact that's what made me decide to get out.' He shuddered at the memory, shaking his head as if to clear the images from his mind. 'They shot him. I knew others had... disappeared, as it were. Found one out in the bush, dead from dehydration. Another died of a snake-bite, one of an overdose of heroin. No doubt all *accidents*. Or made to look so. But they were stories I'd been told, about people I didn't know. Not even sure if they were true or not. Actually witnessing it is a different kettle of fish.'

'I would imagine so,' I commiserated. Although, from previous experience, I knew so. 'What happened afterwards?'

'Nothing. Far as I know the body's still there.'

'Did this body have a surname?'

'Course. Kluger. Dutch descent,' he added. Quite unnecessarily.

'And where exactly is *there*?'

He told me.

So, not only was our Daniel involved with a drugs ring, he was witness to foul deeds. Accomplice was how the law would see it. Maybe I could use that.

'Nasty, nasty, Foxy. Do not pass go,' I said, shaking my head gravely, although I laughed too. 'And if I were able to help in some way... Well..., I'd become an accessory on the one hand, and on the other...? You see the situation you'd put me in? So, before we agree to anything, I need to know more than what you've told me.'

'What kind of more?'

'Well, knowing how they operate would be quite handy. Lets me see where they might be most vulnerable. And who? That might be a good place to begin. Essential I know that. Enemies are one thing, invisible enemies, something else entirely.' I made a pretence of easing my neck, checking the area again as I did so. Clear.

'It's pretty compartmentalized, Roger. I only know about what travels by air. No idea where the stuff comes from originally. As for personnel, most of them we never see. As far as I'm aware, there's just the three of us at the airport, packing drugs into freight shipments. They're extremely cautious, never more than one kilo per item.'

'A kilo? Doesn't sound a lot,' I said.

'Yeah, but multiply a kilo by a minimum of forty per flight, maybe two hundred times a year, and we're talking serious quantities. But not so big at one time so as to attract attention.'

I whistled. 'Slightly in excess of the gross national product of more than one third world nation then.'

'Ain't that the truth,' he responded.

So, I thought, they had shipments leaving regularly. Better than every other day, not counting local distribution. And here was Bob telling me they might make a move soon! In what direction? I was desperately short on facts, but long on speculation. Some of which, I thought, strong enough to make me wonder why nobody else could see it. One thing was for sure, I couldn't afford to loose Foxy, he was my passport to regaining contact. At least a source of information. Of course, he wasn't to know that. Nor would he be allowed to.

'OK, Foxy, here's what we'll do. And for Christ's sake,

133

relax man, give me another laugh. There's no one around, I've been keeping an eye open. Learned that from the Quiller books,' I said.

'This is real life, Roger, Quiller's fiction.'

'Yeah, but close enough to reality,' I assured him.

Not true! Either that, or I'd slipped up, I was later to discover.

*

'Got a surprise for you,' Kim advised on my return.

'Pleasant, I hope.'

'Depends. Dad would like to meet you. Saturday. Ten o'clock. Brekkie at his place. I have an another appointment then, so you'll have to go on your own.'

And I'd like to meet him, I thought. But what I said was: 'Breakfast, at ten o'clock? More like bloody brunch.'

'Aye. But I'll warn you now, Roger, he's an inquisitive sod. Always wants all the details, right down to the far end of a fart. So I'd appreciate your not mentioning certain... er.. aspects of our life-style.' She grinned, patting my thigh, or somewhere in the vicinity.

Why mention that, I thought! "Dad" is a man of the world, I'm staying with you, I'm pretty sure he'll have figured out what we get up to now and again! I just smiled at her.

'You have lovely white teeth, Roger.'

'Hope so. Clean them religiously,' I said. 'Morning and night, ever since I was first able. OK. Most nights.'

'Why only most?'

'Well, there have been odd nights when I've been out drinking, so not capable of anything other than falling into bed.'

'Oh dear!'

' Not too many of those. But of course there were other nights when I had only one thing on my mind, and it wasn't cleaning my teeth!'

'Ah! Like last night, you mean.'

'You telling me I didn't clean my teeth?'

'Certainly didn't.'

'OK. Like last night then.'

'Umm. Oh, by the way, Tony called. Almost forgot to tell yuh. Had a message from Fred somebody-or-other. Works for the police. Two messages, in fact. The registration you asked

134

him to look up was that of a car reported stolen. And he wondered what you'd been up to. Said he'd seen a report "implicating you, in a roundabout way, with a death," were his words. That's a load of crap. You were unconscious at the time.'

'Yeah. Pass that on to Inspector McRobertson will you. Seems he has it in for me.'

*   *

Chapter Fifteen

WHITEFELLA

Bug. That's exactly what it reminded me of; a small black disc with a couple of wires sticking out for legs. It was so well installed I would never have found it had I not been specifically looking. And I'd only been looking on account of a hunch. In this age of miniaturization even something that small could be quite powerful, though it was likely they had a transceiver stashed somewhere close by.

The decision to leave the bug in place was based on something my SAS friend, Mike, had told me some time back: "Remember, Roger, bugs can always be turned. The fact that they faithfully transmit all that's said allows you to feed the opposition whatever it is you wish them to have."

'Even a pack of lies,' I'd added, somewhat unnecessarily.

Of course, being Kim's phone, I'd have to clear it with her first. And that meant letting her in on a few secrets. She didn't need the whole thing. Just enough to satisfy her curiosity.

I made sure we were well away from the house before

raising the subject, hinting that possibly the professor's notes were of value to someone other than the professor. Or at least it seemed someone thought they might be, and that was enough to somehow put me in the danger zone. Not very plausible, but I figured it would do the trick.

It didn't!

'Yuh 'aven't told me all of it, have yuh, Roger?' she said when I'd finished. Womanly intuition, I suppose.

'If I told you all, you'd probably have a seizure. Or maybe kick me out.'

'Like that eh'!

'Afraid so.'

'Kick you out? No danger of that, Roger, love. But I am amazed yuh agreed to whatever it is you did agree to.' She didn't seem at all worried though.

'Yeah, well, with the benefit of hindsight, so am I. But at the time it didn't appear to be anything other than doing someone a favour. I didn't foresee involving someone else.'

'So if yuh feel yuh might be in some danger, why not just drop it?'

'Not my way, love. I made someone a promise.'

OK. So get yurself a bodyguard?'

'In the directory, I suppose? Listed under B?'

'Doubtful,' she giggled. 'Me dad might know. Man in his position must 'ave that kind of information. Could ask, when yuh meet him.'

'I don't think that's necessary,' I told her. 'Besides, I'd prefer to keep this from the old man. I'm sure he'll have enough on as it is.'

Although a light-hearted exchange, Kim could see I was serious, so we agreed the bug should remain, immediately dropping the subject.

She obviously maintained a close affiliation with her father, so what I was asking went against the grain. That she was *prepared* to keep quiet about it said a lot for the relationship we had.

Maybe it was her father who'd had her phone bugged, I thought. Checking on what his daughter was up to, and with whom? The phone by the bed was clear, so maybe that *was* the answer. Kim didn't even question it. In fact I was amazed at how she just seemed to accept things without the need to know the whys and wherefores. Like when I asked her if she knew of a place called Dead Man's Hill. She got out the map, showed me, detailed the quickest route, even offered me the use of the "Ute". Never asked why I wanted to go, didn't appear at all interested in accompanying me. Which was just as well, for she definitely wasn't invited. I decided to set things up, be ready leave very early in the morning, hoping everything worked out OK.

*

You don't have to travel far out of Perth before you're in the country, which was fine by me, for I was a country boy at heart, even though I now lived in London. I'd been raised on a Yorkshire farm, was at home in the country. Or so I thought.

But this was different country altogether. The Australian Outback hosts dangers the guide books omit to mention, ie the local wildlife: snakes so deadly they could almost kill simply by looking you in the eye; monster crocodiles, both saltwater and freshwater, so *they* had you covered no matter where you elected to swim, outside of a pool. And some of the spiders resident around here were best not thought about, so Tony had said.

There were other hazards too, as I found shortly after my arrival in the area known as Willoby Creek. Of this, Dead Man's Hill offered ample proof.

Naturally, I'd expected what Foxy had told me to be close to the truth, had consequently made preparations, taken certain precautions. Which was just as well.

According to Freddie, if you'd asked Freedburg Hoving anything at all about computers, or their peripherals, he'd have gone into a soliloquy on the subject that lasted as long as you were prepared to let it. But on the matter of firearms... well, apart from possibly deducing which end dispensed death, I suspect he'd have known nothing. And although he probably *had* figured out which was the business end, he wouldn't be able to tell you much about that, either, for he was as dead as they come. Had been for quite some time going by the state of his body. And whoever had done the shooting hadn't bothered themselves with such trivialities as muzzle velocity, trajectory, or rates of drop. The professor had been shot point blank, almost between the eyes.

Beneath the body, the bright red stain of what had so recently been a life, had by now darkened considerably; a morphogenetic memorial in the dry earth.

He was also either fast decomposing, or fast food for nature. Which, I suppose, had been the thinking behind leaving him here in the first place. But there was certainly enough left to make identification a certainty.

Foxy and I had arranged a system whereby we could contact each other without resort to the phone - the old dead letter drop, with an added twist I had thought of; never use the same place twice. The message itself contained details of where the next drop would be - and it apparently worked well. For just this morning I had picked up the photograph which he had supplied via that system. I extracted it and made a comparison.

There were subtle differences, I noted. They jumped out at me because I knew what to look for. What to look *at,* in fact. Being an impersonator gave you that. When I wish to alter my appearance, I work on the simple things: hair, beards and moustaches, spectacles, and face padding. Cosmetic changes. So if it was a matter of identity, these were the points to be ignored. For instance, the glasses this man had worn were obviously different from those in the Johan Kluger photograph. The only thing that at first puzzled me about those glasses was, why were they not with the body, but some distance away. They were broken, so I figured they had either been knocked of where they lay, or someone had dropped them there. But the glasses themself didn't mean a lot. So I looked at the things you can't disguise: ears, hands and fingers. Stick to those, and you won't go far wrong.

In this case, it was the ears. Which was as well, for he didn't have any hands to look at! Regardless, in life this body hadn't been a Kluger, it had been a Hoving. Someone had made a ghastly mistake. And I now knew exactly where Kluger was. Or at least where he had been. Not too long ago, either. Not that it mattered to me, I had Foxy instead. But I imagined Bob would very much fancy a chat with our Mr Kluger. Providing he *was* still around. And still breathing.

I thought about these things, and others, as I sat in the

139

vehicle and waited. The silence was oppressively heavy, heat building with time, the persistent buzzing of the flies seeming to reinforce it rather than break it. I cracked open one of the soft drinks Kim had packed in the chilly bin she'd thoughtfully provided. In this climate, that was something else you quickly learnt; never travel without taking the right precautions. Plenty to drink being top of the list.

I thought some more about Kim, too. She hadn't swallowed the story about Professor Hoving and his notes, but she'd obviously decided that if I didn't want to tell her what was going on, she'd accept that. But for how long, I wondered? Which was as far as I got in my deliberations before they finally showed up. All the people who usually arrive after a report of this nature: scene of the crime crowd; photographer; forensic scientists, etc. Also a coroner/pathologist, I assumed. He was bald, wore glasses, displayed an indifferent expression. Not that they were any confirmation. I was basing my assumption on the short white coat he wore, the gloves he was pulling on.

I decided to remain where I was as they got on with their various tasks, but I didn't remain alone for long. Hadn't expected to for, naturally, once the presence of a dead body is confirmed, any live ones in the immediate vicinity become of immense interest. This was especially relevant out here!

I answered all their questions. Not necessarily fully, but in a manner which appeared to satisfy them - for the present. And when I judged the preliminary investigations to be almost complete, I approached the pathologist.

'How's life, doc?' I asked, turning on the charm rather than thinking about what I was saying.

He turned to face me, a quizzical look; realized I was unknown to him.

'Slight contradiction of terms wouldn't you say? Life is not what I deal with a lot.'

'Ah. Right. But can you tell me something about this one, before it ended?'

'We...ll,' he said slowly, as if consulting a mental rule-book. 'Depends.'

'Did he manage to leave a message of any kind do you think, written or otherwise? Any kind of a clue as to what went on out here?'

140

They were questions that apparently fell well within his personal guidelines, for he suddenly continued. Seemingly as if I hadn't spoken.

'The bullet entered here.' He indicated a point on his forehead, left of centre, just above the eye. 'Travelling in the region of 950ft per second - say 650 miles an hour - it drove the bone of the eye socket into his brain, tearing through to emerge a millisecond later out the back of the skull, thus accounting for the redecoration of the brickwork behind, in that gory reddish-grey,' he said.

I was beginning to wonder as to the point of this instant lecture in forensic pathology, complete with graphic detail, when he provided the answer.

'In such cases, of course, death is instantaneous. Previous to that, it appears his arms had been tied, and he'd been gagged.'

Scratch Freedburg Hoving. Nothing there for me. Nothing for the university either. They wouldn't be too pleased about that. But as far as McRobertson was concerned, it seemed he was hopeful of there being something in this for him.

I'd seen him arrive, not long ago. Barely time for a look and a quick report before he spotted me. He came straight over.

'What the hell you doing here? I told you to leave things alone.'

'I just happened to find him. Reported it.'

'Just happened! How did that come about?'

'Touring around. You know how it is.'

'On yur own? I'd imagine tourists to be a bit thin on the ground out here.'

'I'm also a writer, researching a novel. Need to get the feel of the country.' I'd had enough of McRobertson's insinuations and questions, decided to turn the tables.

'How do you think it happened?' I nodded towards where the body had been, now bagged and removed.

'Well, as I'm sure yur aware, he didn't just walk out here and lie down to die of exposure. No footprints you'll notice. Apart from yours. No tyre tracks. Nothing at all to indicate there was ever anyone else around. Interesting, eh?'

141

'Which means there was, of course,' I suggested.

'Well, does it now?'

It wasn't exactly what he said, more the *way* he said it. I decided on what my next move should be, for I felt I may soon be in need of professional advice, as far as the matter of Inspector McRobertson was concerned.

'By the way,' I said, 'that looks very much like the guy I was looking for. The one you were going to ask a few questions about. The University will need to be informed.'

Those words went down like a lead balloon, of course.

I left the area just as soon as I was allowed to.

*

The amazing thing about the names of lawyers, or solicitors, is that they always seem so unusual. How is it you never see Smith, Smith, Smith and Jones, rather than such as Peabody, Proudfoot and Wintersnade. Do they change their names to suit the profession, or what. I pondered on this as my fingers did the walking. Then they came to a sudden halt.

I found it hard to believe a solicitor could possess a sense of humour, never mind two of them! but unless April the 1st fell in October in the Southern Hemisphere, that was the only conclusion I could come up with.

The high-rise buildings of Perth are gathered together as if land were a rare commodity. The offices I sought were actually on St George's Terrace, situated in a block they called Westrell Towers. Nowhere near as spectacular and grand as the name implied.

As I was so close, I decided to take a chance; dropped in without making an appointment.

I checked the listings in the lobby, took the lift to the fifth floor, and had no trouble finding that for which I sought. A polished brass plate revealed the location: Whitefella and Blackfella, Solicitors.

I knocked and entered.

Not what I expected of lawyer's offices, I discovered, finding myself in a deserted reception room. Still, it *was* the lunch hour, and life in Perth is relatively unhurried anyway. Perhaps that accounted for the seemingly easy-going, relaxed attitude on display here, I surmised. Or maybe this firm was under-worked and under-staffed, therefore cheap. That would do me. All I needed right now was some friendly advice. Hoped that was all I'd ever need.

I looked around for a bell push, or some other means of attracting attention, found none. So I was just about to call out, when two of three doors leading off the area opened almost simultaneously. It was like some kind of comedy act. A head peered out of each, both well sunburnt, one substantially more so than the other, so to speak.

Gerald Reginald Gibbs was Whitefella. He greeted me warmly, then introduced me to his Aboriginal partner, Wati Nganyitama.

'Quite a mouthful in court, apparently,' I was jovially informed. 'So Wati takes refuge behind the pseudonym of Ross Grant.'

Gerry was dressed in white; shirt, shorts and knee-length socks. He also wore a blue and red striped tie, but the knot was pulled down to the second button of his shirt, collar undone. Ross, though similarly attired, favoured grey trousers to shorts. His tie was correctly positioned.

Gerry invited me into his office. Once again, a total contrast to the image my mind had projected. Not small, yet richly furnished and carpeted. The walls were adorned with paintings depicting Australian scenes, landscapes in bright colours, reds and blues predominant. Nor, contrary to what I'd imagined, did the firm appear to be short of work. The desk was awash with various papers and legal briefs. Not untidy, either, all neatly stacked.

'Hello, Roger,' he greeted after I'd introduced myself. 'What can we do for you? By the way, call me Gerry,' he said, offering his hand.

I shook, almost wincing in a grip that I imagined had won many an arm wrestling contest. Passing this man in the street, I wouldn't for one second have associated him to be connected with the legal profession at all. The face looked reassuringly lived-in, skin the colour of seasoned oak. His eyes appeared to be permanently narrowed against glare, like he'd spent most of his life outdoors. He gave the appearance of being cheerful and uncomplicated. And once I'd got through portraying the situation that appeared to be developing between myself and McRobertson, I found this opinion to be confirmed.

'Ah, McRobertson, eh.'

'You know him?'

'Know of him, of course.'

'And?'

'Look. Why don't we, you and I, Clive, go down the pub and sink a couple of schooners, along with a pie and peas, then maybe we can discuss the situation in some comfort? I was just on my way,' he admitted.

Clive? He was beginning to sound like Keith Floyd after a couple of glasses of red. Had something of the looks as well, come to think of it.

Once settled, it didn't take long for him to dispel my fears. And well within the hour, for the cost of lunch, the vagaries of the police had been cast aside in favour of the Outback. To him, infinitely more mysterious and exciting.

'This isn't Australia, Roger,' he said, sweeping an arm to take in the whole of Perth. To see this country you need to get out into the bush. Spend a lot of time out there myself. In fact, if you find yourself kicking your heels, be glad to show you around a bit.'

As we made to leave I told him I may take him up on that sometime, bearing in mind that promises made whilst under the influence should not be taken too seriously. Then, as Gerry returned to whatever it was lawyers did after a satisfying lunch and a few schooners, I took myself back to Kim's place, taking it easy on the drive out of town. For I too had had a couple, and I'd been given to understand the police in Oz could be quite ruthless at times.

*

Even in Australia, land of singlet and shorts, I found there were places from which you could be excluded on the grounds of attire so, tonight was to be jacket and tie affair, Kim advised when telling me she was taking me out to dinner. 'Somewhere special,' she said.

Kim wore a stylish, sort of I'm-ready-for-you kind of dress. Low cut top, high cut hem. I saw it as a kind of, "I'm ready for you" outfit. Most other men, I realized, would read into it a similar kind of message. But the look Kim reserved for such occasions soon dispelled any such ideas she may have

144

provoked. "What I mean is, this man, not you lot", it said.

I was beginning to realize what a big slice luck meeting her had been. We appeared to be well matched in some respects, piquantly complementary in others. Though not in the matter of cuisine. Kim's kitchen was stocked with deep-frozen, pre-packaged, lazy foods, and a microwave. To my mind, rubbish. Probably to Kim's also, truth be told, for we ate out most of the time.

As we made our entrance Kim spotted someone she knew, waved vigorously. They semaphored back. I think in reality she was proud to be seen out with me, so the attention she was attracting was really meant to highlight me. She was not to realise I welcomed that attention, was still hoping to be seen by someone who mattered. Although, given recent events, I was pretty sure I already had been.

Kim was obviously well known here, and welcomed, which told me something about her I hadn't suspected. She was not as unsophisticated and naive as she tended to make out. That was just the impression she liked to give, and apparently something she cultivated assiduously.

Against the low bass hum of voices one could discern the clinking arpeggio of cutlery on china, the sounds of a popular and successful restaurant. With prices to match, I assumed.

Once seated, Kim surveyed the wine list , then ordered without reference to me. With due ceremony the bottle was brought and opened. With a flourish the cork was presented, wine poured, viewed, swirled, tasted and accepted. All before we even gave thought to the ordering of food. I was impressed.

Kim closed her eyes, savouring the bouquet before taking another sip.

'Umm, delicious,' she dreamily sighed.

'Surely that must be subjective?' I opined.

'Sub.. what?' she said, running a finger round the rim of her glass as she turned the question over in her mind.

'What you feel is good one day can be less so the next, depending on mood, what you eat, etc.'

'Well, there is that, I ..... Oops. Shit!'

Red wine on white linen is not a pretty sight. White, such as this, not so disastrous. Even so, it barely halted Kim in full flow.

'I just know what I like and what I don't. Penfold's Grange Hermitage, I happen to like very much.'

Grange Hermitage; the name vaguely rang a bell. I picked up the bottle and inspected the label as the staff swung into immediate action. The unused half of the table was cleared, cloth folded back. A clean tablecloth was laid, and the operation reversed, all without disturbing us. The sommelier recharged her glass as the waiter took our order, then the pair of them melted away.

'Impressive, eh. Going to cost a penny or two, I'd say,' I told her, referring to the professionalism of the staff, therefore the quality of the service and food we could expect.

'Dad, not me,' Kim said, taking another sip and rolling it around her mouth before swallowing. 'Yummy, I'd say. And you're right, lover. It is expensive. Scarce too, so get it down your neck.'

'And I always believed the social status in Kirby to be lower than the bottom of the Marianas Trench,' I joked.

'Definitely Woodbine and chip buttie country,' she agreed. 'But we're not all yobbos, Roger. And we can mature with time.'

'I've noticed. So where did you learn about wines?' I asked. But by this time the first course had arrived. Knife and fork were already plugged in to her fists, working on the food, so the question remained unanswered.

'Is everything sweet, sir?' our waiter enquired sometime later.

I looked blankly at Kim for help.

'Strine for, "to your satisfaction", she translated. Then, to the waiter, 'Everything's fine, thanks. Although... perhaps another bottle of Grange...'

'Thought it was scarce,' I said as he disappeared to fulfil the request.

'Getting scarcer by the minute,' she confirmed.

Yeah, and I seem to be doing most of what was required to deplete the stocks, I realized. Not that I minded, for it *was* good. But I was also drinking lots of water, for I'd had an aperitif or two beforehand, didn't particularly fancy wandering the streets in anything other than alert mode these days, for it appeared I had stumbled upon something that made me dangerous to someone. And I knew it had nothing whatsoever to do the professor's notes, or the fact that Grange Hermitage cost the better part of $500 a bottle!

What that someone couldn't know, was that I really had nothing at all, as yet. Some wild ideas, maybe, but nothing solid. It seemed unlikely I would have, unless Foxy could come up with something useful. Foxy, it seemed, had become my prime hope.

*   *

Chapter Sixteen

LATE BREAKFAST

After a reasonably early night, for us, we were awake by seven the next morning. Not real early, though not late, either. We didn't have anything urgent planned, apart from my 10:30 breakfast appointment. Although, I suppose *that* could be classed, urgent in the general run of things. Though apparently not, at least as far as Kim was concerned!

I still wasn't feeling exactly one hundred per cent, naturally, but expected a swim and coffee to improve things somewhat. I suggested this to Kim, but, after my failure to perform last night, it seems she wasn't to be denied. She was already all over me.

'Well,... yes, OK,' she said. But she added a qualification. 'But all in good time, Roger.'

This appeared to be her antidote for a hangover as well. A panacea for all ills! So, the swim was delayed somewhat. Then again, when the doorbell chimed just as we finally managed to struggle out of bed.

Without thought as to where I was, I threw on a

terrycloth robe and went down to answer it. Tousle-haired Kimberley, her face having not yet received its daily quota of cosmetics, appeared at my shoulder as I did so. It was her house after all, her door!

'Oh, oh! Been having a quick naughty then, have we?' Tony guessed, at the sight of us. And, without a word, Kim, from the suffused pink glow which warmed her cheeks, confirmed that, yes, we had.

I invited him in, offered him a coffee which was not yet prepared. Not even close.

''S OK. Don't have the time. Got an appointment in town. Thought I'd better drop this on the way though. Came this morning,' he said, handing me an envelope, postmarked, London.

Good of him, dropping in "on the way" to town. Especially as we weren't. Out here it was so isolated, personal transport was a necessity. Still, it wasn't that much of a detour, if thought about, especially when considering Australian distances.

'Going back to Hedland tomorrow,' Tony continued. 'So, unless you plan on a trip up there, I may not see you for a while.'

'May just do that, if I can fit it in,' I advised. 'Jeez! is that the time? I had just glanced at the kitchen clock.

'I have an appointment, too. And I've yet to dress. Look, how about a drink, Tony? This afternoon?'

So we arranged for sundowners at the Transit Inn, and with that, Tony departed. As did I. Back upstairs.

*

Some things you are able to control, others not. I shaved carefully and dressed smartly, these being things I did have control over, and I saw no point in being at a social disadvantage. I'd also been brought up to believe that punctuality was an expression of good manners, so I needed to hurry.

A taxi dropped me outside the gates at nine forty-five. I paid him off and rang the bell. A camera lens moved like the eye of a Cyclops, and as a result of its investigation, plus my answering, upon being asked to state my name, I was allowed entry to the kind of place that brought to mind such thoughts as, "Nobody deserves to be this rich. And this was only his town house! Maybe a dozen big rooms, I thought, walking up the drive. Extensive gardens were visible, off to one side, plus, as is more or less obligatory   in this climate, a pool area.

I was met at the front entrance and led to an upstairs office by a maid.

The office was luxuriously furnished, with space enough to host a party of at least fifty.

Robert K Hamilton was seated behind a large desk, from which he rose, walking round to greet me. From the clues dropped by Kimberley, he was just as I'd imagined. The face - seamed with exposure, or age - was not just impassive, it was a positive mask of apathy. The sort of face that had been everywhere and seen everything, but which was now attempting to settle into normality. Nevertheless, shrewdness was apparent in the features.

His eyes, a watery, washed-out green, were close-set beneath heavy brows, and he carried a paunch that must have cost a fortune in liquor sales tax. Hard to imagine there being any of his genes in Kim's almost perfect proportions, so maybe she got it from her mother.

'So, Roger Simon McLaren, we finally get to meet. Kimberley's told me a lot about you. Think's a lot of you as well, I'll have you know.'

He sounded like Rod Stewart after a heavy night and two packs of cigarettes. And although it was possible to pick out traces of scouse here and there, it seemed he'd acquired a new accent to match his position.

He looked me over, working from face down; slowly, as though searching for defects. He'd already run a check on me, I knew that. For although Kim may well have told him "a lot about me", as far as she was aware, I was plain Roger McLaren. There had as yet been no mention of my middle name.

None of the usual aura of a businessman was evident; no aggression, no impression of power, etc, all of which led me to expect he would be deadly in the boardroom. Had to be to get to where he was now. Did that also mean he was ruthless enough to be involved with drugs? A natural thought for someone like me. I didn't trust anyone until I knew them.

Hamilton was still an unknown factor, and there had to be big money involved somewhere along the line.

We breakfasted out on a wide, sun-splashed balcony that was lined with clay planters, each filled with brilliantly hued plants and tropical vegetation. Yellow and orange marigolds. Various ferns and palms sprouted from Ali Baba-type pots. Bougainvillaea wound itself around an upright before spreading lengthwise along an overhead trellis to form a leafy canopy. Its pinkish-blue papery flowers shimmered gently in the faint, hot breeze.

This jungle-like profusion of potted plants provided some shelter from the already substantial heat. And out there beyond the confines of the canopy, beyond the flowers and the shrubs, the sun glinted off the Indian Ocean. Placid, with the look of molten silver. No hint at all of the dangers which may lurk beneath the surface: sharks, just daring you to dip a toe. Much like life itself, I thought.

And in this totally appropriate, cloud-nine setting I was able to fulfill a subconscious ambition. One that involved the drinking of champagne for breakfast.

*

After we'd got my autobiography in order, he willingly began on his. That was a surprise.

'Founded my first business empire while still at school,' he said, rudely talking round a mouthful of Eggs Hollandaise, which he proceeded to wash on its way with a slug of Dom Pérignon.

'Used to steal magazines from the newsagent I delivered papers for, selling them to my school-mates. Out here, I started off in property. What I didn't know about the business I quickly learned. Found I was quite good at it. Nowadays, of course, I employ people to advise me. Experts.'

Then came the motor racing - so Kimberley had mentioned it to him - and he was very enthusiastic about the sport.

'Goes back to when they used to race Formula One at Aintree. Track used the same grandstand as the Grand National course,' he told me, talking about times of which I'd only read. We then discussed the current situation in the sport, which led us nicely into the Australian Grand Prix in Adelaide.

Yes, Kimberley and I had reservations. Not only hotel, but access to paddock and pit lane also, if we wanted.

Huh. Did we ever. At least I did.

'Gee. Thanks a lot,' I said, and meant it.

'When you put as much sponsorship money into it as I do, it's not a problem,' he boasted.

He waited until I was about to leave before making his next proposal, causing me to assume he'd been assessing my suitability for the task.

'Having a bit of a reception tomorrow evening, Roger. Like you to accompany Kimberley. If you don't mind,' he added, as if in afterthought.

As he obviously didn't expect a refusal, I didn't give him one. That would have been totally counter-productive. Anyway, I had a feeling this invitation could somehow be of importance to me. There would be influential people present, and whoever was running this thing, money apart, was sure to wield some influence. Besides, as the opportunity hadn't presented itself today, I had some unfinished business to take care of in this house. So I readily agreed.

He didn't elaborate further, so I assumed Kim to already have the details.

*

'Adelaide? Oh, it'll be a suite,' Kim advised when she picked me up in town. 'Don't worry about that. It'd 'ave been a suite if I'd been going on me own. Dad's not daft. He knows the score, just doesn't like me to flaunt it. Anyways,' she said, inadvertently slipping in an unneeded plural, 'he's got his woman living in. You'll likely meet her tomorra.

Oh, by the way, Mcthingy called. Needs you at the cop shop. To identify a corpse.'

We went straight there, but "Mcthingy" wasn't in, so a sergeant dealt with me. A much more civilized option.

'Identification?' I questioned. 'To end his life officially you mean?'

''S right. And you're to surrender your passport.'

'Don't have it with me. I'll drop by later, when I've talked to my lawyer. Meanwhile, you might find this of use.' I handed him the photo of Professor Hoving that Tony had delivered earlier.

Don't know what Kim made of that exchange, but felt there would be questions to answer once we were in bed tonight.

*

I managed to contact Gerry Gibbs by phone. He advised me to hand the passport over.

'A formality. Keep em sweet,' he said. 'Adelaide won't be a problem, I'll see to that. It'll be for the inquest. They just want to be sure you don't leave the country. And I don't think McRobertson'll bother you too much in future, either.' A chuckle came down the line. 'Oh, and I meant what I said about the outback, Roger. It wasn't beer talk yuh know. Just try and give me a couple of days' notice.'

Said I would.

*

I should have checked earlier. There was a message from Foxy. Could we meet, usual place, King's Park. Usual time. Seemed it was urgent.

I checked my watch. Could if I hurried. Something I was usually reluctant to do. Needed time to scout the area. Still, if it was urgent I'd just have to take the risk, this time.

I was going to get a taxi, but Kim said she would take me, then keep out of the way. It was something else that went against my rules, as had been visiting the drop with her. But that didn't really matter, for we wouldn't be using the same one again.

As time was short, I had no choice now, so had her drive past, to drop me up the road. Not great for security, but it was too late for anything fancy or complicated. So, instinct for survival being as strong as ever, I improvised. Cutting through the bush I approached from the rear. I entered via a door marked "Staff", found myself, as expected, in the kitchen. Just two females present, almost too busy to bother with me.

'G'day,' I said, briefly flashing my open wallet, without stopping. 'Special duties.' It was one of those phrases that cover everything and meant nothing.

Unchallenged, I walked through into the restaurant, just as Foxy was preparing to leave. I'd surprised him.

'Jeez, Roger. Thought you weren't coming.'

'I was delayed. Only picked up the message ten

153

minutes ago, but use the big tree next time.' He knew what I meant. We'd previously drawn up a list of sites.

'No matter,' he said. 'Things didn't turn out as planned. I was just about to go and leave another message.' He seemed to be selecting his words with enormous precision. 'No need now. But we'll have to do it again. Give me a couple of days. Say Tuesday.'

'Tuesday sounds fine.'

'Right, Roger, usual time. With any luck I could have some details by then. Maybe some names, maybe not. It's bloody difficult. No one seems to know anything outside of what they do themselves. I don't even know who gives us our orders, but I'm working on it. Should be enough to give you a start. Whatever, after that, it's time to disappear.'

'You think they've rumbled you?'

'Think the time's come to act as though they have. Start asking questions and word soon gets about.' He glanced round quickly, as though expecting trouble to strike immediately.

'OK. How are you off for cash?'

'Huh, cash is the least of my problems. Made two hundred last year alone.'

'Two hundred what?'

'Thou. What do you think.'

'You can't be serious?'

'Come on, Roger. Even to someone like you, two hundred thousand dollars has to be serious.'

It was that. But even more serious was the fact that I had just glimpsed a familiar figure pass by outside.

A man was walking a large dog. Looked very much like an Alsatian.

*　　*

Chapter Seventeen

WARM RECEPTION

I favoured watching the Test Match at the WACA ground during the day, Kim fancied the beach. Naturally, Sunday on the beach it was. OK, Kim's choice it was. But I conceded only after she revealed we'd been invited to accompany her father to Nelson Crescent the following day. He, of course, was a member of the West Australian Cricket Association. Stood to reason, didn't it?

Kim had made a sartorial concession to the heat by appearing in shorts and tee-shirt. Just about! Even so, she remained ornamentally and sexually superior to anything else around. Her clothes could have been designed specifically with this particular body in mind. The pink shorts, she'd told me, were satin, the tee-shirt silk. Sparkling blue letters across the breast suggested I, and everyone else "Go for It. Life is not a dress rehearsal."

No matter, both items stretched and clung in such a way as to make the imagination take flight, her body making emphatic statements beneath the fabric: no underwear, it screamed. I attempted to avert my eyes, but was largely unsuccessful. Kim may have benefited by way of lower body temperatures, the same certainly couldn't be said of me. And, embarrassingly, it showed. Down, boy, I willed. Now is not the time.

After parking the vehicle she tripped away to the loo, and, on her return, wore even less. No less than anyone else, mind, for she was only sticking to the basic rules of Australian beach decorum; if you've got it, flaunt it. This crowd mostly did - have it and flaunt it, that is. All were suntanned. And at first glance many of the women appearing to have misplaced their bikinis. Just like statistics, what was revealed was interesting, what they concealed, vital.

The men were mainly fair-haired and muscular. In fact, I half expected one of them to come up and kick sand in my face.

The relevant Ministry in Australia puts out a health advisory, warning against the dangers of sitting down with a beer and watching the telly, "Life. Be in it", it says. These people certainly were. But, for me, observing her bikini-clad qualifications, Kim was the best thing on that beach. Her figure belonged on a billboard, five times larger than life.

This was my first experience of an Australian beach in full flow, and although it went by the name of Scarborough, it was somewhat different to the place of the same name where I'd been born, back home in my native Yorkshire. Here the sun-drenched beaches were beautiful, no sign of a deck chair, wind break, or knotted-handkerchief draped head, although the odd beach umbrella did provide shade for a few. And almost everyone wore a hat of one kind or another.

'Let's take a dip,' I suggested, once we'd picked our spot and settled. 'I need to cool my ardour.'

'Not me,' Kim replied. 'There's bloody sharks out there.'

'I know, and lots of other nasties too, so I've heard tell. But they don't seem to be a worry to anyone else,' I said, drawing her attention to the multitude of surfers and swimmers.'

'They worry me. That's all I care about.'

Truth be told, they worried me a bit as well. But I wasn't about to admit to the fact. I wasn't afraid, especially as I hadn't actually seen one. But, knowing they were out there somewhere, it did pay to take them into account. Be careful, but don't let them govern what you do. That was my attitude to bullies, terrorists and such. I supposed it could apply equally well to sharks.

There were lifeguards in evidence on the beach, and overhead the media played their part, a TV station's light aircraft assigning itself the role of shark-spotter, whilst no doubt also keeping their eyes open for a story.

'I've heard tell they aren't very intelligent fish,' I assured her.

'Intelligent! They don't need to be bloody intelligent, Roger. All they need to know is how to open and close their mouth.'

'Well,' I said, heading seaward. 'I'm no slowcoach in the water, I'll have you know.'

'Ha! You won't out-swim a shark, that's for sure.'

'No need. All I have to do is to out-swim a few of that crowd.'

We lay there most of the morning, soaking up the sun, blocks, oils, and headgear well in evidence. They worry a lot about skin cancer in Oz, I'd discovered. Apparently the hole in the ozone layer is positioned closer to this part of the world.

'What are those guys out there doing?' I asked, applying yet more lotion to Kim's back whilst at the same time keeping a wary eye on what was going on all around. I think it was application rather than oil that she desired.

She lifted her head so as to peer from beneath the battered straw hat she wore.

'Which guys? Them in t' boats?

'Yeah. Them in 't boats as you put it.'

'They're pulling cray pots. See the buoys?'

Said I did. I watched them closely, but my mind kept going off on a tangent, dwelling on matters other than those in hand.

*

'Hi, Roger. What do you think?' Kim asked as she returned from the bathroom. She reached up and teased her hair. Looked as it would when she'd been to Raymond's, or some such. It was all frizzed up like she'd suffered an electric shock. Intentionally distressed, I suppose you could say. And no, I didn't like it. So, being honest, caring, and knowing how women could be - taking into account I had high hopes for this evening - I told her it was great. Well, she'd obviously done it just for me.

'You don't mean that, do you? Women can tell, you know.'

'Now do I look like the kind of guy who would lie to you about a thing like that?'

'Yes.'

'Oh! All right then, so I preferred it as it was,' I admitted. Nothing else for it. There I went again, with the things that are better for being left unsaid. But she *had* asked.

A flash of disappointment puckered her mouth as she slowly made her way back upstairs.

*

Had I not already been aware of it, the fact that Robert Hamilton was a popular, well-known character, was made pretty obvious. He was also rich, of course, and did wield a little influence, so it went without saying he was warmly greeted by almost everyone. A cheery wave here, a deferential nod there. His hand was shaken enthusiastically, shoulders slapped, invitations offered and dispensed, along with - as is the way with Aussies - copious amounts of booze.

I must say though, as a pair, we also created a stir. In Kim's case, masculine longing. For she wore a white silk dress which revealed a lot of cleavage and not a little leg. It was a longing made keener by knowledge she was unavailable to any of them, causing envious looks to be cast in my direction. This I could understand, for that dress would have revealed a panty-line, had there been one to reveal. That had been my initial thought when I'd first seen her in it.

She'd been in the bedroom at the time, strapping on her Patek Phillipe. I whistled, unable to prevent myself placing a hand on her backside, seeking confirmation. Exploration which, naturally, led to obvious signs of male interest, giving me cause to smile. It was the smile of one who had guessed at something and been proven correct. Which is when I had my second thought.

'Umm.' It was all I could manage, for the thought which took precedence was sinful.

158

'Roger! Nn..oo.' She stretched the word to two syllables, but didn't immediately say much else, apart from intimating that, she couldn't, she wouldn't, we shouldn't. By which time our ardour was not to be denied, so we did. From that point on, the few words to escape her lips were not only crudely brutal, but also superfluous. She was urging me to do what I was already doing.

It was only afterwards that I noticed she'd unfrizzed her hair. Or maybe our performance had unfrizzed it for her!

That put us somewhat behind schedule, but we probably spent as much time worrying about that as an Ethiopian spends worrying about the long term health hazards of smoking.

The crowds had arrived by the time we got there, Kim giggling at the thought of her dad wondering where we'd been.

'Ont' bed, dad. That's where t'dirty sod 'ad me,' she fantasized explaining.

He didn't actually ask, as a matter of fact. I hadn't expected he would. It was his party, not ours. He did introduce me to his lady-friend, Sarah Walker. An attractive, forty-plus woman, eyes the colour of chestnuts. Not bad, Hamilton, I silently extolled. For a man of your age and physique. Don't suppose money even entered into it.

We were then led away and I was introduced to many more guests, and without, I hoped, actually making it obvious, I took note of the type and appearance of the people I met and saw there. I heard lots of names, lost most of them immediately. Directors and managers of this division and that. One of a pair I had no trouble remembering was a guy introduced as Ed Thornton, head of Finance. I was able to raise a laugh at his expense when, after shaking hands, he turned to a man with thinning, sandy hair, and a kindly-looking face.

'Ed Stevens,' he announced. 'My deputy.'

I just couldn't resist it.

'Working, presumably, on the premise that, in accounting, two Ed's are better than one!

Kimberley's father threw his head back and laughed loudly. A genuine laugh. Highly amused, infectious. That's when I started to like him. And that was the point at which the whole atmosphere seemed to change. Whereas previously people appeared to talk in whispers, or out of the sides of their mouths, they now relaxed. Me too. OK, so I forced down a glass or three, just to be sociable. It has been known now and again.

Kim hung on to my arm as if afraid to let go, although she wasn't short-changing herself on the wine, either. On our own now, she was forever directing my attention to various people, whispering this and that about them in my ear; thoroughly enjoying herself, I suppose. She certainly gave every appearance of doing so.

I bided my time, waiting for Kim to excuse herself before making my move. I slipped into Hamilton's office, placing a Singapore Airlines pen in amongst the clutch which inhabited a desk-tidy at his workplace. It should go unnoticed; most of the others looked like give-aways, too, and I knew he favoured the gold fountain pen which he always seemed to carry. I already had a booster secreted amongst the greenery out on the verandah. Green on green.

As Kim returned I dragged us over to the bar, fancied moving off the wine.

'Calvados, please,' I ordered. 'If you have it.'

'Afraid not, sir.'

'Cognac, then? Remy Martin?'

'Would that be with ice, sir?'

'Ice! In cognac? It most certainly would not,' I replied, somewhat forcefully.

He gave me a wan smile. 'Some do, sir.' He sighed, shaking his head sadly at the thought.

'Bloody peasants,' the man next to me muttered. He, also, clutched a brandy balloon.

'Alan Beckwith,' he said, offering me a card. 'Get introduced to so many people you tend forget their names. I do anyway. Besides, there's always the chance a card may bring some business.'

I glanced at it, immediately realized this was a relationship well worth trying to develop. 'Roger,' I replied. 'Roger McLaren. And this is Kimberley. Our host's delectable daughter.'

His eyes appraised her form. 'I'll say. Never had the

pleasure before, Kimberley, although I've been here a few times,' he said. But Kim's attention had drifted to the card I still held in my hand.

'Armadale Air & Marine. Didn't you say Foxy worked for them, Roger?'

The words were out before I realized what she was saying. Couldn't really blame her, she only knew of Foxy as an old friend, nothing of what he was involved in. I hadn't bothered to tell her. Hadn't told her much at all, outside of Professor Hoving. Although I had a feeling she felt there was a lot more to it than a missing university professor, and the package I carried for him. Suspected she refused to pursue it in case it upset our relationship. Well, a mistake had been made, there was no getting away from that. Now it was a matter of assessing the potential damage, or danger. Attempt a little damage limitation.

'Foxy? Don't have anyone of that name working for me,' Beckwith said, frowning slightly.

'That's how he was always known at school,' I replied, brain working overtime in an attempt to save the situation. 'Can't actually recall is real name,' I lied. Couldn't give a false name. Not to Foxy's boss.

Kim looked at me askance. 'You told me it was Dan Reynolds,' she blurted out.

You really should have had that bedtime chat last night, Minerva advised. Too late now.

'Oh, of course. Brain ain't what it used to be,' I quickly ad-libbed. But I knew it was far too late.

'Ah, yes. Dan eh.' I waited to hear what else he had to say, but was alarmed to discover that not only had his loquacity halted, he was awaiting further response from me. For with those words his conversation ceased as effectively as if I'd shot him. He raised his glass and took a sip, closing his eyes as he first inhaled the fumes.

Cool. Feigning a lack of interest. But the silence was becoming ominous. I needed to try and recover the situation.

'We went to the same school, years ago. First time I've seen the bugger since he ran off with my girl in London.' An attempt at humour. Had to throw something into the void.

'Only goes to show,' Alan Beckwith commented. Failing

161

to specify what.

I shrugged and smiled acceptance at whatever. "It does that." It was all I could manage. I really did need to update Kim.

'What line are you in Mr McLaren?' Tangential intrusion, I realized - mention of a totally unrelated topic so as to allow time for thought. *Mr* McLaren as well, I noticed. No longer Roger. His previous bonhomie, it seemed, had faded, and although he did manage to maintain an expression of indifference, I was well aware I'd been cut off from a promising source.

'Line? Oh, er...yes, I'm a writer. At least I'm attempting to be. Was in computers previously.' Probably wouldn't have been a wise move to mention my part-time vocation as an impersonator, so I didn't. And of course, any mention of an SIS connection was a definite no-no!

Unbeknown to Beckwith I was actually watching a rapidly pulsing vein on his temple, and counting. Fifteen seconds. Thirty-five, multiplied by four equalled a high one hundred and forty beats per minute, I calculated. Not as cool as he appeared then. My admitting to knowing Foxy had Alan Beckwith worried for some reason.

Apart from the fact of it being a possible friendship remaining undeveloped, it didn't worry me too much.

Not right away. Didn't, but it should have.

*   *

Chapter Eighteen

TESTING TIME

*T*he sacred turf of Nelson Crescent, East Perth, is home to the West Australian Cricket Association, hence the acronym, WACA ground, which was where we were to be found at lunch time on the Monday.

It was another glorious day. Especially when watching cricket from the hallowed balcony of a Corporate room off the Members' Stand. I couldn't imagine the players agreeing with me though. It was going to be hot out there in the middle. Hotter still for Australia, who, amazingly, found themselves to be in trouble. At home!

Trailing by fifty-five after the first knock, they only had thirty-four on the board in the second, and already two wickets down. OK, so these were only the "B" teams in National terms. But a place in the "B" side was possibly only an injury away from a place in the full Test Team. Not that any of this seemed to bother most of our party. For Hamilton, and many like him, especially in and around Perth, an England - Australia Test Match is a "heads I win, tails you lose" affair. Most, even though now fully accredited Australian citizens, still retained their British passports, therefore saw no shame in supporting whichever side was on top.

Up here on the balcony, despite the heat, men wore lightweight suits, and their ladies were resplendent in silk or cotton - dresses or suits. Nylon-clad legs ended in stylish shoes, and most wore a hat of one kind or another, every cunning device of the milliner's art. Could almost have been Cup day in Melbourne, from what I'd heard, or Ladies Day at Royal Ascot.

Kimberley was as pretty as a cottage garden. A lightweight cotton dress in bright colours, hat that would have done her proud at either venue; Melbourne, or Ascot. The shoes, I noted, quality-wise, were on a par with the rest of her clothes. A matching shoulder bag boasted equal pedigree.

On the whole therefore, a civilized setting, which, come the end of play, was liable to degenerate into a shambolic, though not unfriendly, drunken jamboree. At least down there in the bars and on the terraces.

It reminded me of last night's soiree, though the people here were dressed to be seen. This time in their summer finery. I let my gaze roam unobtrusively around the room, summarizing and filing my observations effortlessly. It seemed that any information my brain found to be even vaguely useful or interesting, it stored for possible future use.

The BOSS-clad Mr Hamilton was talking to someone. Someone who was Bob Hawke! Or, if not, someone of his size, mien, and standing. Then he broke off, walking over to where Kim and I stood.

'Come,' he said, 'Let me introduce you to people.'

First in line was the person he'd recently been talking to. I'd been right then, it was Bob Hawke! Current Prime Minister, and leader of the Labour Party.

As we shook hands he leant forward and whispered in my ear. 'That's some girl you've got there. Drop-dead gorgeous.'

I couldn't have agreed with him more. But from the reactions of him and others, I gathered Kim did not often attend functions of this kind with her father, for few present seemed to be aware of just who she was. Possibly that was why he'd asked for me to escort her last night. He knew she

164

wouldn't attend alone.

From there it was the usual round of greetings and handshakes. Most showing little interest in me, although many men, despite their age, did give Kim a good once over with the eyes. Well, I too thought she was definitely worth it.

There was one person present I recognised from Hamilton's house on Saturday night. We had been introduced then, as we again were now.

`Sorry,' he said, addressing me not at all contritely, `Can't seem to remember your name.'

Shouldn't have said it, but felt like it, so I did.

`If I may borrow from Dickens,' I replied, without rancour, `McLaren is the name. You might remember. It's not a difficult one - Roger McLaren.'

`Ah, yeah, course. Pleased to meet you again,' he said, making it quite obvious that he wasn't by dismissing me immediately.

As we continued to do the rounds, myself shaking hands, or nodding dumbly, I felt I was probably showing as much interest in them as they did me. Though I tried hard not to give that impression. This wasn't difficult, in the circumstances. That is, until we came upon a man in his early fifties. Darkish, thick-set, with bushy eyebrows and a beard. Unimpressive-looking at first-glance. He seemed so dull and boring that one couldn't imagine anything exciting ever happening to him. I suspected, that for such a person a trip to the supermarket would be an adventure.

'Roger, meet Klaus Santana,' Hamilton said. He sounded as if I should be impressed, that the name should mean something to me. It didn't. There again, neither had Hamilton, originally.

"Rumpled" was a word that came to mind when noting Santana's appearance. It wasn't that the clothes he wore were cheap, or badly cut, more that his body appeared to resent wearing them. Even the hat looked as if it should have been on the head of Frank Sinatra.

'How you keeping, Mr Santana?' I used that as my opening, rather than stating how pleased I was to meet him. For some strange reason I didn't feel that I was. Possibly a result of his initial action.

I had been inspected briefly, yet so thoroughly I felt as if I were something being offered for sale. He then shook hands. But just as his smile lacked warmth, his grip lacked enthusiasm. Not a man who took to strangers easily, I decided. In fact, close-up, reading his eyes, I changed my opinion of him altogether. Confirmation of my inner feelings maybe.

They were penetrating eyes, set beneath heavy brows. They watched me as intently as I watched them. Here, they told me, was someone who could easily arrange for you to be shat upon, if you probed too deeply into his background. Whatever that background may be.

Was he as ruthless as that? I wondered, again looking into his eyes. Eyes that had suddenly become as hard as obsidian, and I felt a sharp prickle of antagonism flash between us. Yes, I decided, he almost certainly was. And I resolved there and then to watch out for Mr Santana.

'Ah, yes, the writer.' The voice was silkily hostile. 'Met you at Robert's, you may recall,' he said, revealing the fact that he was much better briefed about me than I was about him.

I nodded, but knew for certain he hadn't been there. If he had I'd have remembered, despite my occasional lapse of memory when it came to faces. Once seen, never forgotten, our Klaus Santana. So, how *did* he know about me, I found myself wondering. More to the point, *why* did he have need to find knowledge about me necessary?

I took Kim to find a seat, and we sat outside and had some lunch. We then watched play for a while, myself explaining the finer points of the game to Kim. She didn't appear to be interested, just happy to have me there for company. I was just as happy, when I thought about it. This I was able to do given such conditions; relaxed; sun; champagne; cricket; along with a pretty girl. Not only was she pretty, together, it seemed, we were able to achieve complete sexual harmony on a regular basis. The first girl in quite a while with whom that had been possible.

*

As was my wont, I arrived in King's Park on Tuesday afternoon with more than enough time to spare, so I wandered around, losing myself to nature and the warmth, concentration possibly slipping ever so slightly. Easily done in this serene ambience,

166

and the added knowledge that England "B" had been victorious yesterday.

I visited the impressive West Australian War Memorial, with its eternal flame, and flags flying. I wandered along a trail which took me right around the circumference of our meeting place, but well distanced from it. Out past the Queen Victoria memorial, eventually ending back where I had begun, in a stand of trees a fair distance from the cafeteria itself, but with a clear view.

From up here - beneath a canvas of deep blue, surrounded by the buzzing warmth of nature, yet still in the city - I could easily see the traffic on roads which scythed unchallenged through the metropolis below. But even though I wasn't quite far enough away for the cars to appear distant and insect-like, I realized I couldn't hear them. Strange. It was like watching a movie where the audio didn't match the visual image, for there *were* sounds, an amalgam of the warm, soft sounds of summer: nature in the raw, the happy laughter of people enjoying themselves. These sounds intermingled, became indistinct.

Even so, I was easily able to define the next two sounds I heard. Minerva, probably unsure as to whether or not I needed the information, offered it anyway; decision deferred to me. The first I rejected: the not too unfamiliar, discordant call a kookaburra. That was reasonably clear, although also distant. The second sound I couldn't do anything but accept.

This was infinitely much closer, therefore certainly more distinct. A cold, hard, snick, close by my left ear! Not the kind of noise one easily forgets. The paralysis-inducing sound of a weapon being cocked with intent, even if it did sound like a weapon with which I was not familiar.

My heart seemed to seize up, starting again almost instantaneously, though it's beat nowhere near as steady as of late.

This, I thought, somewhat wistfully, was not entirely to my liking! For not only was it threatening, it also pointed to a distinct lack of concentration.

I had allowed the surroundings to seduce me. That was what annoyed me the most.

*   *

167

Chapter nineteen

A RIDE IN THE PARK

Whoever was behind the weapon, I assumed he must have been lying in wait, well hidden behind a tree, stepped out behind me as I passed by. Had he been tailing me I would almost certainly have spotted him, for I had been looking. Using the time to good effect, though obviously not good enough by far.

All that is irrelevant, past tense. Now what?

I'd heard that abnormal behaviour in an abnormal situation is normal. Well, this situation was certainly.... if not abnormal, definitely not good.

Not good be buggered! Having a gun stuck in your ear could be quite lethal.

Shuddup! Who asked your opinion? But I did accept the validity of the advice, for it seemed like one of those times when everyone else in the world just disappeared. The laughter had gone, there was no one to be seen, life had suddenly become seriously serious. Just like when you need a policeman and there isn't one around.

One thing bothered me more than any other, that gun.

168

I had never before heard an action like it. Wondered what it was.

Somewhere close-by a clock struck the hour; I didn't count, suddenly wasn't interested in such things anymore. My thoughts centred on the fact that, luckily, I was well isolated from the rendezvous location, rather than wondering who he was, or what it was all about. No doubt the answer to that would be not long in coming.

'Don't have much money, but it's all yours if that's what you're after,' I said, even though I was by then weighing up the chances of tackling him. He was apparently pretty amateurish, at least as far as guns were concerned. Didn't know enough to keep his distance. He was very close to me, I could tell from his breathing, could even smell his breath. Very close then. Too close for his own good. With my skills I knew I could tackle him from here, probably disarm him, too, as long as he was alone. Trouble was, I had an assertive feeling he wasn't alone.

Naturally, being behind me, I had absolutely no idea *of who* he was. But it seemed he knew me, and his first words served to dispel all thoughts of immediate retaliation.

'Just walk over and get in the car, McLaren. And no tricks, or the girl gets it.'

'Jeez. Right out of a cheap movie. Where do they get you guys?' I asked, but I also did as he suggested. I was always prepared to take a chance, as long as it only involved my safety, not so if there was the slightest possibility it could involve someone else's. Now, it seemed, was not the time for heroics. Not if they had Kimberley. Easy enough done, today of all days.

My attention was distracted as a car slid into view, puling up to park at the curb, below our elevated position. I could see the driver, but only his hands and arms, little else. As instructed, I descended the grassy slope towards it, preparing myself so as to get in the rear, or take a chance and make my move.

Then, even as I was still debating my options, a head popped out of the side window to greet me. 'Hello, you old bastard. How the fuck are yuh?'

That's a thing about Australians, they can be so uncomplimentary, often greeting friends and acquaintances by

169

being intensely rude. But in the correct tone of voice! Not so much in the west, but Norman Holman was not originally from WA, I remember him telling me.

My escort was already installed in the back seat, gun no longer evident, leaving me to wonder what the hell was going on.

'Let's take a ride ...er, Roger,' Holman said, indicating I should sit beside him by reaching over to open the front door.

'Don't feel like taking a ride,' I told him.

'Sure yuh do,' he replied, and in such a manner he had me believing I did. Or should! The wide open spaces of the park suddenly didn't seem so friendly and relaxing after all.

'Is this to be the kind of ride from which one doesn't return?' I asked with forced nonchalance, walking round to climb in alongside him. It seemed I had little choice but to comply at the moment.

He laughed at that, a deep, genuine, hearty laugh. 'That's your imagination running wild,' he said. 'There again, as a novelist it would, wouldn't it. But to answer your question. No. We don't play those kind of games.'

It was the answer I'd expected. Naturally, he wouldn't admit to it if they did. But it didn't make me feel any more secure. At least one of them had a gun. And someone round here certainly *did* play those games.

As if to remind me of his presence, there was click from behind. I turned slowly, to find my escort grinning. In his hand he held a kid's toy. One of those joke things that is supposed to sound like a cricket, but *can* sound much more like a gun being cocked, if held close enough, and that is what you are expecting it to sound like.

'Happened to see you up there enjoying the scenery,' Holman said. 'Been keeping an eye open anyway. Got a proposition. Decided to have a little fun with yuh first.' He made the smile last forever, as if we were old buddies.

'About as funny as a Great White in the swimming pool,' I suggested, inwardly heaving a sigh of relief. With earlier thoughts about the type of weapon being unfamiliar now resolved, I realized I was no longer a prospective corpse. It also became obvious that "the girl gets it" line, had just been part of the charade. Of Kim there was no sign, so that was OK.

170

`Seems you have influential friends.'

`Me! I don't know anyone,' I protested. Except maybe someone in the DEA, I told myself. But I couldn't imagine Bob had fixed this, it just didn't fit. Nevertheless, it seemed I was about to be accepted.

We were driving around in the park, slowly. So as I listened to what he had to say. I also kept an eye open for Foxy.

'Got a small package needs delivering in Adelaide. Heard you'd be heading that way.'

'You've got sensitive hearing.'

'I've also got more than one pair of ears.'

'So it would seem.' I decided to take a gamble. Let them think I had no interest in their operations. 'Too bad they don't listen. I told you before, last time fitted in with my plans. Now, it doesn't.'

'Why not? You're going anyway. One more small piece of luggage is all we ask.'

'Must be plenty more heading for Adelaide. Especially that weekend. Twice is pushing the odds too far.'

'No risk at all, on an internal flight.'

'In which case, almost anyone would do. Look elsewhere.'

'Need someone we can trust.'

Umm, interesting. Seems they'd actually got as far as trusting me.'Have to find someone. I'm not interested.'

'You're interested alright.' A simple statement, but one loaded with menace.

Gotcha, I thought. Time to gradually succumb. But he made that a lot easier with his next remark.

'It's worth a thou. Australian.'

'Ah.' A thousand sounded like a lot for such a small task. But a thousand to him was obviously a lot less than it was to me. 'Now, I may be interested,' I conceded. 'Let's hear the rest of it.' Didn't want to push him too far, otherwise he just *may* have got someone else! Although deep down I didn't really think so. Another check, maybe, or had they already taken the bait.

After he'd given me the details, pickup, Adelaide contact etc, I made a show of looking at my watch. Jeez, look at the time. I'm supposed to be meeting someone. Can you drop me at the cafeteria?'

He did so, and I quickly disappeared inside.

I didn't have long to wait, Kim was right on time. I kissed her in a show of affection that was fuelled also by the relief I felt. I then led her to a table with a view. I knew after what had just happened they'd have me under close observation. Making it easy for them helped, though it still took me some time to pick him out. Possibly because of the fact that he was a she! Useful piece of information that. From now on I knew I'd have to be extra vigilant. I was back in the game, I realized, excitement rising. Fear also, but that was controllable, satisfying even, like a drug. I felt light-headed and slightly dizzy.

'Were you really that happy to see me, Roger?'

'Always happy to see you, love. But this meeting was special.'

'In what way special?'

'Promise to tell you about it later,' I said, deciding the time had almost come.

'Yur always going to tell me something later, but it never 'appens.'

This time it will. I mean it.'

Later we were able to check today's allocated drop location. There was a note from Foxy, apologizing for not being able to keep the schedule. He *had* been in the Park, happened to observe people who probably posed a threat to him, so had left, suggesting an alternative time and place. Seems he still didn't have the expected information anyway. Security had been increased, he thought, which told us something. I suspected it told me something different from what it told Foxy, so I left a note in today's drop; suggested maybe he should make a disappearance, along the lines we'd previously discussed. It was beginning to look like I no longer needed his help. He should get out while he still had that option open to him.

All I needed to do now was contact Bob, and make preparations for our departure to Adelaide.

Kim was very much looking forward to it, as was I, both for differing reasons I suspected.

For Kim it was to be a welcome change of venue, as it would be for me, too. But I also had a Grand Prix to look forward to, the first for many years, this one with the added luxury of Paddock Passes. On top of this was the nerve-tingling excitement of what I was sure was to be more than the simple delivery of a packet of a banned substance. For that I would need to remain very much on top of my game.

But we had plenty of time for all that, time also to enjoy ourselves a bit. Now there was no pressure, I didn't need to worry about making contact with anyone, therefore little need to keep watching my back with such intensity. Just relax and act normal, which would take no effort whatsoever. It would allow time for my bruising to clear, which was already happening, probably thanks to Kim and her magic lotion. That, or something else, seemed to be effective treatment, leaving me much fitter than I had been since that fateful day.

What was the inscription Kim's silk shirt had broadcast to all and sundry: Go for it. Life is not a dress rehearsal.

*

Another day over and we were now in bed, snuggled together, relaxing.

'Want to know why I was so happy up in the park?' I suddenly asked. I had promised, so was determined to give her something. I'd been thinking about it, had come up with a story that involved Foxy. Close enough to the truth, but not all of it.

'Ah, not right at this moment, Roger love. There is something else I would rather have first,' she purred, hands exploring under the covers.

'But I did promise. And it could be important,' I told her.

'Oh, and so could this be,' she replied, taking hold of me.

'It certainly could,' I replied. Ah well, I'd made the effort. And I had promised her something!

*   *

Chapter Twenty

PRESENTATION OF CREDENTIALS

Adelaide, SA, is filigreed Victorian balconies and straight streets. It is also wears a green belt of parklands, and is full of churches. In fact, sited on a coastal plain in the shadow of the Mount Lofty ranges, it is known as the City of Churches for that very reason.

South Australia, of which this city is the capital, is the driest state of a dry continent, rainfall-wise. But this has its compensations; there are vineyards galore, with wines to rival the best in the world, so the Aussies would have us believe. Well, they certainly appear to drink vast quantities of the stuff.

There is also the odd pub dotted about here and there, as is the Australian way.

Adelaide, I'd discovered from official sources, was also the home of a company which traded under the name of Freight and Transport International, the chairman of which was a certain Klaus Santana.

Since our meeting at the WACA ground, and at odd times during the past week - a week in which there had been no further contact with Holman, or anyone associated with him, nor with any word from Foxy - I'd been doing a little checking on "Santa", as he was apparently known to most of his contemporaries. The sobriquet, it seemed, was not solely derived from his name, but also because he was known to be was very generous with his donations to charities. But - and this I'd learned from other than official sources - he had to have a darker side, for I'd heard tell certain of his associates were often referred to as "Santa's Claws."

Seemed I'd misjudged Mr Santana. Imagined a lot of people were just as easily misled, his unassuming manner no doubt meant to signal non-threat.

*

Kim, who had been feeling unwell during the flight over, decided to spend the night in the hotel. I told her I wanted to sample the atmosphere, and to check on the best places to watch the race. Some pre race time would hopefully be spent in the Pits and Paddock areas.

As for race locations: `Out here, the pub would be the place to check on anything like that,' she suggested. `You go, love. I'll have an early night, see if I can get over whatever it is.'

So it was that I made the rounds, and I knew which bar to favour immediately I came across it. The place was packed and noisy. Bubbles of sound exploded around the room; raucous, wholesome laughter, the clink and rattle of bottles and glasses, and the talk. Not only that. This was the place to which I'd been instructed to go.

Run on a Sunday, the Australian Grand Prix weekend starts the previous Monday, when aficionados from around the world begin to gather in strength. They already had, for we had not arrived until the Thursday.

The bar was alive with their talk and laughter. Talk which centred mainly on Mansell and Senna; which of them would win this time out, not forgetting Alain Prost. But, as these things have a habit of doing, it drifted off to encompass the relative merits of the heroes of years past: Nuvorali, Fangio, Moss and Clark, as opposed to the present. Whether Fangio or Moss, in their prime, could have outclassed Senna and Co? The usual thing, to which there was never a logical answer. Different times, different cars, different rules, different personalities. Even the tracks were different, so comparison was all but impossible.

I moved around, picking up the odd useful bit of information here and there: the balcony of the Stag Hotel sounded like a popular place from which to watch some of practice, the second day of which would be the faster. Something to do with the amount of rubber being laid on the normally low-grip tarmac.

Then I found what I was after - a crowd that seemed slightly different.

Shouting a round gave me access, but not with any amount of enthusiasm. This was a very cohesive group, yet they didn't seem to be wildly interested in motor racing. In the race, yes, but only peripherally. Certainly not with the fervour shown by the aficionado's. Then I knew why. Knew what they were doing here. They were salesmen. I realized this as soon as I looked in the mirror and saw Norman Holman walk in. He came straight over to join us, effectively bringing conversation in this group to a halt.

I kept my back to him until I was sure, then, hoping to impress, and perhaps gain a few "brownie points", I turned to face him, greeting him like a long lost friend.

`Hi, Norman,' I said, offering my hand. `Long time no see.'

He hadn't been around yesterday, when I'd made the pick-up in Perth, and a full nine days had passed since my pseudo abduction in King's Park, a lead-up to the ensuing conversation, and my recruitment. Anyway, I wasn't sure who was supposed to know about that meeting.

He shouted another round, then joined in the small talk. He obviously didn't require any introductions, or didn't want any. We discussed the merits of our respective hotels, the suitability of Adelaide as host city for a Grand Prix, and the weather. Gentle and irrelevant conversation, until I eased myself close and mentioned the package, now safely stashed in my hotel room. I didn't wish to hold on to that any longer than was necessary.

`Here, tomorrow. Less crowded during the day. Say, after first qualifying. Oh, and don't bring the Sheila,' he added sharply. That sounded ominous, set me to thinking dire thoughts.

As I shaved the following morning I thought about the situation some more, what they possibly had in mind for me. One avenue of thought, brought about by the lack of recent contact, had my cover being blown, and the serious consequences for me had this been the case.

Holman hadn't seemed exactly overjoyed to see me yesterday. And here in Adelaide I was on my own as far as back-up was concerned, for I hadn't informed Bob of this latest development. At the same time, I was fairly confident he would have learnt of it, via his various sources. Even so, I wasn't too happy with the conclusion I arrived at.

They'd have to be stupid to try something like that, really stupid, I told myself.

Are they that stupid, do you think?' I asked the reflection that stared back at me.

Somebody's that stupid, Minerva answered.

It was my first visit to a racing circuit for quite some time, especially for a Grand Prix, and here I was, in the pit lane.

All the remembered excitement returned, and I enjoyed every minute; the sights, the smells, the personalities, the sounds. The sounds particularly; the nerve-tingling, full-throated raucous sound of a finely-tuned V10 at full chat, car teetering on the very limits of adhesion. Couldn't wait for final practice the following day. And still to come was the race itself.

But between now, final practice, and the race, there were other things to attend to, which had meant leaving Kim back at the hotel. She hadn't been a happy bunny about it, hardly laughed at all. But it couldn't be avoided. Anyway, we'd just had the best part of week together, with few interruptions.

`Strewth, that the time? Gotta move on guys,' Norman Holman said, bending to retrieve the briefcase I had brought, which, I noted, had never been far out of his reach since my arrival, and hand-over.

As he prepared to leave, a man along the bar attracted my attention as he drew the back of his hand across his mouth. Nothing unusual in that, except he hadn't just taken a drink, and his eyes were locked on to a point over by the rear exit. Then I noticed the man over there. A big man, gaze fixed on the bar. He gave an almost imperceptible nod of his head.

`Got to take a leak,' I said, excusing myself from the crowd we were with.

I gave him thirty seconds before silently following him out. He had his back to me, the gun in his hand pointed directly at Norman Holman, who faced me.

`Just put the case on the ground and back off,' the gunman advised.

Seeing me appear over the gunman's shoulder, Holman did as he was told. Holding his empty hand up in a gesture of submission he slowly lowered the case to the floor, stepped well clear.

As the guy bent to retrieve it, I struck.

Disarming him turned out to be a simple matter, surprise being in my favour. Along with a certain amount of luck, I'd be the first to admit. An edge-of-the-hand chop to the wrist and his gun skittered away into the shadows. But it wasn't enough deter him, so maybe he, also, realized luck had played a part. Whatever, obviously expecting an immediate follow-up, he quickly turned to face the challenge, momentarily assuming a threatening crouch. It was laughable really, nothing like I'd been taught. Must have picked it up off TV.

`You going to walk away, or be carried?' I asked.

I gather he wasn't best pleased, for he aimed a kick at a place that, had it connected, would have done my love-life no good whatsoever. That I took as a personal affront. Obviously not a man who respected one's more intimate parts. But, as it was where they always aim, I'd prepared myself. In best James Bond tradition, instead of moving away I closed, giving myself an immediate advantage, for he hadn't expected that. The reaction was automatic, unimpeded by conscious thought. Not an innate skill but a knack, a self-taught art. Catching him off balance I grabbed his foot and twisted it hard left. As his muscles tensed to combat the move I quickly reversed and twisted right, so he was now helping me. It spun him round, and I pushed to help him on his way, sending him head first into the wall. He hit at a terrific pace, slithering to the floor. He just sprawled there, looking as if he would not be getting up again for some time.

He'd made the most basic of mistakes; labouring under

the misapprehension that size was a substitute for ability. Entirely the wrong approach. Especially when faced by an executant of Jeet Kune Do, a recent addition to my armoury, though he wasn't to know that, of course.

I retrieved the case, handed it to Holman. He seemed impressed.

`Noticed him making some odd moves in the bar, so I followed him out,' I explained. `People like that think their strength is the be all and end all. They never see it as something that can just as easily be used against them. That's all I did, used his strength.

`By the way, he's got a mate in there,' I added.

`Thanks. But you didn't have to do that. Your job ended with the delivery.'

`I know that. But it seemed like the right thing at the time.' I patted my pocket, and the envelope full of cash it contained.

`Exactly! And it's the doing that counts, isn't it? Most would take the money, turn their backs and walk away.'

He looked me over in silence, obviously deep in thought. It was as though he was deciding on his next words.

`How would you like to work for me? I don't mean as a courier. We have other... er, opportunities. Money's good. Plenty of time for your writing. Good cover, in fact.'

I appeared to deliberate. `What about... er, well, visas and work permits,etc?'

He laughed. `No problem, Roger, believe me.'

I did.

What the hell are you getting into this time? Minerva questioned. *An organisation that can easily obtain this kind of documentation is not only powerful, they had to have some influential people on their payroll as well!*

Nevertheless, the fever of excitement burned as I realized I had once more become a player rather than an observer.

Or had I? I still wasn't sure which way this was going. And I felt the time was fast approaching where I needed to reach a decision. Take a gamble and work from the inside, or call it quits and hand over to Bob? Just two things convinced me. We really didn't have enough hard evidence, and I had taken a decisive dislike to the guy who now entered the picture.

A car drew up at the kerb, two people getting out, one of them familiar. They walked over to where we stood.

`Everything sweet, Norm?' Bruce Jones asked, his red hair now pulled back in a pony-tail. He was careless with his dress, for I also noticed he carried an automatic in a shoulder holster, along with the chip he carried on it. The chip readily apparent, the weapon not easily so. `This prick giving trouble?'

`No worries, Bruce. He's with us. Otherwise I could have been the one in trouble.'

`He did that?' His red beard flicked at the inert form on the ground, disbelief etching itself upon his ugly features.

`Bloody oath.'

`Huh. Want me to finish it?' Jones asked.

`Nah. Secure him and put him in the car, I have a better idea. Let's go, Roger.'

I hesitated, debating the point in my head. Last chance.

'Well, you with us or not. Work for me and you'll need to take orders.'

I made the decision, climbed in the car with them.

I noticed a second car following as we pulled away. The other man I'd spotted in the bar was seated in the rear, which gave me cause for thought. Ours was presumably in the boot, still unconscious.

I suddenly had a very good idea what this was leading to, didn't like it one little bit. It was one of the things I'd been debating with myself about.

Ever since that day in Singapore this affair had taken on it's own momentum, gathering me in. Nothing I could do to alter that now, even had I wanted to. Anyway, hadn't that been the intent? To worm my way in.

I watched closely. We drove past the Botanic Gardens, along North Terrace and on up Summit Road, out into the country. Here, we followed a dirt track, dry and dusty, and then I knew. It was a replay of Professor Hoving's execution, as described to me by Foxy. The knowledge conjured up thoughts and images: the dry, dusty location at Willoby Creek; the pathologist's graphic description; just when I didn't want to be reminded of such things: "The bullet entered here, driving the....

No! Minerva advised. *Stop that.*

I attempted to block the flow. Found it difficult.

At the selected spot - an isolated clearing in amongst the trees - both cars stopped and everyone clambered out. All apart from one prisoner. He was dragged out, struggling, sweating. He'd obviously heard the stories, possibly even witnessed some of them, knew exactly what was coming.

So did I.

A weapon was cocked, causing me to look around. Naturally, it was Bruce. Had to be. Which left me somewhat relieved, but anxious all the same.

`Hold it, Bruce.' Holman's voice.

Here it comes, I thought, just as I expected.

`I think we should give Roger the honour. After all, he was the one who spotted it.'

This was what I'd been psyching myself up to. They'd feel compelled to test my commitment at the first opportunity. Here was that opportunity. Seemed like the fun part was over. Time to go to work now. Present my credentials, as it were. Maybe they needed references for my employment application: Past experience? Has smuggled drugs, and shot someone! How would that look on my resume? Not that I hadn't shot anyone before. I had. But they weren't to know that. Though this would be different, morally. Those others had left me no choice, my life had been at stake. This would be plain murder. Or would it?

With what I took to be a smile, Bruce handed me the already-cocked weapon, flicking off the safety as he did so. He was enjoying this, still didn't trust me, I could tell. Did any of them?

At least I was now armed. The smooth hard weight gave me some assurance, until I noticed the gun I'd been handed was not Bruce's own, that still nestled beneath his arm. Another thing: this gun did not have a full magazine, it was far too light. Probably a single round in the chamber. No. They didn't trust me.

I couldn't see a way out. I was going to have to do it, or be killed myself. No choice. He was one of them anyway, I rationalized. He'd gambled on instant riches and lost. Didn't give a damn for anyone else. How many young lives had *he* been responsible for....

It wasn't working.

"Just do what you have to," Minerva advised.

I recalled Bob telling me the self same thing. Myself more or less agreeing.

The thought returned me to my childhood days, the games we played then. Stalking each other in some disused quarry or after-hours building site. It was much the same kind of thing. Only his time there would be no face-saving call from Mum or Dad, advising it was time for bed, or else! The "or else" for failure to comply here could be infinitely more serious.

The greatest dangers often come from oneself. Inside. The moment you stopped to question yourself at a critical time. I knew that, yet it was exactly what I was allowing to happen. I couldn't afford to let it. I was either in, or I was out. I needed to be in.

More importantly, I needed to remain alive. Him or me, that was the way to look at it.

But of course, there was also the second question that had drifted through my mind. That was still a possibility.

*   *

Chapter Twenty-one

SOME PEOPLE DO THIS FOR A LIVING

I was sweating almost as much as the intended corpse, but that could have been due to the heat of the sun, for my hand was steady. And my aim was true. Couldn't be anything else at this range.

The internal debate was over. If it had to be done, and I now accepted that, no point in anyone suffering. But as a snatched shot at this range was irrelevant, I didn't worry about the finer points: squeezing the trigger rather than jerking it; securing the weapon in both hands, etc. I just wanted it to be over. Needed to appear ruthless. Hoped I wasn't becoming so.

Although the blood roared in my head and my skin prickled, I was in full control. Though I did find it impossible not to swallow hard. One thought helped me. A hope.

I brought the gun up quickly, pointed it, and fired, almost dying of heart failure when the pin fell on an empty chamber. My emotions were in a whirl, but I quickly had it figured, was determined to not let it show. I had been half expecting it; the sharp, dry click of the classic test: loyalty to a cause. It was the thing I had been hoping for all along.

I quickly worked the action, as if clearing a misfire. Pointed and fired again. Again nothing. But I had expected it this time. Knew for certain, for I'd been forewarned; no cartridge had been ejected as I'd worked the slide.

No matter, I still found myself shivering slightly. I felt cold and clammy. Relief, or delayed shock? Didn't really matter. It all worked to my advantage. Pretending to hide it I turned and looked Holman in the eye, held it for a full, silent, three seconds, before letting the gun fall to hang from my finger. I then handed it to him.

`Looks like you're in, sport, if you want it. Make yourself some quick bucks,' he said.

Bruce looked absolutely sick. The guy next to him didn't look too chuffed either! The one I'd run headfirst into a wall. Maybe I'd overplayed my hand there, or he had. How was I to know he'd been assigned a part. Shouldn't have made out like he was about to practice a little Glaswegian folk-dancing on my goolies.

His mate from the bar saw the humour in it. There again, he would, wouldn't he?

It looked as if I'd been awarded my drug-smuggler, second-class, with good conduct badge, for there was much smiling as introductions were made. There were also firm handshakes, impressions of lasting friendship. Except from Bruce, that is. He never so much as made an approach. Gonna get you, you bastard, I thought, and hoped.

As my eyes sought him out, they found his staring back at me, but I was prevented from reading anything in them by the light which was reflected off his glasses. Didn't need to, for his only comment was visual. He gripped the muscle of his right arm with the hand of his left, raising a clenched fist belligerently in the air.

The gesture told me nothing I wasn't already aware of, though it did have an affect on me. Lines from a long forgotten verse by Thomas Brown magically reformed themselves in my mind:

I do not love thee, Dr Fell.....

Despite his apparent lack of intelligence, it seemed Bruce was quite perceptive. I'd have to watch out for that, make allowances.

Inevitably, changes had been wrought upon my character by events of the past, the abnormal now becoming more of a challenge rather than something to be feared; a little excitement. To me danger was an exhilarating experience. I actually got high on it. Nevertheless, I resolved there and then to watch out for our Mr Jones. I marked him as the danger man. The one I would definitely need to take care of, somewhere along the way.

Now that I had been accepted - which had been the purpose of the exercise in the first place - I realized it was possible I didn't need this lot any more. In fact, it could be tying; more of a hindrance. After all, I already had an inside track to information, via Foxy. Not a lot at present, I'll admit, but I had high hopes of Foxy coming good before he went into hiding. On top of which, I had formulated a few ideas of my own. To me they were obvious, but this was the way I worked. Instincts and insights. I find those to be of more help than any vocational training.

Still, there's no such thing as too much information, I decided. For the moment I'd play it their way. Especially as of right now, this seemed the safer option.

During the evening Holman singled me out. He carried with him a bottle of wine from which he poured me a glass, saluting me with his. I returned the compliment, like we were old buddies.

For a moment we took refuge in the ritual of appraising the wine; quite decent, actually. Then he actually volunteered some of that information. To him, I suppose, it was a briefing.

`You'll work under the guise of my company; Outback Express. Sphere of operations, West and South Oz, plus the Northern Territories. That's where you'll be involved. Lots of area, but nowhere near the population figures of Melbourne and the East Coast. That's why we've also branched out a little. Taken in Europe.'

`Yeah, suppose you could call that branching out!' I agreed.

When I judged the time to be right I asked him the question he'd previously declined to answer.

`If hand-carrying is so uncertain on international flights, why the risk? And how come you approached me? Where did

185

that come from.'

`An error. A special shipment, which arrived early. Wasn't due for another week, by which time our pipeline would have been in place. But the Singapore authorities were becoming very nosey, so we decided to ship it out. It *has* happened before, but rarely. As to couriers, well, that's Singapore's decision. We've no idea how they operate. They just advise us which flight to meet, or when a shipment is due.'

So what put me in line for the job, I wondered. But not for long. Bob's department had obviously been aware of the situation, quickly contacted various of their agencies, one of whom had come up with the idea of using me. But that had happened well before I had even set foot in Singapore, I had since learned.

My second question was put to one of the others, when I found myself alone with him, which had involved some previous planning. He appeared to me as one of the more friendly types, which is why I selected him in particular. Fellow known as Julian.

`What about Bruce, Julian. Has he killed do you think? He has that look about him.'

`Hey, don't involve me, mate. That's kind of a personal thing.' He looked decidedly worried.

`Don't see him around,' I prompted.

Before replying, his eyes toured the place as well, as if he didn't trust me. `Nah,' he said, seeming to relax once he'd determined the area to be clear. `He'll be long gone. Doesn't work for Outback, you know. Anyway, I'd not put it to him, if I were you.'

I smiled grimly. `Suppose not.'

No need, I thought. I suspected Julian had already given me the answer. Knew I'd have found out for sure, had I failed to meet today's test criteria.

*

Although the Adelaide race is run through the city streets, it is realistic, not the glamorous joke that Monaco seems to have become. In fact it seemed to have taken over the mantle of Monaco, Adelaide now being regarded as the jewel in the Grand Prix crown. At least as far as Australia was cocerned.

The atmosphere was certainly relaxed. There were

marching bands, low-flying aircraft, and lots of racing. Charity races, touring cars, even a celebrity race for the ladies of showbiz. And was it ever colourful. As for the weather, after Europe this seemed like the promised land, a place where the sun continually shone.

But it never pays to take nature for granted.

Kim and I watched from the balcony of the Stag Hotel, which gave us a good view. Not that there was a lot to see, the Grand Prix rained off after only sixteen of the eighty one scheduled laps, with the pundits being proved correct, Senna declared the winner over Mansell.

Ah well. I was disappointed to be robbed of a full race, as, naturally, would be many others. But at least I had the satisfaction of knowing my journey had served its purpose. I was moving forward.

*

Back at the hotel, I stepped out on to the balcony. I smelt the air - clean and fresh after the rain - and looked out at the panorama. The sky was now blue again, and the birds sang. It made me feel good, for a while. Until I recalled something I'd overheard during the post-race celebrations. A rumour to the effect of there being yet another possible Judas in the organization. More ominous still, was the fact that the name, Dan Reynolds, had been mentioned in this respect. And the thing was, I'd been left with the distinct impression it was intended I "overhear" that snatch of conversation.

They'd recently made two grave errors as far as I could see. One was killing Freedburg Hoving in the manner they had, albeit in mistake for Johan Kluger, the second was allowing me to worm my way in. The first they couldn't do much about, and the police were already on to that. If they eventually uncovered the truth about the second, I could expect them to rectify that, rather swiftly. So I decided on some elementary precautions.

And if I was wrong...?

So what? Minerva chipped in, *wasted precautions should never be regretted. Much better that, than use of the phrase, "if only."*

*

Kim and I had intended to visit "The Circuit Bar" later that evening. A popular place, and one at which some of the drivers and other personalities could be expected to put in an appearance. With the season now over, everyone would be relaxing and partying. Winding down. Naturally the crowd would be rather select at this event, but, as guests of a major sponsor, we had an automatic invite.

It was early when we arrived, so the crowd was nowhere near capacity. I was absolutely parched, about to make my way over to the bar when Kim jerked me to a halt.

Of course! In my haste I'd forgotten to ask what she wanted to drink, I thought. But that wasn't the problem at all.

`Can we go somewhere else, love.' She wasn't asking, she was telling me. Almost demanding.

When I didn't immediately move, she grabbed at my arm and pulled.

`Come on, Roger. Let's get out of here, please.' Insistent now.

I looked around but could see nothing that could have caused her distress. No matter, Kim turned and left, more or less dragging me along with her.

Still thirsty, I was also pissed off.

`What the hell's the matter? Who did you see in there?' I asked, once we were back outside.

`Some arsehole who works for Dad. Evil bastard. You wouldn't know him. Tall. Built like a brick shithouse and ...'

`What! Norman Holman you mean?'

`That's him. But ...?'

I cut her off. `You know him well?'

`We've... managed to bump into each other on various occasions.'

`Subtle difference.'

`I suppose. But how come *you* know him?'

Couldn't very well tell her I now worked for him, so.. `We were introduced,' I ad-libbed. `Told me he ran his own company; Outback Express?'

`So he does. But it's not *his* company. Outback is a subsidiary of Freight and Transport International.'

`Santana's outfit.' I was so lost in thought I spoke quietly, almost to myself. Although it was loud enough for Kim to overhear.

`Right,' she said. Then she dried up.

`So?' I prompted. There was more, and I needed it.

`Well, FTI is part of Hamilton Industries, isn't it?' She spoke like it was common knowledge.

'Well, well. Is it now?'

I had a mind which literally soaked up such information, and retained it. Taken singly, such snippets are useless. Properly assembled and assessed they offer a multitude of possibilities. At the very least, they raise more questions.

That night I found myself unable to sleep, my mind too active. Nothing to do with the incessant noise, or the lights. I could plug my ears, close my eyes to those, but there was absolutely nothing to be done about a mind which refused to shut down.

It was something Tony had said that planted the first seed of an idea. One small bit of information which later filled a blank space, like that niggling but crucial missing piece of a jigsaw. Now, my mind juggling data in the background, it grew rapidly, and spread.

Thing was, to anyone not aware of this operation, the apparently random pieces of data that had come my way over time would forever remain so. To me, they were beginning to make sense; the possibilities becoming clearer.

In theory, I figured I knew how delivery was, or could be, done. What I needed now was proof. And I thought I knew just where to go to get that. If I was right in my thinking, Foxy was no longer important. I wouldn't need any names, these people would supply their own names.

First, I needed to see a couple of people back in Perth. Then I had to check on something else. Rather urgently.

*   *

189

Chapter Twenty-two

OUT ON A LIMB

It happened every time, and I took it as a measure of progress; the closer I got to danger, the more acute became my powers of perception.

It was there, just as I'd envisaged, a message from Foxy. An arrangement for us to meet, usual rendezvous, usual time. Not a clue as to the reason, but that in itself wasn't what was worrying me. The fact of there being a message did!

I hadn't made Foxy aware of my travel plans, outside of the fact I would be going to Adelaide, yet it seemed he knew I'd be back in Perth today, almost fourteen days since I'd last seen or heard from him - and the meeting was scheduled for this afternoon. This, despite my warning him off. Those were the details that served to warn me of imminent danger, or the likely possibility of a set up.

To me, this seemed like a good time to take care of other arrangements I had in mind.

*

I was just about to hang up when there was a click as the connection to London was made.

190

'Yeah.' It was a disgruntled yeah.

'Ah, Mike, Roger. You *are* in then?'

'Of course I'm in. In bloody bed, in fact! Asleep. Or was.'

'Oh, sorry,' I apologised. 'On your own then?'

'As it happens, yes.'

'There you are, then. At least I didn't disturb you in the ... well, you know.' I allowed a chuckle to escape.

'The only thing you're likely to disturb at one o'clock is my bloody sleep. One in the morning, I might add.'

'It's nine here, Mike. Lovely, sunny day.'

'You don't say! Could be due to the existence of time zones, Roger. You know; advance one hour every fifteen degrees of longitude, kind of thing.'

'Exactly,' I replied. 'And now, if you're finished with the geography lesson, I have something which might interest you, if you're ready to copy.'

'Hold on.' I heard a crash, swiftly followed by a muffled curse. Then, 'OK, go ahead.'

Isn't this what friends were for?

*

'It appears the stuff I carried from Singapore was a one off,' I told Bob. 'It's not usually done that way.'

The meeting was again in Bob's room at the Transit Inn. A breakfast conference, which hadn't pleased Kim at all, though she did agree to drop me in town.

'We know that,' Bob confirmed, cricket ball spinning neatly from one hand to the other. 'That's why we had to scratch around in a hurry. Your name came up. Told you we didn't often get the opportunity.'

So, I found myself thinking, they just hadn't bothered to tell *me*. That, and what else?

I'd opened by telling Bob about my recruitment, immediately souring it for him by adding my recent doubts as to their sincerity. Instinct told me the situation had now changed somewhat.

'Something must have happened, between race-day, and my arrival back in Perth,' I suggested.

We'd arranged this meeting previous to my departure for Adelaide. Well before my theories had advanced to their present stage, flimsy as they now seemed, in the cold light of

191

day. So how much of it did I give him? Bob worked on facts, and I only had one.

'What I do know,' I said, 'is that Perth airport alone handles around eight thousand kilos a year.'

'Strewth! Much bigger than we thought,' he said, tossing the ball onto his bed.

'Amazing thing is,' he continued, 'Absolutely nothing seems to have leaked out about this operation. We're talking millions of dollars here, and not a whisper. OK, those involved have a vested interest, which more or less ensures their secrecy. But that kind of money takes some laundering. Which points to power, big business, and authority.'

'Well... I don't have a lot to go on, certainly nothing concrete, but it is possible Hamilton may be involved, or at least companies tied to him. He has the means. And there's no question he has the money.'

'So he's rich. Means nothing. Made most of it during the boom years. Right place at the right time, with an eye and brain to match the situation. In a series of land deals he had amassed a fortune in the days when land could be bought for a few cents an acre, and sold not too long after for thousands of dollars. Oh, there's no question he's a tough operator. Got his fingers in lots of pies, but everything he does appears to be kosher, so far as we can tell.'

'No references to our business on any of these,' I confessed as I handed over the recordings of Hamilton's office-conversations. Could be he's not aware of it. Though I don't see him as the type to be unaware of anything that concerns his business.'

'Ain't that the truth,' Bob agreed. 'So what are your plans?'

'Just carry on. Dig around a little, see what turns up.'

'Good on yer, mate. But be careful. He's very VIP. Well insulated, politically. Have to be bloody solid before we could move against a fella like him. Cast-iron.'

Although he had the weight to lean heavily in places where I had none, Bob seemed somewhat reticent about pursuing the Hamilton angle himself.

'Been warned off, or something?' I had to ask.

'Don't miss a lot do you?'

'It pays not to, doesn't it?'

'It certainly does.'

'Well? About being you being warned off?'

'Something like,' he agreed. 'Been advised to... look elsewhere shall we say?'

'Just as I thought, usual political claptrap, or you asked the wrong person. But, as a private citizen, I'm not so restricted,' I reminded him.

'Bloody oath. Go for it, Roger.'

Now I knew why they needed me. Always the same with government agencies, no one willing to stick their head on the block. They'd use someone like me to take the risk, ready to deny all knowledge if things went badly wrong, jumping in to take the credit if and when I was successful. Well, I could live with that.

'Don't you even have enough to shut down local distribution?'

'Give it away, Roger. Even if that sector of the market were to disappear completely, I doubt they'd go bankrupt. We'd just alert them is all. Distribution is the least of our worries. Cut their supply lines, arrest the ringleaders, distribution and all the rest of it will cease automatically.'

It was fairly obvious they suspected who the bit players were. Enough to cause serious problems if they moved in. But what they were desperately in need of were names. The top people. And the evidence which allowed them to present a case: the hows, whys, and the wherefores. That was my job. Dot the i's and cross the t's.

'Managed to find Kluger, by the way,' Bob said. Ever so casual. He had a way of dropping these bombshells. I imagined he could drop a few more if he wished. Figured he was giving me just enough to keep the operation on track.

'In Singapore,' he continued. 'But he was clean, had to let him go. Had a little bit of a chat first though. Seems they process the stuff themselves, somewhere in Oz. At least he was under that impression, though he had no ideas as to the where. Useful bit of info, that, if it's true. Make that your first priority, verifying it, and finding out where.'

He made it sound like he was talking strategy for a game of cricket rather than infantry tactics.

'I'll try. Can't really see me having much success, though. He worked for them, and if he didn't know... well?' I shrugged and spread my hands in a "what-chance-have-I?" type gesture.

This is what I told him, though I was sure I already had a pretty good idea. Not too difficult to work out, given the necessary data.

"The process of refining heroin from morphine base is both delicate and dangerous. A job for qualified chemists." I recalled reading those exact words in some novel or other. I also remembered some words of Tony's: "We're not as isolated as some. There's a pharmaceutical research facility up there, out in the bush. Distances them from the protesters."

And the authorities, I'd thought at the time.

I decided to keep this to myself for the present. Suspected Bob would dispense with my services as soon as things began to gather momentum. The least he'd do was to withdraw me from the line of fire. Anyway, it didn't all quite gel together yet. I needed more data, and some solid facts.

Why are you being so conscientious? Minerva briefly wondered. *You had to be coerced into this to begin with.*

But I knew why. It was the thought of action that kept me interested. *My* motives drove me now, rather than any priority of theirs.

I doubted I could manage on my own, admitted, but I had a couple of people in mind to supply the kind of help I thought might come in handy. The second of these was next on my list of people to visit. But I did need to keep Bob informed as to my whereabouts, I decided. Just in case we required the heavy artillery. Wondered how to go about that. Then he offered the ideal solution.

'One more thing,' he said as I was about to leave. 'Check with Andy, later today. I may have something else for you.'

'Andy?'

'In the bar, downstairs.'

'Ah yes! OK.' The man had never given me a name.

From a public phone I made a couple of calls, just to set things up, for I felt there was nothing more to be learnt here. In fact I now saw Perth as offering nothing but danger. The

194

answers, I felt sure, lay to the north, and I did have a couple of invitations to visit the area.

*

Gerry Gibbs was waiting in his office when I arrived, but we didn't stay.

'Lunchtime,' he said. 'Well... close enough.'

So, naturally, he took me down to the pub. It was still only eleven o'clock.

After we'd got ourselves settled, I asked if he was serious about guiding me through the outback.

'Sure, Roger. Told you, didn't I.'

'OK, just wasn't sure. When?'

'Just say the word, Roger. Don't have so much on that Watti couldn't hold the fort for a while.'

So I dropped it on him. 'How about this weekend? I'm driving to Port Hedland in the next day or so, to visit a friend. Maybe we could fit it in then?'

As expected, he appeared surprised, yet, at the same time, pleased to have an excuse to get away. It's what I'd been planning on.

'Yeah! Why not then. Hedland's as good a place as any to make a start. Perfect, in fact.'

He said he'd fly up on Saturday. I offered to pick him up at the airport.

'No worries, Roger. We'll meet up at the Walkabout Hotel.'

I then asked if he'd been able to get me the information. Something I'd requested earlier, over the phone.

'Not a problem. It's public knowledge, more or less. Just a matter of knowing where to look, then deciphering what's recorded there.

'In a complicated share issue and merger a few years ago, IF&T became part of Hamilton Industries, through a holding company. They then started acquiring more assets, one of which gave them a major shareholding in AA&M. Since then they've become much bigger. Got themselves into everything, including a major shareholding in an airline. Companies within companies.'

'Ah ha. Just as I imagined. The usual tangle of corporate identities, titles, and affiliations. So what of Slade

195

Laboratories? Any connection?'

'Not with IF&T.'

My heart sank. But only momentarily, for he hadn't finished.

'They do belong to Hamilton though. Through yet another subsidiary,' he told me. By which time he had it figured. 'And they just happen to be located....'

'Out past Marble Bar,' I finished for him. 'Silver Springs. Not too far from Port Hedland, wouldn't you say?'

'And just how would you happen know that? Why would you want to, in fact? What's going on, Roger? What are you up to?'

Said I wouldn't mind taking a look out there, being as we would be in the area, so to speak.

'Not an environmentalist or something, are yuh?'

'Nah, nothing like that,' I assured him. 'I'm a writer of fiction.'

He smiled at that. 'Yeah! So what *are* you looking for? What do yuh suspect?'

He asked a lot of questions did Gerry. There again, he was a lawyer.

'Nothing, really. Just curious.'

'You're more than bloody curious, let me tell yur.'

Perceptive sod too, I thought, deciding to take him into my confidence. Right now. He'd have to know eventually in any case.

'OK, I'm more than curious,' I agreed. So I told him a bit about myself, about what I suspected.

'You know this is police work, of course?' Although not exactly a question, it did require an answer.

'Absolutely. But apart from having enough to do, doubt I have sufficient proof to interest them. Anyway, there's another reason for keeping them out of it. Two actually. It seems possible the Police may be involved. Paid off, anyway.'

'Not inconceivable, in a case like this,' he agreed. 'And the second reason?'

'I represent a Federal agency.'

'Thought there was more to you than just tourism and writing, Roger. Get so you can tell in my business. So what are you planning?' He seemed to be even more interested than

196

surprised.

So I told him that, as well.

When I'd finished, he didn't say a word. But he did question me with his eyes.

'Why the look? What did I say?'

'That's the problem, sport. You didn't say anything. Yet. You did mention how we might get in. Not a fucking word about getting out!'

'Didn't say anything about you accompanying me, either. In fact, it's not even an option. Not inside. Just need you to get me close.'

'Oh! And why not come with you inside?'

'Could say my conduct might offend your professional ethics somewhat.'

'Out in the bush, Roger, I'm no longer a lawyer. Fact is, you may find me rather helpful to have around. Attempting something like that on your own would be crazy. Even for me, alone. You'd have to go back as far as the loaves and the fishes to find a comparable event.' His weathered features displayed no sign of concern whatsoever. Just the opposite, in fact. He smiled, as though the thought of adventure appealed.

'Exactly. And I won't be alone, for that very reason.' I then told him about Mike, his background etc. 'Without him I suspect it probably would be impossible. With him we may just have a chance. Small maybe, but any decision on that will be Mike's.'

*

Leaving Gerry, I made a quick visit to Myers department store. Then I walked up the hill to King's Park.

Today, I allowed myself plenty of time to carry out a thorough reconnaissance. Especially places that afforded someone a clear view of the restaurant, without anyone inside being able to spot them.

I didn't notice anything unusual or out of the ordinary; saw no one looking or acting suspicious. Of course not. I wasn't supposed to. That's the whole idea behind surveillance. I hadn't really expected anyone. Yet. And even if there had been, there was little chance of my being recognised after my brief shopping spree.

The art of impersonation and disguise had at one time

been part of my stock-in-trade. My "treasure-chest-of-make-believe" - as my kit was known - still accompanied me everywhere, and I'd come out of that store looking nothing like the person that went in. All it required was to buy a couple of items of clothing, some accoutrements, make a few facial changes, adopt a different walk, and Roger McLaren had disappeared.

I secured myself away from the immediate area. In a place where I could watch for any watchers, and cover the building itself.

Here I waited.

They started arriving well before the time Foxy and I were due to meet. And they came in force.

But no Foxy. Which told me for sure he'd been blown, and he had talked, or been made to. So as it now seemed altogether possible they intended me harm - a major league piece of inconvenience, to say the least - I quietly and unobtrusively slipped away.

It confirmed what I'd suspected. They were suddenly worried by my presence. They hadn't been. Not in Adelaide. Otherwise I'd never have returned from that trip into the hills. And Holman certainly wouldn't have given me the information he did. No, they had Foxy, all right. That was for sure. He'd set me up as well. Thing was, had he done that voluntarily - in exchange for something - or under duress? Was he with them again, or still with me? I needed to know, for there might come a time when I'd need to count on his help.

Then I realized I did know.

The thing about having an ex-friend for an enemy is that you are probably familiar with some of their habits.

At present, I decided, Foxy was with them. If he saw a way out, through me, he'd be with me.

*

The bar of the Transit Inn was empty, apart from one table in the corner. Here sat a party of lads from my age group; Australians, Americans, and Brits, by the sound of things. From their conversation, I gathered they'd been "offshore".

Andy was behind the bar, and after looking round he acknowledged me with a nod of his head. So I walked over.

Talk at the corner table continued, volume increasing

198

round by round. Now they discussed "offtime", and "per diem rates". Talked of "giving the girlfriend one" when they got home!

'Seismic crew,' Andy muttered, reaching beneath the bar. 'In from the Northwest shelf,' he said, handing me a bag as he did so. 'Present from Bob.'

It was a polythene carrier with Myers plastered all over it, just like any other shopper calling in for a drink might carry. In fact some of the seismic crew did - "one for the girlfriend", maybe? Whatever, theirs were unlikely to hold what mine did. I knew that as soon as I peered in. Beretta .22 , complete with silencer. Small, light, handy. But for what?

'Unusual present, for a collector of information,' I commented. 'Anything on the grapevine I should know about?'

'Nothing specific was mentioned.'

I accepted that. I didn't particularly like guns, but felt better for carrying one, even if I didn't expect to have a use for it. There was no extra ammunition, I noted, so obviously I wasn't expected to have to use it.

Better to be carrying one when you don't need it than not to be when you do, Minerva advised.

'Well, tell Bob I hear there's talk of uncommon activity up the West Coast. Say I mentioned Port Hedland and Silver Springs.'

'Is that right?'

'Just rumours. But tell him it fits in nicely with my plans.'

'And those are?'

'I'm going up there. I intend to take a look at various things.'

'There may be other important points you haven't taken account of.'

'Such as?'

He told me. And he was right.

But I wasn't to find out about that until much later.

*   *

Chapter Twenty-three

COMETH THE HOUR, COMETH THE MAN

Kim's father had done her proud. Although well over halfway towards being grand, her house was in no way ostentatious; despite the fact it was the kind of place an estate agent could truthfully describe as being lavish. A secluded, open-plan, two-storey house, concealed in a bush setting, her nearest neighbour was a good half mile distant. The extensive grounds, though nowhere near the expanse of Hamilton's, were certainly large enough to include a sizable pool. Today though, after dropping me in town, she'd settled for the beach out at Cottesloe - her favourite, apparently. Crowded on a weekend, it was likely to be fairly quiet today.

I'd completed all my business, plus my shopping, and had a drink or two. I'd made my plans and taken out insurance, kind of thing. Even found time to have an interesting chat with that seismic crew. At least *I'd* found it interesting, they probably hadn't. But as I'd been shouting the rounds, they'd accommodated me.

Kim picked me up outside the Transit Inn, right on time, as previously arranged. She had also been shopping, I noticed, placing my bags alongside hers.

'Couple of things you might have forgot,' she said, in answer to my scrutiny. She added a cheeky smile as I opened one of her bags and extracted a bottle of wine. I made a show of examining the label as she drove.

'Ah! A Moss Wood Chardonnay. Perfect,' I said, nodding wisely as though it was the choice I would have made. That I hadn't, had less to do with the amount of things going on in my head than with the fact I wasn't familiar with the local wines. Kim was, so I knew this one would be quite acceptable.

As she parked and switched off, I held out my hand for the house keys. I didn't normally, but today, as we'd driven up, I'd felt it advisable that I open the door. Strange, but I considered it imperative. It seemed my sixth-sense antenna was alive and well.

Kim surrendered them and gave me a look, declining to put words to the question. Instead, she busied herself with the groceries.

I noticed it just as I was about to insert the key. Marks on the face of the key-plate. Scratches. Faint, but bright. Therefore, recent. I noticed things like that. Often looked for them, especially when I deemed it necessary, as had been the case here.

Caution had been called into play even before I stepped out of the Ford. A prickling sensation on the back of the neck and hands had given early warning that all may not be well. A primeval sensation, probably not experienced by everyone, but a sure sign that terminal danger could be imminent. It wasn't training, it was instinctive, almost the same as breathing. And I placed a lot of faith in my instincts, always had. Found it usually paid off. I hadn't stopped breathing yet!

Before inserting the key, I turned the handle. Slowly, carefully. Then I applied pressure.

The door was locked.

'Just testing,' I told Kim by way of explanation. She'd silently interrogated me with another enquiring frown.

'Look here, love,' I said, pointing to the faint scratches. 'Weren't there when we left this morning.'

'So, what's that tell us Sherlock?'

'Tells me someone was here while we were out.

201

Anyone else got a key to this place?'

'Not that I know of.'

My mind quickly took me through the options: an unsuccessful attempt at entry? Or successful? If successful had they had already left? Yes, otherwise the door would likely still be open. In which case, what, exactly had they left with? Or what had they left behind?

I had Kim stand well clear, and with some effort held my emotions in check, managing to remain calm and composed as I slid the key home, then backed away to arms length. I felt like squeezing my eyes shut as I turned it, forced myself not to. My heart thudded wildly, but I was ready for almost anything, apart from what I found.

There was nothing. No bangs, no mess, no one there to greet us, no further signs of entry.

Once inside I relaxed slightly, but my eyes didn't miss a thing. Everything appeared to be as it should to my eyes, but it wasn't my house.

'Have a quick check round, love. See if anything is out of place.'

Satisfied no one was around down here, I dropped my bags in the kitchen and proceeded upstairs.

'What's up, Roger?' Kim called after me.

'Toilet,' I said. 'I'm bursting.' No point causing her to worry unduly.

'There is one down here yuh know.'

'Figured you may want to use that,' I said carrying on my way.

I had a quick look round. No obvious signs of anyone having been up here either, though I'd make a detailed check as and when the opportunity presented itself, would need to have Kim look, too.

I flushed the loo and went back downstairs.

I worked in the kitchen, unpacking, but also carrying out more checks, whilst Kim showered and changed. I also carried out a survey of the full ground floor, disabling the previously discovered bugs, finding no new ones. I checked each cupboard and drawer minutely, looked behind curtains and pictures, examined light fittings and switches. I picked up the phone, listened. Dialling tone, so that was OK. Next I switched on the TV, the remote allowing me to stand well clear. The music system I had to take a chance on, unable to find the remote I switched it on manually. Both systems worked normally.

So, there was nothing. No signs of abnormality, nor of anything missing, as far as I could ascertain.

I'd cover the bed and bathroom when I went up to change.

*

Something didn't fit. I was sure someone had been in the house yet nothing seemed to have been touched. Key-plate apart, there were no other signs of anyone having visited, which pointed to professionals. Yet why? What had I missed? There had to be something, or my senses were failing me. I didn't think they were.

My subconscious must have been working overtime, seeking an answer even as we ate and talked. Kim now wore jewellery, I noticed, whereas she hadn't earlier in the day. That in itself seemed to rule out burglary.

We were both relaxed, each apparently enjoying the other's company, and the wine. Then, during a moment of silence, possibly the result of a guilty conscience, I inexplicably allowed my concentration to slip, forcing a rare *faux pas.*

'If not burglars, what would they want in your...?' Too late. The words were out before I realized what I was saying.

Kim stared at me in disbelief, fork poised, prawn on the end temporarily reprieved.

'In my what, Roger? Who? When?' she said, voice rising, vibrating slightly with instinctive, unthinking anger.

So many questions she sounded like Gerry, throwing a tantrum. But she was right. I'd already hidden too much from her, I realized, not told her enough. This time it *was* her business. It was her house, after all.

'OK,' I sighed. 'Here. When we got back. There were signs of someone having tried to get in. You saw that, I pointed it out.'

'There were no other signs of anyone 'aving been here. I knew yuh were suspicious of somat when we got out of t' car.'

'What made you think so?'

'That's t' first time yuh've ever opened t' door for me. Don't think I didn't notice.'

'Clever you.'

'So who d' you think it were?'

I shrugged. 'It's your house. Who do you think it might have been?'

'How the hell should I know?,' she said. 'Yuh seem to be t' amateur sleuth. Yuh tell me. I take it yuh've had a good look round. Any more o' those bug things?'

'None. I even removed the originals. What about your jewellery?'

'Nothing missing. And I would 'ave noticed,' she said, seemingly very calm about everything.

She would, too. Jewellery was the one thing she really cared for. It had it's own drawer, each piece allocated it's own place in there. I recalled how proud she'd been when she'd pointed it out to me, shortly after I moved in.

'Have to put it down to an unsuccessful attempt at burglary then,' I suggested.

'I see,' she said, sounding a long way from being convinced. Yet apparently prepared to shrug it off as such. At least for the moment.

'You seem remarkably calm about it, love.'

'No point being otherwise, is there. When yuh don't have control of things,' she said. 'Learnt that on t' streets. Needed to in our gang.'

'What? You were in a Liverpool gang? A girl?'

'One of t' most notorious gangs in t' area,' she boasted. 'The only girl, too.'

'How come?'

'Bloody obvious, really. Jimmy fancied getting in me pants, didn't he? He was t' boss.'

I shouldn't have asked, but I did. 'And?'

'No, he niver did, apart from t' odd grope I allowed. kept him interested. Small price t' pay for his protection. No one else dare come near me,' she said, laughing. Which effectively took us away from the subject of prowlers.

But my mind was still troubled.

*

Kim was in the bathroom cleaning her teeth ready for bed when I broke the news.

'Think I'll take a trip up north, love. Any chance of borrowing the ute? A week, max.'

I watched for her reaction in the mirror, a flash of disappointment crossing her face.

'Let me guess. Yuh're going to visit Tony, who just happens t' be in Port 'edland, right?'

'Well... yes, I will visit Tony, of course. But the main reason is to have a look round.

'Liar,' she said, astutely. 'It's Tony all right. Yuh hardly bothered when he was here. Now you want to drive nearly a thousand miles t' visit him. He must 'ave something you need, right? I guessed there was more t' this than just professor what's-his-name and his bloody notes.'

She spat into the basin and rinsed her mouth. 'What's wrong?' she asked my reflection. 'Fed up with screwing me?'

Stupid bloody question, I thought, especially when bent over, wearing a mini and very flimsy underwear.

I moved closer. 'Don't debase what we have, love, you're much more than that. I'll miss you, of course. But I'd like to see more of the country while I'm here.'

'Balls, Roger. If that were all, yuh'd invite me along.'

'No. It's just....' It was no good. I had to give her more than that, even if it wasn't quite the truth.

'All right then. Foxy's disappeared.'

'Ah!' Heavy with sarcasm, like a barrister addressing the jury.

'Yeah. Seems someone's taken him.'

'Taken him? Where? For what purpose? What's going on, Roger?' She replaced her toothbrush in its holder.

'Don't have a clue, love. But I intend to find out,' I told her, starting to massage her back.

'Why not leave it t' cops?' She wriggled her shoulders. 'I take it yuh did inform 'em?' She was conversing with me via the mirror, now checking her eyelashes.

'Not exactly. Thought about it. Decided I'd better come up with something more substantial first. Look what happened last time.'

She knew there was more.

'And?' she posed.

'Natural bloody obstinacy, I suppose. Look, I know it's not been a lot of fun for you, me rushing here and there on my own. Even Adelaide didn't turn out as well as expected. But I promise, when I get back we'll spend time together. Lots of time. Just you and I.'

Although she looked away I knew silent tears were falling, so I wrapped my arms around her, which was clearly what she wanted. Love and assurance. Me too, I suddenly decided.

'Yuh won't do anything foolish?' she pleaded to the mirror, finding her answer in my implacable stare. 'O' course. Silly bloody question. Like asking the frigging Pope not to attend mass! Well... Just take care, love.'

'Will do,' I mumbled, hands wandering lower. 'Goes without saying.'

'What yuh doing, Roger?

'Give you one guess.'

'Umm.' It was more in approval of what my hands were doing rather than in answer to anything I'd said. Now she wiggled her bum. Then she added a thought. 'But not over t' sink, surely?'

'Why not?' I said, continuing my preparations. 'I imagine it's been done before.'

'Not by me it 'asn't!' she adamantly declared. But she made no attempt whatever to dissuade me. Just the opposite, in fact.

'There's always a first time,' I proposed, fumbling her panties down.

'There is that', she purred, helping them on their way, then stepping daintily out of them.

*

I lay there quietly, going ten rounds with my conscience. Here I was, in bed with Hamilton's daughter, the very man it seemed I was after. Was I just using her, or was it truly a loving relationship? And if so, what about....?

I wasn't myself. I was a shadow in a shadow world. The Roger that Tony and Kim saw was the real me, outside of that was a facade. It was a lonely position I was in. Nobody to turn to. Could Kim be of any help? I wondered. She was obviously streetwise.

Maybe, maybe not, Minerva advised. *But as long as she can keep her mouth shut, it wouldn't hurt to see how she reacted.*

Why not, I agreed. She's got to find out sooner or later. Better she hear it from me. So I woke her, and once she was coherent, told her.

First, I told her about Singapore.

She reached over and poured herself a drink, sipping at it, thoughtful.

'Is this the plot for yuh next novel?' she asked. 'Or 'ave you been smoking one of them funny cigarettes?'

'No funny cigarettes,love' I said. 'This is serious.'

Just how serious she was no doubt able to deduce from what came next. I gave her a rundown on my arrival in Perth, the reception I'd been given.

'Norman-fucking-Holman,' she said. 'I might 'ave known.'

'What is it with you and Holman?'

'Bastard... tried to rape me. Twice. Almost put me off men for life. And then you came along,' she quickly added. 'You certainly changed things. For t' better' she admitted.

I'd wondered about that. For at no time during our brief spell together had she surrendered a clue as to why she was still single. And of course, I hadn't asked.

'Dad promised to get rid of 'im,' she continued, 'only it never 'appened. It was t' only time Dad and I fell out.'

She dried up then. Brooding. But she'd planted another seed.

To take her mind off the subject of rape I told her about the drugs, detailed Foxy's role in the affair, but didn't voice my thoughts and suspicions. How could I? Especially as it seemed her father could be heavily involved. In fact there was quite a lot I didn't tell her. Just as well.

She listened in patient, wide-eyed silence to what I did tell her. No doubt she'd by now tied yesterday's break-in to this.

'Yuh've got to be bloody crazy, Roger,' she said when I'd finished. 'They'll kill yuh.' Her concern was obvious.

'That's more than likely, if they catch me. The idea is

not to get caught.'

'Meaning *you're* prepared to kill?'

'Only if I have to. When *not* killing means I'm as good as dead'.

Words like those would put the fear of Christ into most women, I thought. But Kim's tough upbringing again showed through.

'That the reason for t' gun, Roger?'

That took me by surprise, and it obviously showed.

'Yuh left yur bags with me, remember. I took a peek whist yuh was up in t' dunny.'

'It's a just in case thing. Other people could be armed.'

'Bloody hell! So. What are our chances?' she asked.

Our chances, I noted. But she was right. 'In love, war, or the Test series?'

'All three if yuh like. But I'm particularly interested in survival.'

'Me too. Be a disaster if England failed again,' I answered, somewhat facetiously, but it didn't have the desired effect, that of lightening her mood. Instead, she chose that moment to pose another question. It was the question I knew we'd get round to eventually. The one I didn't want to answer. Couldn't, for I didn't yet have the answer.

'Is Dad involved?'

Just like that. Couldn't very well dodge it. No point.

'Can't say for sure, love. But I'm afraid it does seem likely some of his enterprises may be, even though he may be unaware of it.'

Naturally, it went down like a lead fart.

'No!' she screamed. 'Yuh can't believe that. Yuh don't know him like I do. He'd never touch anything like that. Never.'

'I did say he may not be aware of it, love.'

It was obvious she'd defend him, be upset with me for even thinking it possible. I accepted that. And as there was nothing to be gained by possibly making things worse, I didn't respond further. But saying nothing was almost as bad. Female logic dictated that would be the case.

'No, yuh're wrong, Roger. I know it.'

'Let's hope so. Maybe things will become clearer when I get to Hedland. I have this feeling the answer lies somewhere up there.'

'Then I'll just 'ave t' go with yuh.' She stared at the ceiling as she spoke, refusing to look me in the eye.

'No, love, you can't. I won't allow it.'

'Won't allow it! Yuh can't fucking stop me. It's my car, remember.'

'OK, I'll fly up, rent one when I get there. But I'm travelling alone.'

'That's silly.'

'There are lots of words that cover it, but "silly" isn't one of them. It's far too dangerous to take you. Surely you can see that?'

'So it's dangerous. Yuh're going.'

'I have to. Think about it Kim. Our chances will be greatly increased if I go on my own. Taking you will give me two people to worry about. Meaning half my mind will be on your safety, when it should all be on mine. Your way, we could both end up dead.'

'Then leave it t' cops.'

'The cops? Who in particular, Inspector McRobertson for instance? He doesn't even trust me, I certainly wouldn't trust him. Besides, I have evidence whatsoever. Suspicions and theories aplenty. Nothing concrete.'

She pounced on that.

'So 'ow can yuh say Dad's involved?'

'Didn't say he was, love. Said it seems possible some of his companies might be, even though he may not be aware of it.'

'Seems? Things aren't always what they seem, Roger.'

'Don't I know it. Seems an aeronautical engineer once proved that a bumblebee would be unable to fly, power to weight ratio was all wrong. So, obviously, was that engineer.

Now she did look at me. As if I was mad. 'What the fuck has that got to do with drug smuggling, or anything?'

'Look, love, maybe your father's not involved. It's all supposition up to now, no evidence of anything. And evidence is what we need.'

That was enough. Her flash of rage subsided, but she hadn't quite given up.

'I'll be on me own once yuh leave,' she protested. Then

she cried. Real tears this time, washing the emotion from her soul. It really got to me. It always does when the girl I'm with is unhappy.

I held her, pulling her close.

'Hey, come on, love. It'll only be a week. Probably less. And you'll be safe enough in Perth. Don't think they'll bother with you if I'm not around.'

Once I've left, was the implication. But, of course, at the moment, I was still there.

*　　*

Chapter Twenty-four

A MOVING EXPERIENCE

Kim skipped out of bed and disappeared off down the hall, completely naked. It was how we both favoured sleeping. I'd been that way most of my life.

I rolled over to occupy the space she'd vacated. Traces of perfume and natural body odours remained, perfume winning through. It symbolized love and tenderness. The other expressed love also, though less subtly. I savoured its muskiness, now fast-fading, barely detectable, yet it acted as an *aide-memoire*. Not that I really needed one. But it did serve to remind me I was leaving her again. Wouldn't see her for maybe a week.

That was all it took. Especially seeing her skip away like she had. I wanted her. Right now. Couldn't possibly wait another week.

I'd joined her in the shower even before the water had been turned on, although both of us by now apparently were. My ardour was plainly visible. Kim, it seemed, was in like mood, for she immediately took hold of me, gently stroking.

`It's my absolutely, positively, favourite thing. Cross my heart and hope to die,' she said with childish nonchalance, goading me.

Then, inexplicably, she paused, smiling at my obvious disbelief as she released me.

She held up a finger, hinting at the explanation to follow.

`Patience, she said. `Let there be music.'

Music wasn't exactly top of my priorities right at this particular moment. Though I didn't tell Kim that. It would have been churlish of me to do so. Churlish and... what was the favoured phrase these days? Counter-productive? Yes, quite likely. So I decided to let my fingers do the talking instead. But, even as I reached for her, she deftly stepped out of reach.

`Ah, ah.' Now the finger wagged in admonishment. `No music, no nooky,' she threatened, disappearing into the bedroom. Her laughter tinkled after her.

`Music!' I echoed, thinking more about that which seemed to have a pressing priority in my mind.

Then, it suddenly became less pressing.

It was there again, the primeval tingling of neck and hands, mouth filled with a dry, metallic taste. Kim's return, clutching the remote, sparked memories of yesterday. The remote I'd dismissed at the time, because it hadn't been to hand.

My mind was now in overdrive, thoughts a blur as it sought a specific piece of trivia. Something important enough to instantly erase all thoughts of sex!

It seemed more like minutes than nano-seconds.

Then I had it, or Minerva did. *Not infra-red. A radio remote. Type of thing used by the IRA for detonating bombs from a distance.*

'Shit!' It was the only thing I hadn't checked.

I attempted to snatch it out of her hand but Kim playfully jerked it towards herself, her breasts.

`Ah, ah. Mine,' she said, her voice childish, fatuous, thumb hovering over a button.

`Kim! No!' As I shouted I dragged her in front of me, pushing her against the wall. She must have thought I'd gone

212

crazy, or was about to rape her. Then, knowing the remote was beyond my grasp, I reached instead for the taps.

Too late.

Kim's scream was almost louder than the explosion which preceded it. She released the remote, hands now covering her face, sound escaping between the fingers. It pierced my scull like a sliver of ice.

The blast, no doubt dissipated by the partial collapse of a bedroom wall, retained enough power to slam open the shower-room door. It crashed back against its own wall. Shockwaves compressed the air. Air that was hot and dusty. I recoiled from the force. It was like being exposed to a sandstorm. Window glass blew outwards, away from us, a million pieces.

Intense blotches of white light filled my vision as something struck me on the head. Then I was spinning, falling. Kim screamed again as I unintentionally took her with me.

`Roger! No!'

Nothing I could do about it. We ended up as a tangled heap in the shower tray.

Fingers probed my forehead. They were mine. I'd suffered a cut, which, from the amount of blood evident, appeared far worse than it really was, as is normal for a head wound. Blood dripped onto Kim, who lay beneath me. Not an abnormal position for us it seemed, but, in the circumstances, scant protection.

The air smelled of something acrid, choking, causing me to cough. But there was no sign of smoke or flames. No fire. Thank God.

I sat Kim up, wrapping my arms around her. I pulled her close. Hugged her. Felt the rigid fine-boned flesh tremble at first, before relaxing slightly.

`It's OK, love,' I assured her. `All over.'

I pushed apart, inspecting her for damage. Apart from my blood, she appeared to be uninjured. Shocked, certainly. She was now silent; white-faced and wide-eyed, features wild and distorted.

The panels of the shower cubicle were mainly intact, though blown out of their frames. Polycarbonate, I assumed.

Another modern miracle. Shatterproof, yet light. Almost as strong as steel. They, no doubt, had further dissipated the blast, miraculously - magically almost - shielding us from flying debris, protecting us from serious injury.

I kicked our way clear and helped Kim to her feet. This time I succeeded in turning on the water. I ran it warm. I stood there with Kim in my arms, soothing her. The water served to wash away the blood and dust, as well as refreshing the soul. It also flooded the bathroom floor, but who cared.

Head wound aside, we were apparently in fair shape, body-wise, though I imagined there would be some bruising, given time. For me, certainly. I ached from head to feet. But most of that was probably from the almost healed residue of the past episode. We'd been lucky, at least two walls separating us from the force of the blast. Plus, in Kim's case, my body.

Kim, obviously in shock, still had the strength to stand unaided. I dried us both off, then we staggered off to dress in whatever clothes were to hand.

She looked terrible, so I poured her a stimulant - a goodly shot of her bedside Scotch. Naturally, the ice-bucket was empty, so, handing her the drink, I ventured down to the kitchen for some. A wasted journey, I found. By the time I returned she'd drained the glass. At least once. Not a wasted drink though, for restoration was evidently well underway.

Apparently the open-plan lower floor had also helped dissipate the blast - explosive apparently concealed somewhere on the landing, perhaps in the music centre itself, set to detonate on receipt of the radio signal - open space in which searing-hot gasses could readily expand without so much resistance. Of course, windows and doors had stood no chance. Neither had breakables in the kitchen and lounge.

Had it not been for the sheltered, somewhat remote location, the place would no doubt already have been subjected to attention by the emergency services. As it was we were still alone, bush and heavy vegetation no doubt muffling the blast.

`One thing's for sure, you can't stay here. Not now,' I told her sometime later, after we'd made a detailed inspection of what remained of the property. There really wasn't any alternative, I thought.

`God, Roger. Pretty bloody obvious, isn't it. The place is a wreck. My lovely house.'

She was right. It looked like the climax of a high-budget Swarzeneger-style movie.

`I don't mean here in the house, love. I mean Perth itself. Think you'd better come with me after all.'

`It's what you do best,' she said. The surprising play on words proof of recovery. She smiled, but it was a smile that faded almost immediately. Pleasant thoughts seemingly disrupted by those less so.

`You said I'd be safe here.'

`That was last night. Then, I didn't think... er. Well, things have changed now.'

`Hold on! What you're saying is.... No! You're implying Dad set me up to be killed!'

I didn't answer directly. Anyway, it wasn't a question, it was an accusation.

`It was me they were after,' I admitted. `Obviously. But whoever "they" was, they didn't seem to care too much whether or not you'd be around at the time. So I very much doubt your dad was involved in any way.'

`If I come with you, I'll still be around.'

`Yes, but hopefully they won't know where. Especially if we don't tell anyone.'

`Including Dad?'

I felt like saying, "Dad, in particular", but merely answered with a nod and said, `Yes. Including Dad.' Then something struck me, so I added an afterthought. `But just think, this could be more of an indication that your father is not involved, rather than that he is.'

`But....' she began.

I cut her off, stroking her hand so as to soften the criticism. `No conditional conjunctions, love. That's the way it has to be. Anyway, I'll look after you. That's a promise.'

`In that case, how can I refuse. I've heard tell sex can be an moving experience, earth shattering even, but that was a bit too much, and we didn't even get round to the sex. Besides, you're earth-shattering enough not to need gimmicks of that kind.'

There she was again, making light of a bad situation. Forcing herself not to pursue it.

`Hey, listen love. And make sure you do take this in. It's not exactly going to be regatta week at Cowes, you know,' I told her. I had to be sure she was aware of what she may be getting in to. But I'd misjudged her. She *was* aware. Well aware, it seemed.

`Nowhere is it written that if yuh play safe yu'll live to be an 'undred and die 'appy,' she said.

*

Once the decision had been reached, it didn't take us long to collect together what we needed from the remains of our belongings, and load the vehicle. I took charge of the loading, Kim made the house as secure as was possible. There was no reason for us to delay longer than necessary. Just the opposite, in fact. We needed to clear the area quickly. And this we did.

Fifteen minutes and we were on our way. We stopped only once before departing Perth, allowing Kim to arrange for repairs be made in her absence, and to visit her bank. Here her jewellery and other valuables went into a safe deposit. We ruled out informing the police; couldn't risk the delay, nor the fact that they, for sure, would want to know where we intended going. For the same reason Kim had taken the contractor's details, not told them where she was going. She would contact them later. So she told me.

Don't know why, but when Kim was talking to the contractors, I went to a nearby store and bought a paper. I wasn't sure of the reason, for it was something I did only rarely, just to catch up. I put the act down to the old sixth sense syndrome, I suppose.

I glanced idly through it as I waited, starting with the sports and working my way forward, as was my wont. Centre pages, I found, usually contained articles of no particular significance. They had to use something. All those pages, every day, needing to be filled. Preferably with adverts; if not, anything would do. These days the ads seemed to be getting fewer, the absurdity content greater. One reason I rarely bought newspapers.

This one seemed little different. For, as was normal, it

dealt mainly with local matters, of which I would have little idea about, or interest in. That is until I reached the front page.

It wasn't the lead, nor was it given any particular significance. Well it wouldn't be, would it. Just another unfortunate traffic accident.

Although it wasn't really just another accident. Not to my mind. Nor would it seem so to the casualty, for he was dead! Fellow by the name of Andy Mathews. Until last night, barman at a local hotel. The Transit Inn.

It really was time to get moving, I judged. And once you let a thought like that loose in your head, it needed to be acted upon rather swiftly.

*   *

Chapter Twenty-five

DREAMS AND SCHEMES

*T*he beginning had ended with our departure from the confines of Perth. I had a feeling that Port Hedland, a little over a thousand miles to the north, was the place at which the end would begin. Nothing guaranteed. Just a feeling. Very strong at that.

*

As far as roads from Perth to Port Hedland are concerned, the choice was simple. One or other of two! The Great Northern Highway was one: heading inland, sealed for only just over half its length, dusty and dry, passing through, or close by, only the occasional lonely outpost, mining operation, or cattle station. These cattle stations are huge, and it is not unusual to see a sign by the roadside: This marks the southeast corner of Prairie Downs station, and you could drive for thirty minutes, or longer, before sighting, This marks the north east corner of Prairie Downs station!

Or there was the North West Coastal Highway: completely sealed for its entire length, and, as its name implies, tracking mainly within sight of the Australian West coast, passing through major centres of population such as Geraldton, Carnarvon, Wickham, and on to Hedland, with only the odd Roadhouse in between. For us, the better choice by far.

Current events dictated that it would probably be a wise move for us to abandon Perth in a hurry. But as there was no great necessity for our immediate arrival in Port Hedland - our back-up not due there for some time yet - we had elected to take the more scenic, coastal route.

`I wonder where this is leading us?' Kim commented once we were clear of Perth's northern suburbs and heading out along the Brand Highway.

`Leads to Geraldton,' I replied. `Road sign says so.'

`Come on Roger. Yuh know very well that's not what I meant,' she said.

So I did. But as far as the "other" was concerned, this was an unknown journey for both of us. I had little idea of what we were heading into, nor what the consequences were likely to be once we arrived there. But as that wouldn't be what she wanted to hear, I remained silent, deep in my thoughts. I was wondering about other things, such as Andy Mathews. What had gone on before he died? Everyone has his breaking point, and they must have questioned him before arranging his "accident". What had he been forced to reveal, if anything? And why was I being armed, if my role was just to ask the questions, then, if the answers warranted it, call in Bob and his crowd?

Given what had happened to Andy, the question of a gun suddenly appeared to have become superfluous. OK, that gun wasn't an instant stopper, but should I have to use it, it would be very quiet. Not only did it come with a sound suppressor, the magazine was loaded with short, subsonic bullets; low power, low speed, very little noise. But placed accurately, in the right area, they could be lethal. A hit anywhere else would do, even if only to buy time.

Seems I'd been lied to once again! Not unheard of, naturally. Deceit was a continuous necessity in this business. I engaged in it myself now and again. A fact of which I was about to be reminded.

`You lied to me,' Kim said, intruding on my thoughts; or

219

perhaps reading them! `And you nearly got me killed. "Hamilton's daughter in miraculous escape", she said, quoting from imaginary headlines. She obviously wanted some attention.

`Don't get feisty, love. White lies, intended to shield you from danger. And don't forget, it was you who initially invited yourself on this jaunt, remember.'

`But yuh rejected that. Then changed yur mind, insisted I came. So now I'm here, talk to me. Going to be a long drive otherwise.'

She was right, too. Now she was included I'd have to tell her everything. Ideal time. So I started with my background. Told her of my previous experience, and how that had come about.

'Quite a story, but don't stop there.'

`OK, but do you know there an area up here, north of Hedland, known as The Kimberley?'

'Yur shittin' me.'

'No I'm not. Look.' I showed her the map.

'Um.' Unimpressed. 'But yuh was tellin' me a story. So carry on.'

OK. So once I was in a position where it became necessary, I found myself relating to characters in the novels I read; discovered I had a natural aptitude for it. Even got to enjoy it. The excitement and intrigue.'

,Yeah, don't I know it. I'm not so daft, or unobservant as yuh think, Roger. So tell me more about what comes next.'

Couldn't tell her much, for I wouldn't know until we got Hedland. But just to let her know I had some back up arranged, I told her about Gerry Gibbs, and Mike Douglas - my ex-SAS friend - both of whom would be joining us within the next few days. I felt it essential to have Mike alongside, because I wasn't at all sure what I was getting into; and when you put yourself in that situation you'd better have someone you could trust along with you. Mike was that someone. My reliable back-up.

'I'm afraid you'll once again have to remain on the sidelines, love. Hopefully not for long.'

I had to tell her, so she'd know what to expect. Anyway, she had asked. I didn't mind placing myself in the line of fire, but refused to bear the guilt of involving Kim. Not after what happened to Caroline, my last girlfriend. I explained that situation in detail, as well. The whole thing. It helped pass the time, and I'd long since learned to live with it: our escapades and adventures, the dangers involved, that fatal night.

`You mean you blame yourself?' she said when I'd finished.

It was a question I declined to answer. Ultimate responsibility was not something I wished to discuss in the abstract.

`So, what do you have planned? Why the need for those people? Why the trip in the first place?'

`Might sound a bit foolish, love, but I don't have anything planned as such. One or two schemes and ideas maybe. Play it by ear. It's all really just a hunch, but I'm big on hunches.'

'What do your hunches tell you about Dad?'

I figured that would come up again sometime or other, only natural. 'Hard to say, love. But if my theories are correct, some of his companies are certainly involved. Which is not to say he is,' I was quick to add.

`Hope not. If I loose Dad I've got nobody.'

I felt like reminding her that, all being well, she would still have me, but got the impression she was hinting at something entirely different.

*

The town of Carnarvon is located around five hundred miles by road to the north of Perth. North of this is the Pilbara, one of the most mineralized regions on earth. An area bursting at the seams with ore of all types and grades. It is a vast, scarred and ancient land. Sunburnt and brooding. The predominant colour is rust-red ochre. Red rock, the iron content of which was so great, I'd heard it was possible to weld fragments of it together.

After a break in Carnarvon, we set off once more, myself taking a spell at the wheel. And following Kim's instructions, we set off along what was ambitiously still termed the North West Costal Highway - difficult for it to be otherwise really, it was the only road leading north from here, though by now, the traffic using it was becoming rather sparse.

221

Signs along our route gave reference to other small towns and communities, but they were now few and far between. Most remained unseen, way off to the east. Places which bore names such as Paraburdoo, Tom Price - I recalled seeing that name in the newspaper - Onslow, and Pannawonica. Many of these places would not even have featured on the maps of twenty years ago. They were built by the mining companies, as were the railways which served them. The terminus for this rail link, and the main outlet for the region's products, is the town of Port Hedland. Hedland also served as a base to supply the Northwest Shelf oilfields. The very reason for it being our destination.

The emptiness stretched away to the horizon. A vast acreage made all the greater by the realization that it went on and on. Much further than the eye could see. Seemingly for ever. It was eight thousand kilometres from Singapore, and the welcoming atmosphere of TGIF, with its ice cold beer. A further fourteen thousand or so kilometres and I could be in my local, back home. Just the thought had me gasping. I could already feel moisture running between my shoulder-blades, trickling down my sides, for it was hot, hot, hot.

`If you don't see a pub in the next two hundred kilometres, assume we're on the wrong road,' Kim advised, once more seeming to read my mind.

`What! I thought you said......'

`A joke, Roger. The road doesn't go anywhere else. Trust me.'

I gazed at her with new respect, amazed she could actually read a map, not that there was a lot to be seen on it! Basically, a yellowish sheet of paper, a few vague red lines evident.

*

One hundred kilometres later Kim was at the wheel again, I was attempting to get some rest.

`Oh, shit!' she said as the vehicle suddenly lurched, attempting to streak off into the outback before she corrected it. Hardly any different from the road really, just not quite as smooth. Of course, a flat tyre didn't help any!

Her exclamation aroused me, and I quickly adjudged to situation. My feelings exactly, I thought, and piss as well.

222

We were in the middle of nowhere, in the middle of the day sun at its peak. As in most places outside the cities of Australia, the days are hot and dry. The Pilbara took this to the extremes.

`What the fuck am I doing here,' Kim wondered aloud, making it clear she was slumming. And I admit, I wondered the same thing as I got out to change the wheel. I removed my shirt, discovered I'd been right about the bruises. My body once again looked as if it were camouflaged, hurt a little as well. It seemed to be becoming a regular feature. Too regular, I thought.

Kim couldn't help but notice.

`You should be resting, Roger, not bouncing around in the cab of a truck.'

She's a bloody comedian, Minerva piped in.

`Probably,' I told Kim. `But I don't have the time. Need to change this wheel.'

`Yeah! May as well eat while yu're at it then,' she said, unpacking the sandwiches she'd bought and offering me one. They were no longer fresh, but it's amazing how good some things taste when you're peckish and it's the only thing that is on offer. Along with a welcome drink, even though these were no longer cold.

These are precautions you needed to take when travelling in Australia, especially the outback. Forget that and it could be very easy to die!

As we ate and drank, Kim started the inevitable, imaginary menu-making, beginning with a long, detailed description of lobster thermidor, and of succulent steaks. Then of course there was mention of ice-cold beer, swimming pools, cold showers and shade - shade most of all. In our current predicament, all but dreams. But they were dreams which, one hundred long kilometres after we resumed our journey, unexpectedly became reality.

And I'd thought she'd been joking.

There was not so much as the susurrus of a breeze to soften the worst of the midday heat, but suddenly, as if out of nowhere, there was a pub, and that served just as well.

Welcome Whim Creek Pub, read the slightly fading words, painted along the facia. I thought it needed a comma after Welcome, but out here who cared! Part shaded by trees and bush, it sat there in total isolation, albeit to one side of the only road in the area. Any traffic travelling this route, no matter how sparse, would be sure to stop off here. A welcome oasis.

Situated several kilometres from what had at one time been site of the first significant mineral find in the Pilbara - mainly copper, but with small amounts of gold not too far distant - the pub was now the middle of nowhere, the only building in sight alongside this road, although there *were* the twisted, rusting remains of machinery to be seen dotted about the area. Remnants of once profitable ventures.

'Says here there wus once two hotels, plus a blacksmith and cop station,' Kim said, quoting from a guide book to the area, though obviously not verbatim! 'There's also rumours of a beer-drinking camel residing hereabouts. How about that, then?'

'Let me tell you this, there'll shortly be a beer-drinking Roger McLaren at that bar. And that's fact, not rumour,' I said stopping the vehicle close by the door. No restrictions on parking out here.

At first, after the sun's glare, it appeared to be dimly lit, but it brightened appreciably as the eyes grew accustomed. It was as good a pub as any I'd visited in Perth.

With the airconditioning blasting away it was like stepping into another world altogether, a world where already cold beer was served up in chilled, frosted glasses. And never had a drink tasted so good. I could almost imagine it evaporating on the way down, nectar to a parched throat.

'Wanting a room by any chance?' the barman asked.

'Not today, thanks. Heading up north. Will take a couple more beers though.'

'Not signing on at Silver Springs are yuh? Heard they were recruiting, because of the breakthrough,' he said, making conversation as he placed the second round of drinks before us.

`Breakthrough?'

`Yuh musta' heard about it, surely?'

`If I have, I've forgotten. Tell me.'

He spelled it out in detail, as if to an illiterate.

`Yeah. Rumoured to be close to a cure for cancer. Something like that would be worth protecting, I'd imagine.'

'You bet! If that really is the case, the whole world will soon be knocking at Australia's door. But, I saw no mention of any such thing about it in the paper,' I told him, placing The West Australian on the counter. I'd thought I may come across someone up here who may welcome it.

I didn't think for a minute it was anything but a rumour. But it was a rumour that carried a message, as was no doubt the intention. It also appeared to fit well into the scheme of things, as I saw them.

*   *

Chapter Twenty-six

PORT HEDLAND

The Whim Creek halt had set us up nicely for the final fifty or so mile run up the road.

When we finally arrived, there was evidence of the sun's setting; pink and purple brushstrokes against a blue but darkening sky.

Port Hedland, Australia's largest port with regard to export tonnage, and literally a stone's throw from the outback, for immediately outside the town boundaries *was* the outback.

We drove directly to the Walkabout Motel, out by the airport, in South Hedland, selected from the guidebook during our en route planning.

Although we hadn't phoned ahead for a reservation - security the motive here, telephone calls being surprisingly simple to monitor for people who had the means. Needless to say, anyone trying to trace our whereabouts would for sure have the means - we had no problem checking in here. The hotel was of typical old time Australian construction: Wood and stone, with a green, round-edged, corrugated-iron roof and wrap around verandah. And at the rear, beneath the spread of an ancient flamboyant, a beer garden was located under the vast dome of a now indigo sky.

After settling in our room, a quick wash and freshen up, I then proceeded to pass on our contact location, to those who *did* have a need to know.

We then relocated out to that beer garden, seated ourselves beneath a billion stars, seemingly so close you felt as though you could reach out and touch them. A breeze whispered over us, gentle and soothing as a velvet glove, and in this pleasant atmosphere we cast aside thoughts of what was to come, drank schooners of Swan lager instead, and dined on barbecued steaks the size of platters. Not quite up to the standard Kim had earlier dreamed up, but acceptable for all that.

*

Back in Perth, Kim usually wore cotton dresses, or very short shorts during the day, but, as is the way with most monied females, she was a classy dresser when we went out at night, usually something in silk. Up here in the Northwest they dressed differently, somewhat less elegantly, so we did too. She was much more sartorially casual, though tonight, decidedly sexy. When was she ever not, I thought.

Beneath a cotton shawl she wore a halter top and a pair of pink shorts that looked like they had been painted on. She was obviously in the mood for love, but seemed determined to first savour some outdoor dining. So was I, but despite the prevailing ambience, it had taken an excess of willpower for me not to have already dragged her back to our room like some male-chauvinist cave-man. Maybe the heat was getting to me!

It really was pleasant up here in the northern extremes of WA. Peaceful, I thought. Or it could be. So why not just settle down with Kim, forget all about the James Bond stuff?

Yeah, Minerva chided. *Never happen. Four days in Singapore and you were already becoming bored. You thrive on excitement, and danger.*

True, I realized. I was also honest enough to admit to myself that Kim didn't really belong in my world, either. How many times had I harboured similar thoughts about the woman of the moment? At present Kim belonged with me, we belonged together, but not in the world I was about to enter. Anyway, those thoughts were for the future. Tonight, matters were of a more pressing nature, it seemed, and after dining we immediately departed back to the room.

To my surprise, Kim was already in bed, covers pulled up to her freckled nose, smile painted on her face, when I returned from the bathroom.

`Oh,' I said, disappointment evident in my tone, `I was hoping.... well.., those shorts were very sexy. Really turned me on,' I managed to blurt out.

`I did notice,' she said, throwing back the covers and rolling onto her tummy. She still wore them, her buttocks provocatively emphasized by the shiny, tightly stretched material. Like melons in pink cling-film. Much more seductive than if she had appeared simply naked, I thought. I was unable to tear my eyes away. It was a sight I'd never tire of looking at. At least not until I was well over seventy, I hoped.

`Didn't they ever teach yuh that it's rude t' stare,' she asked frivolously.

'I have heard mention of it,' I replied as I shed my clothes. So I stopped staring, and she never once complained about anything I did instead, although it did prove to be a little uncomfortable for me, bruises and all. But we did manage.

And so another day dies in peace, I mused, sometime later. Then I thought about that. Cast my mind back.

Once, not too long ago, they had all ended like this. It was normal. *Had* been normal, back *then.* Now it seemed I'd conditioned my body to expect something untoward to happen, and considering my changed circumstances, that in itself was no bad thing, I supposed. If I thought that way, then I was less likely to be surprised if something untoward did rear it's ugly head.

*

Although mostly sealed, the roads in Hedland were altogether different from those busy Perth streets. Hay Street at rush hour in particular. Up here they saw far less use, and outside the town boundaries it was even quieter still. Wander off either of the two main highways, and you were onto red dirt, with only the occasional car to be seen. The railway was a different matter altogether. Get caught at a crossing when an ore train was passing by and you were likely to be there for some time. They were the longest trains I'd ever seen. Kim, too, I gathered.

'Fucking hell,' was how she expressed herself upon seeing one for the first time, as we drove into town. She had obviously not travelled very far in Australia over her years here. Neither had I during my short time, so I was astounded, too.

OK, so we had to wait awhile. No problem. There wasn't a lot to be done at present, apart from awaiting the arrival of various people who may, or may not, be able to offer help or ideas. And as the first of them was not due before tomorrow night, I'd turned the day over to Kim.

Most of our morning was spent exploring the local area, doing the tourist bit. But I did keep my eyes open. I didn't have anything particular in mind to look for, just whatever may strike a chord. Anything that may possibly provide some kind of a clue, or any helpful information. And I did need to have an idea of the town layout, just in case. I was really just putting into practice the things I'd picked up over time, along with lessons learned from Mike: "Time spent on reconnaissance is never wasted, Roger," and, "You must cover all contingencies," he'd advised, "If you intend coming out on horseback, then the rest of your plan better include finding a horse." Such thoughts were automatic to Mike, slowly becoming so to me, too, which is why I'd invited him out here to join me.

Even though my vigilance had been discreet, I obviously hadn't been discreet enough. And Kim was astute enough to notice. 'Relax love. Nobody even knows where we are yet,' she said.

'Don't they. You sure about that, are you?' I then told her about Andy Mathews, until recently, barman at the Transit Inn, and my Perth contact with the forces that be.

'So why didn't you tell me that before? On the drive up?'

'Didn't really think to.'

'Liar. OK, so we'll put it down t' yuh protecting me from t' truth.' She gave me a smile to let me know she wasn't too upset that I still wasn't including her in everything, including my thoughts. It was her day, and she wasn't going to let anything spoil it.

We ascended the highest point in the area, a conical, building that had the looks of a hatted grain silo. This was the Town Observation Tower, and it overlooked the port area, town, and coastline. At a mere twenty-six metres, it was not exactly the Empire State, but with the surrounding area being almost billiard table flat it did offer a 360 degree view over quite a distance. We then toured the port itself, and saw some of the world's largest ore carriers moored alongside, being loaded. OK, not exactly alongside. Well, they were, but alongside the end of a jetty which stretched out to sea, seemingly for miles. Far enough to where the water was deep enough to accept them. The water depth close in could be anything between maybe thirty feet and five feet, depending on the tide. It was one of the greatest tidal changes I recall seeing, high to low.

Everything round about was coated with the usual film of red ochre dust, apart from the area where solar stills were located. Here, in stark contrast to the huge, red pyramids of iron ore, glaring white dunes of salt also awaited shipment. The area was almost bereft of trees and vegetation.

Towns in this part of Western Australia are mainly single-storey affairs. Bungalow towns. The pub may have had an upper floor, but not too many of other buildings did.

The Esplanade - circa 1904, it said - the particular pub in which we were having lunch, did. Not that it meant anything to us. For as Australian bars don't exactly make females feel particularly welcome, even up here, where normal rules rarely seemed to apply, we again sat outside in another beer garden, beneath the shade of a parasol.

The air almost crackled with heat. The temperature climbing continually during the morning. Now, due to evaporation, clouds were building up out over the sea. Glaring white, billowing, higher and higher until their tops began to flatten out.

Earlier, I'd called the number Tony had given me, only to learn he was offshore, not expected back for two or three days. The guy who answered said he would pass on the message that I was in town. He also gave me the vessel's

Marisat number - for Marine Satellite he advised when questioned - so I could call Tony myself, via satellite, if I wished. Or had a need. At present I didn't, not really. I'd just been establishing my motives for being in this part of the world, my bona fides, should anyone be checking up on me. I was also making sure my presence was known, locally. If you have little to go on, and no more seems to be coming, then surely that's the time to try and make it come. With help it on its way, tomorrow I'd start pushing things even more, I decided. Today was to be devoted to Kim. She'd had a rough time of late, what with the damage to her house and all, and she'd certainly be out of the equation once Mike and Gerry did put in an appearance.

*

With her guide book informing her that the coastline around here was regarded as being particularly dangerous, Kim decided it was to be the hotel pool after lunch. Apparently not only were sharks to be found in abundance in the coastal waters, stone-fish, sea snakes, and the blue-ringed octopus - a rather deadly form of jellyfish - were also likely to be encountered, along with salt water crocodiles.

'Bugger that,' was her opinion. Mine too. Didn't fancy those odds. Anyway, I suspected I was about to have my hands full avoiding trouble on terra firma in the not too distant future. Even though nothing had so far actually pointed to this, it was another of my instinctive feelings. A strong one, too. It had been slowly building during the day, whilst we'd been in town. I'd kept alert, seen no signs of a tail, or of any possible watchers. This would have been difficult anyway, due to the general lack of people. But I still felt uneasy.

Out by the pool I endeavoured to relax and rest. I swam, watched the clouds continue their upward thrust, and I dozed between the periods when Kim insisted on oiling my bruised skin.

'Yell out if it hurts,' she said.

'Don't you worry about that, I will. That's for sure,' I told her. But I didn't, it just felt good. An indication that my body was rapidly healing, I hoped. And what with the sun and her continually wandering hands -'You're not supposed to rub oil down there' - I soon felt it was time to leave this place for somewhere more private. Kim had apparently already decided likewise, for she was packing her things. For her, this was an enjoyable day, that was obvious. It was reflected on her face, and by her actions. She had my undivided attention for a change, and the day was yet far from over.

Back in the airconditioned comfort of our room we seduced each other. We then chatted and rested some, before going at it again. It was a wondrous period of relaxation, my tensions evaporating to her diverse sexual antics.

That evening, we decided to dine in the restaurant, so, suitably dressed, we departed hand in hand, like teenagers on a first date. We were in total harmony with each other, but the mood was about to be broken.

There were two messages awaiting my arrival at the desk. Good news, bad news.

*   *

Chapter Twenty-seven

A STATEMENT OF INTENT

The message from Mike was to the effect that, due to unforseen circumstances, he would not be free to come out and join me. What it actually said was that his arrival in Australia could be delayed by up to ten days. Which, effectively, was the same thing. My hope was that everything could easily be over and done with in that time. Either that, or it wasn't about to happen at all, my theories being way off track.

To me, that still seemed extremely unlikely, or was that just wishful thinking?

That bad news message was a bitter blow. Mike had been my reliable back-up in case of trouble. With his help I could have taken a few extra chances in the hope of pushing things along. With no back-up, my hands were tied. I would now have to play by Bob's rules: collect what data I could whilst keeping a low profile, then pass everything over to him.

I did still have Gerry, but suspected any help he could supply would be limited to a quick look-see at Silver Springs. Provided it was even possible to get close enough so as to allow surveillance to take place. An idea such as that would not have posed a problem to someone of Mike's ilk, he'd been trained by the SAS, had a wealth of experience, probably enough to even have got us inside the place. But Gerry was something else. And even if he could somehow get me close, that would have to wait for at least another day. He wasn't due in until late tomorrow.

Anyway, I first wanted to have a word or two with Tony about a couple of things - ideas that had been developing in my mind for quite a time now - and his vessel was now due alongside the day after tomorrow, twenty-four hours earlier than expected. That had been the good news message.

Even so, the waiting was making me restless, I hated it. Waiting frayed the edges, because it meant the opposition - if there actually was anyone here in Port Hedland - held all the aces. Following such a marvellous day, such thoughts put a bit of a damper on the remains of the day.

Perth had been a warning. What someone was telling me was to leave off and move on. They didn't want me messing in their affairs. They must have realized they'd made a mistake in Adelaide. I could only think that what had happened to Andy Mathews was confirmation of that. He must have suffered, for I was sure my trust in him had been warranted.

A lot more than that, Minerva advised. *It says you're possibly getting too close to some truths, too close to exposing them.*

Yeah, well, just how close? And was I any closer now, here in Port Hedland?

Time will tell.

*

Come morning I had cast the bad news aside, nothing else to be done with Kim around to keep me on my toes. We again spent time relaxing by the pool. Kim lay around, looking good, whilst I studied her guide to the area. I occasionally dived in, just to cool off, then swam up and down for ten or twenty lengths. The bruising was receding, most of the aches were a thing of the past, and I was beginning to feel good again, health-wise. But I was also becoming impatient and uptight. Nor did I relish confronting Kim with what came next. With the memories of yesterday still fresh in her mind, I knew it wouldn't make her the happiest person in Port Hedland, but it had to be done.

'Got to go into town, love,' I told her. 'A few things I need check on.'

'OK. We'll go after lunch.'

'Not *we*, love. *Me*. I have to be alone this time.'

As she looked at me some kind of a nerve throbbed like a pulse in her neck.

'Why alone, Roger?'

'Well, you never know... I told you, I just don't want to involve you anymore than is necessary.'

'But I thought... hoped.. Well, with this Mike guy being out of the picture...'

'It changes things, love, doesn't put a stop to it.'

'Fuck it, Roger. Leave it t' Bob Bottomsworth.'

'Excuse me?'

'What?'

'Bob Bottomsworth. How do you know about him. I've never mentioned him.'

'Didn't need to, Roger. He contacted me, told me a few things. Put me in the picture.'

'Asked you to keep in touch, no doubt?'

'Well.... yes.'

The plot thickens.

It does that. So perhaps I should use this revelation to my advantage; someone to fill in for Mike in case of emergencies. But not yet. Didn't need Bob on my back right at this moment.

'You may as well advise him then,' I told Kim. 'Tell him it's all quiet up here, at present. But I still have to go into town on my own.'

'So what do I do in the meantime?'

'Just wait here, love. Do your own thing for a couple of hours. That's all I'll be.'

'I don't want to bloody well wait here. Anyway, you said you'd look after me.'

'And you'll help me do that if you stay put. Besides, my business is likely to be centred around the bars, where your presence would be a limiting factor.'

'Well sod it, Roger, I've had enough of waiting around. I may just go for a drive. And I'll come back when I'm good and ready.'

'Only a couple of hours, love,' I told her. But it didn't seem to help. The mood swing had been dramatic. I had never before seen her so out of sorts, and she remained so throughout a lunch that was taken almost in silence. The silence from my side was brought about by thoughts of Bob. What had he told her, and when? Why, come to that?

Afterwards, she climbed into the Ute and stormed off before I could stop her. Now she'd left me with no alternative, so I called a taxi and away I went, alone as planned. I hated leaving her like that, but there had been nothing else for it .

I felt terrible. It was like the parting of the ways.

I really had meant it when I'd told Kim I'd only be a couple of hours. And had it been up to me, that's as long as I would have been. How was I to know it would be for what seemed like forever.

*

It had all started with a fella called Tom. At least, after a long, frustrating time, it was Tom that gave me my first break.

Alf had been easy to find. Everyone knew him, pointed him out to me when I asked. He stood at the bar with his mate, both old timers. Friendly, as were most of the people I'd met around Port Hedland. It seemed to be the way. Just hoped these two would prove to have something more rewarding to tell me.

`How's it going?' I asked, parking myself alongside them. Could have used a stool, but there didn't seem to be any available. Standing was a man's thing, it seemed.

`Air fridge,' the one called Alf replied. Or something like that. Had me fooled for a second or two, then it clicked. Fair to middling, I deciphered. As in average. No doubt if I'd enquired what he'd had for brekkie he'd likely have replied, "emma necks", and a comment on the weather would plausibly have revealed, "scona rine", for it was looking like we'd have a shower or two in the not too distant future.

`Shout you guys a beer?' I asked, dropping into the vernacular as I addressed Alf.

`That'd be good. That right, Fred?'

`Bloody oath. Another beer'd go down well, mate,' Fred agreed.

Once in town I'd started off by asking around, trying to gather some information on the chemical facility out at Silver Springs. Prying would be more apt, it seemed, for my enquiries had revealed nothing. The place might never have existed. Everyone I'd approached so far appeared to either, not know, as in - "Wouldn't have a clue, mate"; weren't saying - "Give it away, sport"; were reluctant to do so - "Heard mention of it is all"; or were totally indifferent altogether, as in "Eh?" Even the Commonwealth Employment Services office I'd visited had been unable to help; "Don't recruit locally, mate. Nor through the CES. All handled by some outfit in Melbourne". A blank wall in other words.

Which is when I'd come across Tom. Or rather, he'd come across me. Bit of a bludger was Tom. Likeable old chap though, despite his tendency to be on the scrounge.

I'd been ambling along, deep in thought, just about ready to give up on this line of attack and get a taxi back to the Walkabout, when he sidled alongside. Oldish fella, white beard, white hair sticking out from beneath a greasy, battered hat, shirt and slacks, sandals. Like I say, a friendly old coot. He introduced himself before making his pitch.

`Heard yuh was askin' around. Get any answers?'

`None I wanted to hear. What's with that place?'

`Keeps themselves to themselves, yuh know how it is.'

`And?'

`Me, mate? I don't know, either. But yuh might try Alf. Probably find him down at the Pier Hotel.

`He got a surname, this Alf?'

`Probably.'

I smiled at him, but nothing more was forthcoming. `Here you go then, Tom. Thanks for your help.' I gave him a twenty. Enough for a few stubbies, or a couple of bottles of plonk.

OK, so now I had Alf. Probably to be found at the bar of the Pier Hotel. Probably had a surname. Could even be Probably, but I doubted it. Worth twenty dollars, wasn't it?

So, naturally, the Pier hotel was where I went next. Found Alf. Introduced myself. We shook hands, but he didn't

237

offer me a surname either. But that didn't matter, seemed he didn't know either. Not his surname, any information I was after. But after I'd shouted a couple of beers he did offer information of another kind. Enough to raise the hopes.

`Aw, old Josh'd be the one to know about that. Lived round these parts all his life. That right, Fred?'

`Yeah,' Fred agreed. `Reckon he'd be your man, all right.' Fred didn't look at either of us as he spoke, didn't seem interested, in anything, apart from the amber nectar I was buying. I was still sipping at my first, they were on their third. Admittedly, they were only small glasses, but they must have had a fair few before I'd arrived on the scene.

`OK,' I told Alf. `I'll talk to him. Josh you say?' Didn't see any point asking for a surname. `Where would I find him?'

That appeared to get Fred's attention all right. They looked at one another, questioningly, seemingly deep in thought. It was as if this was the most awesomely complex sentence they had ever been called upon to unravel.

Alf looked me directly in the eye for a couple of seconds, as if he couldn't believe what he was seeing. Then he turned his attention back to Fred. His next gesture was rather more gallic in nature than Australian. As dramatic a piece of body language as I'd ever seen. A kind of pouting, upturned-hands, shoulder-shrugging display that expressed a lot and said nothing. Although his next comment told me he was probably questioning the extent of my stupidity.

`Find him down at the cementary,' was how he pronounced it. `As for talking to him, well, that'd be a neat trick. Died last year.'

`Oh, shit,' I said.

`Probably his last thought,' suggested Alf. `That right, Fred?'

`Bloody oath,' Fred agreed, draining his glass yet again.

The old brick wall syndrome, I mused. Back to the Walkabout then. About time anyway, Kim should be back by now. Probably wondering where I'd got to.

Still on my first glass, I drank up and made to leave, but Alf placed a restraining hand on my arm; possibly saw his next beer disappearing with me.

238

'Nah, don't be in such a rush, young feller. There's allus time for one more.' He stared suggestively at his empty glass, so I wiggled a finger at the barman, indicating I was shouting yet another round.

'You mean there's something else, right?'

'That about gets it. Yuh see, old Josh might have gone walkabout. Still leaves Randy.'

'Randy?' I looked at Alf, aspirations rising.

'Yeah, old Josh's brother.'

*

As so often happens, the next event took place when I least expected it. But maybe I should have, asking questions all over town the way I had been. After all, whispers speak, word travels, if there was anyone around here they would soon have learnt of my presence, which is when things would begin to happen.

I was feeling quite pleased. It had turned out to be a pleasant, if frustrating, afternoon. Frustrating at first, but I felt it had ended rather well.

Randy had related to me tales of people he'd known who had gone to work at Silver Springs, and had simply "gone walkabout," as he put it.

'In what way?'

'Never bloody seen again.'

'Made some money and moved into the cities, maybe?' I suggested.

'Give it away. These guys 'd have bin in touch.'

'And they haven't?'

'Bloody oath.'

'You been to anybody with this?'

'Shouldn't even be telling you. But I figure being a pom, you'll do right by me; keep my name out of it.'

'Fair enough, Randy, I'll do that. You have any names?'

With what he gave me I thought I just about had enough to warrant calling in Bob and his crowd. But before that happened I still wanted that word with Tony, day after tomorrow.

Answers to questions were forming in my mind. Now, with darkness descending like a sultry curtain it really was time for a return to the hotel, and Kim. She was no doubt in a mood already, and doubted it would be exactly the mood I would have wished. My two hours had become three and a half.

Up above, the moon had appeared; no more than a bitten-into slice of honeydew melon.

We'd left the pub and walked to wherever it was Randy hung out. It couldn't have taken us more than five minutes. OK, ten at the outside. Whatever, at the pace Alf travelled that made it not far. Or so it had seemed at the time. But now, after leaving there to walk back to where I could get a taxi, I wasn't so sure. Couldn't quite figure out where I was.

It happened as I was looking round for somewhere from which to phone for a taxi, saw what looked like yet another pub, away down the road. It was that instinctive kind of thing some of us get and some of us don't. Probably goes with the territory in which I was now involved.

I became suddenly aware of how quiet it was. Or did it just appear to be quiet, my mind otherwise engaged, concentrating on other issues, transmitting warnings.

Someone was here, nearby, I knew for certain. I'd been alerted by that unknown feeling which conveys the message that an enemy is close. Not *just* another person. Someone intent on doing you harm.

I don't know what made me aware of it; not sight, because I hadn't seen anyone; not sound, smell, or touch, for similar reasons. How about taste then? Almost, but not quite. The taste in my mouth was possibly a result of their presence, not confirmation of it. Which left me with that elusive, indefinable, but gratifying, sixth sense phenomena.

Still no one was visible, but I knew for sure they were there. Somewhere close-by.

If they were trying to frighten me they were a hundred and eighty degrees out of phase. I'm as tolerant as the next man, probably more so, but if anyone tries to push me around I can become very bloody minded indeed. And tolerance I was just about out of.

Then there was somebody. He stepped right out in front of me as I turned a corner, just like the guy in Perth. Only this time I'd had but one small glass of beer, and a perceived warning, so I was in total control of all my faculties, and on the alert.

Then one became two, the first moving in without so much as a word being spoken as soon as the second made his presence known. Seems he thought he had me by the proverbials. I thought different. When people suspect they have you by the balls is when they themselves are at their most vulnerable, and this guy proved to be not much of a problem at all. He was too out of shape to be fast. So all it required was to use his momentum, a foot in one place, an arm in another, and over she goes. That left his mate, who was much bigger, and looked far tougher. But something told me that's all it was; looking tough was an act. I decided to put him to the test.

From my pocket I produced a knife. Not any old knife, this was a Laguiode (pronounced layole) - named after a small town in Southwestern France where they'd been invented back in 1829. The juniper burl handle was delicately curved to fit the hand, the blade, when opened out, was pointed and dauntingly sharp. The base of the blade on my version was adorned by a bee, the mark of authenticity. It was sleek and elegant. So much so, that in their country of origin they are often used as tableware.

I had always carried a knife, ever since my scouting days. This one had replaced the Swiss Army type I had recently lost in South Africa. And although the Victorinox had been very versatile, the Laguiode was much better suited to an occasion such as this.

I'd never been involved in a knife fight, hadn't much idea of how to go about it once it started - made a mental note to do something about that in the future. What I did know, was how to look as if I knew what I was about: eyes alert, locked on his; body crouched ready to spring; knife projecting from the thumb end of the hand, prepared to thrust or slash; left arm raised for balance, or to protect my body.

I must have looked impressive enough. Or maybe he hadn't a clue either, decided I did know a thing or two, for he quickly backed down. Took me by surprise, really. So, what now?

Buying time whilst I decided on my next move, I told

him to get over next to his mate, who now sat up, seemingly wondering what the hell had happened. That way I could at least keep an eye on them both.

Chastened, if not pacified, he obeyed, just as his mate started to get back on his feet. Instant compliance, which should have served to warn me.

The third one I didn't see, for he came up from behind, ever so quietly, so next thing I knew, I was eyeball to eyeball with the dusty red earth. Then they were punching me, in the stomach and face, kicking me when I was down, picking me up and punching me again. More bruises to join those well on the way to disappearing. My face puffed up like a football and I was bleeding from nose and mouth. One eye closed completely, the other, no more than a slit through which the view was naturally restricted, and somewhat blurred. This was only partially true, for my eyes had closed automatically; protection, the body's natural defence mechanism at work. It was my decision not allowing them to open fully. Let them think I couldn't see. That I was more injured than in actual fact was the case. Create advantages wherever possible when on the defensive. No strength left to try anything physical. Nothing else left to do. This is where I die, I thought. Another planned accident. The taste of defeat was heavy in my mouth - or was that the metallic taste of blood - and my exploring tongue discovered a missing tooth, front left.

Then I truly couldn't see, for a blackness unexpectedly washed over me.

*

When I did come to - had to be a very short time later, for no one appeared to have moved - I felt slightly better. But now my limited vision told me I was looking at the business end of a sawn-off shotgun, the barrel of which flicked to the left a couple of times before centring on my stomach. The gesture needed no words to accompany it. I doubted it was filled with birdshot, either. I recalled once seeing what one of these charged with anti-personnel shot could do to a body. Didn't bear thinking about.

As commanded, I followed where the first one led, the rest somewhere behind me. Not far too behind, but far enough.

Eventually we came to where their vehicle was parked, a shiny Range Rover. I was ordered to get in the back, the two behind crowding in with me.

Not instant death then. And where there's life there's hope, I reminded myself.

They weren't even trying, I realised. Disorientation is a good start towards breaking someone. I knew that, but it was obviously news to these guys. Or would have been. There was no blindfold, no bonds. I was free to move, had I felt capable. Not right now, but I was improving by the minute. Superficial wounds that looked worse than they really were, sandals not best for kicking someone into submission. There again, that shotgun more or less quelled any thoughts of heroics, plus the fact there were now four of them.

We immediately drove off, heading out of town and away from the coast. Inland, where there was a lot of nothing, I knew, thanks to Kim's tourist guide. Not a very comforting thought. Nor was the fact that I was allowed to see where we were going. This told me a lot. Not about *where* we were going - towards Marble Bar, I figured - but it was, to me, a clear indication that I wasn't expected to be able to put the data to any useful purpose. I knew I wasn't expected to return from wherever it was we were now headed.

But my disappearance in itself would serve a useful purpose, if they thought about it. By offing me, they were confirming my theories to be correct. And Kim now knew all about my theories. That would be a big help to Bob.

But, of course, that knowledge wasn't going help me at all. Not in the least little bit.

*   *

243

Chapter Twenty-eight

RED HOT, AND RED

*T*he centre of Australia is known as the Red Centre, for obvious reasons. Not just because it is hot, which it undoubtably is, but because it *is* red. The ground is red, the rocks are red, and, inevitably, the people are usually red; covered with the same film of dust that manages to coat almost everything in the area. The same could be said of the Northwest, for our Range Rover was now red, and clouds of orange dust billowed up in our wake. At least, had it been daylight they'd have been red and orange, tonight though, they were a uniform, dirty grey.

It was apparently still warm enough out there to make it hot in here, for the windows were almost closed against the choking dust. There were five sweating bodies generating heat. It was also very uncomfortable, for despite the ruts, this guy drove like he thought he was Ayrton Senna, but with little of the skill, and we couldn't be doing more that thirty mph! My hands gripped the edges of the seat. It didn't exactly help any, but at least it served to keep my thoughts off food and drink and cool, cool air. My conscious thoughts, that is. Until eventually, inevitably, the heat and the aches gradually receded to a point at which a negative adrenaline rush slowly overcame my will to remain awake.

I began to drift into a state of delirium, my mind's eye throwing up images of airconditioned bars, swimming pools, and a soft bed. I imagined myself laying down on it, just for a minute or two... With difficulty I shrugged it off. For a time.

To sleep now would be foolish, Minerva told me. *That's the kind of sleep from which you never wake.* But it seemed I wasn't listening, and anyway the advice had been wrong. I did sleep, and I did wake up.

*

Although it was much later when I did open my eyes again, three things became immediately apparent: it was daylight; I was no longer in a vehicle; and my eyes *had* opened, *both* of them. But what had caused them to open?

Then I not only felt it, I saw it. A very small rodent was inquisitively nudging my cheek, nose quivering, probably checking to see if I was edible. But he was far too small to have any hope of tackling me.

Then I twitched, and he was gone. Far too quickly for me to think of reversing the situation. That was my breakfast scampering away, soon to be out of sight.

It was hot already, becoming hotter as the sun climbed higher, heat now reflecting of the sandy ground. I could imagine what it would be like in the middle of the day, had already forgotten how cold it had been during the night. So that must have woken me at one time, too, though apparently not for long.

I'd slept at least ten hours, I figured. Not deep sleep for the first part, for I recall briefly jerking awake now and again as we hit yet another pothole or ridge. But subconscious thought told me that had ended long ago. No matter, I still felt terrible. Aches and pains all over.... but I *was* still alive. I was also on my own, in the middle of nowhere. No food, no water, no shade. Alive. That fact alone was worth rejoicing over, though how long I would remain alive I had yet to determine. Yes, determine, for that decision was mine alone. My fate was in my hands, or those of my God.

I looked up at the sky, it was high and blue, and it went

245

on forever, as did the land. In such a vast expanse, were a helicopter were to appear, I imagined it couldn't fail to spot me. And a helicopter could probably cover the distance in no time at all. Wishful thinking all round, as Minerva was quick to remind me.

Helicopter? Don't be bloody stupid. The only people who know your location aren't about to send a chopper to the rescue. And despite the feeling you'll be visible from miles away, you know that not to be the case. To someone up there, looking down, you'll be a minute speck. Hoofing it is the only chance you have.

Two sets of tracks were apparent to my still limited vision, both heading in the same direction, which told me my captors had gone back the way they had come. Probably nowhere else *to* go from here. So, that was one problem solved. It was like they'd left me a map without a scale. I knew exactly the direction in which I needed to travel, just had no idea how far. We'd been on the move for at least three hours that I could remember, but how far had they driven after I fell asleep, before they tossed me out? Too far, I imagined, otherwise I would already have been dead. They had just decided to let nature take care of me, die in my own time, of thirst and starvation, rather than shoot me. Those one-way tracks more or less confirmed that too. I gathered the place they'd brought me to wasn't exactly Australia's favourite picnic location. Nor was I going to be able to catch the bus back, never mind a bloody helicopter.

OK, first things first; an assessment of my situation. Bloody awful, truth be told. Disregard. Where there's life, and all that. I had been in a similar situation and survived, and I'd been in worse physical shape that time, so here we go.

Disregarding the numerous aches, in places I hadn't realized existed, I stood up and looked around. Aches and pain could be ignored, needed to be.

The infinite ground either side was a burnt ochre, the sky deep-blue; colours much enhanced by the dry, clear air. There was very little in the way of bush. But there was life, even out here, as I had just seen.

The immensity of the land was obvious, it just went on and on as far as a fully sighted person could see, and then

246

some. Distances in this country were so vast as to be almost incomprehensible: "Darwin, for instance, the capital of the Northern Territory - an area three times the size of California - is closer to both Jakarta and Manila than it is to Sydney or Melbourne." I remembered Tony telling me that. Which did nothing at all to reassure me given the situation in which I now found myself.

I was well able to survive in hostile terrain - a result of that previous experience, not training - but I wasn't equipped for this. I recall being drenched in sweat, felt like I was dying of thirst already, would eventually do so if things didn't improve significantly in the near future. But it didn't look as if that was about to happen anytime soon. They had cleaned me out. I didn't mind the money so much, hadn't carried a lot anyway, never did these days. What did piss me off was the fact that they'd taken my knife, the most useful item I'd had with me. Even the next most useful thing was missing - my handkerchief. Just as at the seaside in childhood, that handkerchief would have kept the direct sunlight off hy head. Like I said, they'd cleaned me out.

I'd previously dismissed all warnings of heat addled brains, and holes in the ozone layer, to be the rants of jealous friends about to face a northern winter. But, upon arrival in Australia, I *had* taken notice. It didn't take long to ascertain that the stockman's hat was not worn as an item of fancy dress, but as a natural, and essential, accessory. My hat they hadn't taken. Primarily as I hadn't been wearing it at the time!

They had overlooked my watch though, which told me none of them had been Scouts. Not that the time of day meant a lot to me, but direction certainly did. And had any of them at one time been a scout, he'd have known all about the old trick of establishing direction by relating the hands of a watch to the sun's position, taking account of the fact I was now in the southern hemisphere. The fact that it was a digital watch made no difference whatsoever. All it took was for me to draw hands in the sand in the appropriate positions, and bingo. It was very easy to wander round in circles if you had no point of reference, and those tracks could disappear at anytime given inclement weather; which probably meant they could remain for years!

Of course, leaving me with the watch could also mean that they didn't much care if I did know which way was what; that it was impossible for me to reach anywhere on foot from where I was.

I felt like crying out, but a cry for help would only waste itself in this vast emptiness. A waste of energy too. So I used my watch, plotted a course west north west. Just as I figured, it was also the way those tyre tracks led. But one breath of wind and they would likely be gone.

Suddenly my thoughts interrupted were. I stopped, refocused my vision, concentrating as best I could. Nothing to be seen now, but my limited peripheral vision had caught a movement in the distance. I was sure of it. And too far away for it to have been my small mousey visitor.

Straining my eyes, I shaded them against the sun, striving to decide what it was, if anything. A mirage, maybe? More wishful thinking, visual this time? The sun could do strange things to a person, maybe it ... No! There it was again.

Shit! The lazy rolling gait of a camel! In Australia? I hadn't known they had camels here. Still it served to remind me of what I had to do in order to get out of this mess. Catch one and ride it home? Not quite, but I did need to do what it, and that mousey creature, were doing; survive in this wilderness.

I thought about that as I staggered along. No point stopping, I had a limited survival time, needed to make full use of it.

Survival is the same no matter what the environment; adapt to your surroundings, don't fight them. There *was* life out here, I was already aware of that. And it existed because these creatures were survivors. They used this alien world and it's meagre offerings to advantage. I had to emulate them. But not necessarily camels and kangaroos. Plants are what you look for. Birds and animals can move elsewhere if they don't like their present location, plants don't have that option, they have to stay and adapt. That some fauna had also chosen to remain here boosted my flagging morale.

At least my mind was functional, keeping track of things. That was essential too. So I searched around, making sure I only moved in the direction in which I'd decided survival

248

lay, keeping track using my scouting knowledge and watch. Tyre tracks were still visible, just. But all too often those disappeared on patches of firmer ground.

Occasionally I found a few bits and pieces to chew on, some leaves, but mainly they were dry. They'd suffice, until my mouth dried out so there was no saliva to break them down. And in the words of Crocodile Dundee, they did taste like shit, but as long as there was a possibility they'd help keep me alive, I'd force them down. Hopefully there would be other offerings in time, too, providing I kept my eyes open, stayed alert. Small crawly things, some of them slimy; they would all help. Difficult to swallow, but necessary. And there was no point waiting until I became desperate enough not to care what they tasted like, by then it may be too late. Sod's law dictated that would be the least likely time to find anything. Apart from which, I needed to retain enough energy to enable me to compete with everything else around. I wouldn't be the only one looking for a quick snack. That very lucky mousey creature for instance. The only advantage I had was that almost anything would do me, others had the constricting limits of size, dietary constraints, and gullibility to be taken into account. They did have the advantage in that they knew what was edible and what was not. What would help them survive, and what would kill them. I only had my instincts to advise me in that department. And Minerva, of course, which really amounted to the same thing. But sometimes you survive only because you're prepared to die. Danger becomes your friend and ally.

There was no shade, so no point resting during the day. Besides, I wasn't tired. I was everything else, but not yet tired. I'd just slept for I don't know how long. Restless and disturbed, at the start, but after that, the sleep of the dead. Which is what I would be if I didn't motivate myself and keep moving.

As the sun continued the search for the top of its arc, so the shadows moved, became shorter, altering contours as they did so, landscape seemingly changing before my eyes. Features that stood out in the morning sun tended to disappear in the flat light of noon, and vice versa as the sun once again started on its inevitable descent.

I tried to force myself to count steps, not only to keep the mind occupied but also to get an idea of distance covered. In that I failed, miserably. The need was to know what lay ahead, I already knew what was behind.

I continued right through the heat of the day, and it *was* hot. By noon I imagined the temperature to have risen well into triple figures, Fahrenheit, of course. Had to be. And although it was a dry heat, therefore slightly more bearable, it still lay heavy. Forward motion was becoming something of a struggle now; mind over matter.

I was still going as the sun went down, albeit at a much reduced pace. My movements that is, not the sun's. And as that ball of fire finally disappeared over the horizon, the landscape abruptly became monochrome. Then it too disappeared, like a developing photograph in reverse. A darkness as thick as velvet was broken only by last night's moon, that same piece of bitten-into melon. Albeit, maybe a slightly larger bite. But as my eyes slowly adjusted, I began to pick out the stars. It was like they were being switched on one by one. First tens, then there were hundreds, thousands, millions. My estimate kept upgrading itself until the figures became unbelievable. So bright, I had no problem following whatever Town and Country spoor remained, which meant my sight was returning to normal. Confirmation of this was the fact I was able to pick out little pairs of eyes, peering out of the darkness. Breakfast!

As the night wore on it brought with it the cold. Amazing the difference in temperature between night and day in a place like this. It has to be experienced to be believed.

Now I was tiring, but the cold helped me keep going. It forced me on. I had to keep moving to keep from shivering. I longed now for that hundred plus, searing afternoon sun. Found it impossible to imagine how unbearably hot it had been during the day. God, I was beginning to sound like the people back home. First they complain about the cold in winter, then, as soon as the sun comes out in earnest, if it ever does, they complain about the heat. I was just the opposite.

On and on I forced myself, Minerva reminding me of the fact it was either that, or die out here. Die of cold, in one of the hottest places on earth!

The instinct for survival is strong. Even when you think you can't take any more, on the very edge of consciousness, there remains a bit of survival instinct in the very recesses of your mind. It was that which now controlled my movements. Had to be.

It was that same instinct which forced me to look towards the east. Some mysterious impulse warned me that something was happening out there. It was. The first faint glimmer of dawn. I'd made it through my first night. I would make the next, too, and the one after that. As many as were necessary, until I arrived somewhere. That was certainly a fact. The question was, would that "somewhere" be; material, or celestial.

The land was now nowhere near as flat as it had been. That is not to say it was suddenly mountainous, but it had begun to rise and fall slightly, small hillocks and troughs, though that didn't make walking that much more difficult than it already was. No easier either!

Still occasionally looking back, marvelling at the sight, yet moving ahead, I staggered, dragged a foot in the earth, and the next thing I knew I was down there among it. I checked myself over, slowly, knowing there was no damage, delaying getting up again only because it felt so good to be laying down. Just for a few minutes A little rest.

No! Minerva warned. *Get up now, you must. Otherwise you'll remain here forever. It will be your last resting place.*

I knew that to be good advice, tried to act upon it, to rise, but my arms and legs didn't seem to want to obey. I attempted to force myself.....

*

The relentless heat was back, dragging me out of a world where I'd been helping to build an igloo. There had been Eskimos. Polar bears, too. Seemingly so real and alive I briefly wondered if yesterday's sun hadn't been too much for my brain. Decided not, for I was still capable of rational thought. I recalled tripping on the undulating earth, eventually crawling a short distance to the sheltered hollow in which I now lay. Even realized why I wasn't hungry; remembered breakfasting as I walked, or staggered. Some careless, furry creature I'd caught during the night. Snuffed the life out of him, told myself that something else probably would have had it not been me. Didn't make me feel any better, but I didn't feel too bad about it either. Just needed to get it done and over with before I could see what it was. Told myself it was underdone beef, and that had done the trick.

Time to move on again provided my legs would hold me up, if my arms would help me up to begin with. But they wouldn't. I was suddenly frozen to the spot, couldn't believe what my eyes were seeing.

He stood absolutely motionless, staring ahead at nothing I could see, seemingly lost in thought. Probably communicating with spirits of the Never-Never, I assumed. Gerry had told me a little bit about that. I was sensible enough to realize it was based on superstition and the occult. I was also sensible enough not to dismiss it out of hand, for I had my own superstitions, as do we all, if we are honest with ourselves.

After a time, must have been a couple of minutes at least, his head turned, slowly. Not searching, it just sort of tracked round then stopped, facing towards where I lay. The action was both fascinating and chilling, like the turret of a tank, its gun swinging onto a pre-programmed target. It was as if he'd known all the time I was there, yet I was sure he couldn't easily see me from his position.

He didn't hesitate, started to walk forward. Didn't look left or right, just straight ahead. The only spot of any interest to him was the shallow hollow where I lay. Half hidden, I imagined.

*   *

Chapter Twenty-nine

TRICKS 'N' TRACKS

Hard to judge age with his modest beer belly, dark, crinkly, weatherbeaten skin, oddly-sloped forehead, and large flattened nose. He looked right out of the stone age. A modern neanderthal man. His hair, what I could see of it, was a strange yellowy-brown, and grizzled. He smelled of stale sweat, wood-smoke and ash. If pushed on age I'd have guessed at between twenty and fifty.

His clothes weren't right for his shape. The brown trousers he wore were several sizes too large, rolled up at the bottom, rolled down at the waist to make them fit. He had on a red and blue striped sports shirt. At least it gave the appearance of originally being red and blue. Only now it was a reddish, dusty colour - and, despite the temperature, he wore a woolly ski hat. But for all that, to me he was an angel. In fact, more than; an angel with a water bag.

He smiled and passed it to me, never said a word, so I assumed he probably didn't speak much in the way of English, or Australian. Well, this wasn't the time or place to worry about such minor matters, we were communicating well enough already, it seemed.

I raised the spout to my mouth and drank. It was warm, brackish, bitter, and, dare I mention it, tasted like... well, you know what. But after... how long? A day and a half, in this heat, it hit the spot, as they say, instantly reviving me, supplying my body with the moisture it so desperately craved. I sipped at it, rubbed a little on my face. It felt good, but I didn't want to waste too much, didn't know how long it had to last us. I assumed it was now *us;* that he hadn't just happened to be passing by. So I decided I'd better establish our relationship.

I handed back the bag, nodding silent thanks, wondering how to begin. He looked at me, waiting, seemingly sensing I wanted to talk. Almost willing me to. So I did.

`You, I,' I said, pointing a finger, first at him, then myself. `We go? Walk?' I used my fingers again, two of them representing legs walking. `Port Hedland,' I said, pointing off in what I assumed to be the general direction.

He smiled at me, condescending like, a white-toothed smile, I noticed. Probably used some kind if bark for cleaning his teeth; secret recipe, handed down through the generations. I got the impression he desperately wanted to understand me, couldn't, but was determined to try.

`Walk?' he said, miming my finger action. `Port Hedland?' The words were surprisingly clear, yet he looked as if he hadn't understood the name. He then hesitated slightly, as if deciding what guttural utterings to try next. He wasn't, he was taking the piss.

`No bloody way, mate,' he said. `It's miles. Got a car down the road.'

I felt a right prat, told him so. `Didn't think you'd speak the lingo,' I gave as my excuse.

`Bloody Australia, mate. Take English at school. Some of the old fellers maybe don't do so good, but some of us young guys maybe don't do so good in the bush. Swings and dodgems.'

Close enough, I thought.

`Call me John,' he said. 'No way you could handle my tribal name.' He smiled as he held out his hand.

`Roger,' I responded, shaking.

`Yeah, I know. Yuh don't look too crook to me, but

254

better yuh wear this.' He haded me a wooly hat just like his own.

'Eat anything?' he asked.

`Bit of this and that. Bloody starving now.' Part relief at being rescued, I imagined. How could he...? But my train of thought was interrupted.

`Right then, we'll have this bugger. Could use a bit of a feed meself.' Reaching behind his back he pulled out a goanna like he was a magician. Must have had it tucked into the piece of cord that served as a belt.

`What about the car?'

`Nah, don't worry, it don't eat.' He laughed at his joke, then explained. `Car's about ten miles, no point walking, let them come to us.'

`Then? Who are *them?'*

`Couple o' fellers. And Gerry.'

`Gerry! You didn't just stumble across me then, you were out looking?'

`Yeah, we was looking.'

`Of course! That's how you knew my name. Well, John, if we wait here, how will they know where to find us?'

`They'll know. I found yuh, didn't I. Let's light a fire and get cooking, maybe they'll see the smoke.' He winked.

`Light a fire? How do we go about ....? Ah!' I pointed a finger at him. `Two pieces of wood, some dry grass, and kangaroo droppings?' I knowingly suggested.

`Nah, mate. Too bloody difficult, he said, sticking a hand in his pocket then withdrawing it again. `I use these.' He rattled a box of matches at me and laughed again, as though at some secret joke. 'Bet you think we use bloody bark or something to clean our teeth.'

No way I could reply to that.

*

We'd finished eating by the time the next head poked up over the rise. I was taken completely by surprise, for they just suddenly appeared, as if by parthenogenesis, or some means even more removed from reality. I'd neither seen nor heard them approach, although I suspected John had, even though he'd never so much as looked up from his eating, or warned me.

The weather was the same as it had been every other day I'd spent up here; a cloudless sky, blazing sun, dry, still, and hot.

It had been obvious at our first meeting that Gerry had a high regard for this country, especially the northwest. He loved it up here, that was obvious now, too. He understood it. He also understood, and empathized, with it's original inhabitants; the aborigines.

`All they really wish for is to be left alone, with their own land. To do as they please,' he'd told me back there in Perth. 'They don't want modern society with all it's red tape and laws. They have their own laws,' he'd explained. 'Acknowledge that and you'll get on just fine.'

And here we were, getting on fine. Gerry was with me now, John having moved over to join the rest of his group.

They sat upright on their haunches, a little distance away, muttering quietly among themselves. John reached up a hand to remove his hat and scratch at his hair, immediately falling into what appeared to be an earnest discussion between friends, their faces close together, deliberating. So, as we waited for them to complete what looked to be a kind of board meeting in the bush - I imagined John to be relating the tale of how this white fella had thought he wouldn't be able to communicate, for they were all falling about, laughing and giggling. Meanwhile Gerry told me a bit more about himself.

Out in the open this was a different Gerry altogether. He dressed like he'd lived in the bush all his life. `Well,' he informed me when I remarked on the fact, `for a good part of my childhood, I did. In fact I'm a sort of an honorary Abo. I'm accepted. A result of having spent much of my early life among them. I don't need a permit to visit their tribal lands, not in WA, at least. Especially with these fellas, the Nyungar."

Then I remembered seeing that camel, asked Gerry if I'd been imagining things.

'Nah. There are thousands of em. Now feral, they were imported in the 1900s to help with colonization, but once mechanized transport became readily available they were just released and left to get on with it.'

Then I told him how I woke up to find John standing in the near distance, seemingly in a trance.

`Yeah, right. He'd know you were around, somewhere close. Be looking for you,' he said. But he could see the contradiction forming in my mind.

`Not physically looking, in the way we know, he explained. `This is his piece of land, his and his relations, living and dead. He knows everything that happens out here, whether he's around or not. He senses it, feels it, sees it in a dream, who knows. When it comes to Abos, Roger, don't go by what you've heard or presumed, only by what you know, or have witnessed. They believe the spirit can leave the body and go places, travel through space if you like. These are the dream journeys. He took a trip. But he found you, can't argue. with that.'

He was right there. I didn't even want to try. I was just thankful they *had* found me. Especially when Gerry pointed out on the map where we were. His finger traced a route that wasn't actually there, across featureless land. I knew then, just looking at the distance, I never would have made it back on my own.

'Mind you, we did have a good set of tyre tracks to follow,' Gerry added with a twinkle in his eye. 'And they seemed to lead us in the right direction.'

'Ah, right. But what alerted you in the first place? I guess Kim was worried when I didn't show up, came looking for you.'

'Kim? Who's Kim? It was then I realized I had never explained to him about my domestic arrangements. Gerry knew nothing about Kim, although Kim had been aware of Gerry's imminent arrival. This caused me to ponder on the reason she *hadn't* sought him out. But the explanation for that appeared to be answered without the question even being raised.

'John here met me at the airport, told me of his fears. We set off more or less right away.'

So, it seemed my two hours would have turned into something like forty-eight by the time we got back. I was definitely going to be in someone's bad books. Couldn't be helped now. Besides, I had just come up with what I saw as a brilliant idea.

Looking at the map again I noticed there *was* a road

257

marked, quite a way off from where we now were, but not exactly out of reach. If we were to make a small diversion, providing it was possible over this terrain, we could join it, then drive back to Hedland by that route. A much better option, I thought. Especially as it passed reasonably close to a place called Silver Springs.

*

To call it a car would be an overstatement. Once, long ago, it could have answered to that description. By now though it was ....well, not exactly in the first flush of youth. Most of the trim was hanging off. There were some very important-looking pieces hanging down beneath also, from what little that was in sight, but I decided to ignore them. Everyone else was, and they seemed quite willing to ride in it. And I had far more reason to want to ride in it than they did.

Even though all the doors had been left open, it was stifling inside. The seat was so hot the first touch almost burnt my hand, and it was some time before I dare lay my back against the seat backrest. The windows didn't close all the way, one not at all, for it was missing, and it wasn't long before I was as red as the rest of them.

There were three of us in the back, Gerry sat up front with the, er... guide. Driver would be the wrong word entirely in this context, for that signifies some degree of control. This thing wandered from one side to the other without any input from the wheel whatsoever. Any wheel movement was just a correction, which is to say even guiding it must have been very hard work indeed.

`Guess they figured my body would be discovered sooner or later,' I told Gerry, relating to what had happened. `Another accident, rather than a killing. Took what little I had, to make things more difficult.'

`I know mate,' John said. `I saw it all bloody happen.'

`And if he says he saw it,' Gerry quickly added, `then he did. One way or another, fair dinkum. And you'd do well to believe him.'

By now I did. We had to be getting some kind of spiritual help, I figured, just to keep this car going the way it was, getting us to where it did.

When we did stop it was so sudden, in relative terms,

our personal dust cloud continued, swamping the vehicle for a while before clearing enough so we could see. In fact, that cloud had as good as passed us by when we did eventually roll to a standstill.

*

From a distance, the high-security research laboratory at Silver Springs looked like any other industrial complex anywhere in the world. Squat, blockhouse-like concrete buildings, all single storey. With one exception. A miniature control tower which served what from this aspect looked like a small airstrip. None of it looked out of place, until you remembered where it was situated. These were the observations formed when viewing it through Gerry's binoculars. The distance was necessarily great, for all around was almost open land, with only the occasional hillock close by the fence. On this side, anyway. Over on the far side I could make out what looked like an area of bush and scrub, but well distanced from us, as was the security fence which surrounded the place.

'John, any chance we can get behind one of those in daylight, without being spotted?' I asked, pointing at the hillocks.

He stared ruminatively Into the middle distance, his eyes seeming to glaze over. And it seemed an age before he answered.

'No worries, Roger. Easy-peasy, to us fellers. Have to dress you up a bit though.'

*

Inconspicuous was one thing that could *not* be said about the siting of the Slade Laboratories' Pharmaceutical Research Division. There wasn't another building within fifty miles, probably even a hundred, yet the whole facility was surrounded by a substantial chain-link fence. And if I was right in my thinking, there were sure to be other security precautions in place. Electronic listening devices and such. Some perhaps buried. Some perhaps lethal.

'You see any signs of ground disturbance inside that fence?' I asked Gerry. 'Any indication of hidden devices?'

'Nothing obvious. Difficult to tell from where the vegetation begins though.'

I looked across to where a wide strip of healthy vegetation fronted the buildings. Well tended grass and flower-beds. Obviously well watered, which pointed to the likelihood of a borehole.

'Maybe that's the reason for the vegetation,' I suggested. Could be something hidden in there.'

'Could be. But why. All the way out here?'

'Well, there will be government rules on health and safety that need to be complied with wherever chemicals are involved. Location would not necessarily negate those.'

'Suppose not. But just what is in view seems to be taking health and safety to the absolute limit.'

*

John had been right. Easy-peasy, indeed. We were just a group of Abos, wandering around. No challenges, nothing at all. It seemed as if no one was even watching us. Maybe that was what John had sensed. And once we were close, we had cover from those hillocks. No one would see us now even if they were looking. And I assumed there would be cameras of some kind.

I could see no guards, no watchdogs, no activity. Just innocent-looking open land inside that fence, and those buildings.

`So why the keep-em-out hi-tech fence?' I asked Gerry. 'Doesn't look like that's just meant to keep out rabbits, 'roo's. Forget protesters, all the way out here.'

'May be some answers coming up, Roger. Aircraft approaching.'

There was, too, though it was to be some seconds before my ears detected the whine of its engines, by which time we'd changed position so as to remain out of sight of anyone on the airstrip, and hopefully, from the air. Wouldn't do for us to be discovered. Couldn't very well say we just happened to be in the area. I mean it wasn't exactly the kind of area where one just happened to be. Not miles from the nearest habitation. Given the area, I imagined even the indigenous population would be suspect.

As the distant speck grew larger so I was able to bring my powers of recognition into play, aviation being something else I took an interest in. 'Piper,' I announced, focussing the binoculars on the approaching aircraft. 'One of their Red Indian tribe - twin engines.' It was still too distant to put a name to the model, but as it closed, dropping the flaps and gear for a straight in approach, its high tail and turboprop engines identified it as belonging to the Cheyenne range. The airfield was in the same direction from us as that from which the aircraft was approaching, so it didn't pass anywhere near our position.

It touched down with a brief screech of rubber, followed by full reverse on the propellers. It then taxied across to a hard-standing. As the engines slowed to a stop the passenger door opened to form steps, down which filed half a dozen figures.

'What now, Roger? You said you didn't have a plan.'

'I haven't. I'd hoped....' I told him about Mike, and his non appearance. Told him it would be up to Bob in the end. 'Let's just see what happens here. May give me an idea.'

But it didn't. For after about an hour, during which nothing further took place outside, the procedure was reversed, six different people boarding the aircraft to fly out. Obviously some kind of executive crew change. And with no wind to worry about, the machine took off and departed in the same direction to that from which it had approached, without having to pass anywhere near our position. Everything then returned to its previous, seemingly inactive innocence.

We remained in place until well after the sun had set. I wanted to see how it would appear after dark, for night would be the time Bob should make his attempt. If he had any sense. It was the time I would choose. If in fact we could glean enough evidence even to justify an attempt!

What lights there were covered only the area close to the buildings. No guards were visible, just as during the day. So, did that mean there were electronics, maybe explosives? Something to cover the open land which separated the fence from the buildings - a hundred yards, I estimated. Perhaps there was nothing at all. Nothing going on in there that warranted such precautions.

Was I losing faith in my perceived scenario? I didn't think so, for when I got these kind of feelings, more often than not they turned out to be right. Was this to be the time my feelings let me down?

After a while we left, clearing the immediate area to spend another cold night in the outback, only this time we had some grubby blankets and a fire for company.

'Of course, I could still be wrong about that place,' I told Gerry, once we'd settled. 'Maybe there is nothing more to it than the production of pharmaceutical products.'

'Why the wavering, Roger?'

'Well, for a start, at no time during today's aerial activity did I spot a familiar face.'

'Doesn't mean a lot.'

'No, you're right,' I agreed, deep in thought. And, there is another way we could possibly glean more information. A long shot. But first I'd need to find someone with access, then I'd have to return at a later date. I take it a return trip can be arranged?'

'Just say the word, Roger.'

'So, all we need is someone with access. And thereby lies the problem.'

*　　*

Chapter Thirty

DREAMLAND

We'd awoke next morning to discover we had a collective problem. At least, out here in the middle of nowhere, not being able to start the car certainly appeared to be a problem from my point of view, collective or not. Possibly not, for Gerry seemed to be thinking along different lines to me.

'You're not contemplating calling in at that facility to request assistance are you?' I asked. 'Just happened to be passing and our car conked out. Any chance of a push?' kind of thing.'

Gerry never answered, just watched, and pointed.

Our driver, known to me as Henry, was at the wheel, attempting to start the recalcitrant beast. John stood and stared into the open bonnet, did nothing. He seemed lost in obscure thought, or possibly he was willing it into life. In return, the car also did nothing.

I was about to go over and offer advice, but Gerry placed a restraining hand on my arm, motioned for me to stay put. Then a strange thing happened. Without redirection of his gaze   , John reached out and tapped the flat of his hand twice on the front wing, an indication maybe that Henry should try again. This he did, and, amazingly, the engine spluttered half into life. It coughed and rattled, sounding as though someone had dumped cutlery in the tumble dryer in mistake for the dishwasher, but it did run, after a fashion. Then the whole contraption moved, jerking along like a clockwork model in need of rewinding.

`A powerful force, the spirits,' Gerry said.

I searched his face for some sort of humour, saw nothing except certainty of conviction. A little more advanced than Minerva, I thought.

Superstition is easy to dismiss after a few beers in the pub, but out here in the limitless outback, seeing what I had seen, hearing what I'd been told, things took on a different meaning altogether. And with a ride now in the offing, I made no comment, just gratefully climbed in

*

'Still over two hundred kilometres to Hedland, Roger,' Gerry said as we passed the sign for Marble Bar. 'May as well take a break.'

'Yeah, could use a cold drink.'

I knew of this place, had read about it in Kim's tourist guide. Gold discovered nearby in 1891; name derived from the wall of red jasper at the nearby pool, on the banks of the Coongan River. Population: 300, only thirty percent of them white.

But the only place in which we had an interest at present was the Ironclad Hotel, which dominated the main street. It offered air-conditioned shade, chilled drinks, and other than subsistence rations. I munched on a couple of sandwiches, not sure or caring what they contained, and drank what seemed like about a gallon of clear, pure water. At least clear and pure to what we had been drinking for the past two days. I did also down a couple of beers, just to relax the spirit a little, and keep the landlord happy.

'So, how long to Port Hedland from here, you reckon?' I asked the landlord.

'In that,' he nodded at our mode of transport, 'three, four hours, depending.'

'On?'

'Road conditions mainly. And on if that even makes it'

'It'll make all right,' Gerry told him. Then to me. 'But first, to the pool.'

'Don't have time, Gerry. I need to get back as soon as possible.'

'Relax, Roger, there's always time. Has to be in that thing. Anyway, you said you wanted me to show you around.' He smiled as he spoke, well aware that I was just using him. 'Believe me, it's worth it. That right, John?'

'Bloody oath. Ain't bin to Marble Bar 'till yuh've sin the pool.'

So we backtracked a little, and I was glad we had. This was heaven. A wonderful opening out of the dry, scrubby terrain. An oasis of pellucid sunlit water and of gum trees, stark and silvery-white against the deep blue of the sky.

'Marble Bar. That's where the town get's it's name,' Gerry said, pointing to the craggy, red-white striped rock walls. It's actually Jasper, was at first thought to be marble. But the town does have another claim to fame.'

'Which is?' I asked, though I knew he was going to tell me anyway.

'Fact that, between October 31st, 1923 and April 7th, 1924, the temperature here exceeded one hundred degrees Fahrenheit for one hundred and sixty consecutive days.'

'Pretty hot, eh.'

'Enough to earn it the title "Hottest town in Australia,' he said."

I closed my eyes on the scene, losing it in blackness, before opening them again to make it suddenly reappear. It was one of the most beautiful sights I had seen in a while, and that clear water exerted a magnetic effect on me. Doubt if it was a hundred degrees at present out here in the sun, but it was hot. So, without a moment's hesitation I launched myself into the shallow depths, washing away the dust and sweat along with my cares. Thoughts of Silver Springs apart, for some time a nagging concern had been building with regard to Kim's welfare. I could think of no reason why this should be, apart from the acrimony of our recent parting. Now, as I lay there soaking, everything suddenly seemed right again. Even the thought of wet clothes caused no worries. In this climate I would be dry in no time.

Not too long after we were once more underway, Marble Bar having disappeared well behind in our red cloud, Gerry said something in the local lingo and the car once more ground to a halt, as if relieved to do so. I climbed out and looked around. The road ahead was flat red dirt. Dry, dusty, and badly rutted in places. It went on forever. Nor was there was much either side of us either, just scrub and spinifex as far as the eye could see.

Gerry draped himself around my shoulder, his free arm sweeping round to encompass the surroundings.

'That's what you'd have faced, Roger. Like this for hundreds of miles. In fact you can drive for days and see nothing else. Not that there is nothing around. You just don't see them, but they see you.'

'Abos, you mean?'

'Fauna mainly, but yes, the Abos are there as well.'

'Just as well, in my case,' I thought out loud.

'Doubt you'd be talking to us now if they hadn't been,' Gerry confirmed.'

I shuddered at the prospect. An all-round silence impinged. There was nothing to be seen or heard, no matter which direction I faced. Just a vast emptiness that was red-ochre, brown, and black. The low scrub and spinifex provided a contrast of faded yellowy-green, and the panorama appeared to change colour at will, chameleon-like. But I discovered there was sound, once the ears became attuned, like eyes becoming accustomed to the dark. The slow metallic tick of an engine cooling; a light sigh as an intruding breeze briefly disturbed the grass; the cry of a bird; a lizard's click; an abo breaking wind. Loud that!

*

It was more of the same for the next three hours. Hours that dragged inexorably, allowing previous worries to regenerate. And when I finally did arrive back at the Walkabout, it was to discover two things: Tony's boat had been delayed, would not now be in until sometime tomorrow, and Kim was nowhere to be seen.

There had been one more thing. After showering and

shaving I inspected myself closely in the mirror, especially my face. A bit of a mess, but not as bad as it felt, or expected. Some fresh bruising, but the most of the swelling had gone down. But I was heavily sunburnt. Needed to get some lotion on that.

On the drive back I'd already laid my plans for the following day, the priority being to meet up with Tony, so I would now need to juggle things around. I was about to seek Gerry's cooperation on this when, as if reading my thoughts, he saved me the trouble.

'So, how do we gather more information about that place, Roger? Am I allowed to know?'

'Sure you are. In fact, maybe you could organise something that may help.'

'In what way?'

'Well, I was intending going back myself, tomorrow, but I have to meet someone here in Hedland in the evening. Any chance you could talk John into it? I need him to toss some of these as close to the buildings as possible. Amongst that greenery would be idea.' I showed him a handful of the micro transmitters Bob had supplied. Seemed he knew exactly what they were, or might be.

'Ah! Hence the need to find someone with access?'

'Right. A long shot, I know. But they're doing no good in my pocket, and we do need to be prepared, just in case.'

'This time, I take it you do have a plan?'

'A germ of an idea, should things work out the way I'm hoping they will.'

'OK, I'll ask, but I know they'll do it. Be glad to. Probably go straight back, do it tonight, in the dark.'

'No chance that any of them could be involved in any way, is there?' There were times when I regretted my now suspicious nature, but thoughts of what could happen to me if I didn't act in such a manner soon dispelled those regrets. Anyway, Gerry quickly set my mind at rest.

'No way, Roger. None whatsoever. No abo is going to get mixed up in something like this. The elders wouldn't allow it for a start. And even if one was coerced, he'd be unable to hide it. They have no secrets from one other.'

'OK. They'll need to leave a couple of these on our side

of the fence, too. Receivers,' I explained, though I didn't think it was necessary to do so. 'Probably best if the were shaded, to keep the sun off.'

*

I spent the rest of the day making various plans, and trying to track down Kim's whereabouts, without much success. She hadn't checked out of the hotel, nor had she left a message, and as the Ute was nowhere to be seen, I took it she had gone off somewhere.

Later, acting on a hunch, I walked down the road to the filling station, asked a couple of questions, got a couple of answers. Nothing conclusive, but a possibility that only raised more worrying questions.

Utes were to be seen everywhere in Australia, but those with a good looking female at the wheel cut down the odds somewhat. Metallic blue cut the odds some more.

'A stunner of a Sheila? Blue eyes, fair to blonde hair?' the attendant asked in reply to my question.

'Sounds about right.'

'Filled up and took off, this morning.'

'Any idea where? She say anything?'

'Not a word....'

My hopes fell.

'...but she did have Broome circled on her map. Noticed that.'

I bought a map for myself and left, went back to my room and studied it. Broome was close on six hundred bloody kilometres to the north-east! Why the hell would she go there? Or had that been marked for some other reason. Had she really set off back to Perth? That sounded the more logical to me. There again...?

I retired early that night, and although ill at ease with my thoughts, I slept well. First bed I'd been in for days, and was it welcome, even if I did feel lonely in there.

Next morning I called every hotel in Broome - both of them - no one had checked in under the name of Hamilton. I next called the Port Authority here in Port Hedland. The *M/V Wave Rider*'s eta was for 16:00 today.

*

'GPS - Global Positioning System,' Tony explained,

268

'embodies two dozen navigational satellites, parked in geosynchronous orbit, ie, they're effectively stationary in space, positioned to give global coverage, hence the name. The theory is simple, the technology complex. Basically, our antenna picks up data from at least four satellites, ranges and bearings, feeds it to a receiver which computes an accurate position. I could go into pseudo-random-codes, elevation and azimuth, precise dilution of position, and other mumbo-jumbo, but you don't need to know. The system's accurate to less than twenty-five metres. Good enough for most users, but not so the oil industry. We need plus or minus five metres, or better, especially when working near a concession boundary. So what we do is set up a station on shore, at a known location. This compares the satellite derived position to its own accurately surveyed position, computes the disparity, then transmits the differentials to us. You follow me so far?'

`Yeah, I think so,' I said, although my mind was only half with him. Kim was still dominating my thoughts. Broome just didn't add up.

`OK. Now all that's required is to feed corrections and raw GPS ship's position into a computer, the resultant differentially corrected position being displayed on this little gizmo,' he said, directing my attention to a standard colour monitor. So GPS now becomes DGPS - differential GPS. From here we just tell the computer where we want to go, ie, set a way-point, and it displays a range and bearing. It'll do lots more, but that's the basics.'

I was up on the bridge of Tony's vessel, the *Wave Rider*, being briefed by him.

I had arrived at the dock in time to watch the vessel arrive and manoeuver alongside, and that was something to see. By skilful use of the twin propellers, rudder and bow-thrusters, the captain simply "walked" the boat sideways into its allotted berth, held it there until enough lines were ashore to hold it fast. Then, once the gangplank was in position, Tony had waved me aboard.

'What happened to you?' were his first words. 'Yuh look decidedly well used.'

' Careless,' I told him, concocting the lie as I went along. 'Got pissed, then there was a bit of agro.'

269

I was sure he didn't believe me. In fact as good as confirmed it. 'Then fell asleep by the pool, I suppose. Doesn't sound like you, Roger.'

It then seemed he'd decided to let it ride as he led me up onto the bridge to introduce me to the captain.

'No Kim?' he'd asked as he led the way.

'She's er... around somewhere,' I replied.

'Oh, like that eh. Bad day?'

I gave him a weak grin, didn't want to elaborate, tried to concentrate on what he was telling me.

Once Tony had finished with the DGPS briefing, I looked out at my surroundings. It was like a huge floating pick-up truck, the open back deck loaded with a variety of freight. There were sections of heavy pipe, covered skips, shipping containers, racks of bottles for industrial gasses - empty, I presumed, just as the skips would be full of waste material. There were strict environmental laws in operation offshore, I was told, restrictions on what could and could not be disposed of at sea. Apart from food, very little.

At the aft end of the deck, attached to an "A" frame, was something that caught my immediate attention. Something I thought could prove to be very interesting. Should it be what I hoped it was, it could help prove one of my theories correct, or vice versa. I prayed it was.

One way to find out.

'Is that one of those current-meter things you were on about, Tony, out there on deck?'

'Yeah. Recovered it on the way in. That's where the GPS really comes into its own. GPS along with this box of tricks that is. He pointed to a hand-held size gizmo, similar to a TV remote, only larger. There's a transducer mounted on the hull, below the waterline. Select your frequency here, press this button, and provided you are close to the right position, up she pops.

'Simple as that?' I asked.

'Yeah, pretty much so these days. Mind you, we were lucky with this one. So low in the water I suspect it has sprung a leak. Couple more days and maybe it wouldn't have been retrievable.'

Out on deck I noticed the unloading process was

already underway. To these people, time was money.

'Can we take a look?' I asked, my heart in overdrive.

'Sure, if you're interested. But how about later? What I need right now is a cuppa.'

I cursed inwardly. Things were turning out better than I'd dare hope for. This could be the very breakthrough I'd been seeking, and now, all else temporarily forgotten, I was keyed up and ready. Tea was the last thing on my mind, but I had to go along with the suggestion so as to maintain my facade of innocence. After all, who was to say Tony wasn't somehow involved. It certainly didn't seem likely, but I wasn't about to take any chances at this stage. Anyway, my theories had been wrong before, no doubt would be again. But intuition told me they were correct in this instance. Intuition, and the fact that my presence in the area had already led to an attempt on my life.

*   *

Chapter Thirty-one

BREAKTHROUGH

Naturally, Tony gave me the full tour en route to the galley, but my interest in anything other than that yellow tubular item out on deck had waned dramatically. Even though my hypothesis had allocated the current meter as being of possible prime importance in this affair, I had never expected to see one, never mind get close. And now that I had, visions of it disappearing whilst I sat supping tea and engaging in idle chat loomed large on my mind.

It didn't do that, not quite. But by the time we'd had tea, and I'd been kitted out with a hard hat and safety boots - not a lot of good if one of those bloody great steel pipes chose to fall on me, I mused, but rules are rules - preparations were well underway for its removal. And once we got close, I realized just how big it was. At around three metres long by one in diameter, plenty big enough. I couldn't imagine anything that size being completely filled with modern, miniaturised electronics. But of course there was also the recovery system itself, some kind of flotation device. But I couldn't see that taking up much space. Probably a small bottle of pressurised gas and an inflatable bag similar to those in a car.

God. What I wouldn't have given for a look inside. And just maybe..... Then something else came to mind. If it had sprung a leak, allowing enough water inside to almost sink it, surely that water would now be draining out as it lay there. The area around it was almost completely dry. Rule out a leak, Tony old lad. Now I really was excited.

We stood clear as a crane made to lift it onto the back of a truck, parked on the dockside. The second mate was supervising the unloading, and he handed a clipboard to a man who stood close to me, asked for a signature of receipt.

'Got a pen?' the guy asked. I immediately saw my chance, butted in before the mate could respond.

'Here you go. Courtesy of Singapore Airlines,' I said, twisting the top to switch it on, whilst making a show of reading the name on the barrel.

He took it, signed, and made to hand the pen back. I waved it away. 'Keep it. I've got loads.'

'Good on yer, mate,' he said, clipping it into his pocket.

I heaved a sigh of relief. Life is all about chances and opportunities, and this one had been too good to miss; couldn't believe how easily things seemed to be falling into place. I snatched a glance at the clipboard, noted a few details that were written there. Wasn't interested in the signature, just the recipient - Northern Technology.

I learned from Tony that the vessel was being turned around immediately, equipment that was even now being loaded was required urgently offshore. It suited my plans, and after dinner on board I took my leave. Already an interesting day in more ways than one, but what further revelations would it bring? I wondered.

I was continually planning ahead as things developed, so next I needed to speak to Gerry.

Northern Technology's warehouse was easy enough to find; phone directory for the address, map for the location. Gerry and I drove out there for a quick look-see, and what we did see prompted me to make plans for an after-dark return.

*

All that day I had expected, hoped for, word of Kim's whereabouts - a message at the desk, a phone call, her reappearance. There had been nothing. So when it came time to leave the hotel, I was possessed by a growing sense of unease. I realized then that this was the longest we had been apart since meeting up in Perth, and that despite the build up in tension due to what came next, I was missing her. I couldn't entertain the fact that I had upset her enough for this, but if not...? The alternative didn't even bear thinking about.

Evening is normally the time that such worrying thoughts do play on the mind; when you're not doing much of anything, in preparation for shortly doing even less. But not *this* evening. The surge of adrenalin which now coursed through my body was excessive, and excessive surges of that kind are addictive. Only those who have experienced such a phenomena can know how addictive. I had that previous experience.

'You ready for this?' I asked Gerry, once we had parked the hired Ute well clear, made our way back to the warehouse area.

Suspecting the time was drawing near when I may require additional help, I had earlier briefed him as to my suspicions and intentions. I had already made my decision, it was time for Gerry to make his.

'Insurance premiums are up to date, if that's what you mean.'

'Probably as well. So I take it that means you're with me?

'Let's go for it, Roger.'

'Now is as good a time as any. All appears to be quiet, few lights, no signs of security.'

'Doubt they have too many security problems up here in Hedland.'

'We'll see about that.'

The warehouse was sited on an industrial estate out of town, which meant keeping an eye open for guards in any of the nearby compounds, too. Luckily, the one we wanted was on the outer edge of things, which, although it offered them some isolation, also made our job far easier than it might otherwise have been.

Still no evidence of there being any guards. But the truck was there, parked out in the yard. No sign of the current meter.

I checked the area, then the gate.

'Doesn't appear to be wired,' I said. 'And I don't see any cameras, do you?'

'Nothing obvious.'

So, as previously agreed, Gerry stood watch, I got to work on the lock. A simple affair that took but a few seconds of my time.

'There you go,' I said, slipping the chain and opening the gate just wide enough. 'You don't need to come, you know,' I told him, not sure that I wanted to do this to him: possibly place him in danger. And on the wrong side of the law, too.

'It's open isn't it? Get bloody moving.'

'Open, sure. Though I suppose, technically, this could fall under the heading of breaking and entering?'

'Strewth, Roger, there ain't nothing technical about it, mate. It's breaking and entering no matter how you care to look at it.'

So, confident he was well aware of what he may be getting in to, away we went. And after we'd slipped through, I quickly secured the lock and chain, just in case there was a roving patrol, though this was looking less and less likely.

Not roving, not a patrol, but we had barely taken a couple of steps before the warning came. A spot of light appeared briefly, halfway up Gerry's trouser leg. Infra-red beam, and we'd triggered it.

'Jeez! Check that out. Looks like we could have visitors.' The voice emanated from my pocket. The one which carried one of Bob's receivers.

Doubly forewarned, we quickly crossed the open area, rounding a corner of the building in the opposite direction to the only lit window. Once there I peered round, in time to see a door open and another light appear. A powerful flashlight in the hands of a man. Its beam probed the open space, then, apparently satisfied he wasn't about to be jumped, the man followed the beam, went over to check the gate, and its lock.

We, meanwhile, slipped even further out of sight, merging with the shadows. Unseen, yet seeing. And listening.

This wasn't the man who'd made the pick-up today, he, or his pen, had to be inside the building. But this guy was reporting his findings by walkie-talkie; just as effective.

'Gate's secure.' Then, after the beam made another cursory sweep of the area, 'No sign of anything.'

'Yuh sure?'

'Bloody oath, man. Not a damn thing'

'OK, knock it on the head and get back in here. I'm almost done.'

The man disappeared back inside.

'Another bloody false alarm. I keep telling 'em this system's crap.'

'Not as crap as he thinks,' I told Gerry. 'But it does point to the fact there is something here someone thinks is worth protecting.'

'Time to take a look then.'

'Exactly. Follow me, but keep very close to the wall, and be ready to dive for cover.

As we eased our way along, I kept an eye open for possible bolt holes, should we be careless enough to trigger another alarm. If there were any more.

'Over there would be good,' I told Gerry, pointing to a pile of crates.

'OK, that about get's it. I'll have this on the way first thing tomorrow,' my receiver suddenly reported.

Have what on the way to where? I was sure I knew. Certain almost. Felt it ever since I'd first seen that contraption on the deck of the *Wave Rider*. But certainty in my head was not good enough. I needed sight of it, and what it contained, if anything. If it did, and if it was what I suspected, then would be the time to call in Bob and his cronies. Which would then allow me the time to concentrate on the problem of Kim's whereabouts.

The window was high up, but Gerry took me on his shoulders and eased me up. Very slowly, I raised my head over the sill inch by inch, until I could see in. A large open-plan room, but no one, or nothing of importance, in view. I raised myself higher. Still nothing. Higher still, almost at the limit now, and that's when I saw it; not what I wanted. Two men down there, working close in to the wall, which made it difficult for me. But I realized it was also in my favour, one of them would need to look almost vertically upwards to catch a glimpse of me, and there was no reason for him to do so.

One was the man that had been at the dock this morning, but unless he'd left the pen laying around, I already had that figured. The yellow container lay on a bench, partly disassembled. Close-by lay a silver, tubular object, no more than half a metre long, probably a hundred and fifty centimetres in diameter. The current meter itself, I surmised. Very small compared to the size of the yellow container. But was that what they'd been discussing "getting on the way tomorrow?" I could see nothing else. But then I heard something. And it had me frantically gesticulating for Gerry to let me down. Time to head for cover.

'I'll get off then. Don't forget to call before yuh leave.'

'It'll be an early morning departure. May as well stay here the night, just in case.'

'Yeah, right. Don't forget to switch the beams back on once I'm out. I'll give you a blast on the horn.'

By the time he'd exited we were long gone, back into hiding. And we remained there until we heard a car horn sound, a couple of beeps.

'Give it a few minutes, I suggested, 'then we go.'

'Find what you were looking for?' Gerry questioned.

I shook my head in frustration. 'No, nothing. Difficult to see though. They were so close in to the wall.'

'So now what?

'No chance of breaking in, guy's bedding down for the night. Only thing to do is follow him tomorrow. See where it is he's going. That'll give us an idea of what he may be carrying. Can't see a current meter as being any good out at Silver Springs. If he heads in that direction I call Perth, leave it up to them.'

'It'll us mean spending the night out here.'

'Yeah. I'll pick up a few things and come back, drop you at the hotel.'

'No way, Roger. We both need to be here, keep each other awake.'

Now we were aware of the infra-red beam, the source was fairly easy to spot. It was poorly positioned, too low, too far from the gate, so with a little care and effort we were able to step over it.

Correction, Minerva told me. *Not poorly sited at all. Positioned for people breaking in.*

Right! They obviously don't expect anyone to be breaking out.

Back at the hotel we arranged to meet up in half a hour. I had a quick rinse, then half-heartedly started to throw a few essentials into a bag whilst I thought about things. Kim had me worried, but there wasn't a lot I could do about that situation until either I heard from her, or from someone else! And what of Bob? If things worked out as expected, the game was over. I called, told him to get up here. I'd be out at Silver Springs, if he got there by the following morning I'd leave it in his hands. Didn't mention the alternative.

You sure about that?

Bloody Minerva. No I wasn't sure, but that was the way my thinking went at present. Time to go.

Only then did I realize I hadn't yet changed. And what happened next served as a true indication of my current state of mind. I had one leg still in my trousers the other waving in the air, when suddenly the phone rang, taking me completely by surprise. Kim? was my immediate thought. But in my haste to grab the handset I lost balance and fell to the floor, my pockets emptying themselves in the process, loose change etc being scattered every which way. I cursed my stupidity, cursed again once I managed to get the phone plugged in to my ear.

'You ready?' Gerry asked.

'Shit. Would have been if you hadn't bloody called,' I said, disappointment and frustration washing over me. 'Now I've got my kit scattered all over the pissing room. 'Be with you in five.' I hung up, then began to scrabble around, collecting the various bits and pieces together. It took time for my heart-rate to subside to normal levels.

I recovered my radio receiver from where it had landed, but the cover was off and it had ejected its small, button-like batteries. The first was at my feet, and I retrieved it. The second I couldn't see anywhere, and I was tempted to leave it, until Minerva butted in again.

Remember this evening, how valuable that thing proved to be?

There's another, already out in the field.

You sure? And even if it is, you're back here.

Right, I conceded. Could come in handy of course. Anyway, I needed the insurance. By which time I was back down on my knees, combing the floor. Beneath the bed was the most obvious place, but as anyone who has dropped anything round knows, it could have ended up anywhere. Nothing so simple as under the bed then.

They weren't hearing-aid small, these, about an inch across, so I didn't expect it to be as difficult as it was. My hopes rose and were dashed a few times as I continued to find those coins which had so far eluded my original cursory sweep. But then I spotted something beneath the bedside cabinet.

Bingo! And as I reached for it was when I saw the notepaper, upright against the wall. I recovered that, too. Looked to see if it was of any significance.

Shit! Was it ever. A note from Kim. She must have propped it up by the lamp, knowing I would see it. Only it had obviously slipped down the back, so I *hadn't* seen it, until now. But as I read it the heat seemed to drain from my body, almost rendering me catalectic.

What was written there answered the vital question, and I immediately wished it hadn't. For it told me that what I had looked upon almost as a game, no longer was. It had suddenly become deadly serious. Was immediately glad I'd alerted Bob.

I now I knew why Kim had left for Broome. Apparently, I had asked her to meet me there. This caused more alarm bells to ring, for obviously, never having been in Broome in my life, nor intending to go, I had done no such thing.

Which tells you with one hundred per cent certainty that Kim isn't in Broome, either.

As usual, Minerva was right. She was likely to be with the writer of that note. And I doubted she had gone along with them voluntarily.

As further insurance I left one of the Singapore Airlines pens on the bedside table, activated. The last of them I clipped into my shirt pocket.

*   *

Chapter Thirty-two

SILVER SPRINGS

Having had no idea at what time in the morning that truck would leave, we had driven out and parked unobtrusively, close by, the compound's only gate clearly in view. There, beneath the dazzling panoply of the night sky, we'd waited for dawn.

*

It had been a long, uncomfortable night, and I'd spent a lot of the time trying to marshal my thoughts into some sort of order, as well as putting Gerry in the picture. I explained that it was now imperative we go on to Silver Springs. Explained about Kim. Not only Kim, but I reiterated the facts re Simone, and others, long since dead. Kim was now my priority. I couldn't allow anything to happen to her.

It seemed like everyone I'd loved in the past had been snatched away from me. First had been my wife, Simone, knocked down by a truck; Suzanne Daly, a nurse, shot in my bed in mistake for myself; Caroline Dickensen-Maggs, my last girl-friend and intended future wife, killed by a ricocheting bullet. It all took time, and it felt like I was again prising open

281

almost healed wounds.

But I had to get a grip on myself. Neither melancholy nor anger would help solve any of the problems, nor would they help my current plight. They'd be self-defeating.

Reluctantly, before leaving the hotel I'd called Bob Bottomsworth, advised him of my new plans. I did need some kind of back-up, just in case, but also felt the need to keep one step ahead of the authorities. Retaining the freedom to make my own decisions. For what I hadn't yet told Gerry, was that, if at all possible, this time I was going in through the fence. Maybe he had an inkling, for I had asked if there was any way he could contact John. Said I felt he and a few friends could be a great help out there in the bush. Stupid question, really. Gerry was gone no longer than half an hour, returned to say that word had gone out for John to meet us at the Marble Bar Pool.

'Easy-peasy to us fellas,' he said, miming John, when I asked how he'd achieved that.

*

As dawn's orange glow tinted the eastern sky, so the stars went into hiding. The truck remained where it was. Would probably do so all day now, I thought an hour later, as a Ute appeared from between the buildings.

'Bloody hell, Gerry! Just as well we decided to spend the night out here. We could have come back this morning and spent the day watching a truck that was going nowhere.'

The Ute driver was the guy off the dock. I just hoped he had his newly acquired pen in his pocket, even if he was alone. It had certainly been in the room with him, for when he'd called in earlier this morning I had picked up a transmission. Too faint and mumbled to be of any use, so I assumed that it had been some distance away from the phone, hopefully in some item of clothing slung over the back of a chair.

Gerry started our engine, made ready to pull out behind him. I sat alongside, guidebook to hand.

'Stay well back so he doesn't get suspicious,' I advised. We'll see where he goes.'

To me it was obvious, especially so when he turned left on leaving town. He was heading for the Great Northern

Highway, the slightly shorter, though slower, route to Perth - it being mainly unpaved - rather than the Coast Road Kim and I had followed on the way up. But I would have been more than disappointed had he set off in any other direction.

As we came to the outskirts of town I asked Gerry to stop.

'Let him get well ahead, almost out of sight. Then we follow.'

'Looks like he's going for it.'

'Looks like. But we need to be absolutely certain. He could still be heading for Marble Bar, then on south from there.

But by the time we reached Marble Bar we *were* certain, just as soon as we saw him turn off the Great Northern Highway as he left the town. He turned onto a dirt track, heading east. He had now revealed his intentions, abandoning the road to Newman and the south.

Gerry diverted us to the pool area, where we found John to be waiting, as arranged. John and one other.

'Just the two of you,' I asked.

'Plenty more in the bush.'

I knew what he meant. 'Been waiting long.'

'Before dawn, ; he answered.

I was astounded, and it showed.'So what you been doing since then?'

'Plenty for a fella to do out here,' he replied without elaborating.

Soon after we set off again we ran out of black-top. Gerry slowed, and then the car ground to a halt, as did my thoughts. I climbed out and looked around. The road ahead was the usual flat red dirt, and we could see the other vehicle, a moving dust cloud, now some way ahead.

I was about to ask why we'd stopped, but Gerry was already taking a leak.

'Don't look so worried, Roger, no one out here to see me, 'cept maybe an Abbo ot two. That right John?'

'Right enough, boss.'

Could there really be people living out here. There was nothing as far as the eye could see; a flat, dusty dry wilderness pushing in on us from all sides. Not colourless, though. Certainly not that. We were faced by the usual reddish landscape, but when studied in detail, blacks became apparent too, and yellowy greens of the sparse vegetation, brown rocks. Given the overall tone, these individual though few and far between colours seemed to jump out of the scene so as to announce their presence.

Yet even out here I found it almost impossible to feel at risk, let alone in mortal danger.

We piled back in and set off, and soon had the other vehicle in sight. Didn't seem like he was in any great hurry, for we were fast closing on him.

`Can't follow him along here without being seen,' Gerry advised, noting the plume of dust that marked our passage, as well as that of the vehicle in front.

But I had the map out and I'd done my homework. `We don't need to follow, Gerry. Bloody obvious where he's going now. Previously he had three choices, Marble Bar, Newman and down south, or Silver Springs. Now he only has the one. Marble Bar's gone, wrong direction for Newman, which leaves only the facility at Silver Springs. That right, John.'

Nothing else for a whitefella out here,' John acknowledged.

Pass him, Gerry, we'll drive on ahead. Be to our advantage if we arrive well before he does.'

Shortly after we had overtaken and were pulling away, another plume of dust appeared in the far distance, getting bigger with time. Another vehicle, running for Hedland.

'Windows up, Roger,' Gerry advised. Even so, when it eventually passed we were overwhelmed with choking dust.

'Be the same for him.'

'Makes me feel better,' I said. It was also an indication of how far ahead we needed to be were the guy behind not to be aware of our destination, though if he had anything about him he could figure it out just as easily as we had.

As Gerry drove I took out the Beretta. He looked across at me, questioning.

'Expecting trouble?'

'Insurance,' I said. 'If it's their freedom or my life ....? Well, you work it out.'

'They have no choice but to kill you.'

284

'Right, and they won't think twice about it. Which leaves me with a similar choice, hence the gun.'

I did all the checks: slipped the magazine from the butt and checked it was full. 'Always a good thing to make sure everything works before you need it,' I explained. I then emptied the magazine into my lap and refilled it before setting the safety to "on" and replacing it in my side pocket. There was no word from the back seat, but Gerry had a question.

'So what's that all about?'

'Precautions. If a gun is going to jam, nine times out of ten a badly loaded magazine will be the cause.'

'You're familiar, then.'

'If you're ever remotely likely to need one, it pays to be familiar with the one you have.'

'Ever killed anyone, Roger?' I figured that would come.

'I've killed people, sure, and it's not a burden I carry with ease. But that won't stop me doing it again if my life depends on it.'

'Big gun for little bullets,' he remarked.

'You've been watching too many movies, Gerry old lad. Put one of these in the right place and it can be just as lethal as a 357 magnum - the gun immortalized by "Dirty Harry" Callahan. That's a big gun, this is small. It's not necessary to "take someone's head clean off their shoulders" to kill them, you know.'

'Suppose not.'

I took it out again, flicked off the safety, cocked the action, stuck my hand out of the window pointed the weapon at the sky, squeezing the trigger. To me the shot was barely audible over the sound of the engine. Wouldn't have been had I not been expecting it.

'Did you actually fire it?' Gerry asked.

'Yeah, I fired it. You would have heard it too but for the engine noise. The extension is correctly termed a sound suppressor, not a silencer. And don't worry, Gerry, it's not always necessary to kill someone to immobilize them, either.

*

'What conclusions did you reach about Kim, Roger?' Gerry asked sometime later.

'The obvious. She isn't anywhere near Broome. They

285

have to be holding her somewhere in Hedland, or out here. I suspect out here.'

'You think they took her as a warning, for you to back off?'

'Has to be.'

'So why...?'

'A Sheila?' John interrupted. 'There's a Sheila in the compound, for sure.'

'What! You saw her?' I questioned.

'Yeah, I saw her.'

'Not like you or I would see her, Roger,' Gerry explained.

'Yeah, Gerry mate, I did. Through the glass.'

'Hang on... You were inside?' I asked.

'Sure. No problem.'

'OK, John, non of this easy-peasy shit, and forget the dreamtime.' I smiled at him. 'But how did you know there were no hidden alarms, or .... well, that it was safe?'

'Old abo trick, Roger. Let nature take care of things, solve the problem for you.'

'Meaning?'

'We rounded up a couple a wallabies, set 'em loose inside the fence. Wallabies are always going to head for the greenery. All we did was wait around , see what happened.'

'And obviously nothing did. Bloody brilliant. So it is safe.'

'You're not going in as well?' Gerry asked.

'Got too. Don't know when Bob's going to arrive, if he ever does. Things have changed now I know for sure.'

'But it's not necessarily Kim in there.'

'Bloody well has to be, doesn't it,' I said, as if stating a fact. With which Gerry became silent for a while, as did I. Both of us deep in thought.

'I've this asked before, but yuh do have a plan, of course?' he eventually said.

'Of course,' I assured him, my voice full of confidence, avoiding mention of the fact that my plan was to proceed, and see what happened. Anyway, as any military strategist knows, a successful operation requires much more than a plan; it also requires luck and a backup. Apart from the possibility of

286

Bob Bottomsworth eventually putting in an appearance, there was a good chance we had neither.

*

'Over there,' John said, pointing. I looked, noticed an actual clear area, a patch of fence that for some reason the spiders had not draped with cobwebs. And on close inspection, the "reason" became clear. This was the place through which John, along with his wallabies, had entered had entered.

Parking our vehicle well away from the compound, and out in the bush, we made our way stealthily back to the perimeter fence and into hiding.

It had originally been my intention to await the following vehicle's approach, and see if it offered me any opportunity of effecting an entry. But John's earlier revelations had negated the need for such a hazardous approach. And now, looking at the break in the fence, I realized we needed nothing more than the cover of darkness.

John disappeared on some mission or other, and it was almost dark by the time our friend in the Ute arrived. He followed the road around to the main gate and out of our sight, so it was impossible for us to observe the entry procedure. We assumed someone must have been available to open the gate, or he had some kind of electronic gizmo fitted to the vehicle. He certainly hadn't called in... unless of course he'd left the pen behind.

'I think now is as good a time as any,' I suggested.

'Why not wait for the authorities, Roger?'

'Because I'm not sure the authorities are even coming. I still didn't have anything solid when I called Bob. And if they just try and storm the place I suspect by the time they get in, they'll be unlikely to find much that's of any use. What we need is hard evidence, proof.'

'Not just Kim you're thinking about, then?'

'That too, yes. But currently I'm taking a gamble based on available data.'

'And if you're wrong?'

'Well...' I shrugged. 'Tell you what. Let's just say I'd better not be.'

'What can we expect in the way of opposition, do you think?'

287

I caught the "we", decided to correct him.

'I don't expect you to come, Gerry. There's no need for that.'

'Then let's just say there may be safety in numbers.' He grinned when I didn't argue, and then continued. 'Right then, opposition. What's your assessment?'

'Nothing to base an assessment on. Opinion maybe.'

'OK, opinion?'

'Say small to medium.'

'Small to medium! What the hell's that supposed to mean?'

'A step down from a lot.'

'Oh! OK.' He obviously realized I had absolutely no idea. Seemed he was able to accepted that.

Which was the time my receiver chose to crackle into life. After hearing nothing all day I had given that pen up as a lost cause.

'I think it's time you disappeared, Jason, lad,' a vaguely familiar voice said. 'You're compromised, and we can't have you picked up. Leave the country immediately you get back to Hedland, right. For somewhere... well...., out of the way. Know what I mean?'

'Right now? But what about my business, My house and family?'

'Questions, questions. Look you stupid bastard, this isn't some bloody TV soap. Do it, yuh hear? We'll take care of your family.' There followed the sound of what appeared to be drawer opening and closing. 'Here, take this for starters. There's ten thou' in there. Small bills.'

There was a second or two's silence, then: 'Hey, Jason. You forgot something. No honour among thieves, so they say. Sign here.'

Jason obviously did, and just as obviously left his pen behind, for a couple of minutes later we heard...

'I don't trust that bastard. Make sure he's kept quiet. Oh, and don't forget to have them pick up the loot. I want that ten thou' returned.'

Now we had the proof we required.

'Seems like they are expecting us. At least somebody. We must have been spotted somewhere, Gerry. Or has someone else been watching over this operation?

Reckless or not, this was the time for thoughts of retreat, before actually committing ourselves. Once we had, it would then be too late. But... as we had just heard a death sentence pronounced...

Gerry was obviously thinking along similar lines, for he suddenly muttered, 'Fuck it, Roger. Let's go get the bastards.'

Despite the taste in my mouth - bone-dry, metallic - I was in full agreement. 'OK then. This is where it all goes right, or it all goes to hell,' I said, placing the receiver on the ground, close under the only bit of scrub to be seen. Hopefully It would be discovered later, if it all did go to hell.

There was little cover apart from the odd dip and hummock, and the moon moved in and out of the clouds. Buildings apart though, as before, there were no further signs of human presence.

At my insistence, we moved slowly, and kept low. Movement and noise are two of the things that will give you away in the dark. But if you move slowly, keeping as low as possible to the ground, you'll be difficult to spot, and you'll be less liable to make any noise.

We didn't. But something did.

A sudden eruption of sound shattered the tranquillity of the night. Not loud, but in this silent place it certainly didn't go unnoticed. An engine starting up away in the distance. Diesel. It accelerated, along with my heartbeat. Standby generator, probably. On automatic timer, I hoped.

Then, just as the moon slid behind a cloud, I spotted another figure moving around in the dark. Being neither slow nor likely to be silent told me he belonged here, and that he obviously hadn't seen us. He was making his way over to what looked like a wooden hut, raised off the ground, and well clear of the main buildings.

I signalled for Gerry to get down, then remain absolutely still, and to his credit, he obeyed without question. We both slowly sank to the ground and waited to see what happened, praying the moon wouldn't choose this moment to pop out from behind its current cloud. It didn't, not before the man entered the hut and closed the door behind him. It was a door that creaked, I noted. A rusty hinge, lacking oil.

Ideal. Storeroom, or temporary prison, I wondered as we made our way over there, adrenalin pumping into my bloodstream. Even if it wasn't where Kim was being held, at least there was a chance we would have someone to question. That would be a good start.

The distant generator chose that moment to shut down, or be shut down. Probably just a test run, I surmised.

Upon reaching the hut we circled the place, one in either direction, meeting up again in the area of the door. We checked underneath, as well as looking for windows round the sides. There was only one, shuttered and well out of reach; which left the door.

Signalling Gerry to remain outside and keep watch, I eased my way up the steps and put my eye to the keyhole. Nothing. Bloody key in the lock. But I thought I heard murmuring. So I grasped the handle and turned it, ever so slowly. The gun was in my hand, it was cocked, safety off. I was ready.

As soon as I saw the thin strip of light beneath the door go out, I made my decision. Had he heard something, or was he preparing to leave, or maybe retire for the night? No matter, it left me with the immediate advantage of eyes that had already adapted themselves to darkness, albeit for a few seconds. But they were vital seconds. And in that time I had the door open, my victim sighted, and I was in there with him, standing to his rear.

As he didn't have a gun in his hand, I had to assume he'd been about to leave. Well, now I'd be the one to decide on that. First, he had some questions to answer.

I tapped the barrel extension against his cheek, then stepped back. `On the floor,' I ordered, and, after a second or two's deliberation, he made to obey. But he hadn't totally given up, I found, for as I again moved in he struck, like a pissed-off cobra; lightning fast. Almost fast enough even, fingers actually brushing my wrist. But I'd been ready, was faster still. I'd anticipated the move, actually intended for him to make it, for in so doing he'd afforded me reason to shoot. Even if he was now flat on his stomach.

*   *

Chapter Thirty-three

RENDEZVOUS WITH DESTINY

Almost silently the bullet entered the wooden floor, about two inches from his head. It punched a neat hole through which motes of dust now rose, also in silence, visible only as they drifted past the beam of moonlight which streamed in through the window.

'The miss was deliberate,' I informed him. 'And not more than half an inch from where I aimed. Just so you can be sure I'm not quite as unfamiliar with handguns as you would have hoped. Believe me, I can place my shots quite accurately.'

'So can I, fella. Drop the gun.'

Well, that hadn't exactly been a riotous triumph, had been my immediate thought!

The voice came from close behind. So close in fact he didn't have a need to be accurate. I briefly felt the cold steel of his gun as he tapped it on the side of my head.

But, even as he did so I heard the door begin to creak open, which probably served to distract him.

Reacting immediately, I caught him completely

unawares, therefore quickly recovering the advantage. If you hold a gun to someone's head, you either hold them as well, or you stand well clear. Before he realized what was happening, I had moved aside, swung round to chop at where I imagined his wrist to be. It probably no longer was, but no matter, I caught him a glancing blow on the neck when completing the move. It was enough to drop him. But, luckily, this was the moment Gerry switched on the light, and I saw my assailant still had the gun in his hand, and it was rapidly swinging round in my direction. Though nowhere near rapidly enough. No thoughts about it being him or me, I fired one shot, and it almost silently took him square between the eyes.

'Bugger,' Gerry said, involuntarily it sounded. 'You shot him Roger.'

'Pretend you didn't see that,' I replied, noting my saviour's look of distaste. 'Classified information,' I jokingly told him.

'But he's dead.'

'Him or me, Gerry, I said,. 'No time for decisions. That's the way it sometimes goes.'

My peripheral vision caught movement , causing me to react. I swung the gun round, quickly, pointed it with intent.

'And better you remain absolutely still, fella, hands behind your back. Just so I don't get the wrong idea.'

This advice I directed to the guy on the floor, the one who at present remained sound in life and limb.

As he was wise enough to obey, I knelt, knee on his back, frisked him with my free hand, removing from a shoulder holster a SIG-Sauer P226 9mm automatic. Same model as that which had so recently been tapping me on the cheek, and was now in my pocket.

I whistled. 'Hey, a real serious piece of hardware, fella. Especially for a chemical technician to be carrying around.'

I made sure it was safe and handed it to Gerry. He took it reluctantly, like he expected it to go off at any moment.

'I'm a site guard, not a technician,' the man stated. His voice was decidedly unsteady.

'Guarding against what, way out here?'

'We'd received a warning of possible penetration.'

'Not too good at the job are we. I'd suggest you

consider a change of occupation. But first, let's get you comfortable. Then there are questions to be answered.

So, they had been warned. By whom, and of what, I wondered. They were the first questions for which to seek answers.

I looked around the place, seeing it for the first time really. It *was* a kind of workshop, although it did also contain a bed. But it certainly wasn't a place of confinement. Too insecure, and there were too many aids to escape available. OK, they weren't available to the guy stretched out on his back, all he needed was a coffin. And after securing the live one's hands and legs, Gerry and I lifted him onto the bed and propped him up.

'Comfortable enough? I asked, activating the pen, before clipping it back in my shirt pocket. The question was met by a glaring pair of eyes, fierce in their intensity.

This may take some time, I thought. So I asked Gerry to step outside and keep watch. 'Make sure you're not visible,' I said as he left. I then turned my attention back to the guy on the bed.

'OK. Let's start with that warning. What were you told?

As he still displayed a reluctance to respond, I put a shot into the mattress, almost too close to him. But it did have the desired effect.

'Jeez, man, what the hell are you on?'

'I ask the questions, fella. And if you're not prepared to answer, then you'll be of no further use to me. I'll be no worse off if you're dead, too. But that won't do you a whole lot 'o good. Now then. What was the warning about?'

I gather he know believed I was serious, for there was little hesitation.

'We were told there may be an infiltrator amongst the people on site.'

Not us then, someone already here. Which had me wondering if Bob was working with someone else, unknown to me, and had managed to get him employed.

'I don't believe you, fella. But the important question is, where is the girl?'

Nothing. Except the sound of a shot! Again in the mattress, again close enough to have him worried.

'Where is the girl, and who is she?

I pointed the gun threateningly, but now there was no need.

'Hamilton's daughter. She's in the main block.'

'Of her own choice, or...?'

'Course not. Hamilton discovered a few things, was about to blow the whole operation. They took his daughter to keep him quiet.' That was a revelation for the good for starters.

'What operation is that, then?'

'I think you know.'

This shot punctured the wall at the side of his head, causing Gerry to open the door and peer in.

'Everything OK, Roger, he asked, though he had already taken in the fact that it was. The guy was still breathing, sitting up and taking notice.

'No problem, Gerry. Just a little persuasion,' I replied, and the door once again closed on the darkness outside.

'OK, where were we? Ah yes, you were about to remind me of what this operation is all about.' I waved the gun threateningly.

'Fucking hell! Drugs, man. Drugs.'

'Right! Now were getting somewhere. How many people in the compound?'

'A lot. More than is usual.'

'*How many*?' He could see my finger tightening on the trigger.

'I don't know, honest. Thirty... forty, maybe.'

'How many is normal?'

'Twenty, twenty-five.'

Technicians and household, I assumed. I also assumed the technicians were unlikely to be armed. But fifteen more than normal wasn't good news. Sounded like they were expecting trouble of some kind. But from who? That couldn't be for someone who was already established in the compound.

'Why the extra manpower?'

'We weren't told, but the boss is around. Maybe that's it. Only ever seen him up here once before.'

'And who might the boss be?'

'Mr Santana, of course.'

Just as I'd suspected. Come on Bob, I thought. They're all yours. Come and get the bastards.

I then questioned him on the layout, entrances and exits, etc. He responded willingly. Who wouldn't, when they thought they had nothing to lose but their life! And although I never would have shot him in those circumstances, he wasn't to know that.

When I figured I had as much as he knew, or was about to get, which was probably more than enough for my purposes, we gagged him, made sure he was immobile, and as comfortable as possible, and left.

'Better I go on my own from here, Gerry,' I told him, after calling him back in. 'No point you taking any more chances. It does seem they were expecting someone, so I'd better not disappoint them.'

'I could give you some back-up,' he said, casually, and dangerously, waving the Sig around on his finger.

'I think not.' I smiled to soften the criticism. 'No point putting more lives at risk than necessary! What you can do is go find John, then arrange to put a call out to Bob.' I gave him two numbers. 'Tell him we definitely have enough, and it's urgent. Very urgent In fact. Try the Hedland number first. Hopefully he's there by now.'

'Guess it is urgent. When those two fail to report in I suspect someone is going to deduce something other than an unspeakable traffic violation to be the cause. Especially out here.'

'That's quite possible. But hopefully, by the time they *are* missed it could well be sorted, one way or another. Oh, and see if you can do something about saving old Josh, back in Hedland. Material witness.'

With that, Gerry left, last seen heading for the hole in the fence. I had no idea how we were going to get word to Bob from out here, just hoped John had, or that Bob was already on the way. As for Gerry, no need for him to move slowly now for, our two ex-guards apart, there was still no sign of anyone else being around. Worrying, that. And it did point to a real need for me to be extra cautious and vigilant.

After the event, people will always offer advice on what

you should and should not have done. They'll even tell you what they would have done in similar circumstances. But hindsight is filled with logic. What they would actually have done in the heat of the moment is never known.

First thing was a recce of the place, checking that what I'd been told was in fact correct. And after a quick survey, it seemed like it was. So, working my way round to one of the less secure rear exits, reluctantly revealed to me by our captive, I eased open the door and slipped inside. Into a long corridor. Emergency lighting only, I noted, so really a continuation of the darkness outside. Worrying, that!

I quickly assumed a crouching position, back to the wall, gun live, clutched in both hands, pointed at the sky. That way I was ready to point it left or right, quickly and effectively, for I was by now expecting a trap. Well, if expected, it would no longer be a trap, and I needed to carry on.

Counting the one wasted on the drive out, plus the four recently used, I had ten shots left in the Beretta, I calculated. There were times when it paid to know. I had left Gerry with one of the Sigs. He would probably have little use of it outside the wire, but first he'd needed to *get* outside the wire, and you never knew. At present he was my only back-up, and I figured I was about to be in need of some protection.

Still, thinking of the odds I may face, I now wished I'd kept both Sigs.

I waited and listened, counting to ten as I did so. Nothing. No reaction at all. No movement, no noise, no whispered exchanges, no probing lights. The place was unnaturally silent, and I felt very uneasy, but ready.

Were it not for those guards, and an overheard snatch of conversation, now recorded, I'd have suspected the place of having been abandoned.

Choosing to turn left, basically because the corridor ran further in that direction, I eased my way along. I carefully tested each door as I came to it, all were locked. There was only one room left, directly ahead.

Intuition dictated I lodge the spare Sig on a shelf I had noted, above and off to one side of the door. There was no way I'd be able to take them all, even if I had that with me. And it just may come in handy later on. A back-up back-up as it were.

I turned the handle slowly, tried the door, pushing gently. It gave easily, nary a creek or a groan. Ok, so this is the route they wished me to take, I thought, the only unlocked door. So they had left me with no choice in the matter. Better be ready, for anything.

Once again darkness was what greeted me, complete and total. It was cool in here, an indication that it was air conditioned, as it would need to be. Though at present, even the background hum of that had been silenced. I was very uneasy

Perhaps they forgot to pay their electricity supplier, Minerva wryly suggested. A thought which immediately became superfluous, the place suddenly flooding with light.

'Ah! Roger McLaren. At last. Come on in, we've been expecting you. Thought you'd got lost on the way.'

I was glad I'd secured the spare gun, for it would definitely have been of no use to me in here.

'Had to take care of a couple of the hired help first,' I responded, desperately fighting to retain a facade of calm. Inside I was in turmoil. This pointed to something else: the fuse had been lit well in advance of our arrival. Somewhere there was a leak. Not that it mattered now, far too late in the day. But were they also aware of Gerry's presence? If so, it looked like we'd be relying solely on John, unless Bob was by now riding to the rescue. Though I seriously doubted that at present. Only hoped he would receive word soon. For I had as good as given him the OK last night.

They were all present and correct. Well, almost all. A frozen tableau: Klaus Santana, Bruce "Red" Jones, Alan Beckwith, along with Foxy, plus a few unknown others. But the only Hamilton present was Kimberley, and she was tied to a chair.

My heart surged. I raised my eyebrows slightly, but otherwise ignored her. I had no need of that kind of distraction at a time such as this. Yet the scene briefly recreated a vision of Caroline in my mind, the memory not yet ready to let that go completely. Though I was doing my best to avoid situations which recalled the images, this one being unavoidable.

To counter this I pointed the gun menacingly in Klaus

Santana's direction, knowing it was a wasted show of resistance. I was hopelessly outnumbered, and one of them held a gun to Kim's head. All I had was a .22 Beretta, ten rounds, and I was surrounded.

'Foolish gesture, Mr McLaren. Do as we say and she'll be returned with all the pieces joined together. If not..... ' He shrugged his shoulders in dismissal.

'But first, the gun. On the table if you please.'

I looked across to the table indicated, saw there all the evidence Bob would ever need. A stack of what looked like brown building blocks. 'The contents of that yellow tubular item off the M/V *Wave Rider*, no doubt,' I stated. A salvage operation, because they may have been blown? I wondered. Or was this a normal shipment?

'You can see why we needed to silence you. Now the gun,' he said, forcefully, once again pointing at the table.

As Santana waited for me to respond, knowing I had little choice but to, he looked across at Bruce Jones, gave a curt sideways nod of the head. Mr Jones, no doubt being despatched to check my statement, or handiwork, slipped out of the room. Danger man gone.

This was a different Santana altogether from the one I'd met briefly at the WACA ground. He was polite, smiling, amiable sounding, but then he could afford to be, given the current situation. Yet he almost seemed to breathe a sigh of relief as I released the butt of the Beretta, allowing it to swing on my finger by the trigger-guard. I then walked over and placed it on the table.

'And the Sig, if you don't mind. No doubt you relieved our "Hired Hand" of one.'

'No need of the extra weight. I had the Beretta.'

'I don't think so.' He indicated to the man nearest me. 'Frisk him real good.' Then to me, 'Never yet known of a fella in your position giving up on extra firepower.'

Although he was actually right, he was effectively about to be proved wrong, and in front of the "hired help".

'He's clean boss,' the searcher declared, after all but stripping me.

'See how wrong you can be,' I goaded. 'Probably not your last mistake either.'

Santana slowly looked at me, obviously deep in thought. He then told two of the others, 'Outside, quickly. Back to where you found him. There has to be someone else out there. Don't come back empty handed. There is someone, isn't there Mr McLaren?'

I shrugged my shoulders, held my upturned hands out wide. 'If you say so.' I knew they would never find Gerry now, he would be long gone.

Placing the Beretta on the table proved to be a wise move. For despite the fact he was sure there *had* been someone else, the tension now relaxed slightly, and word was given for Kim to be removed from the room. She was duly cut lose and led away, without even a backward glance in my direction. Was that good or bad? I wondered. Rejecting me, or play acting?

'You were quite an adversary, Mr McLaren,' Santana said, once she was clear. Almost too good for us, I'll admit. Dangerous as well. Too dangerous for our operation. You got lucky, found out a bit more than was good for you. A mistake not to pass it on though.'

'You think so? They're already aware of your local distribution techniques; the WACA ground, Adelaide, etc. Anyway, I wasn't lucky. It was you that was careless.'

'Possibly. Though it's of no consequence now. We found you difficult to catch, granted, so we let you catch us. At least we let you think so. That way, we caught you. Heh, heh.'

He so obviously wanted to let me know how proficient he was. He'd become an artist. This was his theatre and he held centre stage. His colossal ego ensured he told all, how clever he'd been, still was. It didn't matter, for I wasn't to be allowed to pass any of it on. I, and probably others too, Kim included, would probably not be leaving this place alive.

What he didn't realize was that his every word was being transmitted and recorded. I just hoped someone eventually found that recording device.

'So where is our Mr Hamilton?' I asked.

'Hamilton? Forget him, he was just a front. A figurehead and a stooge. President, yes. But he had no idea what was going on. And he no longer has control. We do. We could see from the beginning where he wanted to go. All we

299

did was supply the personnel to get him there, along with to places unknown to him. Then the money started rolling in, and bingo! All it takes is a team of skilful lawyers.

'Hamilton was easy, a fool. His aims were too simple: to make good money from a legitimate business. But why settle for a million when it could be ten? Why ten when it could be a hundred?'

I silently willed him to go on, but he didn't. That is, until I enticed him into it.

'And Norman Holman? Don't see him around.'

'Norman Holman! Ah, yes, of course. Slipped up there, didn't you. Much higher up the ladder than you figured, our Norman. Through him lay the way to the top. All your friends needed was five minutes with him. Too late now though. Your friends are no longer coming, and Norman Holman is dead.'

That was a surprise, and a worrying revelation. Not about Norman Holman - it seemed people involved with this organisation and fell out of favour, did invariably tend to end up dead - but the reference to "my friends." Did he mean Bob, or Mike? Was there anyone out there but Gerry, John and his merry band?

I was keeping close watch on everyone, and as soon as an opportunity occurred when I didn't appear to be under close scrutiny, I made brief eye contact with Foxy. Seemed he'd been expecting it, was waiting, so I questioned him, again by use of raised eyebrows. He seemed to respond, for his head seemed to dip in a barely perceptible manner, and then only if you were watching for it. Or was that wishful thinking? Did I have an ally in this room, or not?

'One thing puzzles me,' I said, attempting to draw him out some more. 'Europe. Seems too easy.' I had to get him to divulge as much information as possible, in case the worst came to the worst. Even though I had not yet given up all hope of eventually getting away. I was never one to give up hope while I was still alive.

Santana's ego was such that he fell right in to it.

'Not difficult at all. Limited manpower works in our favour. Impossible for customs to check all incoming flights, so they concentrate on the obvious; those from South America and Asia. Low priority is usually given to flights from

Australia. Then you have the European Union. Common Market; open borders. Most of continental Europe....'

Which was when Bruce returned with the bad news. 'Charlie's dead.'

Well then, Mr McLaren,' Santana drawled. What of the British sense of fair play?'

'Fair play is when both sides operate under the same guidelines. I follow the rules set by the opposition. Can't win otherwise. That's fair isn't it?'

'Ah, but is it legal?'

'Who the hell are you to talk legalities?'

'True. But we aren't employed by any government, or agency. We're not accountable to anyone but ourselves.'

'Me neither. That's why they use me.'

'How much they paying yuh?' This, inevitably, from Bruce Jones.

'Who?'

'Yuh want me to write it out fucking longhand? Whoever sent yuh. The Aussies, the Brits?'

I thought about giving some smart-arsed reply, decided to keep quiet. Non-cooperation usually equated to the rough stuff. No point in that at this stage, not if the only thing at stake was my pride. Especially as the only witnesses to lost pride would be a bunch of thugs.

'They paid enough. There are considerations other than money to be taken into account you know.'

'No matter,' Santana chipped in. 'We'd have paid you ten times as much just to stay away.'

'No you wouldn't. Before I arrived here I knew nothing to be paid for.'

'Same as when you leave here, it would appear. Bring him next door.'

*

It was a big room, completely cleared of furniture apart from groups of chairs set out close to the walls. There were two doors, two windows. Rule out the windows as a possible escape route, probably toughened glass, and they only overlooked other rooms. Which left the doors. The one through which we'd entered I obviously knew about, but to where did that second door lead? was the question in my mind. Wrong location for it to be the one outside of which I had hidden the Sig, so to where? Be good to know, just in case an opportunity offered itself. Any opportunity, no matter how slight. For I had already sussed out the purpose of the chairs, the significance of the otherwise clear room: A smirking Bruce was awaiting my presence.

It seemed there was to be a bout of unarmed combat, which raised my levels of hope somewhat above that of a smidgen.

Bruce, it seemed, looked to have lots of confidence. There again maybe not. Perhaps it was just the confidence of lots of back-up, in case he failed. I think he saw it as an I win, you loose situation. Not me.

The though now gave me more hope, well above that previously envisaged smidgen, for I didn't see Bruce as a one on one unarmed combat practitioner. He was tough with people around him, or with a gun in his hand maybe, anything more I saw as duplicity, or play-acting for his minions, even though at present he did look the part.

You may think that, but until you know for sure, be very wary, Minerva advised.

Sizing the situation up, I already was. A roomful of people, though all well clear of that second door.

But this wasn't a dojo - a training hall. No instructor, no protective clothing, no safety mat to cushion a fall. Nor would there be time limits, or standing counts. This was to be just him against me. My moves against his. Attack and counter. I also knew he wouldn't be bowing politely from the waist and sticking to the rules. This was to be street-fighting dirty, so I needed to make allowances. And if it happened to be me standing at the end, I wouldn't be waiting around for the applause. This could be where the significance of that second door might count. For something. It would be time to run. But to where, and how? No point thinking about it now. Take it as it comes. If the chance offered itself, I'd go for it. But from here on in, one false move and this could be a night with no tomorrows.

He had at least ten years on me, that much more experience. But that also meant his reflexes would be that much slower. Fractions of a second maybe, but in this game fractions can be vital. In my book quick is what counts. The first blows are always demeaning and discouraging. They also hurt the most. Therefore the first blows needed to be struck by me.

He was obviously expecting this to be easy, and final. I was equally determined it should not be so.

'Hi there, pommy shit-head. Guess what happens next.'

I did, immediately assuming a Neko Dachi, a convenient fighting stance; my body aligned centrally to his, balanced, weight on my rear foot, ball of my front foot barely touching the ground. I was ready, was he? The idea is to prepare the body. Too relaxed and the joints are limp and lifeless; too tense restricted mobility. So right away I saw he'd presented me with an advantage, so I took it.

He *wasn't* ready; *too* relaxed, like overcooked spaghetti. And not ready probably related to not very good?

But my Dachi had warned him this was to be no walk over. For he became slightly more cautious. But knowledge of the stance I'd adopted told me he was no amateur, either. Not to be underestimated.

'A fucking expert, eh,' he stated. Slightly taken aback; I could see it in his eyes.

Wasted time and thought, from him.

'Not an expert...' I replied, taking advantage, easily catching him with a Chung Kwon between upper lip and nose; a knuckle chop that really made his eyes water, '...Just very good.' I had plenty of time.

The idea was to get his dander up. That would give me a little more of an edge. And every little advantage added up.

We circled each other warily, seeking the slightest opening. I saw one, let lose a frontal snap kick aimed at his groin. It failed, for he countered with a waving kick known as a Doro Chagi. His subsequent Ashi Sabaki was not the best footwork I had ever seen, but then he may have had other things on his mind. I *was* getting through to him, ever so slightly, and it showed.

He'd even allowed the background murmuring to affect his concentration, whereas I blocked it out completely. Concentration intact. Working on my next move, looking for the opening.

'Shut the fuck up, will yer,' he shouted in frustration to his audience. 'Can't even hear ourselves think.'

'I suspect you'd have difficulty with that in a sound-proof room,' I countered, which, as expected, brought him charging in like a wounded bull. But it was a deceptive action, for at the last minute he converted it to a double-fist punch, almost achieving his objective.

Not bad, I conceded, but rolled out of it enough to turn it into a glancing blow. Even so, it was a mistake on my part, for even the glancing blow bloody hurt. He had strength all right.

He knew it, tried to turn it to his advantage with a continuous technique, but now his flow and timing were way out. Enough even for me to be able to debate my next move before execution: go inside the punch, under it, or outside?

I went inside, at the same time landing a Hook Punch.

It didn't seem to hurt him as much as it should have, but it did tell me something; not only was he strong, he was also fitter than he looked. I'd hit solid muscle, not fat.

Useful information. A slight adjustment in style was called for. Keep him guessing. Go for the bones then. New tactics. You know bones are solid, so a different technique comes into play.

Reading his next move well in advance, I slipped outside a deadly straight line punch, leaving him totally unbalanced as his fist struck blank air. I immediately took the advantage offered, landed a couple of telling blows.

'Bastard,' he roared, and I knew then I had him. He was losing control, which meant a further loss of concentration; the two virtually inseparable. It seemed he was unaccustomed to fighting someone who was prepared to fight back, and knew how. Without a weapon in his hands Bruce Jones was just a schoolyard bully, beating on people who couldn't, or were too scared of him, to retaliate.

In he came again, giving almost as good as he got, but I was still well ahead.

Not if you think like that, Minerva warned. *This is not a points thing. Kill or be killed is what this is all about.*

Right. Statistically, guessing at his age, I supposed

Bruce Jones had probably reached the half-way point in the years of an average life. I determined there and then that, with a little luck, statistics were about to be proved wrong: his end was closer than he suspected. It had to be one of us, and at the moment it seemed my only problem would be getting out once it was done. But by now I had that planned, too. At least I knew which door to head for, Foxy had earlier given me a signal. No movement of his body whatsoever; a couple of quick sideways flicks of the eyeballs and that was it. Almost enough to distract me from the primary objective.

Bruce Jones came in with what could have been a well executed Flying Turning Kick. Could have been good, had his reactions not been so slow. As it was I caught the airborne leg, twisted it sharply and sent him crashing to the ground. That was all I needed. A minuscule amount of time. For a split second he would be powerless; time for the grand finale. Quickly following him down, I selected the coup de grâce to be by way of a Downward Punch to the throat, a killing blow if administered effectively.

I was just about to deliver it, when a blow was directed my way. From behind.

My planned escape attempt immediately became redundant as my world turned to blackness.

*   *

Chapter Thirty-four

HELLO FOXY, AND GOODBYE

*T*ap, tap, tap. It was a noise that woke me, slowly penetrating the depths of my mind.

I attempted to rise to the surface of the blackness that engulfed me. Then I lay there, dragging up images, attempting to make sense of things. Familiar, I thought. Tap, tap. There it was again. Nothing to do with the recent martial arts contest that really hadn't been a contest at all. I wasn't that good, which put Bruce Jones well down on the scale of competence. He was hardly knowledgeable enough to challenge anyone at that kind of thing, let alone someone who obviously had more than a basic knowledge. OK, he hadn't seen me in action in Adelaide, but he had seen the end result of that action. Should have taken note! An unarmed man up against someone with a gun.

Tap, tap, tap. More insistent now.

There was a message there, somewhere. Then I did remember: Tony's. The kookaburras were back. But how... I forced my eyes open and immediately felt sympathy for migraine sufferers.

Definitely not Tony's then. A small, untidy, warm room, again sparsely furnished. Just the bed on which I lay, wrists secured behind my back, beneath me; a door, and a hazy patch of daylight I took to be a window. It was. Low down and with no shutters, so definitely not the wooden shed. My vision at present was not exactly 20/20, and I do recall feeling better. Not too long ago at that. Someone must have knocked me around a bit when I was unable to retaliate, I guessed. The villainous, bullying techniques of a Bruce Jones, I imagined. He'd certainly have wanted to show "superiority" in front of his audience, I assumed. Even if his victim was defenceless.

But back to my current predicament.

I imagined this is what it would have been like for Marie Antoinette while awaiting the guillotine in that small, damp cell - the Conciergerie - even though mine was nowhere near damp. But where exactly was I, and why was I here? Did the fact that I was still alive mean I was no longer in any immediate danger? I somehow didn't think so!

In the background I heard an aircraft take off. The familiar sound of a turbo prop twin. Seemed I was still at Silver Springs then.

Tap, tap. I squinted, shaking my head in an attempt to clear it. It hurt, but it did help, if only slightly. The window swam in and out of focus. No kookaburras in sight, but a hand, fingers tapping on the glass. And behind the hand a face. Vague, blurred, but definitely smiling. Silver Springs all right, and Whitefella to the rescue. So they hadn't got him, after all. Gerry was turning out to be a credible back-up in lieu of Mike, couldn't have wished for better. Could have wished for more of his ilk though, he was thinking. Checking to see if I was in here, and still alive and alone, before charging in.

Provided he was able to free me, that still only made two of us. To face how many? Unless of course John was also lurking out there with the Abbo foot cavalry. And even if Gerry still had the Sig in his possession, it would be hardly likely change the odds appreciably. I mean he never did look very happy with it in his hand, nor competent. Best I could hope for, if it came to it, was that he'd just spray bullets in the right direction, keeping heads down.

Then he quickly ducked out of sight as, with the creak

of an unoiled hinge, the door to my prison began to open. I expected the worst, but instead, into the room stepped Foxy, a smile on his face. It wasn't a cynical or hostile smile, either. It was trusting and friendly, and it told me there were now three of us. Getting better by the minute, for he also had a gun in his hands.

'Come on, Roger lad, get yourself together. Can't manage this on my own, and we need to get you away from here, as quick as bloody possible.' By which time he had released the bindings on my wrists.

'Water,' I mumbled. 'Need a drink.'

'Jeez, Roger. Well bloody hurry will yuh. That red-haired bastard will be here soon.'

There was a washbasin in the corner and I staggered over and helped myself. It wasn't cool, it wasn't clear, but it did help things a lot.

Gerry, I thought. What happened to him? But of course, he wasn't aware of my past relationship with Foxy, so he'd be biding his time out there. Or maybe he was even now creeping round, ready to charge to the rescue.

But I *was* in agreement with Foxy. We needed to get away quick. For I needed to get another message off to Bob, make sure he was aware of the present situation. There were other things to consider, too. I couldn't do anything to help Kim from my present location.

By escaping I *would* be helping. Once I was on the lose, Kim would be safe. At least for as long as I was on the lose. The story about holding her to keep her father in line had to be a load of crap. It was me they wanted control of. They probably had enough on Hamilton - fact or fiction - not to require any such threats. They'd use Kim as a pawn, to bargain with me. I knew too much, so they wouldn't hurt her until I was back in their hands, or silenced. They'd trade my silence for her safety. The longer I could stay alive, and on the loose, the longer Kim remained safe, and the better the chance of our seeing Bob arrive.

Then the question repeated itself, why *was* I still alive. Still couldn't figure that out.

But the answer was shortly to become obvious. And had I been leading the way out of the hut instead of Foxy, it's just possible I wouldn't have been around to hear the explanation.

I was just about to follow him out through the door when a shot rang out. There had been no warning, no challenge, just a noise that echoed around the area like the ultimate pronouncement of death. Seemed like it was, too, for Foxy suddenly buckled at the knees. He then crumpled to the floor, like a puppet whose strings had been cut. And out of the gloom a gun appeared, then a hand. It held a Sig P226, of course.

My first thought was that Gerry had made a drastic mistake. But it wasn't Gerry, was it. Couldn't be, for this gun was held with all the intent of being ready to use, again. And this one was in the hand of Alan Beckwith.

To my mind, it appeared he had been waiting out there. Just listening and waiting. So what of Gerry?

'Never did completely trust old Dan,' Beckwith said, as though talking about a fly he had swatted. 'Seems I was right, don't it now?' He gestured to someone behind him, and three men entered the room. Beckwith's gun now centred on my chest. 'Secure him,' he commanded. 'Never trusted *you* at all. Not fer fucking one minute.'

So, there I was again, hands tied, but now in front. And all I'd gained from my brief spell of freedom was a drink of water, plus another ray of hope that was Gerry, provided he been able to hide in time.

I was now fully coherent, even if I did still have a headache. Foxy, on the other hand, was just the opposite. He lay there, not moving. And, I suspected, he wouldn't be moving ever again.

I'd been wondering about the aeroplane I'd heard take off. Did this mean things were now back to normal, or were they expecting trouble of some kind? Were people moving out? If so, that could also mean other people were about to move in.

Next person to put in an appearance was an unknown to me, but obviously someone of importance.

'Ah, so he *is* still here,' he growled. '*Alive* as well.'

'Surprisingly. Cause for a certain amount of gratitude I would have thought,' I told him.

'Yes, well, you've Mr Jones to thank for that generosity,' he said, his tone implying that if it had been his decision, I would have been down there with Foxy by now.

'In which case I'd say it falls somewhat short of generosity. I suspect he doesn't take loss of face with too much good grace.'

'I suspect you may very well be right about that. Wanted you fully conscious. And I don't expect he will be about to misjudge you a second time,' he told me. On which note, the door creaked open, into the room stepped the person under discussion.

'Yuh can be fucking sure of that.' Bruce Jones spat the words out. No, he hadn't been happy. Still wasn't.

He looked decidedly well used, which immediately made me feel a little better, even if only temporarily.

'Oh, been in a fight have we,' I goaded. I knew I had nothing to lose now. I was as good as dead.

'Got an entertaining little accident lined up fer yuh, sport', he said. 'Entertainment fer me. Yuh get to have the accident. Oh, and I lied about it being little. Fucking huge, you bastard. Believe me.'

Oh, I did. Wondered what he'd come up with this time.

I'd been right then, just as I'd thought. He obviously didn't take kindly to being humiliated in front of what he saw as his underlings. So I could well understand that the next few minutes of my life - possibly the last minutes - were unlikely be the most enjoyable. Not with a psycho like this given free reign. Which he obviously did have. Otherwise, I was absolutely sure I would already have been dead.

Without another word, Bruce turned on his heel and, along with everyone but the three henchmen, departed. The remaining three now dragged me to my feet and forced me out ahead of them. We went all the way through the by now brightly, day-lit compound, and out of the gates at the rear, into the nearby bush, scrub and forty degree heat. This would have been the better side to approach from, I idly thought. A lot more cover here. But now that no longer mattered.

There were still just the three hoodlums and myself, everyone else seeming to have disappeared. Why, and for what reason? There was certainly no one of anyone else to be seen around here. But by the time I'd been lashed to a pole, standing upright, ropes across my chest and upper arms, someone did put in an appearance, as I'd known he eventually would. Once he was sure I was firmly secured, unable to pose further threat to him. Just like any other bully I'd come across.

Out of the distant gates Bruce appeared, couldn't mistake that set of facial hair. And he walked with a strange gait, arms raised in front of him. He held something in his gloved hands, and it was that rather than the heat that had me breaking out in a sweat. A cold sweat. For what he held was a snake.

I recalled Tony telling me that out of the planet's ten most poisonous snakes, seven were to be found in Australia. I now knew for sure I was about to meet up with one of those seven. Which one didn't really matter. In this situation, all would be just as lethal. It would appear I really had upset Brucie boy.

'Lookee here what I found,' he said as he approached, wicked grin etched across his none to handsome features. 'A King Brown.'

He held it up before me, waving it around .Its anthracite eyes stared, tongue incessantly flicking the air, testing for any vibrations which signalled danger. I remained absolutely still, careful not to move a muscle, or even to blink. I just stared back, right into its eyes. It was all I was able to do, but I knew that wouldn't save me. I may have remained stock still, but the snake was now being vigorously provoked.

'What's wrong, lost yur fuckin' tongue, have yuh? Tell yuh one thing yuh pommie bastard. Yu'll not karate yu're way out of this shit.' Heh, heh.

He kept waving the deadly reptile in front of my face. First close in, then pulling it back out of range. It couldn't reach me whilst he had hold of it, for he needed to keep one hand close to its head, to prevent it turning back on himself. But by now it was becoming really agitated, and it writhed and twisted in his hands.

`Spasm, paralysis, death. That's the fuckin' sequence, so I'm told. Takes roughly three minutes. Depending.' A bit snake-like himself, he again spat the words at me, but I was determined not to show fear in front of this man. Not as long as I was alive.

'Depending on what?' I made my voice as casual sounding as possible. Never once deflecting my look from that snake.

'Metabolism, or some such shit. Don't worry yurself over it, fuckhead, yuh ain't got the time.'

In he edged again, now closer still. But not yet close enough. He was enjoying himself too much to let it end quickly. But I knew he'd eventually become bored, and the panacea for this would be to watch me suffer.

He was about to move in again, just as I caught a slight movement off to one side. Then in it came, and I knew this time it was the end, one way or another. I drew my head back as far as was possible, touching the pole to which I was secured. It was as far away as I could manage. Then I watched in fascination as the final act enfolded.

Whilst Bruce and his snake were still a few feet away from me, the incoming missile took Bruce full on the side of the head, one hand instinctively pulling back towards himself, automatically releasing the reptile. The snake was triggered into action immediately it felt his grip slacken. And it turned its attention upon the closest object, its tormentor.

In my mind I saw it in slow motion, even thought it was in fact a blur. The head drew back, jaws opening wide to reveal a yellow mouth, needle-sharp fangs glinted as they withdrew from their scabbards. Then it struck at his neck, again and again. Enough venom to kill ten men, I would have thought.

It happened so fast the snake had completed its task before being fully released. It then hit the ground well before the man, and, threat taken care of, it quickly slithered away.

'Owzat?' I heard a familiar voice call out.

I was so shocked, and grateful, my mouth refused to formulate an immediate reply, so instead, I slowly raised my right forefinger in the accepted manner. Not on high, as that was impossible. But Bob saw it, down by my waist. He obviously approved, for he gave a small nod of his head.

Of the three hoodlums close by, two immediately made to throw down their arms the moment the third pitched forward, a spear suddenly protruding from his chest. But one of the remaining two still followed him down, his head preventing a boomerang from returning to its owner. The Nyungar tribe to the rescue.

It was as if that thrown cricket ball had been a signal (and what a throw! One the likes of Denis Lillee would certainly have been proud of), for suddenly bodies seemed to materialize out of the ground everywhere. There were soon to be helicopters overhead, too, setting down in the compound and disgorging troops. It was like a scene from *Apocalypse Now*. And Bob wasn't waiting around to pass the time of day with me, either, for after retrieving his cricket ball and stuffing it back in his pocket, he took off towards the gate.

At my feet the body of Bruce Jones writhed uncontrollably as the poison entered the central nervous system. His mouth hung open in excruciating pain. The obscene and final throes of death escaping from his mouth. The ugly bastard didn't look much different to what he had in life. But the world was better off without the likes of him, I thought.

All of this was enacted before me, for I remained where I was, couldn't do much else at present, no one seeming to notice, or to bother themselves with my predicament. Then, presumably with everything in the compound more pr less secure, John wandered over, a couple of his mates in tow, one of them apparently the spear chucker, for he now retrieved it, casually wiping the blade on his shorts.

`This white fella one of ours yuh think?' John jokingly asked, pointing a finger in my direction. His friends nodded agreement, each smiling bewitchingly. But none of them moved to do anything.

'Well! Aren't you going to cut me loose?'

The question seemed to precipitate a mute, three way consultation between them. But, after a minute or two, John, still smiling, eventually wandered over and did so.

In the distance I heard shots fired, but generally it all seemed to be over very quickly.

'So what was that all about?' I asked. I was only just coming back down to earth after my adrenalin high.

'Bob said to... entertain you.'

313

'Sure he didn't say *detain*?'

'Yeah, maybe he did. Said they would take care of things from here on in. Something like that. Speak kinda funny at times, you whitefellas.'

That all figured. One reason I'd kept Bob out of it as long as I had.

And you almost overdid it this time, Minerva advised.

'That bloody snake could have still been around, got me,' I protested.

'Nah', John replied, one of the others holding the dead reptile up in the air. 'Not a chance mate. Bloody good feed they are.'

I shuddered at the thought. But I then realised that a couple of days ago I'd certainly have thought different.

'Well, sounds like he does now have it under control. Let's wander over and take a look,' I suggested, when what I really felt like doing was sprinting over there. Felt like, but found I was barely able to move right away. Despite my jovial attitude, for a few seconds I found my legs to be still partially paralysed. The late onset of fear.

A couple of the helicopters lifted off even as we entered the compound.

I eventually caught up with Bob, to discover that, Bruce Jones apart, there had only been four or five fatalities: Beckwith, and the guy I'd classed as "unknown, but important-looking." Seems he was... had been.

'Rather high up in the Federal Police,' Bob revealed. One reason we couldn't run a police op'. Never too sure if any of 'em were involved. Neither of those two were prepared to give up without a fight.'

'Good riddance to both. And I almost cut it too fine calling you.'

'Yeah, yuh did. But we had it covered.'

'You did? How?'

`Had various people watching out for you.'

Should have known. He'd relieved my conscience slightly, but no point telling him that. 'So what took you so long?'

'Our hands were tied: not enough evidence, and too many people in positions of power on the payroll. Had to be a penetration job. One man. You. Once you disappeared inside, we could move in. You were all the excuse we needed.'

'You call that having it covered? Another couple of minutes and...'

`Yeah, well, we didn't expect you to get inside so soon. Thought you'd use these.' He held up a Singapore Airlines pen.

`I did. Should be some interesting stuff on the recorders. There's a couple still outside the fence. John 'll show you. But I had to try for Kim. Where is she anyway?'

'That's the good news. She's OK.'

'That wasn't the question, Bob. I asked *where* she was.'

`Gone I'm afraid, Roger. Flown back to Hedland. It was what she wanted.'

I thought about that, allowed it was probably for the best. I'd contact her later, and maybe we could drive back down to Perth together. See how things went from there. Take it as it comes. But I wouldn't give her up without a fight.

'More good news is the amount of raw product we recovered. Seems "Santa" was really stuffing his stocking this time.'

'My thoughts exactly. And what of the man himself? Where's he?'

'Santana? That's the bad news.'

`Give it to me.'

`He's gone, too. No sign of the bastard anywhere.'

Then I remembered that aircraft departing.

*   *

315

Chapter Thirty-five

ADIEU, KIMBERLEY

Bob had offered me a seat as far as Port Hedland in one of his choppers. Tempting, but I turned him down, choosing instead the discomfort of the road trip. I'd come out here with Gerry, we would travel back together. Besides, it was my signature of the rental slip.

John had said not to bother about him; he and his mates once more dispersing back into the bush. But not before he'd presented me with a boomerang and a spear, the latter complete with the device used for launching them accurately over a distance. 'Both 'bin used in anger,' he told me. But that twinkle was back in his eye.

'A woomera,' Gerry informed me. 'That,' he said, pointing to the throwing device.

Something clicked in my mind: 'Woomera? An RAF missile test site of the fifties.'

'Yeah. South Australia.'

'Apt name then, provided you are aware of its origins. By the way, what happened to the Sig?'

'Junked it. No bloody use to a bloke like me.'

'You did good, Gerry. Without the help you and John supplied, I doubt Bob would have been around in time to save me. Thanks for that. I owe you.'

'No problem, as they say. What of the Beretta?'

'Was forced to part with it. Lying around somewhere back there, I imagine. Or maybe Bob picked it up. After all, it was his to begin with. Imagine he has to account for it. Everything has to be accounted for in government, doesn't it?'

'Unless you are in government, it seems.' He laughed at his remark.

Apart from yet more bruising, and the odd minor injury, I was in fair shape, considering what might have been. But despite this, the agreeable climate, and a country in which I felt I could happily spend the rest of my life, I was depressed. Part of it the winding down process, I knew. An adrenalin low as opposed to the recent high. But this time there were other contributory factors: the principal player had evaded capture, Foxy was dead, but most of all were thoughts of Kimberly, as it seemed she had reverted to in my mind ..... and her father, of course.

Old man Hamilton had been taken for a sucker in a way. It appeared he had never been involved with the drugs side at all, even though it could be argued he had to have been aware of it. And although a court would make the decisions on that, I couldn't see him being handed much of a sentence at all, if any. Providing he came clean.

As for Kimberly, well, I imagined she had enough that was legally hers to see her right for the future. What worried me was the fact she may possibly be without her Dad for a while. Not my fault, but I doubt she'd see it in that light.

Anyway, these matters were not about to be resolved in Port Hedland, for upon arrival there, I was to discover Kim had already left for Perth. A long drive on her own, which told me something of her present feelings towards me.

Bob Bottomsworth wasn't to be found in Hedland either, he too having headed south. OK, him and I really had no more business to conduct, my usefulness being at an end the moment he walked through those gates. Nevertheless, there was a message to say he would contact me once I returned to Perth. Pointless my speculating on how he would know when that event occurred. He'd make it his business to know. Besides, I'd make sure he did. He owed me something. And I'd like a bit of a debrief. There were things to be learned from such as that. There were also questions I'd like answers to, just out of curiosity.

Despite the fact I was looking forward to meeting up with Kim again, hoping to re-establish our relationship, I first decided to take up Gerry's offer and remain in the Port Hedland area for while. I knew she'd need time to think things over anyway.

Gerry and I spent a few interesting days in the North West, soaking up the atmosphere, enjoying the environment, and myself learning a bit about the outback; the flat, dusty dry wilderness that at times still seemed to push in on us from all sides.

Now the pressure was off completely - apart from the niggling worries regarding Kim, and our relationship - I was certainly able to appreciate things more. I had come to love Australia, or at least the little I had seen of it, the West Coast. And it was my intention to take in more of the country before departing. I wasn't in any hurry. Couldn't leave without seeing in the Opera House, the Bridge, the Harbour, and The Rocks; things I'd been advised to see when in Sydney. Maybe even travel to the Gold Coast, and up to Cairns and the Barrier Reef. Be really good if I could coax Kim into joining me. More than good, outstanding. But .... Still, that was for the future.

Meanwhile, we did get up to Broome, an old pearling port, and to where I had supposedly asked Kim to join me. My! Already that seemed so far back in the past.

Then it was on to Derby, before finally flying all the way up to Darwin in the Northern Territory. We then returned to Port Hedland, where I had arranged to meet up with Tony.

It was the end of his current spell offshore, and he had two weeks off, so we all flew down to Perth together, and I again found myself staying up in the hills at Maida Vale.

Bob was not long in contacting me, but I experienced difficulty when attempting to contact Kim. Her house was still under repair, in the hands of contractors, and she had apparently gone elsewhere, as well as going ex-directory! Not a good sign. But, of course, ex-directory posed few problems for Bob, and he, after some unexpectedly necessary persuasion, reluctantly provided me with the number.

'Like you said, those recording devices proved to be very interesting. Good thinking, Roger, getting him to talk like that.'

'Wasn't difficult for someone with his ego. Difficulty would have been in trying to stop him. Of course, he didn't realize it was all being "taken down, to be used in evidence," as it were.'

Bob chuckled at that. 'Yeah, right. It also provided us with the time to move in.'

'I was aiming for that as well. But have to admit, I'd almost given you up for lost. Ended up pinning my hopes solely on Gerry and his abo friends.'

'Yeah. Great mob to have on your side. We'd have been struggling a bit without their help, for sure. Anyway, a successful conclusion. Though it's depressing to think that what we've achieved will cause no more than a hiccup in world supply lines.'

'A big hiccup, I would have thought. Especially as far as your part of the world is concerned.'

'Well, there is that. Plus the fact that there are a few openings in places both high and low. Did I mention that your friend Robo was deeply involved?'

'Robo?'

'Inspector McRobertson.'

'Ah! Can't say I'm surprised, or sorry about that. And what news of Santana?'

'Not a lot. He's apparently either in Sydney, Singapore, Tahiti,....'

'What makes you think so?' I interjected, or attempted to. But Bob carried on as if I hadn't spoken: 'Capetown, Delhi, Auckland, Tokyo, or Rio. Take your pick.'

'You mean he bought all those tickets?'

''S right.'

'In his own name, of course. Using a credit card?'

'Right again. And get this, they were all used.'

'Then forget it. That's what I'd do if I wanted someone to waste time looking. Those are places he isn't. He'd pay cash, and he'd use an assumed name, in a passport he no

319

doubt held.'

,Exactly, Roger. But we'll catch up with the bugger eventually. 'Till then.... By the way, stick this in your pocket. Yuh've earned it.'

'Thanks,' I said. 'Come in handy on my travels. Especially if I can talk Kim into joining me.'

'Huh! Good luck with that.'

It wasn't the way he said it, it was the look he gave me that wiped the smile off my face. What did he know that I didn't? Only one way to find out.

'Hello?' Just that. If you knew the ex-directory number, presumably you knew to whom you were speaking. But the voice was confirmation enough; it immediately set my pulse racing.

'Hi, Kim. Roger.'

'Yeah. Recognised the voice.' Not at all enthusiastic. My presence at the end of the line obviously didn't have the same effect on her as hers did on me.

'No need t' ask how yer came by this number.'

'Guess not. Do you mind me calling?'

'Why d'yuh think I went ex-directory? Yuh bloody well used me, Roger, then left.'

'Is that what you think?'

'Don't matter now. It's over.'

'Couldn't we discuss it, face to face, over a drink, maybe?'

'What's the point? Nuthin' to discuss.'

'Maybe not, but... well, I'd like to see you before I leave. Can't just walk out on the past few weeks without saying goodbye. And in my view they were glorious weeks. Thanks to you, I might add.'

It seemed to help, if only briefly.

'Transit Inn. Half an hour. And it will be goodbye, Roger.' She hung up before I could ask if she was to allow me half an hour to put my case, or to be there in half an hour. Didn't really matter. The prospects didn't sound all that promising. But I left immediately.

I was already seated in the bar, drink to hand when she walked in, and I was astounded, though attempted not to show it.

Just so I didn't get any wrong ideas, I assumed, she had dressed for the occasion, as she usually did. Only this time the clothes were fairly baggy, and the sparkle seemed to have vanished from her eyes. As for the lipstick, that appeared to have been applied in the middle of having a fit. All in all, right now she possessed the sexual charm of an ice-block. Though I knew it was an act that was quite at variance with her character. She didn't look too comfortable with it, either.

I stood up and smiled, kissed her on the cheek, which she allowed. She didn't return the smile, and I didn't ask how she was, that was obvious. My hopes plummeted.

'Can I get you a drink, love?'

'Coffee, please, Roger.'

Roger! So I hadn't been totally dismissed, I mused as I went over and ordered the beverage. And had there been a hint of moisture in those eyes?

'You OK, love?' I now ventured to ask, placing the cup before her.

'No, Roger, I'm not bloody OK. Was. But you refused to trust me.'

'Just being cautious,' I admitted. 'Don't even trust myself in that kind of situation. You are your father's daughter after all.'

'No cause to abandon me.'

'Not true. I was...'

'You abandoned me, Roger.'

She sipped at her coffee as I attempted an explanation, but I could see it was falling on deaf ears. It was as if thoughts conjured up by the meeting had been dredged from the scrap heap of memory. All negative. Her attitude got to me, readily eroding my enthusiasm. So much so, I eventually felt forced to concede defeat. Maybe time would ease the hurt she felt, maybe not. But I knew the moment of parting was upon us. Probably for the best. A one way relationship stood no chance whatsoever.

`What will I do now?' she said, almost to herself, and for a second I detected a faint glimmer of hope. But it wasn't a plea for me to remain. On that front, the shutters were down completely.

In which case, I thought, the perfect answer would be to quote one of the most famous lines in movie history, but I refrained from doing so, offering her a simple shrug of the shoulders instead. Besides, I did give a damn.

I gave her my address and phone number. 'In case you ever find yourself in London, without a friend. Call. I'll probably be around.' And on that sad note we went our separate ways.

But I hadn't given up totally. I did try calling a few times, but all I ever got was the answer-phone. It seemed Kim *was* now back on her own. At least as far as she was concerned. And it appeared that was the way she intended things to remain. Just like when I'd first met her, on the flight from Singapore. What had been the cause that time, I wondered. Norman Holman, she had told me. Well, no need to worry about him any more.

She never once returned my calls, and in the few days I remained in Perth I never saw her again.

One week later, after saying my goodbyes to Tony and Gerry - the former with a backyard barbie, the latter, a pub meal of pie and peas - I flew out of her life and on to Sydney. In the end things had not turned out anywhere near as well as I'd planned, or hoped for, and I was by now depressed enough to lose all interest in Australia. So, after a couple of days in the city I boarded another aircraft, for home. I did try calling from the airport, and this time she answered. But it was only to say goodbye. Although she did add a "Thank you for calling, Roger".

I'd ruled out a "Singapore Stopover" on the way home. After all, what would I want with a copy watch when for the same price I could buy one which kept me in touch with my biorythmic cycles, and the phases of the moon? Instead, I elected to continue in the direction in which I was pointed, across the Pacific, through America, and over the Atlantic.

Long hours in the air allowed me time to gather my thoughts together, sort them into some kind of order. I made copious notes on the sequence of events whilst things remained fresh in my memory. The pencil literally flew across the paper - physically, too, I guess - words forming in its wake, and that of the aircraft. Phraseology, spelling and punctuation were unimportant at present, plot, characters, and scenario

322

were. Syntax and grammar could be corrected and honed later, as the manuscript came together. Once back home there would hopefully be enough to present to Freddie, my agent. Needed to have words with him, too.

Thoughts of a possible second book spurred me on, and during our west to east progress we crossed paths with a sun that soon set behind us, creating darkness out there. It was a molten blackness that, although sprinkled with stars, remained deep and mysterious. A thick night through which the aircraft bored a steady passage, heading for its rendezvous with the runways of Heathrow. And by the time we began our descent, I was well on the way towards achieving normality for myself.

*   *

Chapter Thirty-six

LOOSE ENDS

Darkness and I returned to the East End of London at the self same moment, it seemed. There again, it *was* the back end of the year, when it hardly ever got fully light.

The same old thoughts returned once the aircraft had descended low enough to take in the sights on the approach to Heathrow. Here I was, home again, along with all the feelings that are generated by the sight of that familiar landscape sliding past beneath the wings as the aircraft exits the cloud-base on its descent. The green of England; rolling countryside; a patchwork of fields and woodland; the occasional golf course; farms, pastures and open country; rivers, lakes, towns and villages; castles and cottages. Is there anywhere so green and peasant as England? Whose words had those been? I tried to recall.

The romantically rural eventually gave way to green-belt suburban, to semis and urban terraces. Then along came London and its environs: the Isle of Dogs and the silver thread of the Thames; Westminster; Twickenham - stadium apart, row upon row of identical houses lining narrow streets along which were parked a rainbow necklace of toy-like cars - and the castle at Windsor, if approaching from the west. A football ground passed by, still way below; twenty-two colourfully striped insects moving purposefully about in pursuit of an invisible ball.

Up here the smooth, aeronautical lines were about to be broken as slats and flaps emerged from the leading and trailing edges of the wings, spoilers above; the geometry of low-speed flight. Beneath us, unseen, but felt and heard, the undercarriage would be sliding and locking into place, multiple four-wheel bogies ready to support that which the wings would soon be incapable of supporting as airspeed was allowed to bleed off. Lower and lower we edged, as if feeling our way down, a perfectly controlled descent, vortices spiralling away behind in our turbulent wake.

Buildings: houses and shops; a school; commerce in its many guises; traffic-filled roads, their vehicular traffic moving along at a crawl . All flashed past, for even low speed flight in a large jet is well on the way to one hundred and forty knots.

Impressions from the air. OK, no longer was it that legendary land of Shakespeare and Nelson; of Kings, Queens, and pageantry; of traditions and moral values. They, it seemed, belonged in another age. Today it was the weather; the NHS; trainer and tracksuit fashions; designer stubble - a cop-out for not bothering to shave, that, a lack of personal hygiene, or lost pride in one's appearance. It had all come about with the general lowering of standards; lack of self respect, and esteem. It was becoming a, bugger you, what's-in-it-for-me, society. That was how it appeared to me in my present buoyant mood. But I was well aware of this impression not being mine alone.

*

After the usual trials and tribulations of arrival: immigration, then the long walk to the baggage hall, the wait, customs, the queue for a taxi, and the ride into the city, I had the taxi drop me in Aldgate, right outside my not so humble abode. I paid him off, then fumbled through my luggage for a key. Letting myself in to comfortable and familiar surroundings.

325

The scattered pile of mail I shuffled aside with a Bally shod foot. Mail I'd get round to later, once I was settled.

After dumping my bags, I immediately went to switch on the heating. Despite the cold, it felt good to be back. No matter where and how far I travelled, this, after all, was home. At the present moment, anyway. I'd been having plenty of thoughts about that whilst in Australia, too.

That mail, the unpacking, the laundry, could all wait. What I needed first was a good cup of tea, which of course entailed a quick trip to the corner shop for milk, plus a few other essentials. Maybe call in for some fish and chips on the way back, too, but I knew they would not be as good as those I had so enjoyed in Australia. Or was that the rose-tinted glasses syndrome kicking in?

Tomorrow I would pick up Caroline's Ferrari from the garage. At least the Ferrari that *had* been Caroline's, was now registered in my name, I having been named as beneficiary in her will. I had also inherited Caroline's dog, Copper, and Polly, her parrot; would need to pick them up from Freddie's, which is where I had left them on my departure. There was also the matter of a house along Chelsea Reach, a magnificent pile that had also been bequeathed to me, its future yet to be decided. I was still in the process of debating whether or not to upgrade, move in there and put this place on the market, or something entirely different.

*

Two days, and it was as if I had never been away; two weeks of hard graft and I had enough of a manuscript on the hard-drive to enable me to present Freddie with a synopsis, along with a few sample chapters.

Once I had, he told me he liked what he saw, and so, apparently, did the publisher. He even enquired as to whether or not the novel could be completed in three months.

I hated deadlines, so did Copper. He seemed to understand that I was not to be bothered when writing, so he usually stayed put in the bedroom, to where I banished him. I say usually, for it was now really his decision to make, I'd found upon my return. I could shut him in there, but it seemed Freddie had taught him a few tricks, the most aggravating being that he could now open the door and let himself out.

Jump up, paws on the arm of the handle, and with the door opening outwards, bingo! But he only seemed to use his recently-acquired skills on those odd occasions when he realized he'd been forgotten, or maybe when a visitor called. Which didn't often happen. I usually preferred to meet people in the pub.

*

Things had gone well, and at the end of a day two months later, they showed promise of becoming even better. Needed to, for with the book almost finished, now would begin the downward slide, unless I again found something with which to keep myself occupied, to combat it. A new lady-friend, perhaps? Although at present I had not met her!

I did have one idea up my sleeve though. But that would entail a trip up north, to visit my parents.

When one lived alone, which is what I'd once more been reduced to, one could starve and live in squalor if one so chose. I didn't, but certain things *had* been neglected over the weeks of writing, I realized. I was out of Calvados for a start. But produce of the Cognac region had in the meantime served, when necessary. Although that too was now getting low.

Deciding to award myself a night off, I poured myself a reasonable shot, switched on the TV and flicked through the channels. The usual unimposing selection of repeats was what greeted me.

So, nothing on the box, no girl, lonely house, lonely me. Lonely, and becoming a little depressed, despite the cognac's attempts at reviving me.

Bound to happen in time, especially so after the company and excitement of those weeks in Australia.

The weather outside didn't help, either.

OK, I wasn't quite alone. I had Polly and Copper. But as the conversations you can hold with a dog, or parrot, are liable to be pretty limited, and unilateral, I debated going out to Macdonalds, or the pub. Maybe both, I decided.

I was making preparations for such an engaging night out, when the phone rang. No it didn't, it tweeted, like a monotone canary. Something Polly had not yet learnt to imitate.

My heart missed a beat temporarily. No one had called me for some time, so the sound brought on feelings of mild excitement. Who could this be?

I picked it up, not without a slight feeling of optimism, I admit.

'Hello? Six one two five four two,' I intoned, as was my wont. It confirmed to the caller they had reached the number they had dialled. And provided they had dialled correctly, they knew to whom they were speaking.

In this instance, the other party instantly hung up. Wrong number, I surmised. So, optimism proving to be unwarranted, I prepared to continue with my dressing.

Then it tweeted again, almost immediately. Now I *was* intrigued. I once more dumped my coat, picked up the handset.

'Hello?' I didn't bother repeating the number, suspecting it to be the same person calling, having dropped the previous attempt for some reason.

'Hi, Roger,' a familiar and rather welcome voice greeted me. And I was immediately overcome with the thankfulness of a prayer being answered. This could be like wining the National Lottery.

''Appen to be in London, all alone. Can I interest yuh in dinner.'

I could barely believe it, after all this time. Hah! Could she ever! Wondrous thoughts engulfed me.

'Well... not really,' I found myself answering, feigning indifference. 'I was just about to prepare something for myself. Tell you what, though,' I added, as if the thought had just occurred to me. 'Why don't you come round here?'

'Yuh can cook, as well?'

'When one lives alone one must at least learn basic cooking skills,' I replied, laying it on a bit thick.

'Oh one must, of course,' she mimicked. 'What did yuh 'ave in mind?'

'To be honest, I thought a cheese sandwich, a bottle of wine, and you. But I'd be prepared to linger. Could even substitute Bœuf à la bourguignonne de Riz for the sandwich. How's that grab you?'

'Bonza. Whatever it is, I'm on my way.'

She hung up before I could give her directions, so I assumed she'd already done her homework on that front. Things did sound promising then.

I began preparations immediately. Out of the freezer came the home-made Bourguignonne. Into the microwave. It went. I prepare them in my spare time, keep a selection of about half a dozen for just such an occasion. Although such occasions happened but rarely when I was in writing mode.

A pot of rice would only take twenty minutes, ten if that also went in the microwave. Set the table, open some wine, and, bingo!

I looked around, wondering if she would see the room as I did; clean, though cluttered, and badly in need of decorating. And if she didn't? Well... it was home to me.

I checked my wine rack. Bugger! All one bottle of it, and that a Chardonnay. With beef bourguignonne? I self-questioned. Or maybe that was Minerva. Whatever, it would suit our needs. From previous experience I doubted food and wine were foremost in *her* thoughts, either.

Everything was under control and bubbling away merrily. Then the doorbell rang. Sooner than expected. Much sooner, in fact, thus raising my hopes. If she was this keen to rush over, who knew what the evening may have in store, I thought, as I wandered over to let her in. There again, I doubted Kimberley would fly twelve thousand miles just to invite me to dinner. And on the phone she had sounded like she was back to her old self. The Kim I had come to know so well, before....

Too long the easy life; thoughts of caution and security - such as a quick peep through my door spy-hole, or using the chain - had tonight been superseded by those most basic of romantic emotions.

Until I opened the door, that is, to be faced by.....
'Klaus Santana!' I exclaimed. Thoughts awhirl.

Too late now. For I found myself staring at the business end of yet another SIG-Sauer P226. And this one had what looked very much like a Ceiner sound suppresser fitted to the barrel. Fifteen shots and no one would hear a thing.

Panic was not a word with which I associated, that way

only led to deeper trouble, possibly fatal. Take time to think things out, if there isn't time, make it, that's my motto.

Exactly. What I needed to do was to play on his ego again, get him to tell me how clever he had been in finding me. Calling on the phone first to make sure I was home.

Meantime, I was slowly being forced back into the room, Santana's eyes flicking here and there, taking in everything as he moved forward. He reached back and closed the door. And he was even cautious enough to maintain some distance between us. He never so much as smiled, or uttered a word, just kept advancing as I backed up.

There was a sound from the bedroom, a snuffling noise. Copper, upset at being precluded from welcoming our guest. I saw a slight chance about to present itself. Prepared myself for what I prayed was about happen.

'Who's there?' Santana questioned sharply. 'I understood you were alone.'

'Understood? You've obviously not been talking to the right people,' I replied. Confusing him couldn't possibly make my situation any worse, and if I didn't come up with something quickly, I was probably as good as dead anyway. So by now I was back in full attack mode, primed for the slightest opportunity. All it needed was for Kim to arrive. For the bell to ring.

But then Santana himself provided me with a possible alternative. Couldn't have been better.

'Tell them to come out,' he advised. 'Right now.' He had a murderous look in his eye, and I knew I didn't have long. Decision time.

'OK, come on out,' I called. Which was the exact moment the door bell *did* choose to ring.

This was truly a real bonus, and I almost felt sorry for Santana.

Obviously not used to handling such think-quick situations, he immediately became confused. I, on the other hand, had been trained to make the most of such opportunities, which handed me the advantage.

Santana briefly turned to look at the front door, changed his mind as the bedroom door suddenly flew open and Copper came charging out, fast, seemingly furious. It briefly reminded me of my first visit to Caroline's apartment - now seemingly a long, long time ago - this forty pound bundle of hair flying at me in the same way, a fearsome sight, especially so if you didn't know him.

Santana had obviously anticipated an upright being, therefore his first shot was far too high, just as I'd hoped. Now he was fractions too slow in swinging the gun back in my direction, and lining it up, for I was already well on my way before he realised his error.

By the time he was able to get off a second shot, both Copper and I had already hit him, the shot going well wide. Not only that, the gun was dislodged, flying from his hand to go skittering across the floor, therefore all sense of self-importance that comes from carrying such a weapon immediately disappeared with it.

Now he was even less of a match for me than had been Bruce Jones. And Santana knew he didn't have someone able to hit me over the head if *he* looked to be losing. Which, I suspect, he already knew was about to happen.

He was now fighting for his freedom, which gave him added strength. But my strength was born out of anger, and he would have needed to be twice the man he was to stop me.

Knowing his only chance was to stay close, he desperately attempted to do this, thus limiting my options. It may have worked had he been *able* to stay close, but I didn't allow that. And even as I broke his grip and prepared to deliver a knock-out blow, I noticed Kimberley was in the room with us - and obviously dressed for this particular occasion. It distracted me only slightly.

But not only had I noted Kimberley, I saw she'd bent down and scooped up Santana's gun. It was pointed right at him.

Without taking my eyes off Santana, I told her, 'Good move Kim,' for she had once again become Kim, rather than Kimberley.

'Don't move, Sant...' I began. 'Oh, shit,' I exclaimed, for the moment a gap had opened between us, Kim squeezed the trigger, not one, but two shots taking Santana full in the chest. I like to think it was good shooting rather than luck, for both shots passed me by, though far too close for comfort. But the most worrying thing was the fact that there had not been a need to shoot at all.

Too late now. Santana was down. And, like many people who had chosen to tangle with me, it didn't look like he'd be getting up again. But I couldn't call an ambulance in the circumstances, that would certainly have led to Kim being arrested and charged. Which left only one person *to* call: the late Caroline's father, Lt-Colonel Sir James Dickensen-Maggs. My mentor, and contact with the SIS. I picked up the phone and dialled. When he answered I explained in no detail whatsoever what had happened, but at the first mention of Santana, he'd told me to stay put. He'd resolve to get things organised.

So, after greeting Kim and getting her a drink, we sat to await the response team. But there *was* a question needed answering.

'Why the hell did you shoot, love? He wasn't going anywhere.'

'That's not very nice, Roger. I just saved your life.' She sounded like she really believed it, too.

I looked at her and smiled, for I understood. This was the guy that had arranged for her to be held captive, who had threatened her father, used him, almost earned him a jail sentence. Now, seeing him as a possible threat to *our* welfare, she had snapped. OK. Why not? Who was to know any different.

'Yes, you did, and I'm grateful, I said, kissing her affectionately and pulling her close. It was a real kiss this time, to which she responded with much passion. The rest would have to wait, I decided, breaking off whilst I was still able, though still hugging her.

'As for him,' I indicated over her shoulder, to where Santana's body reposed in death, 'I think we'd better get our story sorted before anyone arrives.'

I finally released her, and we reluctantly parted.

'He was unarmed, you'll notice. So we'd best at least provide him with a knife.'

I went into the kitchen and returned with the one I used

for peeling and chopping. A real Crocodile Dundee affair, probably as sharp, thought not quite so big. I also brought an onion and my chopping board. 'For authenticity,' I told her, cutting the onion in half.

Kim stood and picked up the knife, holding it like she really meant business. She had me worried for a moment. But her thinking was spot on.

'For authenticity, she repeated, making a couple of slashes in my clothing. But she was a little too enthusiastic, one of them drawing blood by mistake.

'Oops! Sorry, Roger. Is it..?' She was fighting off breaking into laughter. Placed a hand over her mouth to suppress it.

'Ah, what the hell. A minor wound. It too adds authenticity.'

'You're sure?'

'Of course I'm sure. Too late if I wasn't! And a spot of my blood won't hurt the plot one iota. So, all that remains is to wipe it clean of your prints, mine are OK. They will be expected. Then we plant it in... Was he right, or left handed?'

''ad t' gun in his left 'and as far as I recall. Just a brief glimpse as I came through t' door.'

'So he did. But could that have been because he thought he'd need the right hand to open the door?'

We came up with nothing definite, so I elected for the left on the premise that, as he had rung the bell, he wasn't expecting to have to let himself in.

'OK. When the gun was knocked out of his hand, he immediately grabbed the knife which was on this table. You walked through the door, quickly took in the scene. As far as you were concerned, he posed a serious threat to me. And, with the gun almost at your feet, you didn't hesitate.'

It sounded a bit weak to me, but apparently not to Kim. Anyway, in such situations things do happen very quickly. And not always for the best. Rational thought can be squandered in the quest for speed in a desperate situation.

Yeah, It should suffice, I decided, And it was the best we could come up with the time available.

Not a problem anyway, it seemed. Our story of events was listened to, recorded, and apparently accepted. The

333

"response team", which included someone from the Australian High Commission - whom I doubted was one of their diplomats - took care of things without too much fuss.

After they had cleaned up and finally departed, I discovered the rice to have ended up more like pudding, and the Bourguignonne to be ruined, not entirely unexpectedly. So we did end up with a cheese sandwich and bottle of wine, after all. Wrong wine for the cheese, but neither of us seemed ravishingly hungry, though we did fervently devour each other. First with our eyes, then the hands, then... Yes, this was the Kim of old. Fully recovered, fit, and extremely energetic as it happened. I don't think she had seen much action in recent times, for she behaved as if there would be no tomorrow! And apparently, the kitchen table was also a first for her.

'Thank you Roger,' she said as we lay in bed. 'Not for that, although I did need it, love. But for saving me from myself when we first met. Didn't realise the situation I'd let myself slide into. And sorry about Port Hedland. Wasn't really sure what I was doing until too late, and you'd left.'

I kissed her, told her that was all in the past.

Much later, we discussed other things: hotel rooms, as opposed to Kim sharing my bed for a longer period than we'd just had together, for instance. Sod the book. Given the current situation that could wait a little longer. Probably be able to squeeze another chapter out of this performance.

I eventually took Kim up to Yorkshire for a week. To show her around, and to look around myself, for I was also thinking of possibly moving back up here. Not too seriously mind. It was an idea that had implanted itself whilst I'd been in Australia; open spaces and countryside, as opposed to concrete and steel.

She enjoyed herself in Yorkshire, but I gathered it wasn't a place where she could ever live, given the vagaries of the weather. She was happy enough in London alright, for quite some time. But even there she eventually began to feel the pull of Australia. That was now her home. And as I had made no moves towards a lasting relationship, she gave me her contact details, invited me to visit, any time, packed her bags, and we said our goodbyes with the usual enthusiasm.

It was over three months later, just as I was planning to leave for a holiday in the Caribbean, that I received a call from the Colonel.

'Just thought you might be interested, Roger. Klaus Santana was right-handed. By the way, have a good holiday. Governor of the British Virgins is a close friend, so, should you feel a need to call on him for any reason....' He hung up.

I guessed they'd figure it out, eventually. He was letting me know they had, and that it was covered. After all, a bullet - even two - was far cheaper than a lengthy court case it was still possible to lose. Especially so in this day and age of political correctness. And of course, it also gave them something else to hold over me, should the need ever arise.

Kim apart - she had declined an offer to join me - I hadn't mentioned a word about going away to anyone else. I had only finally decided, and made the booking, just over a week ago, so assumed the Colonel to have added the last just to let me know he was keeping a finger on the pulse, as it were.

I realised, far too late, I should have used a different travel agent this time, after the Singapore booking set-up. Anyway, did it really matter. And why should I ever need to call on a Governor. Of the British Virgin islands, or anywhere else, come to that?

*   *